Mr Oliver's Object of Desire

V G Lee

Published by Ward Wood Publishing
6 The Drive
Golders Green
London NW11 9SR
www.wardwoodpublishing.co.uk

ISBN 978-1-908742-58-2

British Library Cataloguing in Publication Data. A CIP record for this book can be obtained from the British Library.

Designed and typeset in Garamond
by Ward Wood Publishing.

Artwork: London skyline in watercolour background
© Domiciano Pablo Romero Franco ID 35064128
Supplied by Dreamstime

Cover Design by Ward Wood Publishing

Printed and bound in Great Britain by
Imprint Digital, Seychelles Farm,
Upton Pyne, Exeter EX5 5HY.

Mr Oliver's Object of Desire

Chapter 1

1975

Imagine this if you will: an immaculately dressed middle-aged man wearing a navy Aquascutum raincoat and neat trilby hat. He is five feet ten inches tall. His figure could be described as 'spare' which has a preferable dryer sound to it than the word 'lean'. This man has retained his hair although the original blue-black colour now has to be helped along with a product called Grecian 2000.

He – I am leaning on the balcony rail as the cruise ship Artemis sails into the port of Southampton. Wistfully I watch the tiny moving figures on the quayside. They remind me of the two much loved Lowry prints hanging on my wall at home: insubstantial characters in sombre coloured clothes anxiously hurrying this way and that.

The memory suits my present dark mood just fine – I am not the madman I was last summer but nor am I the sane Sydney Oliver of previous years. For months now the proverb 'Out of the frying pan and into the fire' has formed a musical refrain, march time, in my head. Subject to fallen arches, I missed my stint of National Service; even so I believe I can appreciate how a battle-weary soldier might feel with yet another difficult campaign ahead of him. I take a deep breath and straighten my shoulders. Common sense tells me life needn't be such a struggle. Common sense supplies further proverbs: 'It's always darkest before the dawn' and 'Every cloud has a silver lining'. I remain unconvinced.

'You forgot Napoleon and Josephine.'

I turn my head. A smiling Doreen Mildmay, silver fox fur jacket thrown over her shoulders, is walking towards me. This may seem ungallant but in the grey morning light her heavy make-up reminds me of a Kabuki mask. Under each arm she carries a large wicker donkey.

Reluctantly succumbing to the tide of Doreen and donkeys I'm forced to step backwards into my cabin. 'Actually Doreen,' I tug the belt of my raincoat tighter, 'I had decided to leave mine on board. I have such a small flat.'

She leans them against my suitcase. 'Don't worry. There's plenty of room at my place. I wouldn't get rid of them for all the world. I'm just a sentimental old fool.'

'I wouldn't dream of encumbering you with my donkey,' I quickly respond.

Her eyes twinkle up at me. 'No, you're supposed to say, "Doreen, you're a woman in your prime."'

'You are indeed.' My voice sounds stiff and insincere although Doreen could easily be classed as 'a woman in her prime' if your taste leans towards well-corseted women of fifty.

Dropping her jacket onto my bed she sits down. 'Care to join me?' She pats the counterpane.

'I'm afraid it's almost time to disembark.'

'We've got at least three-quarters of an hour. Come on. Take that raincoat off and make yourself comfortable.'

'I'd rather keep it on.'

'But why?' Doreen leans back against the headboard and lets her high-heeled shoes drop to the floor.

'I'm not someone who lounges on a bed mid-morning. There are some character traits you'll have to accept about me. I'm a man of fixed ideas.'

'You're a daft so-and-so,' she says but her expression returns to being that of the sensible, maternal Doreen who over the past few days has encouraged me to lower my guard. She sits up, slips her feet back into her shoes and straightens her sheer stockings in a business-like, unsensual way. 'Fair enough. Shall we take a final stroll on deck?'

Doreen crosses to the dressing table, intently studying her reflection in the mirror as she re-ties a Hermès scarf, Audrey Hepburn fashion, over her burnished, lacquered hair. I drape the fox fur around her plump shoulders. It is only when finally we both stand side-by-side on the balcony again that I realise I've been holding my breath for several minutes.

For the best part of a year my life has consisted of a series of both personal and professional disasters that even in retrospect seem somehow unavoidable. This particular disaster, as in the 'Considering a move to Yorkshire for a trial period with a woman I hardly know', had been the indirect result of a weekend spent with my old friend Steve Chambers while at my lowest ebb.

It had been a desperately hot day when I'd set off to visit Steve. I'd woken that Tuesday morning just after nine. Accusingly I'd stared at the alarm clock, then shaken it. The clock continued ticking. I checked the alarm. It had run down. I – Sydney Oliver – had overslept. In my entire career I'd never woken after nine before. It seemed catastrophic: an end to all normal life and the beginning of a descent into an uncharted hell. I'd fallen back against the pillows and attempted to reason with myself. Surely sleeping late didn't automatically mean that I was becoming a man who couldn't get out of bed in the morning. Did it?

Musing over this disturbing possibility, I discovered a whole section of the populace that I hadn't known I despised. People who slept late were lazy, feckless and no doubt wore the previous day's underwear *and* their socks in bed. The clock's hands moved round to – five past ten! How was I going to get out of bed? How had I got out of bed in the past? I needed some impetus. At that moment of despair, as if by divine intervention, the telephone on my chest of drawers rang. Steve Chambers had saved me from staying in bed forever or at least until the need to use the bathroom became critical.

'Old buddy,' Steve said.

'Ah Steve.'

'Now I know how busy you always are but I wondered if you'd like to come down and look over my new venture. I'd welcome your input. You might even want to sink a bit of money into it.'

Under normal circumstances, I would have brusquely replied that I was *very* busy and had no desire to sink my hard earned cash into any hare-brained scheme that Steve might suggest.

'I could pop along this afternoon.'

Steve sounded pleased as well as surprised. 'That's great. Brockstead in Hertfordshire. Pick up a train at Liverpool Street. There's a telephone box outside the station. Just ring and I'll be with you in a matter of minutes.'

We'd known each other since the early nineteen-fifties, nearly a quarter of a century and although I couldn't hand on heart say I liked Steve very much, he was dependable. Whatever my situation

– and there had been several low points over twenty-five years (only none as low as this particular one) – Steve's situation had invariably been worse.

Steve was always on his uppers, always finding himself disappointed in a sure cert. Just popping into hospital for a snip here, a biopsy there – having to lay off alcohol, cigarettes, sugar. He'd been left high and dry or taken to the cleaners, been two, three and four-timed, had his heart broken, been sorely disappointed. In the short term, Steve could be relied on to make any problems I might have, seem trivial.

Just before two o'clock the train pulled in to Brockstead. The station was small and appeared unmanned, confirming my opinion that once again Steve had landed himself in some benighted hole. However, it was clean and the telephone box un-vandalised. On the second ring a woman answered. 'Hello, this is the Canal Club. You're through to Reception.'

'Can I speak to Steve?'

'Sorry?'

'Steve Chambers.'

'*Mr Chambers*. I can give him a message.'

'Could you tell him Sydney Oliver is waiting for him at the station?'

'Certainly, sir. Mr Chambers will be with you shortly.'

I'd felt my first pang of unease, that Steve was now an obviously respected Mr Chambers. Dismissing this pang, I stepped out into broiling sunshine.

From my late twenties onwards, I have considered myself an urbane, sophisticated man who only ever left London to arrive in the South of France, Spain or Cyprus, so it was with some misgivings I assessed Steve's neck of the woods. There was nothing much at all apart from a small parade of shops and a Post Office, flanking an empty dusty road.

In the distance I heard the sound of a car engine starting up. The sound continued, settling into an oncoming purr. Slowly a car drove towards me, the sun glancing off its gleaming bodywork.

Steve leant out of the car window. 'Hop in, old buddy.'

I hopped in. 'Very nice car, Steve. Whose is it?'

'Mine, all mine.' Steve's voice was warm and confident. 'Two-tone metallic finish, Special Edition Ford Capri. This year's model.'

Steve was going to let me down. The signs were there in the car with us. Steve's forearms were deeply tanned. His hands resting loosely on the steering wheel looked more like those of the film star, Steve McQueen. He wore jeans and a Wrangler checked shirt over a black t-shirt. For a fact I knew that Steve was fifty-seven. What had happened to his paunch? How had his legs grown longer? What the devil was he doing wearing hand-tooled cowboy boots?

That morning I'd chosen a formal dark suit and, as a concession because I was leaving London overnight, a mid-blue shirt instead of smart white, gold cufflinks of course and a tie of course. My socks were a subdued charcoal grey worn with black leather lace-up shoes. Sitting next to Steve, I felt diminished – a ventriloquist's dummy of a man, sinking deeper and deeper into Steve's racing green upholstery. How had I come to this?

We pulled into The Club carpark. 'I appreciate you coming up at such short notice,' Steve said. 'Usually you're up to your eyes at The Store.'

'I don't work there anymore.' I tried to say this casually – a throw-away line. I didn't succeed.

Steve switched off the engine. 'Has something happened?'

'I was sacked. Last November.'

'But that's months ago. Hell Oliver, when were you going to tell me? Are you jobless?'

'Yes,' I said.

'But you're the best god-damn general manager in London.'

'I'd rather not go into details. Let's just say, I behaved like a fool.'

Steve gave me a keen look. 'Was a woman involved?'

I nodded.

'Well okay. Let's talk inside. Do you need to freshen up?'

'Not really. If I can park my briefcase?'

'Leave it at the desk. They'll take it up to your room.'

Steve took charge. Looking back I'm amazed. I didn't appreciate it at the time but that moment seemed to mark the change to a different, reliable… caring Steve. I followed him blindly; to reception, the bar and out onto the busy Club patio overlooking the canal.

It had turned into a stifling afternoon. My carefully arranged Brylcreemed waves were starting to melt, a blue-black strand of greased hair repeatedly falling forward over my sweating forehead. Steve indicated two rattan sun loungers beneath a canvas umbrella and I sat down feeling like a fish out of water. I was surrounded by relaxed people in summer clothes; noisy holiday-makers, perched on the prows and cabin roofs of their brightly coloured barges, passed by on the dark green water. They all seemed so very different from myself – uptight man in a formal suit.

'I'm not much of a sun worshipper,' I said.

'What about all those hot countries you go to every year?'

'That's different. On holiday one wears swimming trunks. There are umbrellas, a swimming pool… '

'I could lend you a pair of trunks but you might look kinda… '

'No, no. I wouldn't dream of it. Not appropriate.'

'It's cooling down now. Refill?' Steve waved to yet another passing barge family of mother, father, three children, baby and barking dog.

'Better not. Is it strictly necessary to wave to all and sundry?'

'Makes good business sense. Those people are the future and my game is leisure, old buddy. Back in a moment.'

(If I've given the impression from my recollection of Steve's conversation that he was American – he was not. Nor to my knowledge had he ever visited the United States. However, he was a keen film fan, with a particular admiration for Kirk Douglas, John Wayne and Charlton Heston.)

I watched him lope inside, tossing greetings right and left, not a bead of perspiration on his tanned face. Undeniably Steve was doing well. His name was in the club brochure as 'Marketing Director'. I accepted that every dog must have its day but why must Steve have his now? He'd become a popular fellow. Being popular suited him. I remembered treating him to drinks and dinner at La Bussola in Long Acre when he had looked unkempt and shabby, looked like a man on the slide. Now the breeze off the water ruffled Steve's still thick, still chestnut brown hair. *How the mighty have fallen*, I'd thought before realising that I referred to myself.

Steve handed me another beer. 'Take some time to wind down

and loosen up,' he said before stretching out on his adjacent chair.

Six months earlier and I'd have curtly told him to 'cut the platitudes'. Instead I meekly replied, 'Easier said than done.'

Steve chuckled as if I'd made a joke. 'Oliver, you're going to be just fine.'

No, I wasn't going to be 'just fine'.

'I am terribly unhappy,' shot out of my mouth before I could swallow those words back down as I'd swallowed them dozens of times over recent months. Absolutely shamed and disgusted with myself I put a hand over my eyes.

Steve – well Steve was terrific, reacting in a manly responsible fashion that completely belied the frivolity of those tan cowboy boots. Slowly sipping his drink and apparently concentrating on the view of the water, almost to himself he'd said, 'Let's go see what the cook-house has rustled up for tonight.'

We had an excellent dinner in The Club dining room. Talked about our boyhood – a subject never before even touched on between us – which was comforting and anxiety free. Steve said his mother was still alive, living at the Elephant and Castle and he worshipped her cotton socks although maybe if he'd worshipped her cotton socks less he might have had a more successful life.

'I'm talking the fairer sex here.'

'Ah, the fairer sex.' I could see that Steve was disappointed with my lacklustre response.

'You've always seemed to have your share, old buddy,' he prompted.

'I don't know about that.'

He tossed his napkin on the table and sat back in his chair. 'I'm here to listen.'

Nobody had ever said those words to me before or needed to. I felt acutely embarrassed, but avoiding Steve's eyes I began to talk.

'I've had a couple of affairs lasting about a year each. They did not prove successful. I've never lived with a woman, never wanted to. I've been sexually involved and that level of involvement has suited me down to the ground. Not very impressive. Nothing much there to be proud of.'

Steve whistled. 'I remember seeing you with several crackers in the fifties and sixties. Always some dolly bird on your arm.'

'They meant very little. My career, The Store, came first. That's where I found my stimulation.'

'Did you never fall in love, get your heart broken?'

'Never until now. Steve, I don't know if I can talk about this – about her – over dinner, in bright light.'

'Let's get our coffees in the Lounge. Brandy?'

I'd waved a hand as if to say, you deal with it. Head down, I followed him out of the dining room.

We had the Lounge to ourselves. The evening was still and warm and most of the diners had taken their drinks outside. Steve pulled up two leather armchairs and positioned them by the open window so we had a view of the canal, dusk settling. Our drinks came.

He let a few minutes of contemplative silence pass before broaching the subject again. 'Stop me if you really don't want to talk about this but I think I know who you've fallen for.'

My hand stretching out to reach for my coffee cup faltered in mid-air. 'I can't see how that would be possible.'

'I believe I saw her once.'

'When? Where?'

Instead of the coffee, I picked up my brandy glass and swallowed half of it.

'It was last year. I'd just landed a management position here. Couldn't believe my luck and wanted to share it with someone. I came into The Store. I didn't bother telephoning. I'd intended to give you a surprise, treat you to lunch. Show you a side of Steve Chambers that wasn't always looking for a handout. You were talking to a young woman – early twenties, maybe even younger, long blonde hair?'

I nodded.

'Stunning but a little too thin for my taste. It looked like you were reading her the riot act. She was staring at the floor, kicking the toe of her shoe into the carpet. You didn't see me although I was only a few yards away. You were totally concentrating on her. And then when she walked away – your face was a picture.'

'What sort of a picture?'

'Hungry. Desperate. Kid shut out of a sweet shop. I decided to leave lunch for another day.'

Later, slightly unsteadily, I'd found my way to a bright bedroom of primrose walls and leaf green paintwork, with twin beds and ensuite facilities.

On the spare bed, along with that month's issue of Men Only, was a brochure cutting extolling the delights of a cruise to Madeira. With absolute disinterest I'd read, 'Witness the bejewelled city of Funchal by moonlight, climb to the summit of the world's second highest sea cliff, plummet down mountain paths on a wicker sled…'

On a sheet of Canal Club note-paper, Steve had written, 'I'd skip the wicker sled if I were you – don't want to end up with a plastic hip. However a change is as good as the proverbial. As Dylan Thomas used to say, *Time passes.*'

Old habits die hard. I removed my jacket and hung it up in the narrow cupboard. Methodically I undid my shoe laces and slipped off the shoes, then I loosened my tie. With great care, as if every small movement was capable of causing pain, I lay myself down on the bed, my hands linked across my stomach. I wasn't drunk, or if I was, my thoughts remained remarkably clear.

Chapter 2

1975

Six weeks later, ten days ago to be precise, I found myself boarding The Artemis, a hardback copy of Constantine FitzGibbon's, *The Life of Dylan Thomas*, borrowed from Steve Chambers who was something of a Dylan Thomas fan, packed in my hand luggage.

'You'll find you've got quite a bit in common with old DT,' Steve had promised. (The only common ground I discovered with old DT was that both of us had curly hair and neither had gone bald.)

From day one of the cruise I'd set myself a routine to give some semblance of a man cheerfully occupied; a man on his own but not necessarily lonely. First a leisurely breakfast, remembering to summon up a smile, followed by a polite 'Good morning' to the other breakfasters at my table. Then a stroll around the Lido deck, swinging my rolled copy of the previous day's Telegraph. In the afternoon, if the weather was good, I changed into longish beige linen shorts and one of a selection of shirts I'd brought in a tropical print. Late afternoon was spent in my cabin trying unsuccessfully to nap.

It was almost a relief to get ready for pre-dinner cocktails in the open-topped Crow's Nest Bar. I could ignore everyone, just stand at the ship's rail looking thoughtfully out to sea as I sipped a dry martini. On the second day a woman did join me, also looking thoughtfully out to sea as she sipped *her* dry martini, but I adjusted the angle of my head so my profile was partly averted. Just a small realignment but after a moment she got the message and moved away.

Evenings were spent in the Port Bar, the only bar below sea level. It was a dark and womblike place where I could nurse a pint of beer and return to my newspaper to dismally consider wars, famines and the ponderous activities of Edward Heath.

I saw a certain synchronicity between us – both unmarried, lives devoted to our careers, Heath losing his job as Prime Minister within a very few months of my own dismissal as The Store's general manager. Both of us finally brought to our knees by a woman. But there the similarities ended. Doubtless Heath was upset, even devastated, but at least there was no broken heart to contend with.

By day three, sitting alone in the Port Bar facing a false window painted to look like a starlit sky, I felt I had established myself as a serious man with much on his mind. No one would approach such a man and anyway the Port Bar was generally empty till after eleven o'clock when the dances, concerts and shows finished.

For the first time since I'd come on board, I allowed my contrived expression to slip. It was a relief to let my facial muscles return to the place they truly wanted to be – heading downwards. I could have cried. I could have laughed at the very idea of a man like myself crying. My body was tired, my face – particularly the skin around my eyes – felt stretched and sensitive.

Keep going Oliver, I told myself.

I raised my glass to salute my reflection in the false night sky. That face in the glass, it didn't look so very old? I wasn't so unattractive, was I? Della, my head saleswoman, had nurtured a crush on me for years. A crush lasting that long would surely be considered 'love' – wouldn't it?

I couldn't summon up the comfort of Della's adoring face; instead I saw again the tender curve of Claire Daker's stubborn chin. Her unbelievably blue and hostile eyes. How she'd hated me and how I'd come to perversely savour that hatred.

'Are you all right, dear?'

For a second I didn't react. I was so utterly absorbed in my own thoughts. Finally I raised my head, immediately recognising top quality cashmere in a deep expensive shade of claret. A low scoop neckline revealed the upper two thirds of what would be considered – if you were a 'breast man' which I'm not – an extraordinary pair of breasts. I had the wild thought that I was being offered the handsome décolletage of at least Madame de Pompadour. It – they – filled my entire field of vision. I was fascinated yet somehow appalled. With a huge effort I dragged my gaze upwards.

'Only you don't look too bright. You've got a real sweat on. I won't stay if I'm *de trop*. The name's Doreen Mildmay.' The woman held out a plump, heavily jewelled hand.

'I'm absolutely fine.' I took her hand and then found it impossible to disengage, rather like shutting my own hand into a mouse trap only not painful.

'I couldn't help noticing,' she continued, 'from where I sit at the Captain's Table, that you always look so sad. I've said to myself, Doreen that poor man's lost a tenner and found nowt. You see I've had my fair share of sorrow so I can recognise unhappiness when I see it.'

'No really –'

'What I'd suggest,' and here she held up her free hand so that a rainbow prism bounced off the large diamond on her third finger, casting almost a biblical light over myself and my beer glass, 'is hot tea and brandy. That beer will do you no favours. Just sit there and let me sort it out.'

'But –'

She was gone, rat-tatting her way across the parquet floor on high stiletto heels. Her voice carried back to me, admirably assertive, 'I couldn't care less what your normal bar policy is, I want a pot of tea for two and double brandies right now – I'm paying enough for the privilege so hop to it sunshine.'

On automatic pilot I assessed her: I estimated that she must be in her late forties, early fifties; dark brown hair, cut, styled and dyed at a top class salon. A trim figure apart from those astounding bosoms, obviously expensively corseted to retain such ballistic missile proportions. Her clothes were of a superb quality – probably from Harvey Nichols or some similar high-end store. A navy moiré silk skirt with fan pleating, heraldic Hermes scarf tied to the strap of her navy patent leather handbag, navy patent sling-back shoes. (I have a fondness for patent but can recall only one period some ten years ago when patent leather has actually represented 'high-fashion'.)

In my head I totted up the cost and choice of her clothes, general presentation and her reassuring self-confidence and decided that Doreen Mildmay was a woman of depth and taste.

'Little toe-rag.' She put the tray on the table and sat down. 'Said he couldn't leave his post at the bar to rustle up a pot of tea. You'd think he was Horatio sodding Nelson.' She poured the tea, adding two sugars to each. 'There, drink that. Follow it up with the brandy.

What's your name, pet?'

I hesitated. This was exactly what I'd hoped to avoid – intimacy. A stranger's assumed right to know about me. But her eyes were kind. I checked again – kind and encouraging.

'Sydney Oliver – fashion retail. I was known as Mr Oliver.'

'Oliver.' She rolled my surname around her mouth as if sucking the liqueur from a dark chocolate. 'Oliver. Sydney Oliver. Very nice. Very refined. I'll stick with the Oliver if you don't mind. All my life I've had a thing about Oliver Cromwell. Now there was a real man. My late husband was a Peter. That name makes me think of separated milk. I don't know why.' She trailed off, her lips settling into a thin line.

I realised that her lips were in fact thin lines, their apparent generous fullness achieved by mulberry coloured lipstick.

Fair enough, nobody's perfect, I thought. My own hair, eyebrows and moustache received help in remaining their rich and lustrous black.

We sat surprisingly companionably, facing each other across the bar table. Doreen began to talk about her house, her friends and her two sons.

'Junior is the apple of my eye. He's twenty-four now but all I see is the little boy he was with his blond curls, running up to his mummy for a cuddle. Get that drink down you.'

Brandy is possibly my least favourite tipple but as Doreen had almost finished hers I felt it only polite to drink mine.

'Between you and me,' she said, 'I'm not over-fond of my eldest son Carpenter. He was his father's favourite and a little sneak. I like to speak as I find, and I've found that once a sneak, always a sneak.'

Although failing to recall any sneaky children in my own youth who had grown into sneaky adults, I nodded. 'And what did your husband do?' I asked in an attempt to lighten the conversation.

She snorted. 'Sod all. I did the work, he spent the money! You may have heard of Mildmay Executive Properties?'

I admitted that I hadn't.

'We're very big in the north of England. I was even voted Business Woman of the Year in 1964, for the whole of west Yorkshire. Carpenter runs the company now but he doesn't share my drive and enthusiasm.'

Intrigued, I leant forward. 'So, why did you give it up?'

She shrugged. 'I'm still the Managing Director. It's my name on the company cheque book.' For a moment the expression on her face was wistful. 'You know I travelled all over the country promoting our executive houses but an evening came when I was on my own in a hotel dining room full of couples.'

Our eyes met. Both of us had experienced evenings like that.

'The next morning I rang Carpenter and told him he had three months to learn the business.'

Doreen continued to talk. Sometimes she did ask questions, sometimes even waiting for my answers.

The ship rocked gently. My fears of unwelcome intimacy receded. Sipping my third tumbler of brandy I began to think that Doreen Mildmay – provided I could control our acquaintanceship – might just make the cruise bearable.

*

Some hours later, back in her luxurious ocean-view cabin on 'A' Deck, Doreen Mildmay prepared for bed. She had bathed, moisturised and powdered her body as always. Naked, she stood in front of the full-length mirror and considered her reflection.

'All gone. I've just about lost the lot. Thank god I can't see the back of my thighs. What a bloody waste. What a crying shame.'

She smiled grimly then leant forward cupping her large breasts, imagining them descending onto Sydney Oliver's face. She thought of his luxuriant corrugated waves, his distinguished blue-black widow's peak, the trim moustache and the short black hairs on the back of his hands.

'A wolf's hands.'

Immediately he became a handsome wolf, padding – panting at the edge of a forest. He raised his head, nostrils flaring as he caught the beguiling scent of Estee Lauder's 'Youth Dew' wafting from where Doreen waited in the open doorway of a small log cabin. A restless Doreen, her senses stirred by the night and the awareness of a wild, male presence. Oliver/wolf loped across the intervening scrubland, rearing up at the sight of Doreen who now wore a revealing black chiffon nightdress. Doreen stepped back into the cabin, half-fainting gracefully onto a soft hand-woven rug – as Oliver's wolf tongue rasped against her bare neck, his wolf hands reaching for her breasts.

She turned away from her reflection. Folded over the back of a chair was a candy-striped nightshirt. She'd bought several for the cruise on the advice of her friend Laverne: 'Doreen they're a fun option and hide a multitude of sins.' Doreen slipped it on, making a mental note to tell Laverne that she, Doreen, was not a 'fun option' sort of woman. She poured herself a brandy from a small decanter and lit a cigarette. In bed with only the side lamp casting a warm glow over her banked pillows she banished thoughts of Laverne and settled down to a more realistic daydream. This time she was in her bedroom at home. She sat at her dressing table, brushing her thick dark hair with a silver-backed brush. Her nightdress was again of black chiffon with loose full sleeves and a pale green satin ribbon tied under the swell of her breasts.

Behind her, the bedroom door opened. Oliver entered wearing a dinner suit.

She stopped the dream and rewound. Behind her, the bedroom door was kicked open. At the dressing table, hair brush raised so that the thin voile sleeve of her nightdress fell back to reveal one startlingly white shoulder, she paused. Oliver stood – lounged in the doorway, slightly dishevelled, still in a dinner suit but his bowtie and top four shirt buttons were undone.

'You little bitch,' he said – no, he growled.

In the mirror she watched him steadily as he moved towards her. Doreen laid down her hair brush. She felt heat emanating from his approaching body. For a moment, he stood quite still and then his rough hands clasped her shoulders… roughly. Impatiently he pulled at the delicate cloth of her nightdress. It tore. A moment of reckoning. Oliver's eyes met hers in the mirror. Doreen's magnificent breasts were bare – quivering, begging, aching for Oliver's… rough wolf's hands.

'I must sleep,' Doreen told herself and surprisingly, once she'd extinguished her cigarette, put down her brandy glass and switched out the light, she slept very well.

Chapter 3

1974

I'd worked in Ladies' Retailing since I was fifteen years old, starting as a stockroom boy at Madame Baldwin's Millinery in Waltham Abbey. From there I edged into London, spending an unhappy six months with Burton Tailoring where I discovered not only a disinterest but an aversion to the male body, clothed or unclothed.

Over the years I've realised that otherwise intelligent people make assumptions – that just because a man is fastidious regarding his own clothes and possesses an interest in female fashion, he must be a homosexual. This is such a narrow stereotype and in my case totally misplaced. This is not a case of my 'protesting too much'; it is a statement of fact.

At nineteen and with some relief I joined Swan & Edgar of Piccadilly. For a time I was content to be a junior buyer of ladies' accessories. It was a useful stepping stone for the ambitious young man I was. But the store was too large, elderly and set in its ways – rather resembling the coterie of grim-faced women running each department – all apparently united in *not* promoting my interests.

It was by accident I came across The Store. I was on my way to meet a twenty-two -year-old Steve Chambers for a drink at the Hog in the Pound pub in Mayfair.

This remains a tale I like to replay in my head. Imagine this: a backdrop of snow falling gently on Oxford Street, one of the busiest fashion malls in the capital. Yes, the pavement was a perilous mix of slush and ice but I was impervious to it. I was young – too young to worry about broken limbs or a cracked skull. I remember glancing at a store window and then skidding to a halt, mesmerised by the display. A beautiful manikin, modelled on the cool blonde style of Grace Kelly, lounged in a silver sleigh against padded cushions. She wore white velvet – a hooded cape trimmed with seed pearls. Her chin rested on one elegant hand while in her other negligent hand she held a posy of red silk roses. A blossom had been allowed to fall and it lay against the fake snow like a spot of blood.

Foolishly emotional perhaps, but I felt a stab of bitter-sweet pain in my chest, just from looking at something so perfect. The sheer whiteness of the tableau stung my eyes and I'd blinked before noticing a small hand-written card in the bottom corner of the window: 'Temporary Under-Manager required for the Christmas period. Apply within.'

Moving swiftly forward to March 1974 when I celebrated my fiftieth birthday – a good month for me, although my beloved London was in chaos with strikes, power cuts, political upheaval and the ever present threat of IRA bombings. The Conservative government in its wisdom had introduced The Three Day Week – an attempt to cut the nation's electricity consumption, resulting in many small businesses being forced to close. The Store rode out the disruption, remaining open by means of limited power supplied by a small generator, the use of candles, and the staff being allowed to wear their coats, scarves, gloves and even hats indoors.

Naturally, as Manager of The Store, I went through the motions of anger and irritation. Had anyone asked me for an opinion on The Miners' Strike, I would have said in a voice of contained fury, 'Those bastards are draining the life blood out of the country. I'd put the lot of them in prison and throw away the key.' But really, I couldn't have cared less. Inadequate heat and light was little more than an inconvenience. Perhaps for the first time in my life, I felt invulnerable.

On my birthday, contentedly alone in my Earls Court flat, I poured myself a glass of *Château La Conseillante* from the Pomerol region in France. A case had been presented to me at the previous year's staff party, just one of several tokens of appreciation from Head Office for outstanding sales figures in that financial year.

Sipping my wine from a Waterford crystal glass (one of a set of six with decanter) I could honestly claim to be a happy man. Over thirty years, determinedly and, I might add, with a certain flair, I'd worked my way up my chosen career ladder. Gradually I had metamorphosed from 'young Oliver' to 'young Mr Oliver' to the blissful moment, when an impressive weight of gravitas had settled comfortably on my padded suit shoulders and I had become just 'Mr Oliver'. That name meant something in ladies' retailing. It cut past underlings and got straight through to the men who mattered.

I had finally become a man who mattered.

Standing at the window, gazing down on the busy, moving traffic below, I saluted just some of my haute couture idols: Dior, Balenciaga, Balmain, Chanel. These were the designers who had first dazzled me as a young man and to whom in my heart I had remained true. The bias cut, a dolman sleeve, the magical texture and sound of crêpe de chine, and so much more to do with style and fabric still retained the power to make my head buzz pleasurably and moisten my eyes. True, The Store no longer boasted a Model Gown showroom, standards had definitely dropped during the nineteen-sixties but there still remained the Bridal Salon, stocking arguably the finest range of wedding dresses and accessories in Britain, if not the whole of Europe.

In this benign and self-congratulatory mood, my thoughts turned to the previous afternoon. An incident of seemingly little importance, yet I'd been oddly affected by it. Only in retrospect, months later, did I realise that this was my very first encounter with Claire Daker.

Whenever there is a royal or celebrity wedding, in real life or on film, no matter how hush-hush the details of the dress, The Store prides itself on having a copy of the bridal dress in their main Oxford Street window within twenty-four hours of it going public. The previous year, Princess Anne's wedding to Mark Phillips had seen a phenomenal rise in bridal sales and the year before that there had been the fictional Mafia daughter, Connie Corleone's wedding dress from the film The Godfather.

So far 1974 had been barren. No really big weddings within cinema or royalty. In a few minutes, I had a meeting with Mr Stanhope, our Sales Director, and Miss Frances the Chief Buyer and would need to come up with some ideas.

The lift doors opened. Absorbed in my thoughts, I stepped inside and pressed the button for the fifth floor. Nothing happened. I pressed again then looked at my watch. Damn it! Ten past one. Limited electricity till late afternoon. I'd have to take the stairs.

During the power cuts, the windowless back staircase was lit by candles placed in tins on each bend; however, that day I pushed open the Fire Exit door and found myself in a candle-less gloom.

Confidently I took the first flight two-at-a-time but as I rounded the second bend I came to an abrupt stop. Above me was darkness. I paused, allowing my eyes to become accustomed to the absence of light before setting off again at a slower, more cautious pace. Arriving at the next corner, I was reduced to clutching the stair rail, but it was only on reaching the first slippery faux marble steps between the fourth and fifth floor, denoting the Management Suites, that I experienced any real apprehension. Below and above me lay total darkness. Even the stair rail seemed inadequate. Supposing I stumbled, went hurtling backwards, knees, ribs, chin cracking on every step? I was no longer the carefree, careless young man who had kicked his way through the ice and slush years earlier.

'Who's there?' A young and frightened female voice called out from several feet above me.

I was about to shout back, 'It's Mr Oliver,' but decided that my name probably invoked dread in at least half the hearts in The Store. 'Don't worry,' I said instead. 'You're quite safe.'

'I hate the dark.'

'Yes, it is a bloody nuisance. Nothing to be scared of though.' I tried to sound reassuring. Where exactly was the voice coming from? 'How far are you from the top?'

'Fifteen steps. I counted them.'

'In that case you've got about twenty-five more steps down before you reach the third floor. After that it gets a bit lighter.'

'What if I fall?'

'Just hang onto the rail and be careful.'

No response. Silence and a flowery scent. I inhaled. Nothing expensive but not unpleasant. The person would be a junior. One of the typists or someone on the switchboard. Her voice was unfamiliar, or perhaps that was because from fear it was pitched high.

'Look, I'll hold out my hand.'

'Who are you?' She sounded suspicious.

'Jim. I work down in Dispatch.' In the darkness, I'd smiled at my glib lie.

'Do you have a family?'

I was astonished. What more did the young woman want? I was offering her a hand on the stairs; surely it wasn't necessary to provide a character reference? But perhaps it was.

'I live in Lewisham, quite near the station. I've a wife, a boy and a girl. They're in their teens. I'm hoping the boy – Philip – will go to college. Get a better job than his old dad.'

I liked the idea of having kids. Kids. For some foolish reason I wanted an opportunity to use that word.

'And the girl?'

'Jenny? There's talk of an engagement but her mum and I feel she's far too young. Get a couple of GCE's under her belt before any of that nonsense. Our kids are nothing but a worry but we wouldn't be without 'em.'

In the darkness, I could sense her considering.

'I'll lead you all the way back down if you're frightened,' I offered.

'That's very kind of you, but no. If I can just take your hand to the next flight of stairs, where you said it gets a little lighter.'

I stretched my arm upwards and waved it, making a breeze. A small, thin-fingered hand took hold of mine.

'Ready,' she said.

Feeling the smooth surface of the wall on the right-hand side, I began to retrace my steps until finally the wall fell away, dropping down into the stairwell.

'We're at the corner. Hug the rail. Feel with your feet till you reach the next step. Even go down on hands and knees if you're scared of falling.'

She passed me. Her fingers slipped out of mine. 'Thank you, Jim,' she said.

I called after her, 'And what's your name?'

'Hush,' she said. 'I need to concentrate.'

Her steps grew more confident and I knew she'd reached the dimly lit staircase. The sound of her footsteps faded away. Cautiously I made my way upwards and pushed open the door, stepping out into the brilliant light of the fifth floor. The feeling of satisfaction, an undeniable warmth, had remained with me.

Oh, and the wedding dress to mark 1974? We did our own approximation of Anne Boleyn's wedding dress – the highlight of our most successful bridal window ever.

Happy Fiftieth Birthday, Mr Oliver.

If I were to pinpoint the moment when I became less content, it would be a few months further on. The sixteen-week miners' strike was over, electricity production had returned to normal, Harold Wilson (a man I rather liked for his pipe smoking, although I didn't quite know why as I'd never personally felt the desire to smoke a pipe) was prime minister and leader of a Labour minority government – I was looking forward to the return to 'business as usual'.

'How would you feel about a teen boutique?' Miss Frances asked, pausing on her way through the Bridal Salon, although the salon wasn't on any immediate route either to the lift or to the outside world of the West End.

I'd glanced up from my copy of the new Spring-into-Summer Bridal catalogue. 'Annoyed,' I'd answered with just the hint of a smile. At that time, Miss Frances was possibly the only woman apart from my mother that I might have admitted in the privacy of my own thoughts, to respecting.

'Why so?' Miss Frances admired the stack heels of her leather boots in one of the salon's floor to ceiling mirrors.

'The Store already does extremely well without such a thing. There are more than enough teen boutiques in this area to satisfy several populations of 'teens'. Nor would our loyal customers appreciate hordes of teens running riot, trying clothes on willy-nilly. You get my drift?'

'I take your point.' She veered several yards to my left and ran her index finger over a glass display cabinet.

'Was there anything else, Miss Frances?'

'I don't think so. Just thought I'd touch base.'

With some admiration, I watched her retrace her steps down the Salon staircase and head in the direction of the coat department; an extremely stylish woman who I liked to think shared my love for garments of the highest quality.

Della, my manageress and reliable right arm, glided across the expanse of cream carpet to my side, her expression one of concern. 'Problems?'

'Nothing I can't deal with. I think I've nipped that little nonsense in the bud.'

'What little nonsense would that be?' She brushed an invisible speck of dust from my jacket sleeve.

'A teen boutique! I didn't have a fight on my hands for most of the sixties to succumb to the idea now. Let the teens slog up to Miss Selfridge.'

'We don't want to be overrun by hippies either.'

'Hah! Over my dead body.' I thrust away the image of lying comatose on the shop floor as long-haired hippies wearing gold and orange kaftans scrambled uncaringly over my body in their desperate rush to reach a teen boutique.

Tanned and firing on all cylinders, I arrived back from holidaying in Cyprus to find a large plasterboard structure being erected in the middle of Daywear.

'What the devil's this?' I barked at the carpenter.

'It's the teen boutique.'

'We'll see about that.'

Three minutes later I stood in the doorway of the fifth floor Buying Office bestowing on Miss Frances the full force of my anger.

'How dare you!'

'Mr Oliver.' She rose swiftly from behind her desk. 'My, you do look like a bronzed god. Sit down. Can I get you a coffee? Tea?'

'I said I would not accept a teen boutique in my store.'

'There is no need to shout.' Miss Frances closed her office door.

'If you persist with this ludicrous project you'd better look elsewhere for someone to run it. I have no intention of wasting my precious time trying to second-guess teenage fashion.' I spat out the last two words.

Over the rim of a pair of ridiculously ostentatious spectacles her eyes danced with amusement. 'I couldn't agree more.'

'What does that mean?'

She sat down, gestured for me to do the same.

Ungraciously, I fell into the chair facing her.

'It means that you and I are in total agreement.' Another smile. 'Of course, we must look elsewhere for someone to run the boutique. Head office had no intention of burdening you with a very tentative step into the youth market. It's a junior management job. A young woman's job. '

'A young woman?' My voice drowned out the piped sounds of Mantovani crackling over the intercom. 'It has taken me years to learn what a manager needs to know. How can a young woman pick up that kind of experience?'

I waited furiously as Miss Frances made a church steeple of her fingers. 'She will be under your guidance. When not occupied with the boutique she can help out around The Store. The Bridal Salon is always very busy. An extra pair of hands will come in useful.'

'She's not setting foot in my Bridal Salon,' I roared.

I immediately regretted roaring. Her smile had changed to one of deep hurt and bewilderment. Shaken by the force of my anger I tried to construct a more measured approach. 'I assume you already have someone in mind?'

She nodded.

'How old is she?'

'Early twenties. It's hard to tell these days, isn't it?' Miss Frances's smile returned. 'She's supremely capable. I've had my eye on her for some time. Excellent references. Cut her teeth at Marks & Spencer. Stood in for the manageress of their Hackney branch when she came down with chicken pox, and Hackney is no picnic.'

'Hackney is a long way from the West End. The Store isn't the place for a cockney-voiced oik who can't tell the difference between polyester cotton and cashmere.'

'I assure you that this young woman can tell the difference.'

'She's far too young.'

'Finger on the youth pulse.'

I snarled inwardly and couldn't resist clicking my fingers derisively at Miss Frances. 'I wouldn't give tuppence for your "youth pulse".'

She'd laughed as if I'd said something immensely amusing. '*Formidable*, Mr Oliver! Trust me. The two of you will get along splendidly! I expect you'll learn something from each other. You're never too old or too young to learn. Don't you agree?'

What could I say? *No, I don't agree.* But if I said that, where to from there?

Miss Frances referred to a pink file on the desk in front of her. 'C.M. Daker. I believe that's Claire with an 'i'. The boutique won't be ready to open till mid-August at the earliest but she's all yours from next week.'

'So there's to be no more discussion? It's a *fait accompli*?'

'The Board has decided. It's out of my hands. Now I'm afraid…' She looked at her over-sized wrist watch.

'Don't worry. I'm going. Good-day.' Instead of my words coming out clipped and forceful, they'd sounded slightly American, the sort of lazy 'G'day' my old friend, Steve Chambers might trot out before ambling off to a bar or three.

I stood up, smiled grimly, tightly, haughtily. Inside I yearned for a convenient sword to fall on. That would teach these head office simpletons a lesson. But witnessing their discomfort wouldn't be so enjoyable from a hospital bed, or worse, death preventing me from seeing it at all.

*

Miss Frances closed the door on Mr Oliver's furious footsteps and returned to her chair.

The damn cheek of the man bursting in like that!

Nobody, not even Mr Stanhope, would ever enter her office without knocking first. She had set this protocol in stone several years earlier. As chief fashion buyer to the fifth largest London store, she required time without intrusion for 'creative thinking'. It was understood that she possessed an artistic temperament – to function at the high end of the fashion retail sector, her privacy must be respected. With a contented sigh she let her eyelids droop.

Miss Frances was a woman prone, in her own words, to 'girlish crushes'. She wasn't ashamed of this, in fact it was a side to her emotional character she liked and approved of. Even now, she continued to think fondly of Audrey Wisbeech, her very first crush from junior school. She had initially been drawn to Audrey's brightly coloured tam o'shanter. In retrospect her fascination with the hat may have been an early indicator of what would eventually be a career choice in fashion.

Audrey had been a quiet little girl. Miss Frances couldn't recall Audrey actually speaking but she did remember the two of them sitting on the stone steps of the Girls' toilets, taking turns to plait each other's hair. Audrey's hair had been a very ordinary mid-brown and quite short so it took no time at all to make her plait.

Miss Frances tilted back her head. She could still feel the tug of Audrey's gentle hands moving over her scalp: stroking, dividing into sections and then slowly, sensuously weaving her hair into a long thick rope. She shuddered pleasurably.

Enough of that, Fran! Miss Frances opened her eyes and drew the pink file towards her. Claire Daker stared back from a small photograph paper-clipped to a new employment contract. *Nothing gentle about that young woman's face*, Miss Frances thought.

Restlessly she crossed to the open window and looked out over Hanover Square to the boarded-up building that had once been 'Danny La Rue's', a nightclub owned by the female impersonator. She'd often seen him getting out of a taxi before a show. He looked surprisingly tall and manly, impeccably dressed, with thick iron grey hair. Not really flamboyant apart from the little touches – a brightly patterned shirt worn open-necked or with beautiful eye-catching ties: always smiling, particularly gracious and generous to cab drivers. On several occasions Miss Frances had watched Mr La Rue laughingly wave aside ten pound notes, the drivers pulling away slowly with cheerful cries of 'Thanks guv'nor'.

Those days were gone. Miss Frances returned to her desk and picked up a small silver-framed photo of a young woman sitting on a rock with the sea behind her. The woman wore shorts and a boy's Fred Perry shirt. Gus.

If anyone asked, Miss Frances always replied, 'My sister. There's very little sibling resemblance.' She would smile to indicate a private family joke built up over years around sibling resemblances. They were not sisters.

What were we then? Sporadic lovers with very little love involved.

They'd shared a one-bedroom flat in Canonbury. Gus had insisted on single beds. 'I don't want anybody imagining that you and I are a couple,' she'd said several times at the beginning and laughed. Quite a cruel laugh – Gus was capable of cruelty but only with someone who loved her.

She remembered Gus taking her to the Gateways club in Chelsea for her twenty-seventh birthday.

'Wear a dress,' Gus said.

'But I never wear dresses. What about ski pants and a satin shirt?'

'Wear a dress.'

Miss Frances bought a dress: sleeveless, fitted, in silver-grey Shantung silk.

'You'll knock them dead in that.' It had been one of the rare occasions when Gus had seemed to see her as a woman rather than a lowly side-kick.

'But I don't feel like me in it.'

'What's so great about feeling like you?' Gus had turned away from her to look at her own reflection in the bedroom mirror. 'The club's a dive but that's half the charm. The butchies line up on one side, femmes on the other. Some of the women feel intimidated. They don't like being stared at. I want all the attention I can get.'

Gus wore a lime green dress with a cowl neckline. It was a style nobody wore anymore – or that's what Miss Frances had privately thought, until her visit to The Gates. As she'd followed Gus down the steep stairs she'd been aware of a sea of faces turning to look up at them – women wearing dresses just like Gus and men in suits – only of course they weren't men.

Gus was popular with everyone. Her address book bulged with cards and slips of paper scrawled with names and telephone numbers.

Gus told her they might see Dusty Springfield or even the British film star, Diana Dors. They weren't there that night. The room was full of smoke and noise and hard assessing glances.

'Come on.' Gus's smile was huge. 'Let's go to the bar.'

'I'll give you the money. Get me a gin and tonic. One for yourself.'

'But Fran, crossing the floor, standing at the bar – it's all part of the excitement – getting noticed.'

A woman in a dinner suit grabbed Gus by the shoulders. 'Sweetheart, you look gorgeous.' She'd swung Gus into an ugly grinding dance, their hips glued together. Over her partner's shoulder, Gus made a face at her, *what can I do?* As if she was helpless. Gus was never helpless.

How Miss Frances had hated that evening.

She returned the frame to her desk. For twelve years she'd

thought of Gus as the love of her life but now she wondered. If Gus hadn't died, would she have gone on loving someone who didn't love her back?

Until Friday lunchtime exactly a week ago, Miss Frances hadn't even known of Claire Daker's existence. She'd been standing in the cafeteria doorway staring at the menu-board and debating whether to opt for a light salad or 'Dish of the Day' which was shepherd's pie with grated cheddar cheese topping. One would be tasteless and watery, the other delicious and fattening. As she mused she became aware of a pair of citrus yellow knee-socks leading to tasselled loafers standing next to her own tapered trouser legs and tan ankle-boots. Her gaze had travelled higher, absorbing a short pleated skirt and an ill-fitting blouse in a yellow and grey dog tooth check pattern. Straight away, she'd recognised that the clothes were poorly made and of cheap material. The loafers were almost certainly from Saxone's, the shoe chain-store. It would have been easy to dismiss the entire ensemble as a rag-bag of badly put together items but instead she'd experienced a sense of unease.

Miss Frances prided herself on perfect presentation, from her elegant cap of burnished burgundy high-lighted hair down to her expensive shoes and boots. She personified an image of a fashionable yet stylish young woman who had money and knew how to spend it for maximum visual effect. For once her confidence was rocked. Compared to the girl standing next to her, Miss Frances was no longer the youthful dynamic fashion-buyer guaranteed an upward trajectory – at thirty-six she was verging on middle-age.

How old was she? Nineteen? Early twenties? And if Miss Frances had noticed her, how long would it be before someone else noticed her? Mr Stanhope, or worse, the Managing Director himself. New blood. Fresh blood. Miss Frances felt suddenly bloodless.

In her head a silent film began to play: the girl wearing a Victorian nightdress perched on the edge of Miss Frances's desk. The ruffled collar of the nightdress framed her face. She resembled a beautiful, angelic choir boy. In front of her, Mr Stanhope dropped to his knees. He took one of the young woman's feet in the palm of his hand, holding it as if he cradled a beautiful and fragile flower. With reverence he'd pressed his nose against her instep and inhaled. The expression on Mr Stanhope's face was one of complete intoxication.

Youth and beauty, an obvious flare for fashion – somewhere alarm bells were ringing. Behind them Miss Frances thought she heard the words 'Get rid. Danger.' She'd shivered with apprehension, but also, for the first time in some years, she experienced a thrill of excitement.

Miss Frances had taken her place in the queue for food behind the girl. As the queue moved forward she tapped her on the shoulder.

The girl half-turned to face her. She was very pretty – eyes of an extraordinary blue.

Miss Frances held out her hand. 'I'm Miss Frances. You are?'

'Claire Daker.' She'd briefly touched the tips of Miss Frances's proffered fingers.

'Claire Daker.' Miss Frances stared hard at her from behind the mirrored lenses of her brand-new Revo Classic sunglasses. 'You have a certain style.'

'Thank you.'

'Where do you buy your clothes?'

'Here and there.'

'Is that in the Kings Road?'

The girl had grinned. 'Yes.'

'I must pop in one lunchtime.'

Claire Daker had reached for a tray and stepped forward to be served. She tossed her pony tail almost as if she was flicking Miss Frances away. Her hair, the colour of cream, grazed Miss Frances's nostrils. She would later swear that she had smelt warm grass, the scent of freesias with a base note of Miss Dior perfume.

Chapter 4

1975

'Not much but my own,' I say, ushering Doreen into the hall. 'Would you like a coffee? Only powdered milk I'm afraid.'

'I don't think so.' She extracts a small lace-trimmed handkerchief from her bag and dabs her nose. The gesture somehow implies dissatisfaction.

'Earls Court isn't really the West End, is it?' she'd observed moments earlier as I'd paid for her taxi.

'Well, no it isn't,' I'd agreed.

Carrying several store carrier bags and Doreen's overnight case (she is staying at a hotel near Piccadilly Circus) I follow her into my lounge.

Frowning, her gaze rakes the room. 'So austere, Oliver. And gloomy. How have you borne it?'

Up till that moment, I had 'borne it' rather well. I am proud of my home. Who would not relish the opulence of solid oak furniture, dark brown leather chesterfield sofa with matching armchair and a coffee table fashioned to look like several antique leather-bound volumes randomly stacked on top of each other? Answer: Doreen.

After disembarking from The Artemis, we'd gone our separate ways. I'd already booked a Bed and Breakfast for myself in Southampton for the night as I had no pressing need to hurry home. As I saw Doreen off on the London train she'd once again brought up the idea of my staying with her in Yorkshire for the summer.

'Doreen, give me a couple of weeks to think about it.'

'What's there to think about? I'm offering you the holiday of a lifetime – all expenses paid – in the fabulous Yorkshire countryside.'

I'd chuckled as if appreciating a joke, although I could see that she was deadly serious. 'Just a fortnight. After all, I can't just up sticks.'

'What does "up sticks" mean?'

'Go away on a whim?'

'Oh, I like the sound of that.'

Fortunately, at that moment the train had begun to pull out of the station.

Three days elapsed. Common sense had almost reasserted itself and then Doreen telephoned – she was coming to London at the weekend to buy a couple of summer outfits. The weather in the north was perfect; the long range forecast set fair, what earthly reason could I have for remaining in London?

Give in, Oliver, I told myself. *Go with the flow*. All my life I'd lived by my own rules but suddenly I was being torn, tossed and tempted in every direction – I had a foolish flimsy reason to believe that Claire Daker might now be in Yorkshire. Of course even if she was, all I had was a needle in a haystack's chance of bumping into her.

'I'll stay overnight in a hotel and help you pack,' Doreen prompted.

By the time I put the receiver down I'd agreed to stay at her house for a minimum of two months. I slumped back into the armchair and let my tense shoulders relax. Gradually a sense of good cheer washed over me, which is not quite the same thing as happiness but even so was very welcome. That sense of good cheer lasted right up till Doreen's arrival at my flat.

'I suppose I could run down for a pint of fresh milk from the newsagents?' I try to sound cheerfully brisk.

Doreen turns towards me, her expression softening. 'You've been through life's mill, haven't you, pet?'

I shrug politely. I am often at a loss how to answer Doreen's more searching enquiries.

With a determined smile, Doreen approaches my three age-spotted George Cruickshank illustrations, the only pictures in the room. 'And are these the prints you were telling me about?'

'They are indeed. Exquisitely executed. I'm rather a fan of Cruickshank.'

She studies each drawing, tracing their individual titles with a magenta tipped, index finger: 'A Pickpocket in Custody', 'The Last Chance', and 'Bill Sikes Attempting to Destroy his Dog'.

This last picture in particular makes her shudder. There is a rough-looking thug and here is his cowering dog. Despite never having owned a dog, Doreen has told me that she is definitely a dog woman. Had her first husband been more of a manly man, she likes to imagine that they might have attended pheasant shoots. She can picture herself with a camel-haired coat thrown about her shoulders and an adoring gun dog at her feet.

'I hope this Sikes character didn't kill the poor animal.'

'No. But I'm afraid the dog dies attempting to reach his master after he accidentally hangs himself trying to escape.'

Doreen is appalled. 'The dog hangs himself?'

'No, Sikes hangs himself and then the dog dies.'

Quickly she steps away from the picture. 'That's a dreadful story. It's a shame nobody thought to call the RSPCA.'

'It's not real, Doreen. It's from Oliver Twist. Dickens, you know?'

'Oh him. I could never get on with Dickens. I'm not a great one for the printed word especially when it runs to over a hundred pages.' She wrinkles her nose as if an aroma of age and criminal deeds emanates unpleasantly from the prints. 'How old are these?'

'Quite old,' I say with satisfaction. 'I have a couple of excellent Lowrys as well – Lancashire scenes of course. They're in the hall. Worth quite a bit in today's market.' With a sinking heart I watch her again wipe her fingers with her handkerchief.

'And were you thinking of putting them into auction?' she asks.

'They belonged to my late father.'

'Well that's all right then. No hurt feelings. Personally I lean more towards Romanticism and *Art Nouveau*.'

It is at this baffling moment of misunderstanding, that I register a feeling of real alarm. Doreen in her perfectly cut red gabardine suit and fox fur jacket does not go with my beloved flat. This is my castle, my masculine domain. In my mind's eye I'd always intended my home to resemble a gentleman's club – a place to relax, shake out the newspaper and smoke a fine cigar. Never have I arrived home without experiencing a sense of welcome.

After all, what and where was Yorkshire apart from being a large area where people prided themselves on speaking their minds, somewhere to the north of London?

'What I meant was, Doreen… my dear,' I say carefully, 'these prints have sentimental value. I couldn't possibly sell them or leave them here when I may be away for a substantial amount of time. I won't take many possessions to your home but these must go with me, the Lowrys as well as the Cruickshanks.'

The corners of her mouth droop. 'But they're so depressing.'

'But not to me.' My tone is gentle yet firm.

Doreen crosses the room to the window and lifts the net curtain. When she turns back she is smiling. 'I'm too used to getting my own way. What a spoilt Doreen, I am. Of course your pictures must come with you, and any other knick-knacks if they'll make Mildmay's feel like home.'

I realise that I've been waiting for Doreen to refuse, to hand me the perfect excuse to call off this ludicrous escapade. It surprises me that I actually feel a sense of relief. Doreen is being reasonable. I am even able to regain a feeling of mild fondness for her.

Doreen stands in front of me. She closes her eyes, raising her pink powdered face to mine. 'Ollie kiss Dorie.'

Extraordinary how rapidly my feeling of mild fondness can vanish – if she'd only have patience and wait for me to initiate physical contact.

The very first time Doreen kissed me we were standing outside the Sé Cathedral in Funchal, Madeira's capital city.

'Apparently this cathedral's got a beautiful Moorish ceiling and carvings in ivory and local cedar.' She'd brushed her lips against my mouth as she'd reached for the guide-book in my jacket pocket. 'Shall we have coffee and a pastry first?'

Automatically, I'd jerked my head away. The easy familiarity of her kiss had left me confused and out of sorts for the rest of the day.

Now I consider Doreen's heavily lipsticked lips and again find them unenticing.

Her eyes are closed, she grasps my shoulders.

My hands are obliged to do something. They flutter like two desperate birds before settling lightly on her waist.

Doreen kicks off her high-heeled shoes. Suddenly she is three inches shorter. Instead of her waist, my hands now cup the outside of her breasts.

'Yes, yes,' she whispers. 'Take me.'

With my face pressed into Doreen's lacquered hair, I mumble, 'Not now.'

'Yes, now.' She tugs at the belt of my trousers.

'No, Doreen. Stop it. We hardly know each other.'

'We spent ten days together on the cruise. It doesn't take that long for me to make up my mind. I want you, Oliver.'

But I don't want you. I can't quite bring myself to say those words, although common sense whispers that it would be better in the long run if I did. I set Doreen aside and position myself with the chesterfield between us.

'Doreen, we discussed this on the telephone. I'll come up to Yorkshire and stay with you for a trial period. We'll take things slowly, familiarise ourselves with each other's… ' I trail off, 'peculiarities' being the only word to present itself.

'But I'm ready to go the whole hog, Oliver. We're not getting any younger.'

'I'm sorry, Doreen, this is all I can offer at the moment. I hope you can understand and respect my good intentions.'

What I would really like to happen, is for Bill Sikes to swing in through the window, hit me hard over the head with a stolen candlestick and then drag me back out of the window never to be seen by Doreen again. Alternatively, for her to meet that same fate.

It is my turn to walk across the room, lift the net curtain and stare out. With my back to her I say, 'Doreen, as I've explained several times, I am a man who has received several major setbacks over the last two years. I can't emphasise enough that I need time to recover my equilibrium.'

'Of course you do, my darling.' She jumps off the sofa and takes a step towards me. 'But are we talking days, weeks or months?'

'I have no idea.' I take a deep breath and turn to face her. 'Supposing I said never?'

'I wouldn't believe you.' Doreen juts out her chin, smooths her hair and skirt. 'But you're quite right, I'm not helping matters, am I?'

'Not really.'

Her bosom rises and falls. 'I am a passionate woman, Oliver.'

'I'm aware of that.'

'Are you passionate?'

'I'm capable of passion.'

'That's all I need to know.'

The tension has faded from the room. 'Perhaps a cup of coffee, Doreen?'

'You're the boss.' Doreen salutes me and marches smartly towards the kitchen. 'Where do you keep that powdered milk?'

Left alone, I slump into the armchair. Beneath my suit jacket, my shirt, my cotton vest, my heart pounds. Increasingly I feel trapped in a parallel universe. Surely a duplicate, confident Mr Oliver still reigns supreme over the The Store? Della will be trying to catch his eye with a flourish of tanned cleavage; Rosa (I glance at my watch) will even now be rushing in with his mid-morning coffee and bacon sandwich from the Copper Kettle in Hanover Square. And Claire Daker, my nemesis, what would she be doing at this very moment?

My heart slows, the dampness on my forehead dries. I can hear the cheerful sound of rattling crockery coming from the kitchen.

Tunelessly, Doreen sings out, 'Night and day, you are the one.'

I quite like her tuneless singing. Yes, I can enjoy romantic messages from Doreen – provided she remains in another room.

For lunch, I take Doreen to a small trattoria on the Earls Court Road.

'Not expensive,' I tell her. 'But it does serve authentic Italian food.'

'I'm not sure I like the sound of that.' She smiles up at me. 'I think I might prefer unauthentic Italian food. I could have knocked us up something in your kitchen. Much more intimate. Vesta does a very nice *Spaghetti Bolognese*. It comes with a sachet of parmesan.'

I have no idea who or what Vesta might be but feel too weary to ask. 'Trust me, Doreen.' I give her a reassuring smile. 'You'll enjoy the food.'

This is the only restaurant I ever visit, generally eating alone. For a change I am sharing a table with a well-dressed woman. The tension in my neck that I'd felt all afternoon begins to recede. My father had a saying: *Reflected glory is no glory at all*, which I can't disagree with. However, under the restaurant's subdued lighting,

Doreen looks attractive and very, very rich – just basking in the warmth of her glory does me the power of good!

'Doreen, I can recommend the *Asparagus alla Milanese* followed by *Veal Escalope*.' (I have been ordering the same dishes for twenty years and still find them delicious.)

She looks unconvinced. 'My late husband Peter always ordered *Steak Diane* for the two of us when we went out for dinner, but I'll give this a go.'

I suggest a bottle of Merlot.

'I'd rather have a light Chardonnay.'

One bottle becomes two. I begin to feel kindly disposed to everyone in the restaurant. Doreen is truly a queen amongst women.

She pushes away her plate. 'Most pleasant. Simple but tasty. I don't know what your thoughts are, but we could skip pudding and go straight to coffee and brandies.'

'I don't normally drink spirits at lunchtime.' Even to my own ears, my tone sounds prim rather than assertive.

Her fingers rest lightly on my leather watch strap. 'It's gone three o'clock. As far as I'm concerned, that's late afternoon.' She holds up her hand and shouts, 'Antonio, two brandies over here with coffees. Chop-chop.'

While admiring her confidence in dealing with the waiter, I wish she wouldn't keep calling him Antonio. His name badge clearly states Giorgio.

Under the table Doreen caresses my right knee.

I steel myself not to tense. *Has the woman not listened to a word I said earlier? Or is this just a reassuring friendly pat, perfectly acceptable between friends?* I realise that I have no idea what the difference would be between a caress and a pat!

The waiter puts two glasses of brandy in front of us.

'Cheers,' Doreen says. 'Here's to holidays.'

'To holidays.' Doreen's hand has left my leg and suddenly I am in a holiday mood.

'Oliver… pet,' she leans towards me. 'I did intend to book into a hotel for the night… '

My spirits soar even higher at the prospect of having my flat to myself again.

‘ …but I’ve left it rather late. Perhaps I could sleep on your sofa – I’m only a little titch?’

My spirits plummet. Courtesy demands that I open my mouth and assert, ‘Doreen, I wouldn’t dream of letting you sleep on the sofa. You must have the bed. I’ll be perfectly comfortable with the sofa.’

‘But your great long legs will dangle over the arm.’ She hesitates. ‘Of course we do have an alternative?’

‘Do we?’ I’m fumbling in my jacket for my wallet.

‘It’s somewhat indelicate.’

‘Please Doreen, what alternative?’

‘We could just… ’ She shrugs her shoulders. ‘Pop on our pyjamas and bunk in together.’

Perhaps it is the quantity of drink, but the thought of us both changing into serviceable nightwear and ‘bunking in together’ seems a surprisingly comradely concept.

‘You on your side, me on mine. Why should I waste money on a hotel when you have a perfectly comfortable double bed?’ Doreen drapes her fox fur over the back of her chair. ‘Think about it while I’m powdering my nose.’

Late evening: I emerge from the bathroom. My head is throbbing. At some point during what remained of the afternoon, Doreen has spirited away my tailored Egyptian cotton pyjamas with the cloth-covered buttons and replaced them with a pair in yellow silk. The jacket is of a karate-style with black piping and a black sash.

‘You look terrific.’ From the depth of the chesterfield, Doreen applauds the new pyjamas. ‘Very sexy. That colour suits you.’

From my fashion retail background, I know that yellow is possibly the worst shade to be worn next to a sallow, ageing skin. The tie sash won’t remain tied because the silk is too slippery. Only a man like Sean Connery with his film star tan and admirably hairy chest could have carried off an open karate pyjama jacket. Already the jacket is parting to reveal the triangle of grizzled hair between my nipples, which is the colour that the hair on my head would now be, left to its own devices.

I have always been sensitive about the proportions of my chest. During my early thirties I’d tried the ‘Charles Atlas Dynamic

Tension Fitness Programme' guaranteed to turn a scrawny weakling into a muscle man. I *had* gained muscle on my arms and legs but my chest remained puny, a mismatch to the quite fine proportions of my limbs. 'You look like Ernest Hemingway at his most virile,' Doreen says.

'Do I?' I can't help but feel flattered.

'My late husband was a big fan. Saw all the films, had all his books. For whom the bloody bell rings, Ta-ta to Arms' Doreen's words are slightly slurred. 'Want a last little drinkie before bedtime?'

'I think I'll hop straight in.'

'You do that pet.'

With trepidation I push open the bedroom door. From the lounge, Doreen has brought the table lamp and draped a rose-coloured chiffon scarf over the shade. The room is now suffused in warm amber light. To combat the unexpected chill of early summer, she has positioned the small electric radiator that I only ever use on very cold days, at the foot of the bed. Curtains drawn, sheets turned back, pillows plump and inviting, I enter almost hesitantly, fearful of disturbing Doreen's thoughtful appointments. Climbing into bed, my feet meet a hot, hot-water bottle wrapped in a towel. I realise that I'm smiling. What heaven. What luxury – only spoilt by having to share the heaven and luxury with Doreen.

Half-an-hour later as I'm drifting off to sleep, she joins me. She wears a sensible, unthreatening nightdress and carries two mugs of hot chocolate.

What a thoughtful woman Doreen is capable of being.

She puts the mugs down next to the bed.

I fold back the bedcovers on her side.

Decorously, Doreen climbs in next to me. She arranges her pillows into a more comfortable sitting-up position and stares around the bedroom with satisfaction. 'Better than paying for a hotel, isn't it, Oliver?'

'Indeed it is.'

'Shall I pass you your hot chocolate?'

'If it's drinking temperature.'

'I used half boiling water, half powdered milk.'

Admirable woman!

We sip our drinks in companionable silence.

'And do I taste whisky?'

'Just a small tot. It will help you get a good night's sleep.'

I dutifully continue drinking while wondering when or if I will ever come round to liking spirits.

'And tomorrow we're off to Mildmay's,' Doreen says. 'I can't wait.'

'I'm looking forward to it.' And I am.

She takes my empty mug and places it next to hers. 'Oliver, this afternoon while I was packing up your clothes and a few knick-knacks I thought you might like to keep around you at Mildmay's, I did some thinking.'

'Ah.'

Doreen reaches for my hand and squeezes it.

'I want you to know that I do appreciate your need to recover your equilibrium. No man wants to be rushed. From the start you've made that very clear.'

I flap my free hand, 'All in the past.'

'No, I accept I've tried to barnstorm you on several occasions, that dreadful evening on the Artemis.'

'I have erased the incident from my memory.'

'At the time –'

'Completely erased.'

'But at the time,' she repeats. 'You did say that we were more than just friends.'

'And so we are.'

'Good.' Doreen strokes the line of her neck.

'Yes indeed.'

'Only while you're recovering your equilibrium, I hope you can spare a little sympathy for your Doreen.'

Beneath the sheet and blanket my feet twitch.

'You see, my late husband starved me of affection. God only knows how we produced the boys, but I'd like to think – if we do get on – that together we – perhaps could make up for the years I've wasted.'

'This is the moment to make your position clear, old buddy. Be cruel to be kind. You're offering her nothing but a bum steer.'

If I had to hear Steve Chambers' voice in my head, I wished

Steve would dispense with the 'old buddy'. And surely this was the worst possible moment to make my position clear? *Doreen, I realise we are both in our nightclothes and sharing a bed, which pre-supposes a close relationship, and that you would be invaluable as a mother, housekeeper, Bridal Salon saleswoman or nurse, but these foolish things aside, I cannot ask you to be my partner in any biblical sense.*

'Doreen… '

'Yes, my little love.' She turns towards me, searching my face with tender eyes.

I don't much care to be called 'my little love' but again feel the moment is wrong to take issue with this term of endearment.

'This is all very new to me.' I wave a hand to encompass Doreen, the scarf on the lamp and the functioning electric radiator.

The wine and brandy at lunch, another bottle when we'd arrived back at my flat and the whisky now, are finally having an effect. Words present themselves that are entirely unsuitable.

'I've had affairs with many other women; many, many other women,' I say. 'But have never felt the deep, sincere regard that I feel for you, dear Doreen.' I wave my hand again.

'Thank you, my darling. No, not just "my darling" – you truly are my very own little love.'

'Maybe so. Maybe so. I just do hope –'

'Hope what?'

My eyes smart with unshed alcoholic tears. 'That you won't find you've bought a pig in a poke.'

'I'd love a poke from a dear little piggy.'

'Goodnight, Doreen.'

I ease myself down under the bedclothes. As expected the silk karate jacket slithers upwards so that much of it is lodged around my neck like a muffler.

'Goodnight, Oliver,' Doreen says, leaning over me.

I do my best. I shut my eyes tight and as I press my lips against Doreen's lips I think of Claire Daker.

Chapter 5

1974

Carrying the telephone in one hand, Miss Frances stepped out onto the terrace. She looped the wire behind her chair and sat down at a wooden table large enough to comfortably accommodate a dinner party for eight guests. It never had.

In front of her she spread out the contact sheets for The Store's new bridal wear catalogue. As she studied each photograph with a magnifying glass for faults, she mused on whether Margo, her favourite model, was still credible representing a mother-of-the-bride. Nearing seventy, Margo should really have been modelling grandmother-of-the-bride-clothes but with careful lighting she still passed for mid-fifties or even fifty.

But not for much longer. Who would replace Margo? Surely Margo was irreplaceable?

Distracted by the view of distant hills glimpsed between the trees, Miss Frances pushed the photographs aside. She'd bought the two-hundred-year-old cottage to share with Gus eight years earlier. Initially Gus had wanted a *pied-a-terre* in Brighton but for once Miss Frances had been determined. She'd grown up in Yorkshire; Hampsthwaite – just a village but she'd been happy there.

'Gus, Brighton is much the same as London but with sea,' she'd said.

'Which is why I like it.'

'But I'm paying for it.' And surprisingly, Gus had backed down.

Together they'd planned the renovations, for once in agreement about restoring the rooms as near as possible to their original form and decoration. Even when Gus became ill she'd still enjoyed discussing plans for a small herb garden at the front, a second bathroom in the eaves. Plans based on a certain set of circumstances. On her own, Miss Frances found she couldn't care less about a herb garden or a second bathroom.

The cottage stood on a wooded slope and for most of the year it was concealed from the road behind a tall hedge of roses. That had been part of the appeal for Miss Frances – the notion that the two of them were alone together in a forest. Within a few steps of their garden gate, the trees formed a canopy and a path took them between banks of wild flowers and high hedges of blackberry bushes.

The isolation had been part of the charm for Gus as well, but for different reasons. It was only after her death that Miss Frances realised she had not been the only one to wander alone in the 'forest' with her girlfriend.

Miss Frances smiled ruefully. She remembered a similar morning of bright early summer sunshine in their first real holiday at the cottage: from the then un-renovated kitchen, the cheerful sound of Gus whistling 'Oh what a beautiful morning' while burning their toast. Even now, years later, Miss Frances still preferred her toast burnt.

'This is the life.' Gus had said, waving her slice of blackened bread at the view. Her ability to live in the moment would have been endearing, except for the fact that any one of Gus's special moments was just as good as all her other special moments. There were other cottages, flats, chalets even caravans and camp sites where she burnt toast and announced with great good humour, 'This is the life.'

That had been a hard lesson for Miss Frances to learn.

She thought about Gus's death quite objectively now. In retrospect she wished that Gus had died suddenly and hadn't felt the imperative to cram every bit of living into her last ten months.

She'd accused Miss Frances of being selfish. 'You should want what I want, not what you want. I'm the one who's bloody dying.'

It had taken Miss Frances three years of therapy to understand that Gus may have even loved her. But being loved hadn't automatically meant that she was the one Gus wanted to see when time was limited. Her company could be saved for when Gus was too ill to get out of bed. Sometimes Miss Frances had day-dreamed of sitting at Gus's bedside, trying to coax her into swallowing another teaspoon of yoghurt. While Gus slept, she would remain quietly reading a novel, watching over her. She imagined the two of them together, window blinds drawn against the afternoon sun and the only sounds perhaps a machine for monitoring breathing or heartbeat. Macabre, but she saw a Gus reduced to white and grey. This woman who had always been as 'brown as a berry' – which was a stupid sentimental phrase but described her so well. Berry-like. What did a berry represent – something light-hearted, ephemeral, pleasant to look at and taste? Gus.

Even now, it seemed extraordinary that none of this ever happened. Gus had never seemed too ill to stay in bed – not even in that last week in Harrogate Hospital.

The nurses had moved her to a private room. The casement window was open, the bed ignored. Gus sat on a hard hospital chair, her elbows resting on the sill.

'You'll catch your death of cold,' Miss Frances was about to fussily say. She stopped herself, but Gus wouldn't have minded. She might have even laughed.

Miss Frances kissed the top of Gus's head, touched her lightly on the shoulder.

'Get me a chicken sandwich from the canteen, Fran.'

'But you can't eat it.'

'I can still smell it. *You* can eat it.' Gus's voice had been warm and affectionate.

Like the eager puppy Miss Frances imagined herself to be, off she scampered up three flights of stairs to the canteen. She'd hurried back with the sandwich, smiling triumphantly.

'Chicken sandwich coming up!'

The familiar figure of Gus remained seated at the window, elbows on the windowsill, shoulders and head leaning forward as if to feel the breeze on her face but the woman she'd known and loved was gone forever. Miss Frances didn't immediately call someone; instead she closed the door and sat on Gus's bed. She waited, and although nothing happened she didn't wait in vain. She chose to think that the spirit of Gus could not yet be too far away, surely there were a few moments left of her company. Only when Miss Frances was quite certain that she was alone in the room did she open the door and make her way towards the nurses' station.

Miss Frances realised with surprise that she wasn't crying. Usually when she re-played that last day in her head, she was ready to howl.

A jay landed on the stone birdbath. He was a regular visitor.

Miss Frances wondered where the jay went for water in the weeks and months when she wasn't there to top up the birdbath. She must sell the cottage. It held too many memories and most of them sad. Sometimes on starless evenings, if she woke in the night, she was nervous being there on her own. She'd get out of bed and double-check that the doors and windows were locked. When Gus had been with her, she'd never worried.

Coming back from the kitchen with a fresh cup of coffee, she found herself thinking about the Daker girl. She imagined leading her out onto the terrace to meet Gus.

'This is Claire Daker.'

Spontaneously, Miss Frances burst out laughing. Gus's expression would have been a picture, as she took in knee socks, the short skirt, glossy white-blonde ponytail, and of course the ten years or more age difference.

'Excuse us.' Gus would wheel Miss Frances round and march her back into the kitchen. 'Are you mad? That girl is totally unsuitable. Fran, you can do better.'

Miss Frances drew the telephone towards her. She opened her Louis Vuitton address book and found the number. Smiling, she dialled the Jean Peterson Model Agency.

'It's Miss Frances. The Store. Put me through to Jean please.'

The mother-of-the-bride shoot would have to be done again. She needed someone younger. Nobody was irreplaceable.

Two days later, Miss Frances returned to London. She felt energised. Thinking about herself as she walked along Oxford Street, she came to the conclusion that a page in her life had been turned, while serendipitously, a door may have also clicked open.

From the Copper Kettle she collected her regular cappuccino before sweeping into the staff entrance of The Store. As she approached the lift, the doors opened. With amusement she noted how lesser members of staff rarely wanted to share it with her. She heard a voice shout, 'Hold on.'

Ignoring the voice, Miss Frances pressed the button for the fifth floor.

Before the lift doors could close, an ankle-strapped shoe jammed between them, an angora arm snaked into the lift and shouldered the doors apart.

'I said, "Hold on!"'

'Claire, I have a meeting at nine-fifteen. I haven't got time to wait at every floor.'

Claire pressed the third floor button.

Miss Frances successfully concealed her pleased smile. 'It's only about a dozen stairs. Someone your age shouldn't need the lift?'

'It's at least two dozen stairs and I'm walking about all day, thanks very much.'

The doors opened and Claire stepped out.

Miss Frances pressed the fifth floor button again. 'I'm promoting you. You're going to manage our new boutique. Meet me on the Mezzanine floor at one.'

'One o'clock is lunchtime,' Claire protested as the lift doors closed.

At one-fifteen the lift doors opened on the Mezzanine floor and Miss Frances stepped out. Claire peeled herself away from the wall. Pointedly she looked at her watch.

'Claire, if I wanted to keep you hanging about all afternoon, as head buyer that would be my prerogative.'

'It would also be very inconsiderate of you.'

'The higher you climb, the more inconsiderate you can afford to be.' Miss Frances pushed her tinted glasses up above her fringe. 'Follow me.' She led the way along a corridor. Outside a pair of heavy metal doors she stopped and lightly touched Claire's arm. 'I'd advise you to take a deep breath before you go in. It can be pretty suffocating until you reach the windows.'

Miss Frances took her own deep breath and pushed the doors open onto a billowing world of white. She stepped forward. A second later, all that remained to show that there had ever been a Miss Frances was a row of tightly packed bridal dresses swaying slightly in their polythene shrouds.

Claire inhaled, lowered her head and followed, finally breaking through the rails of dresses into space and sunlight. On three sides of the room, cardboard boxes were stacked to the ceiling. Two battered wooden tables faced each other in front of the window. In a chair behind the far table a plump woman in her forties sat sewing. She had a pretty but bad tempered face framed by crisp black curls.

'Claire, this is Mavis,' Miss Frances said.

Mavis gave an acknowledgement but made no attempt to get up.

'Mavis is a marvel. Not only does she check all our mail-order garments, she tickets and prices everything that comes into Mezzanine. Mavis, you will help Claire, won't you? She is our *ingénue.*'

Mavis removed several dressmaking pins from her mouth and adjusted the tape measures looped around her neck. 'I don't intend to play nursemaid.'

'Heaven forfend that you should play nursemaid, Mavis.'

'Excuse me, Miss Frances but I thought I was going to be the boutique manageress not an ingénue.'

Miss Frances inclined her head as if Claire had said something profound that warranted consideration. 'You are indeed.'

Mavis scraped back her chair and got to her feet. 'But that's what it will amount to – me playing ruddy nursemaid.'

Removing her spectacles, Miss Frances began to polish their lenses with the hem of her eighty-percent cashmere, twenty-percent man-made fibre, maxi-cardigan. 'We all have to make sacrifices.'

'This isn't going to be my office, is it, Miss Frances?'

'Well, yes it is Claire, and a very generously sized office.' Miss Frances unfurled her arms into the immediate space.

'It's a stockroom.'

'That doubles as your office. We've found a filing cabinet for you.'

'What about a desk?'

'A table offers so much more room to spread out on.'

'There's no chair.'

'There is a chair. We just need to locate it.'

'It's at the back,' Mavis said. 'I use it to keep one of the doors jammed open if it gets too stuffy.'

'Excellent. Mavis.' Miss Frances turned back to Claire. 'When you've settled in, come and find me. We'll go downstairs and I can introduce you to Mr Oliver. Till the boutique opens you can help out in the Bridal Salon.'

'Help out in the Bridal Salon? You said I'd be managing the boutique.'

Miss Frances could almost have laughed at the expression on Claire's face. Really, she was such a delightfully ungrateful young woman. 'All in good time.'

Chapter 6

1975

Carpenter closed the front door and stood very still, an unopened telegram in his right hand. He held the envelope up to the light filtering in through the faux-mullioned panes of the hall window. For some reason he felt this was the kind of action a man might make when receiving a telegram. He glanced over his shoulder. Both the dining room and kitchen doors were shut. In a low voice he addressed the crystal chandelier immediately above his head: 'Look god, I don't want anything unpleasant to happen to Ma, but couldn't you just extend her London trip for a few more days? Give us all some extra peace and quiet?'

He tore open the envelope. His shoulders slumped. 'God, you never fail to disappoint me, not that I believed in you in the first place.' Carpenter gave the chandelier a long, hard stare before striding back down the hall and barging into the dining room.

'Junior, read this.'

His brother, Peter Mildmay Junior, sat at one end of a long, highly polished table, a copy of British Vogue wedged between his breakfast bowl of Shredded Wheat and the milk jug. Junior, at twenty-four, was six years younger than Carpenter. He was slender (almost girlish in Carpenter's opinion) with silky light brown hair that sometimes in sunlight shone a watery green.

'Not now, Carpenter. How do you think I'd look in a zippered jumpsuit?'

'Ridiculous.' Carpenter dropped the telegram in front of a double-page spread of young men wearing zippered jumpsuits.

'Go easy, you're dislodging my sugar.' Junior put down his spoon. 'Oh, it's from Mummy. Why didn't she just telephone?'

'Yes, it is from "Mummy".' Carpenter's voice was grim. 'And Mummy likes to go for the maximum dramatic effect.'

'Darlings, shopping trip successful!' Junior read out. *'Carpenter; please meet the 3.15 train tomorrow (Tuesday). Will be bringing home someone rather special. Love and kisses. D.'*

Junior laid the telegram on the table and began to carefully segment the remaining Shredded Wheat. 'I'm not happy with that,' he said.

'With what? The telegram or your breakfast?'

'Both. Obviously Mummy bringing home an unknown "someone rather special" is disturbing, but honestly Carpenter, I do like the sugar to retain an unbroken crust as I work my way through it.'

Carpenter rubbed the side of his face, 'So, is that it? She's never brought home someone special before, which means he must be pretty bloody special, our financial future could be hanging in the balance but your prime concern remains your breakfast?' Pulling a packet of cigarettes from his jacket he rested his buttocks on the table edge.

'I wouldn't smoke if I were you. She'll smell it on the curtains as soon as she walks in here.'

'I'm shaking in my shoes.' Carpenter put a cigarette between his lips but didn't light it. 'If she *is* serious about someone we could be left penniless.'

'But I am penniless. Even if I desperately wanted a jumpsuit I couldn't afford one. I rely on what Mummy gives me. At least you have a salary.'

'I earn a salary. I work bloody hard for this family. She sits on the money like a broody hen on a clutch of golden eggs.' Carpenter hit the table with his fist. Sugar from Junior's Shredded Wheat rose in the air; British Vogue toppled forward.

'You have just ruined my breakfast.' Junior threw down his serviette in disgust and stood up. 'Honestly, Carpenter, all this fuss. Mummy just might have found a genuinely nice old chap who will make her happy.'

With surprising grace for such a tall man, Carpenter dropped his unlit cigarette and grasped Junior by the collar of his shirt, lifting him several inches above the carpet. 'I couldn't care less if she's fallen in love with Albert Schweitzer; he's not getting his feet settled under this table.'

'You're hurting me. I'm losing all feeling in my toes, ankles and collarbone.'

Carpenter lowered Junior to the floor. 'You're pathetic.'

'No, you're pathetic. And a bully.' Junior stepped out of Carpenter's range to straighten his collar and tie. 'I intend to tell

Venables to put some champagne on ice.'

'Do what you like. I haven't got time to argue. I'll be back around six.'

He left the room. A few moments later the front door slammed.

Junior retrieved the cigarette from under the dining table and considered it thoughtfully before dropping it into the breast pocket of his shirt. He walked over to the window. Carpenter's silver-grey Mercedes sports car rolled smoothly across the gravel drive and out onto the Burnside Road.

Carpenter had lunched well but unwisely at the Templar's Arms on Laverne's Alpine lamb pie with a Swiss cheese dressing, followed by apple strudel. He'd washed this down with two pints of Thwaites Best Bitter and now, at only three in the afternoon, with tea and rock buns on the three-thirty tea-break horizon, he was on the verge of falling asleep at his desk.

Carefully, he balanced an open file, his pen and an estimate for sandstone paving on the black leather chair arm before swivelling the chair to face the window. If Monica took it into her head to peer in through the glass at the top of the door she would assume he was mulling over some knotty problem to do with the estate they were building near Harrogate. Thinking of Monica, he smiled drowsily. How she'd changed. It was hard to believe that only a matter of months ago Monica had been at least a stone-and-a-half heavier. The temp agency had sent her over as a stand-in for Enid, his last PA who had gone for a month's skiing in Chamonix. He'd almost sent her straight back but hadn't been sure if he could reject an employee on the grounds of weight.

Of course, Doreen had wanted to know all about her. 'I don't want you falling for some little trollop while Enid's abroad.'

'She's fat, Mother.'

'How fat? Voluptuously fat? Hideously fat?'

'She has a double chin and her skirt is fastened at the waist with a chain of safety pins.'

Enid never came back to Burnside. She married a ski instructor and settled in France. Carpenter found he didn't mind at all. He warmed to Monica which was about as much affection he was willing to admit to. In a matter of weeks Monica lost her double chin and he found he quite missed it. She became alarmingly thin and he wondered how he'd manage if she died, and in a fit of anxiety he made her his permanent PA. He watched as she flowered, blossomed – became the kind of woman that men like Ned seemed to find attractive, but he still yearned just a little, for the earlier, bigger version of Monica

He hadn't given Doreen an update.

'Is the temp still the size of a house?' Doreen sometimes asked.

'I'm surprised she's not bigger.' Carpenter had mastered a careless laugh. 'Considering the amount of cake and buns she tucks away morning, noon and night.

Only half-awake and not wishing to disturb this pleasant state he turned his head fractionally. In the outer office, Monica sat at her desk, head bent over the typewriter, hands flying across the keys. She was a fiendishly fast typist, but whatever was she typing all the time? At most, on a busy day, he only dictated half-a-dozen letters.

Deciding to join a spoken French class with her had been a mistake. When they'd first discussed the possibility at Easter, it had been snowing and the extreme weather had created an easy camaraderie between them. Just before eleven she'd suggested that in view of the wintry conditions she would buy toasted buttered muffins instead of their usual rock buns. Really he should have been the one to brave the snow, but Monica was wearing thick-soled boots. He'd looked down at his expensive brown leather brogues and said nothing.

Normally they took their breaks separately but that morning he'd stood at his open office door to eat his muffin, coffee cup resting on the filing cabinet. They'd started discussing holidays. Monica wanted to go to Paris while he fancied a leisurely tour of some French vineyards.

'I'm joining an Adult Ed. Spoken French class at the college in April,' she said.

'What would "Adults" cover?'

'Adults.'

'Really? Would I be considered too old to be an adult?'

Monica had raised her eyes towards the ceiling and failed to answer.

Carpenter imagined himself walking, no strolling, into Burnside Technical College, a couple of books under his arm, a notebook and a Parker fountain pen and propelling pencil in the top pocket of his tan corduroy jacket. A vista of friendships beckoned. A whole spoken French class of friends who would toss out cheerful comments: 'Hi there, Carpenter, done your homework? A swift half later?' He would smile, make a joke or shrug, in a relaxed, don't give a damn kind of way

The class was already on term two. To catch up, he and Monica had decided to speak French during working hours, apart from when he needed to dictate a letter or in an emergency such as the building being on fire or his mother arriving unexpectedly. Six weeks later Carpenter knew how to *ouvre la fenêtre* and *fermer la porte* but there was a limit to the use of such phrases unless the building really was on fire.

Reluctantly he checked his watch. Any minute now Monica would come in for his tea order. They were back with the rock buns. He would have liked to ask for a toasted buttered muffin but she might think he was making some sentimental reference to that wintry morning. Did she have a boyfriend? What was 'Do you have a boyfriend?' in French? Not that she was his type. Half-asleep he began to list reasons why Monica wasn't his type: too young, too tall, too thin, chewed gum. Although in trying to give up gum she'd now begun to smoke cheroots. His mother would prefer a gum-chewing woman to a cheroot-smoking one. Carpenter heard the outer, outer door click open.

'Are you Carpenter's new office girly?'

He recognised the hateful, smooth tones of Martin Renshawe.

'I am Mr Mildmay's PA and secretary, Mr Renshawe. You asked me that the last time you called in.'

'Well, Mr Mildmay's PA and secretary, can you tell your boss that *Doctor* Renshawe would like a word with him.'

'I'll check if he's available.'

'I can see him through the glass.' Martin raised his voice. 'Carpenter, you old dog, what are you up to in there?'

Monica stepped in front of Martin Renshawe and opened Carpenter's office door. 'Doctor Renshawe *pour vous, Charpentier*.'

Martin Renshawe squeezed past her and bounded across to Carpenter's desk. Adopting an expression of a man interrupted while in deep thought, Carpenter slowly rose to his feet.

'Why, Martin, how nice to see you. You've caught me up to my eyes, I'm afraid.'

They shook hands. As always, Martin Renwhawe tried to crush his fingers and almost succeeded. Carpenter steeled himself not to yelp.

'Grab a chair Martin.'

Martin grabbed a chair; twirled it till it faced backwards then straddled the seat.

Carpenter sat down. 'So Martin? To what do I owe this pleasure? I hope Junior's not proving a hopeless case?'

Martin scrunched his forehead attractively. Carpenter knew for a fact that Martin Renshawe was teetering on fifty. Just when was he going to start looking middle-aged?

'Junior? Not a hopeless case at all. A charming boy. A few more sessions and I'll have the lad straightened out.'

'And Madge? She's well?'

'Never better. Actually I popped in to have a few words about Burnside's damnably seductive First Lady.'

Carpenter narrowed his eyes to signify bafflement.

'Your gorgeous mother of course. Laverne tells me she's bringing home a man-friend.'

'Did she really? Good grief.' Carpenter flinched inwardly at the idea of his mother and a 'man-friend'.

In a graceful sequence, Martin leapt to his feet, turned his chair the right way round, sat down again, rested one ankle on the knee of the other leg, tweaked something invisible off the rib of his black silk sock before saying, 'Sorry Carpenter, you can't kid a kidder. I'm afraid the cat is well and truly out of the proverbial bag.'

'I've no idea what you're talking about.'

'You did know your mother has got herself engaged?'

Carpenter's heart missed several beats. This was worse than he'd imagined. Surely any affair hadn't reached that advanced stage? 'Of course I knew,' Carpenter replied smoothly. 'I just wasn't aware my mother's relationships were common knowledge. However I'm thrilled for her.'

'I wonder if you are.'

'Well, I've said I am and you'll have to take that as the truth. Now I'm sorry, but I have an important meeting this afternoon.'

'You and Junior are as close to me as my own sons would have been… if Madge and I had been so blessed.' Martin passed his tanned hand in front of his eyes as if to brush away tears. 'All I'm asking is that you both watch your backs. Lover boy will expect to be head honcho.'

'I do appreciate your concern. If you'd just excuse me… ' Carpenter opened the office door and looked out. 'Ah, *Monique, quelle temps est nos prochain rendezvous*?'

'*Temps est* weather, *Charpentier, heure est* time.'

'Well, *quelle heure est nos derniere* appointment.'

'*Dix minutes* and I think it's *notre.*'

'*Dix minutes! Sacre bleu! Etes-vous certainement ce ne'est pas cinq minutes?'*

'*Non. Dix minutes.'*

'*Merci.*' Carpenter returned to his desk and picked up his file and fountain pen.

'*Entre nous*,' Martin quirked an eyebrow at him, 'I find French quite a sexy language.'

Carpenter bared his teeth in a smile. 'Nothing sexy about good business sense. Naturally I voted for the Common Market.' For a moment he was jubilant. Martin Renshawe demolished. For a fact he knew that Martin had voted against, on the grounds that Burnside would be overrun by foreigners who smelt of onions and garlic. How he disliked the man. Since childhood, he'd felt dogged by the big generous figure with the big generous features.

Incredibly quickly, Martin regained the upper hand, just by smiling back at him with an apparently genuine smile. 'Let's keep this *tête-à-tête* about the interloper under wraps, shall we?' He threw a fake punch at Carpenter's shoulder.

'Fair enough.'

'Good. We're singing from the same hymn sheet, you big streak of lightning!'

Carpenter ached for a loaded double-barrelled shotgun.

Chapter 7

1975

'You'll love Mildmay's,' Doreen informs me, leaning her head back against the white linen antimacassar of her First Class seat. 'It's ideally situated.'

Ideally suited for what? I wonder, but I smile back at her and very slightly incline my head forward. Ten minutes earlier I'd become aware of a nagging pain at the base of my skull and realised that I'd probably nodded and smiled more since meeting Doreen than in my entire life.

'I can't wait to introduce you to the north.'

'Ah, the north.' I turn to stare out of the window as if we were already there rather than just passing through Stevenage.

The train enters a tunnel. I can clearly see Doreen reflected in the dark window. Dreamily, she has begun to stroke her neck, fingers trailing across her skin to linger in the V of her silk blouse. I know that she is trying to attract my attention – would the woman never stop thinking about sex? We emerge into daylight again and I concentrate my gaze on the countryside.

Lines of drab houses have given way to fields and trees. I spot several brown-and-white cows mooching near a hedge. I've never felt the inclination to pat a cow before but suddenly I find myself thinking that to pat a cow's nose might be an enjoyable experience.

An hour passes. Now I can see distant small hills that seem more like mountains and I am assailed by an unfamiliar, almost boyish sense of adventure. I have always associated the north of England with rain, snow and cold, wet feet. But even that prospect no longer daunts me. For the first time in my life I'm considering the possibilities of Wellington boots and Arran knit socks. An entire new wardrobe beckons. How might I look in a sports coat? Or a lumber jacket thrown over a virgin wool shirt in a sombre tartan? Why must the tartan be sombre? A bright Scott Red tartan would suit my newly and attractively weather-beaten face. (Obviously I'm running ahead of myself here, however I do retain a light tan from the Madeira cruise.)

Perhaps I could even become a man who rolls up his shirt

sleeves (meticulously) to reveal hands and forearms made muscular from wielding an axe.

'Are there real fires at Mildmay's?'

Doreen frowns. 'We've not got through the summer yet. Why would you care about real fires?'

'I just like the idea of them, that's all. Chopping wood. Filling up a coal scuttle.'

'When Peter died I had Scandinavian electric panels fitted throughout. The local paper did a feature on them. They're cleaner and far more reliable.'

'I was rather hoping for something in the inglenook line: an open grate or perhaps a log-burning stove.'

'Then you'll be disappointed, although I do have stylish Berryflame Magicoal electric fires with genuine teak surround in the lounge and the study. Cost a small fortune but they create a certain ambiance, and where bodily warmth is involved, it's money well spent.' Like a small inquisitive animal, one of Doreen's hands begins to travel breastwards again.

I feel my buttocks clench apprehensively. As a man who had never experienced nervous buttock clenching before I wonder if this might have an adverse effect on my general health. Or might the effect be positive? Might my buttocks become the tautest buttocks in the land?

'And your house, Doreen – is it in a village?'

'Outskirts.' Doreen crosses her legs. 'It's set in a cosy nookery of executive style mansions. That's how the estate was described in the sales brochure.'

As I watch her mouth continue to move, I find myself absently thinking, surely she means 'a cosy nookery of thatched cottages'?

'So your house is on an estate, Doreen?'

Doreen appears offended. 'We're not talking "council estate" here – this is executive housing at its finest.' She reaches for her handbag. 'And you'll adore my friends, Michael and Laverne and they'll adore you.'

'They are?'

'The couple who run the Templar's Arms pub. They're always saying "What this place needs is new blood".'

'Metaphorically?' I try out a dry chuckle which Doreen ignores.

'And then there's Martin Renshawe. He's a dear family friend, also a psychiatrist. My son, Junior's under him at the moment.'

'But the Thwaite Templar you've mentioned, that *is* a village?'

'You do go on about the village element, Oliver. There is – was – a village. It's had some re-development but we still have a village green, a village pub, and a village cricket team. Is that enough "village" for you?' Doreen picks up her handbag and clasps it against her stomach, drumming out an irritated tattoo against the leather.

'More than enough. This is a big step I'm taking. I'm a man of fixed ideas.'

'Yes, yes. So you keep saying.' She stands up. 'I'm just popping to the Ladies' powder room.'

Although I'm thinking that Doreen will be sorely disappointed by British Rail's Ladies' powder room I say nothing. Left to myself, I cogitate on the surprising phenomenon that I appear to be developing a sense of humour, in direct contrast to Doreen who does not seem to have any sense of humour whatsoever. I can't really add 'sense of humour' to my list of our incompatibilities, because if and when my life improves, I may return to being my familiar acerbic self.

I move on to dissecting Doreen's responses so far to my queries about Mildmay's. Generally I'm satisfied. Already I can see myself partaking of a pint of local beer in the no doubt rustic pub, bonding with her pub-landlord friend Michael over a mutual interest in French wines. And Martin Renshawe. I warm to the name. It sounds innately masculine.

I believe I'm feeling better. In the countryside I will recuperate. Imagine this: its lunchtime and I'm taking a leisurely stroll to the pub, exchanging neighbourly greetings *en route*. 'I'm up at Mildmay's. Bit different from London but Thwaite Templar certainly has a charm.'

I could even include Doreen in my perambulations. Brisk walks, several brandies and she might set off to her own bedroom satisfied with a chaste peck on the cheek.

My eyes closed, I visualise my new accommodation, executive but in the Tudor style. Possibly a lake, swans reflected in still dark water, stone bridges overhung by blossom. Did lakes have bridges?

Trees – those pale green drooping ones associated with water. Perhaps tucked in next to the pub would be a corner shop with mullioned windows and displays of old fashioned sweets: pineapple chunks and bulls' eyes. I'd buy a quarter of Tom Thumb Drops and take them home to Doreen by way of an inexpensive yet thoughtful gift.

'The moment I get home, I'm writing a letter to Harold Wilson about the state of that bog.' Doreen has returned from British Rail's powder room.

I kept my eyes shut. 'Please, Doreen.'

'Please what?' She tosses her bag onto the seat next to her.

'Please don't use that word.'

'What? Bog? I call a spade a spade and a bog a bog. You may be a man of fixed ideas – well I'm a woman of fixed vocabulary.'

I hear her fall into her seat. Underneath the table between us, her knees press against mine. Something flutters against my cheek. Startled, I open my eyes to see Doreen's fingers moving towards my nose. I brush her hand away but it only travels back as far as my neck.

'I was just getting to know your face.'

With part relief, part apprehension, I note that Doreen's mood seems to have taken a turn for the better.

'You're a funny chap, Oliver. Such a combination of forceful and sensitive, sophisticated and unsophisticated, yet you can spot a cashmere mix at twenty paces.'

I can't help feeling flattered at the novelty of someone finding me so complex. For a second I am able to enjoy being cared about. It is as simple as that.

'In the early days, my husband used to say having his neck stroked drove him wild with desire,' Doreen says and the moment is spoilt.

I remove her hand from my neck and clumsily kiss the palm before leaving it on the table. I would have to learn romantic, parrying tactics.

'Different strokes for different folks I suppose.' Had I inadvertently made another small joke?

Thinking positively, the only barrier standing between me having at least an enjoyable holiday seems to be Doreen's infatuation. Surely it wouldn't be too difficult to move our relationship on to one of friendship? Set in place certain strictures? After all I would be Doreen's house guest. It seems perfectly reasonable to expect that my body should remain forbidden territory whether clothed or unclothed and I would do my best to keep it clothed when in Doreen's company. Doreen's body must remain clothed at all times and kept a minimum of four feet away from mine. No, make that ten feet away.

'I will have my own room at Mildmay's?'

'The study's all yours, Oliver.'

'I mean my own bedroom.'

Doreen frowns. 'We got on perfectly well last night, didn't we? You slept like a baby. I woke up twice to use the bathroom and you were fast asleep.'

I concede that my sleep had been excellent. I did feel refreshed, better than I'd felt in several months.

'There you are then. There are plenty of spare bedrooms at Mildmay's if you really need a room of your own, but let's give the joint sleeping arrangements a chance.'

The other passengers in the carriage seem to have fallen unnaturally silent.

I wish that Doreen would lower her voice.

'Is that an okay for another night or two?' Doreen demands loudly.

'It is, Doreen.'

Across the aisle and to my left, a bearded man raises his eyebrows before lowering his head behind a copy of the Telegraph.

I sink back in my seat and close my eyes again.

*

Doreen rummaged in her handbag but only for something to distract herself. Oliver seemed determined to fall asleep rather than sit up and talk to her. It was now late afternoon and she badly needed a proper drink. In the disgusting toilet she'd swallowed all three of the vodka miniatures she carried with her when travelling, in quick succession.

They hardly touched the sides, she thought.

She wished she had another miniature. At that moment what Doreen needed was to find a tiny Gordon's Gin bottle tucked into a compartment of her handbag that she hadn't known existed. She could imagine the sensation of her heart lifting with pleasure. When they got home, she would have to cut down. It would be easier.

I drink from loneliness.

But was Oliver the answer? She doubted it. On board the Artemis, she'd been convinced that Sydney Oliver was the man she'd been waiting for all her life. She'd even written something along those lines on a postcard to Laverne. God knows what the postman had made of that. Probably told half the village. Not that she minded half the village knowing. She'd gone on a cruise to find romance and to all intents and purposes, that's what she'd found. If he'd only be romantic.

From what little he'd told her about his departure from The Store, a young woman had been involved. Probably some little gold-digging tart trying to get off with the boss and he'd been sucked in. Men were such fools.

Doreen looked fondly across at Oliver.

He was smiling in his sleep. The sun through the carriage window had turned his skin to a parchment colour. The shade of old people's faces.

But was the sun making her skin look like parchment too? Doreen took out her travel mirror, her Estée Lauder rouge and lipstick. Not a moment too soon: her top lip was about to vanish. She drew it back in. Smiled at her reflection. She was every inch the successful, attractive woman returning home triumphant.

Doreen leant forward and gently tapped Mr Oliver's hand. 'Darling, we're almost there.'

*

As the London train pulled into Harrogate Station, Junior Mildmay – pale and slender – lay draped across Doctor Martin Renshawe's bronzed body, like whitebait resting on a heavily smoked kipper. Limbs entwined, they occupied a small rubber dinghy, inflated on the floor of Martin's consulting room. The room was pleasantly warm, with the afternoon sun streaming through the partially closed Venetian blinds and falling in narrow stripes over the naked couple.

Martin flexed his bicep, resisting the urge to draw Junior's attention to its perfection. For some years now he had admitted to being on the cusp of fifty. He hoped to continue with this admission for several more years, priding himself that physically he was in his prime. His body was toned, athletic and tanned from being a keen and competitive tennis and squash player. In the privacy of his walled terraced garden he liked to sunbathe as near to nude as his wife Madge would allow, which entailed a small towel, firmly tied, low on his hips.

During the autumn and winter months he helped his tan along with the expert use of a sun lamp set up in their spare bedroom. Madge sometimes commented that they looked as if they inhabited two different hemispheres. 'Don't you feel embarrassed, everyone assuming we take separate holidays?' she'd asked him. 'Correction: everyone assuming you holiday abroad while I stay at home?'

Martin invariably guffawed heartily. 'Not in the slightest. I have the hide of a rhinoceros.'

A woman less sensitive to Martin's feelings might have said, 'Well, yes you do.'

'Martin, that was marvellous.' Junior traced 'J' in the sheen of sweat on his lover's hairless chest.

With a complacent smile, Martin surveyed the ceiling rose and replied in a rich, deep voice, redolent of Paul Robeson (one of his wife's favourite singers as long as Robeson stuck to show tunes rather than spirituals), 'Yes, we are rather good together. Now make yourself useful and get my ciggies from my jacket pocket.'

'I hate this damned dinghy.' Sullenly, Junior stepped over the side. 'If anyone looked through the window, they'd think we look ridiculous.'

'Fortunately we're not at ground level. Don't sulk, my little sea urchin. The dinghy muffles the sounds of our joyful copulation.'

Junior smiled down at him. 'I like being your little sea urchin.'

Martin watched him lightly cross the room. Junior was like a sprite, or a fawn. Some creature one might imagine glimpsing in woodland at dawn or dusk. It was impossible not to care about him.

Junior climbed delicately back into the dinghy, settled himself under Martin's arm before taking a cigarette from the packet and lighting it. After two puffs he positioned it between Martin's full lips.

Martin blew a stream of smoke towards the window. 'Shouldn't you be in Harrogate today meeting your mother and her new boyfriend?'

He felt Junior's body automatically tense.

Junior made a strange, small noise. 'Ngah!'

Gently, Martin peeled open Junior's clenched fingers. 'This won't do. Your mother loves you. She will always love you.'

'She wouldn't love me if she knew about us.'

'There's no reason for her to ever find out. It's our secret. You like sharing a secret with me, don't you?'

'Yes.' Junior pressed his lips against Martin's tanned neck, his forehead against Martin's jaw line. For a moment he felt that it was possible for him to physically merge with Martin, sink into him. He knew that Martin would never leave Madge. But when the two of them were in the dinghy, in each other's arms, Junior believed that Martin did truly love him. A bit. Which wasn't enough. Not nearly enough. But he was young. He could hold on. He mumbled into Martin's neck. 'Carpenter's collecting them from the station. I believe the plan is to annoy Mummy so much that she has one of her tantrums. The new boyfriend will realise what a mistake he's making and return to London by the next train.'

'It will take more than your brother or your mother behaving badly to shift him.' Martin eased Junior away from him and reached for his underpants. 'Come on. Time you went home.'

'Five more minutes.' Junior linked his hands behind his head and watched Martin getting dressed.

'Not even five more minutes.' Martin thrust his fingers through his thick, slightly long, brown hair. He wondered if he should have it cut really short. A crew cut or even a Number Two? First he'd have to check the back of his neck for signs of ageing. 'Does Carpenter have a plan B?'

'Not yet.'

The bus was already at the stop. As Junior stepped onto the platform he recognised the conductor. 'Hello Gary.'

Gary grinned and handed him a ticket.

Junior pulled out a handful of change.

'You're all right, Junior. Put your money away,' Gary said cheerfully. He rang the bell and the bus moved off.

Junior took the steps to the upper deck two at a time and slumped into a seat at the front of the bus. Seeing Gary had made him feel guilty. They'd known each other at school. Now Gary was married, had a house and a car. Gary was an adult.

The moment Junior passed his driving test, his mother had promised to buy him a car. But he'd given up on the lessons. The driving instructor had body odour. Anyway, he didn't really want the responsibility of owning a car. Supposing a tyre burst on a wet road? He could be killed or scarred for life. At best he'd have to change the tyre and then drive to his destination in wet, muddy clothing.

The bus's route doubled back past Martin's consulting rooms. Junior stared down, hungrily hoping for another glimpse of his beloved.

Sure enough, as the bus slowed, the front door opened. Martin, wearing crisp white shorts, an aertex shirt with a leaf-green pullover slung about his shoulders, stepped out onto the pavement. Under his arm he carried a tennis racket. He lifted his face to the sky and seemed to find the afternoon pleasing.

Junior rapped on the bus window. Martin didn't hear him but set off briskly in the direction of Burnside Leisure Centre. Junior turned to watch him, kept on watching until Martin finally turned a corner. He wouldn't allow himself to wonder who was partnering Martin for tennis.

Junior was romantic. He believed in 'Everlasting Love', 'Puppy Love', 'Sugar Baby Love', 'April Love' and even 'Love grows where my Rosemary goes'. There seemed something rare and precious about Martin having been part of his life for as long as he could remember.

Junior's first Martin memory was from his fourth birthday. He didn't remember the actual day at all, only in the evening, lying in bed and the bedroom door opening. A rectangle of orange light had fallen on the carpet. He'd shut his eyes pretending to be asleep as a wonderful smell entered his room. Years afterwards he'd broken the smell down into aftershave, cigarettes and clean, warm skin. The smell that came with Martin Renshawe.

'Don't pretend, Junior. I know you're awake.'

Junior had opened his eyes and seen a man's big face. Even then that face must have been familiar. Martin had known Junior's parents from long before he and Carpenter were born. The light from the hall had made the face golden. The voice too, had sounded golden. At that early age, well before Junior could read, he knew his colours.

The golden face came close to his. Gleaming in the man's eyes were pinpoints of light, his lips were moving. Had he been singing a lullaby? He could almost imagine Martin capable of doing such a thing.

Once, early on in their relationship, he'd tried to get Martin to think back to that night. 'I was four years old. Surely you remember bringing me a book?'

Martin had looked annoyed. 'I don't want to think of you being four years old. Can we drop it?'

Junior still had the book, *The Illustrated Peter Pan*, with the inscription 'To my favourite godson'.

Another memory – from long before his family had moved to Mildmay's. He'd been sitting on a rug in front of the fire with crayons and paper. Carpenter was already in boarding school. Mummy was out. There had been a time when she'd hoped to become a Conservative Party candidate, when it had felt as if she hardly lived with them anymore.

His father and Martin were sitting in armchairs, reading the newspapers but noisily, teasing each other as they often did. Suddenly it became very quiet in the room. He'd looked up. Martin was leaning forward, holding the flame from his cigarette lighter to Junior's father's cigar. They were like seated statues. Then the flame burnt Martin's fingers. 'Damn it,' he'd said. Both of them laughed. They'd looked at him as if suddenly remembering that he was in the room. 'Get on with your drawing,' his father had said.

From the bus window, Junior could see the sun, a flaming ball of golden-red sinking down behind the distant hills, turning them from dusty green to rose-coloured. Junior imagined sitting with Martin on one of those hills, still warm, after dusk. Martin had known him for twenty-four years. Surely it was impossible to know someone that long without a bond developing?

Junior stood up and rang the bell. The bus turned the corner and Mildmay's came into view. There were no cars in the drive but Mummy and possibly this Oliver would be on their way. Carpenter would be on his way. He wished Martin, someone, would rescue him. Keep him in a safe place.

He jumped off the bus and waved to Gary. At Mildmay's open iron gates he stopped. The last thing he wanted to do was go inside.

Chapter 8

1975

At Harrogate Station, relaxed and almost optimistic, I hurry along the platform to commandeer the one visible porter while Doreen goes in search of her eldest son.

'Ah, my good man! If you could just take those suitcases and few packages out to the forecourt for me.'

The porter doesn't reply but sets off with his trolley towards my sizeable stack of luggage.

'And Mrs Mildmay's hold-all.' It had been on the tip of my tongue to say, *and my wife's hold-all.* 'Mrs Mildmay is a friend. Have you heard of the Mildmay family? I believe they hold quite a prominent position in the local community.'

The porter continues loading.

'We mustn't forget my pictures.' I smooth their brown paper packaging fondly. 'I'm not an artist, you understand. These are family pictures. Not of my family. In my family. As it were.'

Roughly he forces the pictures down between my suitcases and Doreen's hold-all.

'Any room on your trolley for my briefcase? No? Not a problem. Should I follow you? Yes, that is exactly what I'll do.' I am now talking to myself. The loaded trolley is already several yards ahead and making for the exit. With briefcase under my arm I hurry after the porter.

I find the man's taciturnity pleasing. It was what I'd expected from a Northerner. My father had been taciturn although born and bred in Palmers Green. By comparison I'd appeared almost garrulous. My mother – also a person of few words – died when I was seven years old. I still cherished a daydream of a gentle and affectionate woman who, had she lived longer, might have transformed my gloomy boyhood home with love, warmth, jugs of flowers on windowsills and a cat on a mat. Had all these wonders been available, I wouldn't have minded a silent home in the slightest.

On the train I had reached a decision – I would treat staying with Doreen and her family as if holidaying in a foreign country. It would be a chance to get to know the area, appreciate a different landscape, maybe a more rural way of life. I can't deny that I also retained the foolish hope of glimpsing Claire Daker, but I refused to let myself dwell on this possibility during daylight hours. Determinedly I dragged my thoughts back to Yorkshire.

I imagined the community to be rugged. The women – I discounted Doreen – would have a dependency on aprons, stout shoes and keeping a clean front step. The men would be big, dour and as honest as the day was long. I liked that phrase. Was it a northern phrase? I was ready for flat caps, braces, farm carts drawn by shire horses, steam trains, black puddings, mill-owners, in fact I imagined the whole of Yorkshire to still epitomise the early twentieth century world of the recent popular Hovis television advertisement.

Keen to absorb more local colour I catch up with the porter. 'This is my first visit to your fine county,' I say breathlessly.

He shrugs. I resolve to shrug more.

As we step out from the gloom of Harrogate station into bright sunlight I am smiling and, even at my most even-tempered, I don't smile often.

'Those two are having a right barney,' the porter observes.

My smile remains in place for another second as I savour the words 'a right barney'. Then I recognise Doreen's voice.

'How the hell do you suggest we fit three people and a lifetime of luggage into this bloody tin can?' She is kicking the front tyre of an open-topped, two-door Mercedes sports car.

I stride forward, hand outstretched. 'I'm Sidney Oliver and you must be Carpenter.'

'He's up to his usual undermining little tricks so we'll save the civilities for another day.' Doreen stares with open venom at her son.

With her hands on her hips and chin jutting forward, I am reminded of a bull fight I'd witnessed in Alicante some years earlier. The bull fight had been thrilling – Doreen as an angry bull, less so.

'Doreen, calm down. I'm sure we can all fit in.'

'Just keep out of this… Oliver… pet.'

'But Doreen –'

'I won't tell you again. This is between me and my swine of a son.'

'I'd do as she says,' the porter advises.

Resigned, I turn away and make myself comfortable on a wooden bench. Carpenter unlocks the car boot and throws it open. 'Surprisingly roomy,' he says.

'It does look roomy,' I call out. I can't help but feel sorry for him.

'Please mind your own business, Oliver?'

But I can't. After all, my luggage is *my* responsibility. 'Really Doreen, from over here it does look a sizeable boot.' I'm inclined to laugh. Having lived in London all my life I've never found the need to learn to drive. I know nothing about cars and boots. Why couldn't we just hop in a taxi? Fifteen yards away and to my left a line of cabs waited.

Now Carpenter is making a complete buffoon of himself by lowering his head and shoulders into the boot to demonstrate just how much space there is.

He emerges. 'There's the bucket seat as well, Ma.'

'Give me the keys.' Doreen sounds more weary than annoyed. 'Pack what you can in the back. Bring the rest home in a taxi.'

'But it's my car. Why can't *you* bring the rest home in a taxi?' His voice is almost tearful.

I feel obliged to turn away rather than witness a tall, well-built man being vanquished by his tiny, well-built mother.

'Because I don't want to. It's as simple as that.' She turns to me. 'I think we're ready to go now.'

Carrying her travel bag and my donkey, I climb into the car. In silence we wait while Carpenter fits in the rest of the luggage. Finally, with everything except the pictures packed away, Carpenter comes round to Doreen's side of the car and says plaintively, 'You can't lend me a tenner for a cab, can you? I came out without my wallet.'

'I'm afraid not.' Doreen hits the accelerator hard.

It is getting dark. We are driving at over sixty miles an hour down a narrow road. I am fleetingly aware of trees, hills and a pale navy sky intermittently punctuated by the lights from clusters of houses. *I expect these are hamlets*, I'm thinking, but my earlier optimism has evaporated.

I wish Doreen hadn't left the station so abruptly. The drive could have been enjoyable with the car roof up. A chilly breeze whistles around my ears and my hair is being blown about. I feel I should say something to her about the arbitrary way she'd addressed me outside the station, but her profile is set and implacable.

I try to ignore the niggling drone of Steve Chambers' voice, *Hey old buddy; you can't keep fiddling while Rome's going up in smoke.* As I fall fast asleep the thought occurs to me that I've heard more from Steve over the last weeks than during our entire friendship.

With a start I wake as the car turns sharply in through tall iron gates. We are approaching a large house; the front door is open and light streams out over the gravel drive.

Doreen brakes, and before the car seems to have come to a complete standstill, she has thrown open her door. 'Come on Oliver. Leave everything. Venables will deal with the suitcases. I need a drink.'

Easing myself from under a suitcase I climb out. I follow Doreen up a flight of gleaming marble steps, her expensively corseted buttocks being the only familiar landmark in an alien landscape. For one moment, I have to fight an overwhelming desire to press my face against them. Not with any erotic intention, but for comfort.

'And this is Venables, my housekeeper.' Doreen waves in the direction of a trim grey-haired woman wearing a navy blue shirt-waister,

'How do you do, Mrs Venables?' I hold out my hand.

Mrs Venables ignores both me and my hand. Doreen has her full attention. 'Lovely to have you home again ma'am and can I say how pleased we are –'

'Not now Venables. We're going straight upstairs. It's been an exhausting day and we are very weary. Please, rustle up some sandwiches, a pot of tea and my usual times two.'

At speed, I pursue Doreen up another wide staircase, carpeted with an opulent pattern of gold medallions on a deep red background. Just to keep up I find myself breaking into a trot. My tired brain recognises regrets like shadowy wraiths, travelling past me, heading in the opposite direction. I imagine Della and Gwen, my favoured sales-women, their mouths opening with astonishment: *Where's the fire, Mr Oliver?*

This corridor is larger than my Earls Court flat, medallions giving way to thick, cream-coloured carpet not unlike the one in my beloved Bridal Salon.

In front of an open door, Doreen stands waiting for me. 'Shut your eyes, Oliver. I want it all to be a surprise.'

'Well, if I could just negotiate the corridor first.'

As I reach her, she takes my arm and squeezes it against the side swell of her breast. I'm thinking, *What am I? Man or mouse?* But obediently I close my eyes and shuffle forward. Never in my life have I shuffled but I find it's not easy walking into unknown terrain without being able to see where I am going.

'You can open them now.'

On opening my eyes I again experience a sense of *déjà vu*. Doreen's colour scheme – turquoise, cream and gold – is exactly that of the Bridal Salon. I try to disengage my arm from hers but Doreen's grip tightens.

'Fitted wardrobes.' She leads me across the room.

I see myself reflected in the mirrored doors. I am dragging my feet like an old dog on a leash.

'In the style of Louis XIV. Melamine of course – it's so much easier to keep clean. His and hers.'

'Very sumptuous, Doreen.'

Doreen's bed is huge. At least six feet across. Carved into the headboard is a muscular lion locked in mortal combat with an eagle. Neither appears to be winning.

She lets go of my arm and sits down, plucking at the creamy counterpane. 'You bought this for me in Madeira, do you remember?'

'I do indeed,' I say heartily. I feel exhausted, apprehensive, hungry, thirsty, but definitely not hearty. The bed is a monstrosity. I am in a Whitehall farce, a Carry On film, but certainly not a kitchen sink drama!

'I won't bite, you know,' she says, smiling ruefully.

I sense a change in her. A softening.

'I am sorry, Oliver. And embarrassed. That was the first time you've ever seen me in a temper. Not a pleasant sight, but my son would try the patience of a saint and I'm no saint.'

I don't know what to say but at least it is a relief that safe, maternal Doreen has returned.

From behind a mound of cream satin scatter cushions she produces two small teddy bears with red velvet hearts sewn on their chests. One says, Ollie, the other, Dorie. My spirits dip again.

'Do you like them? I thought I'd consign our wicker donkeys to the conservatory as they're not really tactile. I got Venables to commission these from a little shop in Skipton.'

'They're charming,' I say. 'Most thoughtful. You are a… ' I dismiss living wonder as over the top, decent woman as under the top, almost settle on constant revelation but am saved by Mrs Venables arriving with a tray.

Silently, face impassive, she crosses the room, placing the tray on a low glass coffee table that stands between two velvet armchairs.

'Will there be anything more, ma'am?'

'No. Goodnight, Venables.'

'Goodnight, ma'am.' She inclines her head in my direction.

'Good night, Mrs Venables.'

Without replying, she closes the door behind her.

'In future, call her Venables, Oliver.'

'But that would be rude.'

'That's what Peter used to say, but she's a member of my staff, almost an inanimate object.'

'I can't think of people as inanimate objects.'

'You surely didn't think of your shop staff as human beings, did you?'

'Sometimes I did.'

Doreen is on the move again, pouring out large brandies.

'Just a small one please, Doreen.' I sit down in one of the armchairs. It is almost too comfortable. I prefer the austerity of my leather armchair at home.

She continues to pour.

'Help yourself to sandwiches.' Doreen places a full brandy glass next to my side plate.

'I will indeed.' Although I'm ravenous I make no attempt to reach for a sandwich. I press one hand against my forehead and try to concentrate on my own thoughts rather than Doreen's moods and movements. I am not behaving naturally and have not behaved naturally in weeks. The words coming out of my mouth aren't my words. The tone of my voice isn't right. I do not use agreeable phrases like 'I will indeed.' With shame I recall approaching the porter at Harrogate station and calling him 'my good man'. I would never have spoken to Fred or Jim in Dispatch like that. I might have been sneering, insulting, peremptory but never patronising. What was wrong with me? How had the steel vacated my body and will?

'You're tired, pet. Let me pile your plate for you.'

For the moment there is no escape. My bewilderment is finally eclipsed by hunger, thirst and fatigue. I eat four sandwiches, ham and mustard. They are delicious. Possibly the best sandwiches I've ever eaten. I follow them up with two cups of tea; strong, a delightful shade of tan and again better than any tea I'd drunk before.

I notice it is one o'clock in the morning. Normally I am in bed by ten thirty. Where are my pyjamas? Would I ever see them again? I wouldn't even mind wearing the yellow karate style pyjamas again, if I could just sneak off to bed. Not this bed. A camp bed in a well-ventilated store cupboard would do.

I look at Doreen. Her eyes are half closed and she cradles her empty brandy glass in her lap.

'Doreen, I really think I'd be better off on my own tonight.'

'I wouldn't hear of it.'

'But you must hear of it.'

Her eyes open. 'But I won't. Come on, Oliver, stop this foolishness. Be a man for heaven's sake. Another drink?'

'I'm swimming in the stuff.'

She returns our brandy glasses to the tray and then crosses to the bed. From under one of the pillows she draws out a green chiffon nightdress and holds it against her.

'What do you think?'

'I think it's far too late at night for chiffon.'

Surprisingly, she laughs. 'I'll slip into something more

serviceable, shall I?'

She throws the nightdress onto the chair and picks up one of the teddy bears, kissing it on the nose before tucking it back beneath the counterpane. The other bear she brings over to where I'm sitting.

'Ollie kiss Dorie?' She holds the bear up to my face.

Reluctantly I peck at its snout.

'Oh, kiss your Dorie Bear properly. A big, grown-up bear kiss.'

Surely she doesn't want me to give a teddy bear a proper kiss? I can't bring myself to think the word passionate. I am exhausted. There isn't a drop of passion for anything except sleep, in my entire body. I look into her expectant face, into the expectant face of Dorie Bear and seriously consider slithering out of the armchair to collapse gently on the deep pile carpet. *So much excitement, the old angina kicking in…*

'Never mind, Oliver.' Doreen's voice is gentle. 'Let's go to bed. We've got the summer to sort ourselves out.'

*

Doreen woke early. The first light of dawn was creeping through a gap in her 'Country Floral' lined curtains purchased from John Lewis the month after Peter died. She'd had the entire room redecorated – spent a wonderful few days with Venables, bagging up Peter's clothes for a charity shop in Harrogate. Getting rid of his shoes had been the best thing. They were enormous. Like boats. He'd had to buy larger and larger sizes when his feet and ankles had become swollen.

Why must the dead leave a legacy? Doreen slipped a satin cushion behind her head.

All her post-Peter refurbishments, embarked on to erase his memory were a constant reminder that there had been a Peter and a death.

For a few years, at the very beginning, he'd loved her. She was convinced of that. At first she'd enjoyed being loved. He'd called her his 'pretty munchkin'. Of course a time came when she'd absolutely detested him calling her that. What woman wants to be known as a 'pretty munchkin' once they reach their thirties?

Bottom line, I married him for his money.

Doreen leant on her elbow and looked down at Oliver. Her expression softened. He lay on his back, his hands clasped across his chest.

He looks like a dead Pharaoh, she thought, *so dignified and aloof.*

His eyes were shut, not even a tremor of his eyelids. Was he pretending to be asleep? No, he'd never allow his mouth to hang slackly open like that if he were awake. She tried to peer into his mouth to check out the colour of his tongue. He had all his own teeth. From forty onwards Peter had had a denture at the top. To annoy her, he'd move it around in his mouth. Disgusting.

Doreen fell back against her pillows. The clock said six-ten. The taste of brandy was still on her tongue but she welcomed the reminder. Had Venables offered her a glass at that very moment she wouldn't have said 'no'. But not with Oliver lying next to her.

Across the room she could make out the footstool where he'd had left his clothes the night before. Each garment meticulously folded: his underpants, vest and socks straight into the laundry basket. Observing his slow, precise movements around the bedroom, she'd felt exhausted by the effort needed to keep her temper.

They hadn't recaptured the camaraderie of the previous night in his Earls Court flat. He treated her as if she was a lioness waiting to spring, and perhaps she was.

So far sex was a washout. Non-existent. It could all be so different. Of course she had only herself to blame. She always jumped the gun. Half-past-one in the morning, what had prompted her to say as she'd turned back the bed covers, 'Don't worry Ollie. I won't force foreplay on you.'

He'd looked bewildered, as if she were speaking in a foreign language.

'Foreplay, pet. You know, cunnilingus –'

His face had gone absolutely beetroot red.

'I call a spade a spade, sweetheart.' She'd reached out to grab his hand but he'd shied away from her.

'You can call a spade what you like, Doreen, but I'd rather you kept it clean.'

'Most men find mucky talk quite an aphrodisiac.'

'Then I'm not most men.'

No he wasn't like most men. With Oliver, the harder she tried the more unwilling he seemed to get to grips with her. And yet, she reasoned with some higher deity floating in the region of the bedroom ceiling, so much of her strained to be got to grips with.

There had been that awkward evening on board the Artemis when she'd gone to his cabin.

He'd half opened the door and peered out at her. 'Doreen, I'm afraid I'm already in my pyjamas.'

'Well as long as you're not in the nude.' She'd pushed past him and walked in. 'I can't get this bloody necklace clasp undone.'

'I'll just put my dressing gown on,' he'd said.

'Don't be silly. You're not the first man I've seen in his night clothes.' She'd turned her back on him and held up her hair.

He'd been nimble-fingered whereas she'd hope he'd fumble with the tiny clasp and that would have developed into an excitable tussle between them.

'There Doreen,' he'd said, holding the necklace out to her.

'My hero!' she'd said bitterly. She'd wound the beads around her fingers before tossing them onto his bed.

Glimpsing her reflection is his full-length mirror had given her confidence. Who was that attractive, dynamic woman with the satin of her cocktail dress creased alluringly across her hips? She'd turned and kept her gaze locked into his.

He hadn't moved

She'd imagined he was waiting for her to come to him. Wasn't that what real men wanted? Had the cabin been larger she might have dropped down onto her knees and crawled towards him, rubbed her forehead against his legs like an amorous cat.

Instead, all guns blazing she'd crossed the cabin, put one hand on his shoulder and the other on the top button of his pyjama jacket. She'd expected the button to slip easily from the button hole – it didn't. She'd found herself fumbling desperately with it while he stood as rigid as a guardsman giving her no help at all. In the end she'd stepped away from him and held up her hands in good natured defeat.

'Oliver, are you super-glued into that jacket?'

'Not at all, it's just that –'

He'd looked almost boyish in his obvious embarrassment.

She'd retrenched – asked for a brandy – insisted he have one with her.

He'd seemed to relax. 'No brandy I'm afraid. Just a rather good Merlot.'

'A glass of Merlot will be perfect.' She couldn't stand red wine.

While he'd fussed with glasses and opening the bottle, she'd sat on the edge of the bed. Thinking hard always worked for Doreen, and often afterwards she'd wonder why she didn't think hard more often. Almost immediately her brain supplied a memory of her late husband droning on about how he'd calmed terrified horses when he'd been on veterinary service in Egypt during the Suez crisis.

'They become submissive if you whisper gently in their ears.'

At the time she'd remembered saying something smart like, 'I'm not surprised they calmed down, my only surprise is that you didn't put them to sleep.'

He'd shrugged and given one of his tight, hurt smiles.

But now she tried the same whispering technique on Oliver. As he poured the wine, holding the wine glasses up to the light to ensure that they were equally filled, she started to quietly talk about her sons. How she missed them. How she'd only come on the cruise because her close family friend, Doctor Martin Renshawe had told her, 'Doreen, I don't like to see you looking so lost. You're normally bubbly, so full of life.'

Oliver put their glasses down on a small table near the bed, then he'd sat next to her.

'I have felt lost,' she said. 'Knowing my boys don't need me anymore. Oliver, do you know how it feels not to be needed by anyone?'

'Yes I do,' he'd replied gruffly.

Gently and rhythmically, she'd patted his knees as she continued to talk, her voice pitched low. 'It's bloody lonely. Some mornings there hardly seems a reason to get out of bed. You ask yourself, what's it all about? You work hard all your life, try to build something worthwhile that's there for the sharing and then you find there's nobody who wants to share it with you. Everyone's getting on with their own lives and only "yours truly" is left high and dry.'

'You're absolutely right of course. My feelings exactly.' He touched her hand. She let her fingers link with his.

'We're a sad duo,' she said.

'We are indeed.'

Doreen felt the warmth of his shoulder as his body relaxed against her.

He squeezed her fingers.

She squeezed back. The cabin was silent. Not even the sound of their breathing. She let go of his hand and gave his knee a reassuring pat but this time she let her hand rest a little higher up.

'Oh, Oliver,' she said.

'Ah, Doreen.'

She picked up the note of strain in his voice. At any moment he would be on his feet and telling her it was getting late and they'd both want to be fresh in the morning. It was now or never. She pretended to reach for her wine glass. Instead she turned towards him, thrusting her hand under the hem of his pyjama jacket and into the warmth of his flies.

He couldn't have reacted more violently, bucking like a maddened bronco. Arms flailing he leapt to his feet, leaving Doreen to fall sideways into the void his body left behind.

From a prone position at the foot of his bed she saw him rushing towards his cabin door, as if his pants were on fire.

With breathless solemnity he swung the door open. 'Doreen, will you please go back to your own cabin?'

She got to her feet and smoothed down her skirt, 'But why?'

'You don't seem to comprehend that I'm a broken man.'

'But I'm trying to mend you, pet.'

'Attempting to sexually assault me will not help.'

'I was just giving you the green light.'

'I'd rather we stayed at red for the time being.'

That 'for the time being' held out hope. She reclaimed her wine glass and gulped it down. In front of the mirror she tidied her hair while Oliver hovered near the open door.

'We're still friends?' she asked over her shoulder.

He'd hesitated.

'Oh come on. It was just a bit of fun. No harm done.' She turned and gave him a light, friendly smile. 'I'm not leaving till you say we're pals.'

He frowned but nodded. 'Yes, of course we are.'

'A tiny bit more than friends?' she wheedled.

'A bit more.' He almost managed a laugh.

'I am sorry. I thought it might help. I'm not one for finesse. I've never held back. If I want something I go for it. Take it as a compliment.'

She could see her words sinking in.

His frown cleared.

Doreen stayed in bed a few moments longer watching Oliver's face. His responses or lack of response bewildered her. *Surely any man worth his salt would like his private parts stimulated?*

She could give up on him. Hand him his marching orders, but there was something about him that charmed her. Something about his reserved manliness that appealed to a girlishness in her, that she'd imagined lost a long time ago.

God, I'm in for a long haul, she thought.

But what alternatives did she have? The days of men queuing up to squire Doreen McCardle around Harrogate were long gone. She leant forward and whispered in his ear, 'Sydney Oliver, you don't stand a chance. I always get my man.'

Chapter 9

1975

I am lying in Doreen Mildmay's bed. I check beneath the bedclothes. All is in order. My pyjama cord, tied in a double granny knot has not been tampered with.

I hear three peremptory raps on the bedroom door. Quickly I prop myself up on the bank of pillows, drawing the counterpane over the upper half of my body so that only my neck and head are visible.

'Come in.' My voice is a querulous bleat rather than the authoritative growl I'd intended. I recall Doreen's instruction of the night before.

Be as brief as possible with Venables. Do not engage in small talk. She really does prefer it that way.

The bedroom door opens and Mrs Venables glides through the curtained gloom towards me.

'Mrs Mildmay asked me to give you a knock at ten.' She lowers the tray onto the bed. 'Three slices of medium brown toast, marmalade and a pot of tea. Is that correct, sir? I can rustle up bacon and eggs if you want.'

'No thank you Mrs Venables.'

'I'm surprised you don't want bacon and eggs?'

'Just not hungry.'

'I hope you slept well after your long journey?'

'I did indeed.'

'Shall I open the curtains?'

'Please do.'

Mrs Venables tugs back the heavy brocade drapes and grey wintry light filters into the room. She stares out of the window before turning back to me. 'Not a very nice day I'm afraid. We get a lot of wet weather up here in summer.'

I have a sudden distressing image of myself, bundled up in the counterpane, resembling a papoose, or worse a pupa, but no longer a man. The door clicks shut behind her.

I let a full two minutes elapse to ensure Mrs Venables isn't biding her time outside in the corridor before popping back in a final attempt to surprise a fuller response from me, then throw off the bed covers and get up. I slip on my new maroon silk dressing gown, bought in Harvey Nichols especially for this holiday.

Despite the grey light, despite the drum of beating rain, I suddenly feel as if I'm a small boy on Christmas morning, a smile of delight ready on my lips as I advance towards the window.

Initially my view is impaired by the vast quantity of net curtaining – far more than the Drapers' Bible's recommendation of two-and-a-half times the window width – that had gone into creating such abundant fullness. Impatiently I pull the net to one side and stare hungrily down onto a four-lane stretch of highway.

Directly across the road, behind iron railings and an imposing gate, stands a large detached house. A flight of marble steps lead up to an impressive front door flanked by Doric pillars. Although bone tired the night before I recall similar pillars on each side of Mildmay's marble steps. I press my cheek flat against the glass and look to the left. Another identical house. I look to the right. And another one. A sign on the grass verge says, Mildmay Executive Properties. From the height of the shrubs and trees bordering the individual drives I judge that the estate of executive houses is no more than five years old.

As I recognise Carpenter's car turning into the drive I take a step backwards. Arms clasp my waist and I am literally slammed against the window pane.

'Mrs Venables!' My voice comes out in an unmanly shriek as I find myself struggling with the net curtain and alien limbs.

'Did I surprise you, my little love?'

'Doreen, it's you.' Her breasts press against my shoulder blades. I keep my conversation conversational as I try unsuccessfully to ease myself free. 'Your Mrs Venables is rather a gloomy character, isn't she?'

Her hips mould to the shape of my buttocks.

'She does the job she's paid for. I neither need nor want Venables being cheerful all over the place. Let her be cheerful on her own time.'

She squeezes me even tighter.

Again I buckle forwards. 'Steady on, Doreen, you'll have me through the window.'

'Don't be silly. All our houses are fully double-glazed,' but she loosens her grip and I'm able to wrench away from her.

I rush back to my breakfast tray, remove it from the bed and place it on the footstool next to my designated armchair. I sit down. Out of harm's way.

'This looks delicious.'

'Do you want me to butter your toast?'

'No, thank you.'

'Silly Ollie bear.'

'Possibly.'

Doreen sits on the bed, kicks off her shoes and wiggles her stockinged toes. 'So, first impressions?'

Waiting for inspiration to strike, I munch my toast in a slow and thoughtful manner. Challenges, changes are being forced on me and I have no idea how to respond to them. Why wasn't I able to treat Doreen as I'd treated everyone in the past? With the unadorned truth, that I'd hoped for country cottages, fields, cows, sheep and perhaps a horse or two.

I feel homesick for the noise and movement of London; jostling, shouting – people under cars and leaning out of windows – and there *are* trees and birdsong, sparrows and pigeons, parks, lakes. Too much noise sometimes, too much dirt, but the interest value had always outweighed any irritation. I had felt alive walking back and forth from the tube station, hopping on a bus. In London, I'd had a purpose. What purpose had I here?

Carefully buttering another slice of toast I try to choose the right words. 'I don't mind saying, Doreen, I'm extremely impressed.' These are not the words I want.

She beams at me. 'Oh I'm so pleased. I'm ecstatic. We'll get the party out of the way and then the two of us are going to have a splendid time.'

'What party would that be, Doreen?' I wipe my fingers on a linen serviette. I'm imagining a small soirée of Doreen's closest friends, the cream of the county.

'Can we talk about it later? My boys are waiting for us downstairs and you're not dressed yet.'

'Fair enough. You're not planning anything too lavish, are you?'

'You're going to be annoyed with me.'

'Why ever should I be?'

She stands up. 'Should I wear the matching jacket or is that too formal?'

I set the tray aside. 'Can we talk for a moment about this party?'

'I'll wear the jacket.' She opens her wardrobe. 'It's an engagement party.'

'Really? For whom?'

Doreen breathes in before fastening the jacket's three jet buttons. 'It's meant to be fitted. How do I look?'

'*Who* is the engagement party for?'

'Us.' Her tone is defiant.

In a reasonable voice, with only the hint of chiding in it, I state, 'But Doreen, we are not engaged.'

'Oliver... pet. Throwing a party to celebrate having a house guest isn't really worth hiring the Côte d'Or Hotel ballroom for.'

'Then why bother with a party at all?'

'I love parties.'

'Then have one. You can afford it. But not to celebrate your engagement.'

'Our engagement. It's just a figure of speech.'

Appealing to Doreen from the depth of an armchair, I am at a disadvantage. Now is the time to stop being reasonable and walk about in an authoritative manner – I stand up. 'I am not engaged to you, Doreen.'

'You're sleeping with me.'

'But that's all I'm doing.'

She dabs her eyes with a tissue, which affects me not one jot. In a very short space of time I've seen Doreen adopt many different emotional states. She presents them to me as if conjuring rabbits out of a top hat, whichever one she imagines will secure her own way.

Now she looks up at me tremulously. 'Could we not just go along with being engaged for a week or two?'

I actively dislike Doreen being tremulous. 'Whatever for?'

'Because all my friends think we're engaged.'

'Why would they think that?'

'I told them we were.'

I try to step aside as Doreen runs at me, but too late, her arms are around my neck and she is sobbing into my dressing gown lapels.

'I know I shouldn't have said we were engaged, but I'm a silly Doreen. I wanted to come back with a handsome fiancé. I've been so long in the wilderness.'

Her tears leave me unmoved but the bit about being so long in the wilderness hits home. This could just as well apply to me. More so. At least Doreen has a family and friends.

'Just for a week or two, Oliver? What harm could it do?'

'And after a week or two, how will you feel when these same friends commiserate and whisper behind your back at your broken engagement?'

'But you might find you enjoy being one half of the premier couple in the Harrogate environs.'

This is true. I did rather like being half of a premier couple. I remembered the morning on board the Artemis when I'd been elevated to sit next to Doreen at the Captain's Table, how I'd immediately felt the sense of a wrong being righted. And only two days ago in the Italian restaurant, imagining that the waiters were seeing me in a different, more enviable light just because I was accompanied by an expensively dressed woman.

I remove Doreen's arms from around my neck and move away from her. 'Very well.'

Her eyes widen in surprise. 'Darling.' She raises herself on tip-toe and I fear another physical onslaught.

Like a lion tamer, I pick up the foot stool and hold it in front of me. 'A week or two only. If it doesn't work out, if either of us wants to call it a day, let's hope we can shake hands and get on with our lives without too many recriminations. Is it a deal?'

'My little love.'

'Never mind that, is it a deal?'

She puts one hand on her hip and thrusts out her breasts. 'So Oliver, are you asking me to marry you?'

'No I am not!'

'But we are engaged?'

'For a week.'

'You said two.'

She squeezes my arm.

Nice Doreen. Doreen happy for the time being.

Doreen and I hold hands. We are standing in Mildmay's generously proportioned hall. A few feet away the lounge door is slightly open. I know this is the lounge because on the wood panelling is a small onyx plaque, with LOUNGE etched in gold leaf. Doreen is speaking to Mrs Venables and doesn't hear a young male voice, coming from the other side of the door, ask, 'So what's he like?'

'Pretty unprepossessing. Dyed hair, dyed moustache, possibly fake tan, good suit and shoes.' I recognise Carpenter's voice.

'Ready to meet my sons, Oliver?'

'Lead on.' *Fake tan indeed!*

Doreen pushes the door wide open. 'Good morning, boys.'

Carpenter and her younger son both stand self-consciously, one each side of a drinks cabinet, like two life-sized statues. On it, between them, the neck of a champagne bottle emerges from a silver ice bucket. Crystal champagne flutes of a far better quality than my own Waterford glassware are lined up and ready.

'This is my fiancé, Sydney Oliver. Oliver – you've already met Carpenter – enough said.' She waves a playful finger at him. 'And this is Junior. My youngest. Got a kiss for Mummy, darling?'

Junior, a pallid, slight young man, hurries forward to kiss Doreen on both cheeks. 'Mummy, you look radiant. We had no idea the two of you were engaged till Doctor Renshawe enlightened us.' He pumps my hand. 'Thrilled to meet you, sir.'

'Call him Oliver, darling.'

'Should I? Is that really okay?'

'Of course it is,' I respond jovially.

It is Carpenter's turn to step forward. 'Sorry about the little misunderstanding yesterday. Congratulations.'

'No problem. It's nice to meet you both.'

At that moment Mrs Venables appears in the doorway. 'Should we assemble, Mrs Mildmay?'

Doreen glances at her watch. 'We'll just have a couple of drinks. If you and the rest of the staff could wait in the hall till we're ready.' Doreen pauses to give Mrs Venables a moment to back out of the lounge. 'Carpenter, if you could pour our drinks? We'll have a toast and then I'll introduce Oliver to everybody. Won't that be lovely, darling?' She smiles at me.

I summon what best I can describe as an approximation of a smile before I realise that all happiness and animation have drained from Doreen's face.

She inhales deeply. 'Has someone been smoking in this room?'

Carpenter looks blank but uneasy. 'No. Of course not. We know the rules.'

'I don't doubt that you know the rules, but have you been abiding by them?' Like a small, brightly-coloured bloodhound, Doreen makes her way slowly towards the bay window.

A pulse begins to throb above my eyes. Another scene is brewing. What an extraordinary woman Doreen is. She should have worked for MI5 or the French Resistance. She should have been anything that required courage, tenacity, single-mindedness, passion. As a home owner and mother of two grown sons she is wasted.

'Doreen, is whatever you're doing really necessary?'

She ignores me, picking up the hem of one of the curtains and holding it to her nose. In an almost thoughtful tone she says, 'This curtain reeks of cigarette. Someone has recently been smoking in my lounge and I hope they own up before I get annoyed.'

'I can't smell anything.'

Doreen looked at me as if I'm a complete stranger, or worse, a member of staff. 'Of course you can't smell anything. You're standing a million miles away. Please don't interfere.' Her gaze moves past Junior, settling on Carpenter, whose fingers are tightening on the neck of the champagne bottle.

'But Doreen,' I remonstrate. 'You yourself like a cigarette last thing at night.'

'Pet, if I wanted to burn this whole house down I could, because it's my house.'

Carpenter drops the bottle back into the ice bucket and makes a move towards the door.

'Stay right where you are.' Doreen's voice is the hiss of a venomous snake.

Carpenter halts.

Doreen holds the curtain up to the window. A small beam of daylight shines in through a perfect circular burn, and there on the sill is a cigarette butt.

'Carpenter, you have ruined my curtains.'

'Ma, I've never smoked in here. I promise you. Junior, will back me up.' He looks pleadingly at his brother who turns away.

'Don't you dare try to implicate Junior! These curtains are made from an Arthur Sanderson fabric that cost me several hundred pounds and were made by a seamstress the like of which I will not find again –'

'Really, Doreen,' I remonstrate.

'Shut up! Carpenter has broken one of the cardinal rules of my house and then lied to me. In front of you, my fiancé and a treasured guest. In front of someone I wanted to impress with the love and trust that is inherent between mother and sons.'

'But I'm really not bothered.'

'Thank you.' Her voice is icy. 'I'm relieved that you're not bothered. Somewhat disappointed but still relieved. Unfortunately I am bothered that my eldest son has shown himself up as a lying little swine. I'm bloody bothered.'

There is a moment of stillness in the room. I entertain the inconsequential thought; this is what is meant by a tableau and then, as if a starting pistol has been fired, Doreen sprints across the room, reaching Carpenter before he can make his getaway. 'You're going nowhere, Sonny Jim,' she shouts.

I too am on the move. I grip Doreen's shoulders and try to disengage her from her son. 'Doreen please, this is no way to behave. I thought the morning was to be a celebration.'

'I'll teach him to ruin my curtains and make me look a bloody fool.'

'Good heavens, woman – a piddling cigarette burn isn't the end of the world.' I tug at Doreen's jacket and a jet button pings off and rolls on the floor.

'My jacket!' she screams, letting go of Carpenter's pullover. 'You've ruined my jacket.'

'For god's sake – I'll sew the button back on myself.'

'How dare you lay your hands on me? How dare you tell me how to behave in my own house? I've never taken orders from any man and I'm not starting now.'

'I wasn't giving orders, I was only –'

I recoil as she pushes her white pinched face into mine.

'Don't think you can come in here and lord it over me like you could with your little shop girls. You've got to earn that right and so far by my reckoning you've earned nowt.'

The 't' of nowt sends a spray of spittle onto my chin. I step away from her and retrieve the button from under the coffee table. I have the strangest impression that I am taking part in a Russian melodrama – an aristocratic subaltern required to relinquish the field of battle with dignity. I feel an overwhelming urge to click my heels together and make a low bow to the assembled company. I do neither. With quiet dignity I place the button on the mantelpiece.

'Excuse me, Doreen. Gentlemen,' I say before leaving the room, closing the door carefully behind me.

As I turn towards the stairs, there is the sound of glass shattering on the other side of the door.

Chapter 10

1975

Leaving Doreen's lounge, I had intended to dash upstairs and pack while Mrs Venables booked a taxi to take me to the railway station. However, as I attempt to cross the hall I encounter her blocking my flight.

'Ah, Mrs Venables – just the person I needed to see. I wonder if you could call a local taxi firm. I need to return to London urgently.'

'Whenever you and Mrs Mildmay are ready, I can organise Dobbs and Pandora for the introductions.'

The thought of pushing my way through a line of Doreen's minions while carrying suitcase and overnight bag is unappealing. I square my shoulders, plunge one hand into my jacket pocket and raise my left hand authoritatively, in the age-old British stance beloved of kings and princes – or at least as old as the invention of the jacket pocket. 'There will be no staff introductions this morning. I advise you to go about your usual duties. Get me a cab, prepare lunch, clean windows.'

Mrs Venables seems to literally digest my words, her jaw moving as she shifts them around in her mouth. 'If you don't mind, sir, I'll just stay put till Mrs Mildmay comes out of the lounge.'

'But she is unwell.'

'Mrs Mildmay is often unwell and then suddenly she's as right as rain again.'

'How will I get to Harrogate station?'

'There's a telephone in the lounge.'

The lounge is the last place I want to return to. For the moment I am beaten. 'Is there a pub nearby?'

'Turn left out of the gate, keep going for five hundred yards and you'll find the Templar's Arms. Stay on the inside of the grass verge. It's been raining so the cars will probably try to soak you.'

'Why ever would they do that?'

'Just a bit of fun.' She looks up at the hall clock. 'You'll miss lunch if you go now.'

'I don't want lunch.'

'Mrs Mildmay won't like you to miss lunch.'

'Well Mrs Mildmay will have to put up with it.'

I struggle with an immediate feeling of anxiety at the thought of Mrs Venables repeating this to Doreen. Probably embellishing. *He said you'll just have to bloody put up with it. You can like it or lump it.*

From the lounge there is the sound of approaching footsteps. I don't want to see any member of the Mildmay family ever again or at least not for several hours. I stride across the hall and fling open the front door.

'There's an umbrella in the elephant's foot,' Mrs Venables calls after me.

'I don't mind a drop of rain.'

Almost running, I reach the grass verge and turn left. The earlier rain has stopped but the grass is long and wet. I regret my thin-soled shoes and summer-weight suit. Fifty yards from the house I slow my pace. It isn't a busy road but the few cars that pass actually do seem to swerve towards the puddles, sending up sheets of filthy water. As I glance back to check I'm not being pursued, a builder's lorry soaks me. I am drenched right through to my underwear.

Houses give way to sodden fields and hedgerows. Just as I begin to query whether Mrs Venables meant me to turn right rather than left, I round a corner and there is a large Swiss chalet-style building. A swinging sign shaped like an enormous cow bell welcomes me to the 'Templar's Arms'.

Warm orange light streams encouragingly from the chalet's windows. I feel a sudden yearning for Steve Chambers to be waiting for me inside. Steve in check shirt and jeans, cowboy boots resting on a gleaming brass fender surrounding a roaring log fire – *Hey, how you doing, old buddy?* Steve tapping a double gin and tonic, ice and a slice – *Get one for yourself and a chaser for me.*

Before meeting Doreen I was never a man who drank during the day, but at some point during my miserable fifteen minute walk, I had begun to regain the feeling that I was on holiday. My old self, that Mr Oliver who had ruled The Store with an iron hand, would have considered my present position untenable. Having hit rock bottom and then finding there is still a long way left to fall, I am finally beginning to see my position as a challenge that is not without humour. As I step into the pub I am actually looking forward to something in a sturdy pint glass.

The Templar's Arms does not disappoint me. The bar is of highly polished dark wood with glass panels at the front etched with flowers. On the wall hangs a large photograph of a snow-covered mountain signed by Christopher Plummer and Julie Andrews.

I've seen a number of Christopher Plummer's films but make a point of avoiding anything containing Julie Andrews, particularly if she is required to sing. Hers is the type of voice I least like – high pitched. There are other photographs: Julie Andrews meeting the Royal family. Nobody had autographed that one. Christopher Plummer opening an alpine garden centre. A large pin board devoted to faded newspaper cuttings about both of them.

'What do you think of our *Sound of Music* memorabilia?'

Startled, I turn quickly, almost colliding with a plump, middle-aged woman with blonde plaits which should look ludicrous but don't. She wears a low-cut blouse.

'Extraordinary.' I feel as if my response has been highly amusing.

'We love the Alps. Michael and me, we're cold climate people.'

'I think I prefer the heat of the Mediterranean – when suitably dressed of course.'

The woman begins to polish the optics. 'I wouldn't give you tuppence for the Med. We went to Greece once. Michael said it was like spending a week in Dante's Inferno. Are you a fan?'

'I rather like Cyprus.'

'Are you a fan of *The Sound of Music*?'

'No.'

'I expect you're more into James Bond?'

'Not really. Could I have a pint of Guinness, please?'

As she pours she studies me. 'You'll want to get out of those trousers.'

'Just a drop of rain. Dry in no time.'

Setting my drink in front of me she leans her bosoms on her folded arms and leans *them* on the bar.

I avert my eyes to the snow-topped alp above her head before realising it resembles a large breast dipped in sugar. I believe I would be perfectly happy if I never saw a woman's breast again, be it clothed, unclothed, silhouetted, swelling or even just bearing a passing resemblance.

'Take your drink over to the fire and dry out – but don't singe yourself.'

I pick up the Guinness. 'Thank you.'

'I like a man who says "thank you". So many just help themselves without a by your leave.'

There is no answer to this. I decide to revert to Doreen's recommended approach by keeping communication to a minimum. I whistle through my teeth.

'Will you be wanting anything in a basket? I can offer you chicken pieces or a burger.'

I execute a brisk head shake combined with a rueful smile.

'Okay. Just give me a shout if you need a re-fill. I'm in the kitchen peeling spuds. I'm Laverne.'

I am pleased to find a blazing fire with a brass fender and a large ginger cat in front of it.

'Hello there, puss,' I tell the back of the cat's head. 'What's your name?'

The cat continues to stare at the flames.

'Fair enough.'

We share the fire. I first dry my front, then the back of my trousers before finding a cushioned banquette in a wooden cubicle. The banquette is stained but comfortable and, for the first time in many days, I begin to relax. Three times I call Laverne away from her spuds to pour me another Guinness. I'm plagued by a dim memory of Doreen having a friend called Laverne, but this Laverne seems far too nice to have anything to do with a woman like Doreen. Although, I add to my internal dialogue with myself, Laverne is an uncommon name.

Around me, the bar begins to fill. I like the sound of background voices, fancying that they have a softer, friendlier burr than London voices. Gradually, the urgency of my desire to flee Mildmay's starts to fade. An aroma of frying chips permeates pleasantly from the kitchen. I am almost tempted to try out 'anything in a basket'. Perhaps it would be possible to return to the house during the afternoon and insist on a pot of tea and a ham sandwich followed by a nap? Surely Doreen owes me that much after her appalling behaviour?

On finishing my third pint I begin to meditate on happiness and whether, up till this moment, I have ever experienced it. Even at this distance I can feel the warmth of that fire on my face. My trousers are dry. I would like to take that ginger cat home. Do all these things equal a state of happiness?

I sniff the air as Laverne delivers a tray of chicken legs and chips in raffia baskets to the neighbouring cubicle.

'There you go, ladies. Enjoy.'

As Laverne makes her way back towards the bar, tapping the empty tray against her thigh, I watch her appreciatively. She is a fine looking woman. I think what an attractive accessory an apron is, the ties enhancing her small waist, the ruffles of the apron framing her generous hips.

'I don't think I can eat all these chips, Roberta. I wish Laverne would offer a quiche option,' says a gentle voice on the other side of the partition.

'For goodness sake, Madge,' barks back a louder female voice. 'Quiches may have their uses but they can never replace a staple diet of meat, veg and potatoes. They've been fobbed off on us by the French and I wouldn't give French cuisine the time of day.'

'I believe they're quite the coming thing,' Madge says.

'The coming thing! You can't eat something because it's the "coming thing".'

'Martin says quiche and salad are a healthy alternative.'

'If your Martin told you arsenic was a healthy alternative, no doubt you'd eat it.'

'Roberta, I'm not a complete fool.'

I consider intervening on behalf of the gentle-voiced Madge. I've taken an instant dislike to her opinionated friend. But what do I know about quiches apart from a certainty that they are yellow, round and soggy? Instead I drain the very last of my Guinness and, with some difficulty, get to my feet, waving my arm in the direction of the bar to attract Laverne's attention.

'Just what do you think you're playing at?' The woman with the large voice is looking up at me, a fork-full of chicken and chip poised in front of her mouth.

She's wearing a suit of brown bonded jersey, possibly my least favourite fabric. I'm not even certain that it really is a fabric.

'We are trying to have a private *tête-a-tête*. Could you sit down and stop gesticulating?'

'Do leave the poor man alone.'

'Why can't he leave us alone?'

'I just wanted another drink,' I say quite pleasantly.

'I'd imagine that you've had more than enough.'

'Roberta, stop it now.' Madge pulls at her friend's sleeve.

'Oh, you're such a soft touch.'

I adjust my head to face the bar while still observing Madge. A rather nice face. Narrow shoulders, a positively admirable pigeon chest clothed in a soft lavender-coloured jacket. Pure wool. An understated Peter Pan collar peeps out from between the jacket reveres, fastened by an amethyst brooch. Quality if somewhat old fashioned. Possibly Windsmoor or Berkertex? Why couldn't Doreen take a leaf out of this woman's book? Why did Doreen always try to cram so much into so little space?

From the bar, Laverne spots me. 'Another pint, dear?'

I nod and sink back onto the banquette. With no real sense of urgency I am aware of discomfort in my bladder area.

Laverne places another Guinness in front of me.

'I don't know if I've got enough cash to pay for this. I seem to have left my wallet in my other jacket.'

'On the house. I'm on my ten-minute break. Move up.' She squeezes into the banquette next to me.

The kindness of strangers – it makes me almost tearful. As I edge further along the seat, I realise that the discomfort in my bladder area is becoming acute.

'You're new around here, aren't you?' Laverne asks.

'On holiday. Staying with a woman friend.' I decide not to mention Doreen by name.

'A woman friend, is it?'

I find this a difficult question to comprehend but answer, 'It is.'

'And why has your woman friend let a handsome chap like you out on his own?'

Another difficult question; however, as is the way with alcohol, time speeds up and when I glance at my watch I realise that ten minutes have passed and, although I've no idea what my answer was, Laverne has now embarked on a story about the pub's resident cat. 'We thought he was a tom but he's just had kittens.'

'Laverne,' someone shouts from the crowd around the bar. 'Can we have some service?'

She pats my arm. 'You'll have to pop in again when it's quieter. Bring your friend with you. I'll introduce you to my husband, Michael. He's my third.' She stands up.

I can't explain what prompts me to grasp her hips and pull her onto my lap, but fortunately Laverne doesn't seem to mind at all.

'You cheeky devil.' She gives me a loud and hearty kiss on the lips.

I pull her plaits and give her a loud and hearty kiss back.

A shadow falls across the table. Laverne turns her head and looks upwards, then smiles delightedly. 'You're home. We didn't expect you till the weekend.'

'Just what the bloody hell is going on?'

I know that voice…

Laverne bounces playfully on my knees. 'Don't worry. He's nothing I can't handle.'

'*He* happens to be my fiancé,' Doreen says icily. 'I'll thank you to get your arse off his lap.'

The Lounge Bar falls silent.

Laverne scrambles to her feet. 'We were only larking around.'

Everyone seems held in mid-action, mid-conversation – a glass raised, a head turned; a chicken drumstick pauses inches away from Madge's open mouth.

Wanting to laugh, I open my mouth to say, *Mea culpa, mea culpa*, but no words emerge. With drunken clarity, I know exactly the dilemma being worked out behind Doreen's sunglasses and I feel sorry for the Doreen she is. As drunk as I am, I have no doubt of her inner struggle before her face relaxes into a warm smile.

'Laverne, forgive me.' Doreen holds out her hands and extends her smile to the attentive audience. 'I've been beside myself with worry. My fiancé is a complete stranger to the area. A hundred times in the last hour I've imagined him lying injured and bloody in a ditch.' She manages a small, anxious laugh.

The silence breaks. Conversations resume.

Laverne grasps Doreen's arm. 'Darling, we were so thrilled to hear your news.' She looks down at me. 'But whatever was he doing wandering about on his own?'

'Men.' Doreen shrugs. 'You send them out for a packet of tea and they end up in the nearest pub. Laverne, if you could ask Michael to help Oliver out to my car.'

'Of course. I'll be two ticks. If I'd have known –'

'Thank you.'

Doreen rests her buttocks on the edge of the table, effectively blocking me from public view. I tweak the hem of her jacket.

'Not now, Oliver darling,' she responds in the tenderest of tones.

Madge, the timid woman from the next table says gently, 'Congratulations Doreen. Martin told me your good news the other evening.'

'Why Madge, how nice. My fiancé had a touch of pre-wedding nerves. Men just can't take the strain like we women. We work horses.'

'I need the lavatory,' I whisper loudly.

'Then go, my darling. But hurry up.'

'I don't think my legs will work. Doreen, I really need to go now.'

'We will be home in less than five minutes,' Doreen whispers back, her face stiff from smiling.

'I can't wait five minutes.'

'Please try to wait.'

'I can't.'

Again I sense Doreen desperately working out her best plan of action. In a loud, cheerful voice she announces, 'Oliver, before we go home I think it would be a good idea if you pop to the Gents. Madge, you wouldn't mind giving me a hand helping my fiancé to the lavatory, would you, he's more than a little inebriated?'

At a stroke she's won over the whole pub. Won me over. Won over Madge Renshawe.

'Of course.' Madge lays aside her drumstick and wipes her fingers on a paper serviette.

'I don't think that's a suitable task for you, Madge,' her bossy friend Roberta says. 'I've served in the navy.'

'But Roberta, *I* am a married woman.'

Doreen puts her hand on Madge's shoulder, almost as if anointing her. 'I'd prefer Madge. She is a family friend.'

Roberta manhandles the table out of the way, then Doreen and Madge each take one of my arms and haul me to my feet. My legs buckle but Doreen is physically strong and Madge stronger than she looks. Together they support me towards the Gents. Someone flings open the door and in we go.

'I hope it's clean,' Laverne calls out from behind the bar. 'Michael's on his way.'

'I think a cubicle rather than the urinals, don't you, Madge?' Doreen says.

Using my head as a battering ram they get the door open and me inside.

'Thank you, Madge, I'll take over now.' With some difficulty Doreen shuts the door of the cubicle with the two of us squashed inside.

'Doreen, how do buckles undo?' I ask, fumbling with my trouser belt.

Just lean against the wall and I'll sort you out.'

'Most irregular.'

In spite of herself, Doreen begins to laugh. 'Should I point Percy at the porcelain?'

'I can manage.'

'Then I'll wait outside. Do what you have to do and do it quickly.' She lightly pinches my arm. 'I am so sorry for this morning.'

'Please Doreen; I have got to pee now.'

'I'll keep Madge company then,' she says cheerfully.

Under normal circumstances I would have been incapable of urinating, knowing that two women were just the other side of a thin plywood door, but I'm so drunk it doesn't matter to me in the slightest. There is just my feeling of absolute relief.

'My Martin's always desperate to go and then finds he can't,' I hear Madge observe.

Doreen answers, 'I do appreciate your help, Madge. I owe you one.'

'Don't be silly. I'm sure you'd do the same for me.'

I try not to snort with laughter.

'Of course I'll expect you and Martin to come to the party. The invitations should go out this week.'

I flush the toilet and shuffle out.

'I don't feel too good, Doreen.'

'Better get you home then.'

Chapter 11

Lying on a leather sofa in a darkened room, I wake from a deep sleep to a blinding headache. I am in the study. Someone has put a damp cloth over my forehead and I experience a moment of confusion before remembering the pub and three pints of Guinness drunk on a relatively empty stomach. As if I'd been a mere bystander, I recall Doreen and a mouse-like woman helping a man – me – into the lavatory. With a groan, I roll onto my back and re-arrange the cloth against my throbbing forehead. My free hand drops down and touches metal. I lean on one elbow and peer over the edge of the sofa. A bucket has been placed on the rug in case I'm sick. Taking care to move my head as little as possible, I lower my body down again and close my eyes.

For months I've denied myself. No what-ifs. No looking back. If any chink has appeared in my armour, any word or image prompted a memory, I have stifled it.

Now I say the name aloud. 'Claire Daker.'

I am standing at the top of the Bridal Salon staircase looking out over the shop floor. How many times had I paused in exactly that same spot taking in everything that went on in my small yet highly successful empire? But at that particular moment I'd been waiting for something to happen. I'm certain that my heartbeat had accelerated in anticipation.

At the far end of the ground floor shopping area, a door leading to the stockrooms swings open. Miss Frances steps out, a slim, pleasing figure in a well cut trouser-suit. Accompanying her is a young woman, white-blonde hair tied back in a pony-tail. It seems to swing almost defiantly. Talking animatedly to each other, they stroll past the shell of the Teen Boutique, through Day Wear and Ladies Fuller Fashions, until finally they reach the foot of my staircase. Both look up at me. Only Miss Frances smiles.

As they climb the stairs, I turn my back on them, busying myself with re-arranging a display of bridesmaids' gloves.

'Mr Oliver,' Miss Frances sings out.

I allow a few seconds to pass before turning round. 'Why Miss

Frances,' I reply as if I hadn't already seen her.

We embrace coolly, neither quite landing a kiss on the other's cheek.

'Have you met Claire Daker, our new boutique manageress?'

'I don't think so.'

The young woman holds out her hand.

I thrust mine into my jacket pockets.

'I know you'll both get on like a house on fire.' Miss Frances beams at me. 'Claire, Mr Oliver is the fount of all knowledge regarding our beloved Store. Mr Oliver, you will find this clever young woman invaluable. Please use her.'

'If I'm to have someone thrust on me by Head Office –'

'Never "thrust". Proffered. I will leave her in your safe care.'

'Now just hold on – I insist on some further discussion…'

Miss Frances gives me one of her undeniably charming smiles. 'I'm afraid further discussion must wait till Monday. I'm spending a long weekend at my cottage in Yorkshire.'

Standing side-by-side, Claire Daker and I watch her run lightly back down the staircase.

'So, Miss Daker?' My gaze travels upwards, taking in knee socks, short tartan kilt, cheap angora jumper, and settles on her sulky face. 'Have you ever been into the Bridal Salon to see what exactly goes on? Or anywhere else in The Store?'

'Until very recently I was snowed under in the Complaints Department.'

'That's a "no" then?' My nostrils pick up her scent – cheap, flowery… familiar.

Taking her by the elbow, I steer her across the vast expanse of cream carpet towards the mirror-glass walls at the back of the salon. With my free hand, I shove aside a glass partition to reveal dresses in white, cream and palest pink. I push open another partition and then another.

'Gosh,' is all she can come up with.

'Della, Gwen,' I call out. Like exotic birds, copper and ebony plumed, my two chief saleswomen step out from a curtained alcove. 'This is Miss Daker.'

'I hope you'll call me Claire.'

'No, I don't think we'll do that. Let's keep to Miss Daker, shall we?' I release her elbow. 'Ladies, *eventually* Miss Daker will be managing the Teen Boutique. Till it's ready she'll help out here. Any questions?'

'Is it okay to send her to the caff for our coffees when we're busy?' Gwen asks.

I look at Claire. 'Well?'

For a moment she seemed uncertain and then she gives them both a friendly smile. 'I'd be happy to go out for your coffees. Of course, providing I'm not too busy myself.'

She thinks she's won a point.

'In that case,' I say, 'will you get my girls a couple of coffees right now? Rosa at the desk will give you petty cash.'

'But it isn't busy.'

'But it is.' A mother and daughter in raincoats and holding dripping umbrellas are trailing damply up the staircase. 'We have customers.'

Round One to me.

The pain above my eyes is receding. It no longer hurts to lift my eyelids. I stare at the picture above the fireplace, of a galleon battling against a frothing sea, which immediately reminds me of Doreen. Not actually Doreen, but her breasts battling against the jet buttons of her tight fitting jacket earlier in the day.

Steve Chambers once described me as 'a buttoned-up kind of guy'. At the time I'd been irritated, but I realise now that Steve hit the nail on the head. This doesn't necessarily make me the best of company, but a general manager isn't required to get on with everybody. He has to be able to say and do the unsayable and undoable, to make sweeping changes, root and branch cuts, hire and fire. Had I been dictating my memoirs to a sensibly shod and dressed secretary, I would have stressed that being 'a buttoned-up kind of guy' didn't automatically mean that I would be passionless. No indeed!

I remove the cloth from my forehead. I feel hungry. Am I like someone who has been very ill and then one day finds his appetite has returned? Was I getting better?

Surely not? An impossibility. Unwanted.

*

In those first weeks after her arrival on the shop floor, I believed that I hated Claire Daker; however Miss Frances had told me to 'use' the girl and by god I did just that.

At least twenty times a day, I summoned her down from her eyrie on the mezzanine floor: to meet me in the Bridal Salon, at the cash desk, out on Oxford Street to review The Store window displays. How I relished keeping her waiting while I attended to everybody and every last damn thing first. When I was finally ready, I'd treat her with contemptuous courtesy that would have reduced any other member of my staff to tears.

I considered her to be a thorn in my side. I no doubt said as much to Della. Pluck out that thorn and the implication was there – I would be restored. To what exactly? Good humour, confidence, sanguinity? Not for one moment did I spot what probably everyone in the building must have seen – that in my own tortuous kind of way I was falling in love.

A Monday morning came when I walked through The Store humming. I took the stairs up to the salon two-at-a-time. As I reached the top stair, metaphorically a flood gate inside my chest opened. God almighty, it sounds like sentimental twaddle but my heart told me what my brain refused to believe. Suddenly I knew why Sunday, normally my day of rest – newspapers and colour supplements, slippered feet up on either the leather *pouffe* or the sofa – had seemed so interminably dull. There had been no Miss Daker to take to task. I had mooched around my flat wishing the day away. In anticipation, I'd gone to bed early.

Della stood in front of a mirror, her face turned towards me in welcome, mascara brush poised in mid-air.

'Ring Miss Daker. Ask her to meet me in bridal immediately.'

'No need. She's on her way down with a consignment of bridesmaids' baskets.'

'And in future confine your make-up to the Ladies Cloakroom.'

'But the light's awful in there.'

'Is it too much to ask for you to perhaps make your face up in your own home and in your own time?' I'd responded silkily.

'The light's awful at home as well. My Stan goes in for subdued lighting.'

'Does daylight never filter through a window?'

'Not really. We're one of a block and there's a block opposite.'

'Get Miss Daker down here – now.'

'She's just stepped out of the lift.' Gwen, her coat half off, rushed past us. 'Sorry I'm late, Mr Oliver.'

I couldn't have cared less that Gwen was at least an hour late for work and this was becoming a habit. My attention was caught by the sound of light footsteps on the stairs coming down from Mezzanine. The side door into the salon opened and there she was, her arms full of pink and blue raffia baskets. I drank in her annoyed expression, her gleaming blonde hair, that sullen lower lip. Oh, I was so pleased to see her. You have no idea, unless you too have been wildly in love.

'Mr Oliver,' she said and sighed heavily.

'Good morning, Claire.'

Della, Gwen, they heard the note of tenderness in my voice. My change of heart could not have been made clearer had I swung from the chandelier and roared, 'Claire my reluctant darling, my own one. Fly with me to my one-bedroomed bachelor apartment in Earls Court and let me shower you with the love of my declining years. Let us be united and let no man put us asunder.'

Time stood still. The bridal women were… gobsmacked: Gwen rising like Venus from the waves, out of a froth of white veiling she was attempting to fold, and Della faltering as she gathered her make-up into a quilted purse. She'd looked at me and no doubt recognised the foolish look on her hero's face. All those decades I'd spent building up an impenetrable façade, shattered in a moment.

'Did you want something, Mr Oliver?' Claire had asked. 'I was just dropping these off before going out to the Copper Kettle.'

I stepped towards her.

She took two steps back.

My hand shot out and gripped her shoulder. In a quiet, firm voice I said, 'From now on, I want you down here where I can keep an eye on you.'

'But –'

'Do you understand? Yes or no?'

'Yes, Mr Oliver.' She twitched away so that my hand fell to my side. Carefully, she arranged the bridesmaids' baskets on the glass counter before looking at her watch. 'And now it's my tea break.'

'You don't need a tea break.'

She tossed her ponytail defiantly. Her gaze met mine. 'I don't need a tea break. But I'm entitled to one.'

Round Two to Claire Daker.

Chapter 12

1975

Carpenter eased open the middle drawer of his bow-fronted, flame-mahogany bureau. There had to be an item of clothing suitable for the French class. Each week he'd found himself surveying the other students and wondering, *Just where do these people find such god-awful outfits?* Surely he must have some god-awful outfits of his own? Yet even amongst his oldest clothes there was nothing that could be called 'casual' or even 'smart casual' – a term he'd recently heard Oliver use when describing a jacket he was thinking of buying.

Carefully, he arranged his pullovers into three neat piles on his bed: grey fleck, beige fleck and brown fleck, crew-neck and vee-neck in style. Each one was as pristine as the day it had left his favourite menswear shop, Austin Reed of Harrogate.

These days, Carpenter found it impossible to think about clothes without also considering his mother's fiancé. He doubted whether Sydney Oliver even owned anything quite as casual as a pullover. In the short time he'd been at Mildmay's, he'd worn formal suits every single day, changing for dinner into an even more formal suit. A fresh shirt morning and evening. To give the old devil his due, he'd brought a touch of urbane elegance to their family dinner table.

Carpenter caught his reflection in the mirror and straightened up. He must improve his posture. That was another thing: Sydney Oliver's ramrod-straight, military bearing. There was a man for whom slumping was an impossibility. Could slumping be caused by an over-dependency on pullovers? Carpenter liked his clothes new and expensive. He also preferred them a size larger than was strictly necessary, disliking the pressure of firm waistbands or a collar pressing even lightly against his throat.

One by one, Carpenter returned the pullovers to the drawer. Reaching the very last one, in the very last pile, his heart lifted as if acknowledging an old and beloved friend: his university cricketing pullover. He shook it out. Frayed at the wrists – good. Discoloured but not dirty – good. On the small side – not so good. He would have to wear it over a shirt.

Lighting a cigarette he went over to the open window. From his bedroom he had a view of Mrs Venables' bungalow roof, the kitchen garden and fields, and there she was, pulling up something green and leafy for their dinners. Pity there wasn't time to get her to turn his turn-ups down.

'Can I come in?' Without waiting for an answer, his mother pushed his door open.

Guiltily, Carpenter tossed the stub of the cigarette out of the window before turning around. 'Excuse the mess, Ma. Just having a tidy up.' *Why the devil did he always feel the need to make excuses for being alive?*

It was unusual for her to search him out. Ill at ease, she drifted from chest of drawers, to his desk, to the mantelpiece, picking up a framed family photo, his hair brush, cufflink boxes, before putting them back in the wrong place. What did she want now? So many of his childhood memories had been coloured by his mother's anger and dissatisfaction. He pulled out his desk chair and sat down.

She reached the window.

Carpenter tensed. Would she spot his cigarette butt smouldering on the gravel below? He dreaded a similar recurrence to the row over the ruined curtain. That nasty little trick had to have been down to Junior. He should have said something to him, but his younger brother somehow always seemed so vulnerable – not much of a life: no job, no money of his own, and no picnic being a mother's boy.

As Doreen turned her back on the view, Carpenter breathed a sigh of relief. Even with the light behind her, Carpenter could see that she looked tired. He wondered if she'd been drinking. Sometimes, even first thing in the morning, he was sure he picked up a combination of perfume, face powder and alcohol.

Holding out her hands as if appealing to an audience, she announced, 'Carpenter, I don't want to embarrass you but I have to talk to someone.'

'I'm not embarrassed.' He was upset. His mother was rarely vulnerable, and to have her confiding in him now felt unbearably painful.

Doreen drifted across the room. 'Do you mind if I sit on your bed?'

'Of course not.'

She perched on the edge.

He thought that she almost always perched like a stocky little bird. She was incapable of relaxing, only of pretending to relax.

Doreen picked up a book from his bedside table, smoothed out the turned-down page marking his place before snapping it shut.

'Talk away. I'm listening,' Carpenter said gently.

'But will you be able to understand?'

'I'll do my best.'

Positioning his chair so he could still obliquely see his mother's face, he tried to concentrate on the familiar view of the garden.

She appeared to begin in the middle of an ongoing train of thought. 'Of course, the maddening thing is I really feel Oliver is capable of giving me what I want. It's just that he keeps putting up barriers.'

'Then don't give him reasons to put up barriers.'

She flapped her hand as if brushing away an annoying fly. 'We won't get anywhere if I don't make a move. I'll be living the same sort of sterile life I lived with your father. I could just about stand that because I didn't love him.' She shuddered. 'Sometimes he gave me the heebie-jeebies.'

It no longer hurt Carpenter when she dismissed his father as unlovable. He didn't know whether he believed her or not. He was almost sure he remembered times when there had at least been affection between them.

'You like to dominate, Ma. The bloke you've chosen doesn't want to be dominated.'

As if on cue, he saw Sydney Oliver stroll across the lawn, heading towards the wooden summer house.

She leant forward, her hands holding her stomach as if in pain. 'You're a man. What do you think he wants?'

He really tried to think. Never mind Sydney Oliver, what did *he* want? At this moment – for his mother to leave him alone for at least twenty-four hours. Ditto for the fiancé!

'He looks a bit browbeaten, a bit knocked about. I should say he wants someone to look after him and be his friend.'

Tears filled Doreen's eyes but didn't fall. 'I would do all that. But is it too much to ask for him to sometimes take the upper hand, treat me as a desirable woman?'

The last thing Carpenter wanted in his head was the image of his mother being treated as a desirable woman. Abruptly he stood up and risked taking a pack of cigarettes from his desk drawer.

'Cigarette, Ma?'

'I wish you'd stop.' She took one from his packet.

He lit it for her, and then lit his own, blowing the smoke towards the window. There was now no sign of Oliver, but the summer house door was open. Carpenter rested his elbows on the windowsill. The landscape was turning to gold, yet he never travelled close enough to see the wheat, ripe or unripe. The summer sky was a brilliant blue, yet he rarely took the time to look up at it. He thought of his desire to look 'smartly casual' and wished he didn't care so much.

'Ma, I think that you could answer his needs but he can't answer yours. Perhaps nobody can.'

Behind him he heard the rustle of clothing and knew his mother was searching for her handkerchief, but he wouldn't look at her. Better to see her angry, drunk, or both, than crying. She never cried. Until recently he would have laid money that she never would.

'I could be wrong of course,' he said.

'You're not wrong.' Her voice was moving towards the door. 'I expect you think I'm disgusting to want passion at my time of life. It's not just now – I've always looked for it. Somehow I've never brought that out in anyone.'

'Whatever you say, Dad loved you.'

'Not in any way that I wanted to be loved. Your father was chilly. He told me he had a 'quiet burning' where I was concerned.' Her voice was bitter.

'Ma, I'm sorry.' If only he could turn away from the window, walk over to his mother and hug her, but his body felt incapable of movement.

'The thought of living and dying without ever having passion in my life makes me feel quite desperate.'

Carpenter was aware of a light draught as his bedroom door

closed. He remembered how resentful he'd been at his mother managing to find someone special. A fiancé. A stuffed pig served up on a silver plate with an orange in his mouth.

Her handkerchief lay next to the bed. He picked it up. It was bone dry. So she hadn't cried after all. What a fraud she was.

He lit another cigarette and watched Mr Oliver carry a deckchair from the summer house and place it in a patch of late afternoon sun. The man looked somehow ill at ease, unused to gardens and open air perhaps. Carpenter felt something like affection for him. He moved away from the window.

If his mother could find herself a boyfriend, however unsatisfactory the relationship, what was the matter with him? There had been no one in his life since the six month fling with Enid, the PA before Monica. Was that why she'd gone off with the skiing instructor? Had she grown tired of waiting for him to turn their fling into at least an affair?

Breathing deeply, he inflated his chest with air and flexed his arm muscles. They were becoming flabby. He should join the gym at the leisure centre in Burnside. But then he might bump into the vile Martin Renshawe, or worse, the even viler Ned Barber. Apparently *he* was a pool attendant in the evenings. Why in the world did Monica find the man so amusing? Someone who had named his ramshackle junk shop on the Skipton Road, 'Bewitched, Bothered and Bygonerie'?

Carpenter kicked off his shoes and lay on the bed, his head and shoulders against a pillow. That first Friday of the college term, Ned had made an excellent impression.

There's a chap I can do business with, he'd thought. *A chap who's not ashamed to wear a club blazer.*

Ned's blazer had been immaculate, navy with an armorial embroidered in gold and red on the breast pocket. Something nautical, maybe a ship's anchor? Plus a club tie. A different club, air force, but he'd immediately assumed that a man like Ned would be gregarious – might belong to a variety of clubs. Knife edge creases to Ned's Bedford cord trousers. The whole outfit a bit old fashioned for a student evening class, but fine were they to share a future tipple in a wine bar or even dinner at Harrogate's premier hotel, The Majestic. At the time Carpenter had sentimentally thought that he would almost be willing to lay down his life for such a man under battle conditions.

'So, you're something of a wheeler-dealer in the antiques trade, eh Ned?' he'd imagined saying, accompanying the comment with a light friendly jab to Ned's ribs. Monica would see him in a different light: Carpenter Mildmay, man's man and all-round good sport.

The following Friday evening, Carpenter arrived at the college ten minutes early, intending to initiate a conversation about cars, antiques or restaurants. But where was Ned? Surely he wasn't that hippie drawing a cartoon of a man with his head between his legs, on the blackboard?

'Up his own arse,' the hippie scrawled next to the drawing. He'd tossed the piece of chalk into the waste paper basket and swung around.

'Carpenter, my old mucker,' he'd drawled.

The hippie wore several days' growth of beard, a stained polo neck jumper that almost reached his knees, dirty jeans and rope sandals.

'Ned?'

'As you live and breathe.' Ned looked over Carpenter's shoulder. 'Monica, you gorgeous minx.'

Carpenter held his breath, waiting for Monica to verbally crush Ned.

She'd laughed as if genuinely amused. 'You fool.' Her tone was warm and familiar.

With the intuition of the thin-skinned, Carpenter felt certain that at some point during the intervening week, Ned and Monica had arranged to meet, sat in a coffee bar talking intimately, made each other laugh, found mutual interests, common ground, shared the bill, possibly a tea cake, hopped on the same bus, agreed to reconnoitre after class, spend Christmas or the New Year together. He couldn't bear to look at either of them. He stared at the floor as Ned ambled past him. All he absorbed was the image of Ned's tanned bare toes.

He had found a chair and desk on the other side of the room. Avoiding them, his eyes had focused on the blackboard. The cartoon man wore shoes tightly laced, his trousers ended above the rib of his socks. Ned had cleverly caught something foolish about his posture that was familiar. Carpenter had felt as if icy water was trickling down his back as he recognised himself.

What a cruel bastard. How had Ned concluded that someone he'd hardly said two words to was 'up his own arse'? Carpenter looked at the cricket pullover lying on the chair – would that dispel 'up his own arse-dom'? He thought not but it was worth a try.

Chapter 13

1974

Miss Frances rarely smiled. Smiling didn't suit the position of a Chief Buyer. She could allow her eyes to warm, signifying approval or amusement, but the distribution of her smiles was kept under tight control. She admired Mr Oliver for the self-same discipline.

It was early August and the Teen Boutique was ready on schedule – no more than a plasterboard and plywood shell wedged between Accessories and Lingerie but it faced the store's glass double-fronted doors. A young woman pausing on Oxford Street to admire the Summer Bride window display might well glance in and murmur, 'Hmm that looks interesting. Must check it out.'

Miss Frances stepped inside the boutique. All her own work. She had fought the management board, including that dinosaur, Oliver, and she'd got her way. From concept to construction, the boutique was her personal creation. With pleasure, she inhaled the smell of fresh paint as she surveyed the finished room and found it pleasing: the walls of matt silver, the ceiling black and patterned with random showers of silver stars.

Mr Stanhope, the Sales Director had suggested further expanding the night sky theme into science fiction. 'Planets suspended from the ceiling by invisible threads? A dalek might be amusing by the door.'

'Young women aren't interested in science fiction,' she'd said severely. 'Anyway there isn't a door. The boutique interior needs to be fully visible.'

Annoyingly he'd persisted, musing over the heroes in his collection of Marvel comics. 'Funnily enough, although I can't stand spiders, I have a particular affection for Spiderman.'

'Really?' Miss Frances considered just what job Mr Stanhope might have been suited for had he not been the nephew of the present managing director.

'Yes.' He'd rubbed his chin and smiled at the memory. 'I've bought a Marvel comic a week since I was twelve years old. Keep 'em in airtight polythene bags. The early ones must be worth a fortune by now.'

Fortunately Mr Stanhope rarely needed a reply. Men were so childlike and yet often ended up in positions of power. She would never have reached her present position if she'd moped aloud over her own personal favourite, aspiring secret ballerina Moira Kent, from her Bunty comic.

She adjusted the wig on the Twiggy mannequin, bought at a snip from the boutique manageress at Marshall & Snelgrove. There was a small chip across the bridge of Twiggy's nose, but apart from that you would never know that she was nearly ten years old. Miss Frances had half-expected Claire Daker to make a comment of the 'Twiggy is so sixties' variety but no, with great enthusiasm Claire had dressed the fibreglass model in purple suede gauchos, candy-striped, halter-neck top, with a diamante studded dog-collar around her neck.

'I can't imagine that even our younger customers are ready for dog-collars,' Miss Frances had protested.

'Dog-collars have been stocked in Miss Selfridge for at least two seasons. They look fantastic. Trust me.'

Those last two words had caught Miss Frances by surprise. Of course they were meaningless – just a glib phrase that a careless young woman like Claire might utter. But they made her perceive the gulf between them, not just in years, but worlds apart. 'Trust me' was something Miss Frances would say to a lover, or a lover to her. 'Trust me' was promise of a future, even if the promise turned out to be a lie.

'I'm sure you're right, Claire,' Miss Frances had replied.

'I might buy a couple with my staff discount.'

'As long as you don't wear one to work.'

'But why not?'

Miss Frances's tone had been cold. 'It wouldn't be appropriate.' She'd been tempted to add 'Trust me' but didn't.

Claire hadn't argued, which was a relief.

Miss Frances had allowed her gaze to soften. 'You can always use your staff discount in Daywear. They have some very trendy dresses in at the moment.' She'd regretted the word 'trendy' the very second it left her mouth.

Claire winced. 'I'd rather die than wear anything trendy from Daywear.'

Claire was certainly attractive, often amusing, admirable when standing up to Mr Oliver, but after several weeks, Miss Frances still felt that they were no closer. She was almost intimidated by the young woman. Miss Frances knew that her own tough, sophisticated exterior was just that – an exterior. Claire Daker was cool. In a few years' time she could imagine her sitting completely at ease, in smoky Soho jazz clubs, making everyone else feel overly voluble just because she said so little. Somehow Claire was rather special. Della, the store battle-axe was certainly won over, and Mr Oliver…

Miss Frances bent down to adjust Twiggy's legs so that the mannequin's knees almost touched and the feet pointed inwards in approved gamine style.

'When are we opening?'

She felt her cheeks reddening as if Claire had overheard her thoughts. She straightened up. 'Saturday-week, I believe. The twins, Teddie and Babs from the Beverley Sisters are coming in at eleven to cut the ribbon. Quite a *coup*!'

'The Beverley Sisters!' Claire looked appalled. 'But Miss Frances, they're my mother's generation.'

'The Store is very fortunate that they could make time for this. The Bevs are about to set off on a nostalgia tour of the Far East.' Miss Frances read disdain in Claire's extraordinary blue eyes at the word 'nostalgia'.

'But you said the boutique was about youth and fashion. Everyone will laugh. We'll look stupid – as if we're completely out of touch.'

'Oh Claire!'

'I'm serious. You asked me to do this job and I don't intend to be just a token "young person".'

'Of course you're not.' But Miss Frances felt slightly sick. If she thought about it, and she hadn't up till that moment, a 'token young person' was exactly what she'd meant Claire to be.

'Miss Frances, you're not listening to me.'

'I am.'

'The Beverley Sisters are at least twice the age of some of our customers.'

Miss Frances put her hand on Claire's shoulder. 'Sit down.'

'There is nowhere to sit.'

Miss Frances moved a pile of t-shirts from a wooden display case. 'Sit on this. You don't weigh more than a sparrow. The glass won't break.'

Claire took a paper tissue from her skirt pocket and wiped her eyes before sitting down. Either she was upset or very angry. There was no tell-tale smear of black on the tissue. Miss Frances could have sworn the girl wore mascara. Her eyelashes were always so enviably thick and dark.

'I *was* listening and of course you're right. We didn't think this through properly but crying instead of arguing your case is rather disappointing.'

'I wasn't crying.'

'Well that's a relief.' Miss Frances's lips twitched. 'So, who would you suggest instead of The Beverleys, taking into account that The Store and its management are old-fashioned. What about Cilla Black?'

'No!'

'Lulu?'

'These are all singers from your generation, not mine.'

'Thank you, Claire. Perhaps *you* could come up with a suggestion?'

'If we've got to have someone old, Dusty Springfield's okay.'

'She's only thirty-six.'

'Exactly.'

'That's young by the standards of many of our customers.' Miss Frances was thirty-seven. She tried to keep the hurt from her voice.

Claire's top lip curled. 'Compared to anyone buying clothes in a boutique, Dusty Springfield is ancient. But okay.'

Miss Frances's heart began to beat faster. Somewhere at home she still had Gus's address book. She turned her head so that Claire couldn't see the excitement in her eyes. 'Dusty Springfield might be available.'

'But what will you do about The Beverleys?'

'I shall cancel them.'

Claire's eyes widened. 'Won't you get into trouble?'

'As head buyer, I can do what I want.' She paused for a moment, enjoying the return of her power. 'Claire, I'm well aware that I'm out of touch with those things that women your age want, in fashion, music, practically right across the board. That's why I chose you to manage this venture.'

Claire kicked her heels against the display cabinet. 'Thank you.'

'I promise you that we won't have The Beverley Sisters opening the boutique. However, if we can't get Dusty Springfield at this late date, we may have to open it ourselves. Will that be so bad?' Miss Frances smiled. Immediately she tried to withdraw her smile and failed.

'No, the two of us will be fine.'

'I will see what I can do. I used to have a few show-biz friends back in the day.' Once again she sounded horribly old-fashioned. She saw herself as Claire must see her: out of touch, one foot already in middle-age, stuck in the jargon of the fifties. She could have howled and beaten her fists against her Jaeger blouse front. Should she desert Jaeger?

But wait, Claire Daker, her protégé, was grinning back at her. 'That's fantastic, Miss Frances. Do you know Diana Dors?'

Miss Frances inclined her head. 'Yes. Actually we did meet. Just the once. It was some years ago.'

'Tell me.'

'She came to my friend Gus's funeral. She said a few words.'

'I'm sorry.'

'All water under the bridge.'

There was a staccato rap on the plywood frame. The entire boutique shuddered. Claire looked over Miss Frances's shoulder, her expression hardening.

Miss Frances turned, smoothing back her hair. 'Mr Oliver! We are honoured. We hardly expected to see you in the boutique at this preparatory stage.'

Mr Oliver stepped across the threshold, slowly, almost menacingly. The boutique seemed suddenly crowded. His dark suit, dark hair and moustache, dark glowering expression, absorbed the light.

She had a moment of insight – *Mr Oliver is a creature of the night* – before dismissing this as prompted by an unhealthy interest in

Hammer Horror films. He was a man like any other who possessed an unreliable temper. She could handle him. She always had done in the past. Giving him a rare warm smile, she waved in the direction of the Twiggy mannequin. 'As you can see, we're almost ready for business.'

'Not much stock.' His eyes raked the small room. 'The place looks half empty.'

She shook her head. 'You must remember, teen fashions take up far less room – less cloth, smaller sizes. Even our maxi-coats come in lightweight fabrics.'

She threw Claire an inclusive glance. Claire chose not to catch it.

'When are we expecting our jersey pinafore dresses in, Claire?'

'This afternoon. I'll have them priced and on the shop floor in time for the opening.'

'Bravo.' Miss Frances clapped her hands. She knew she was overdoing the bright charm but it seemed impossible to do otherwise. She turned to Mr Oliver. 'You see, everything under control.'

Very slowly, Mr Oliver turned a full circle, taking in the mirrors, the racks of dresses, rails of separates, the neat but packed display cabinet, finally stopping to face Claire Daker. 'I was beginning to think you'd taken yet another extended tea-break,' he said. There was an intimacy in his tone, as if he and Claire were alone in the room together. Claire crossed her arms defensively across her chest.

'And yet here Claire is, Mr Oliver – hard at work.'

He continued to look at Claire. 'But is she hard at work? As far as I can see, subject to the late arrival of some pinafore dresses, she has nothing much left to do here.'

'She? Surely it should be Claire or Miss Daker?' Miss Frances's voice was reproving.

He clicked his heels together. 'I stand corrected. Miss Daker, when you do find a gap in your busy boutique schedule, we're almost out of Anne of Cleves head-dresses. A dozen boxes by the weekend, please.'

How extraordinary the situation was, Miss Frances mused. Just on the other side of the boutique shell, the business of The Store was proceeding as normal for a busy Thursday late-night closing. If all three of them were to fall silent they would be able to hear the conversations of the customers, the sound of the cash register being rung up, the crackle of wrapping paper and the hiss of polythene. Instead they were fixed in this ill-natured scene.

'That requires a response,' Mr Oliver said.

'If I have time,' Claire answered.

'You really are an annoyingly lazy and impudent young woman.' His eyes remained fixed on her face.

Miss Frances stepped between them. At school she had shone at Piggy in the Middle. Although short, she'd been agile and capable of leaping high into the air to intercept the ball. Later in life she hadn't enjoyed the experience half as much, playing Piggy in the Middle to a succession of Gus's girlfriends or would-be girlfriends. She had dealt with them; Mr Oliver couldn't be more formidable, could he?

This much she knew – Mr Oliver lacked friends, lacked an ability to make friends. Somewhere under his suit jacket, shirt and no doubt vest, he suffered. There had been a conversation between them once, at a Store Christmas party, when both had come clean about ambitions being achieved at the expense of friends and family. Miss Frances hadn't told him about Gus, but she'd held the knowledge that she at least had someone in her heart, as he'd said the one word, 'Sublimation'.

At home she'd looked the word up and found that Sigmund Freud defined sublimation as 'the process of deflecting sexual instincts into acts of higher social valuation'. She thought she knew what both Freud and Mr Oliver had meant, but was unsure whether it truly applied to her.

'Mr Oliver, Claire and I have so much to do. Perhaps one of your wonderful sales staff could order the head-dresses? We do want this venture to be a success, don't we?'

His face was set into its most implacable expression. He would know she was manipulating him. He was a clever man – even her friendliness would be recognised for the bluff it was.

'I don't know that I care either way,' he said.

'As a favour to me?'

Almost imperceptibly, his shoulders relaxed. 'I'll see how Della is fixed for time. Just this once. There is no point keeping dogs and barking myself.'

He turned to leave. Twiggy's outstretched hand grazed against his shoulders. His body tensed. He looked straight at Claire.

In his eyes, Miss Frances recognised a brief flash of yearning, as if he'd imagined that Claire had leant forward and touched him. She took his arm again and steered him towards the doorway. With his shoes facing in the direction of the shop floor there was no option left to him but to leave.

For five more minutes Miss Frances and Claire Daker worked quietly together, Claire unpacking boxes of t-shirts, Miss Frances writing out price tickets. At four o'clock Miss Frances looked at her watch and stretched.

'I hate him,' Claire said. 'He gives me the creeps.'

'I'd say he was lonely.'

'He's lonely because he gives everyone the creeps.'

'Now there you'd be wrong. You must get that all the time, though. Men liking you. You're so pretty.'

Claire didn't answer her. She went behind the cash desk and came back with her purse. 'Do you want a tea? Coffee?'

'Let me buy it. We deserve a break.'

'No,' Claire said firmly. 'I'll buy it.'

Chapter 14

1975

'Aren't you coming to French?' Monica appeared at Carpenter's elbow as he swung open the door of his sports car. 'Honestly Carpenter, I do wish you'd told me yesterday, I could have brought my bicycle.'

'What do you mean?'

'You're wearing a cricket pullover. I assume you're going to play cricket?'

'And you are wearing a maroon cloak and beret. I wonder what assumption I should make about that outfit. At the end of a long working day, I've simply chosen to wear something I'm comfortable in. This happens to be an old favourite from my university days.'

'I didn't know you'd been to university?'

'There's no reason why you should. I've never mentioned it before.'

Carpenter resisted the urge to tug at the frayed hem. The pullover wasn't comfortable. It *was* too small for him. At a stroke Monica had wrong-footed him – his mood had switched from almost cheerful to feeling a complete fool.

They got in the car and he switched on the engine.

'Carpenter –'

'Do you mind very much if we don't speak? I've got a splitting headache and I'd like to concentrate on my driving.'

He turned out onto Burnside High Street. From the office the college was walking distance yet he never chose to walk.

'Fair enough.' From her shoulder bag she took out *Claude et Béatrice sur la Plage* and began to read.

'Would you like a cigarette?' Monica asked without looking up from her book.

'No thank you.'

'You don't mind if I have one?' She opened a packet of Gitanes.

'Actually I do. They smell disgusting and anyway we're there now.'

Monica dropped the packet back in her handbag. 'Oh, look.

There's Ned's car.'

'Hardly a car,' Carpenter said sourly.

Ned had parked his scarlet, open-topped Morgan F Super three-wheeler in the 'no parking' zone in front of the college steps. He was immaculately dressed in a navy and grey pinstripe suit, a black homburg worn with the brim dipping down over one eye.

'Doesn't he look fabulous?'

'He looks like a two-bit gangster.' Carpenter pulled into a space on the other side of the road.

'Then I can be Bonnie to his Clyde Barrow. Faye Dunaway wore a beret in the film.'

'Huh! You're no Faye Dunaway.'

Monica ignored him and climbed out of the car.

Watching her cross the road, Carpenter realised that with her page-boy hairstyle, Monica did look like Faye Dunaway, only younger and prettier.

'The divine Monica!' Ned shouted, raising his hat.

Reluctantly Carpenter locked the car and joined them.

Ned saluted him. 'Well, if it isn't our greatest living Yorkshireman.'

'I have no idea what you're talking about.'

'Harold Wilson's favourite cricketer. Yorkshire's very own, fiery-tempered Fred Trueman. I'm not mistaken, am I?' Ned wiped an imaginary cricket ball on his thigh and mimed bowling it across the road.

'Most amusing.'

'I try to please.' Ned took Monica's hand and slipped it under his arm. '*A bientôt.* Pub later, Fred?'

Dismissed, Carpenter was forced to dawdle behind them. Whatever could Ned be saying to make Monica laugh? Their heads were almost touching. Going up the college steps their hips did actually bang together. They laughed even more.

'I'm just picking up some books from the library,' he called after them. 'See you in class.' He willed Monica to at least turn her head or wave. She did neither.

For one-hour and fifty minutes Carpenter sat in the college library before returning to his car. He read page eighty-seven of *The Cruel*

Sea five times before Monica appeared, unaccompanied. He pretended not to see her till the moment she rapped on the window.

'Ah, Monica. You startled me.' He pushed open the passenger door. 'Sorry I didn't make the class – got engrossed. What do you think of Nicholas Monsarrat?' He waved his book at her.

'I don't.'

'Was I missed?' He managed to keep his voice light and careless.

'No.'

As he manoeuvred the car out into the line of traffic, he spotted Ned bounding down the college steps in his rear-view mirror.

'I don't think I'll come to the pub tonight. I'll just drop you off. I'm sure Ned will give you a lift home. As I said earlier, I've got a couple of work problems –'

'Oh shut up Carpenter. Can't you bear to be teased on any level at all?'

'I have no idea what you're talking about.'

'Yes, you do. Ned was just joking with you earlier.'

In his rear-view mirror, Carpenter saw Ned leap over the side door of the Morgan and land neatly in his driving seat. Why hadn't he left *his* canvas roof down? But was he capable of leaping over the side door with grace and accuracy? He doubted it.

A double-decker bus stopped to let the Morgan out.

He was sure he heard Ned shout, 'Nice one, squire.'

'Men don't "just joke" at another man's expense. Particularly someone like Ned Barber. They do it for a reason.'

'And what would that be?' Monica sounded bored.

'To make that man – me - look foolish.'

'Honestly Carpenter, you're so...'

'Say what you want to say. Everyone else seems to.'

'It's just that you don't mind dishing it out, but you don't like having it dished back.'

'Dish it out? When do I ever "dish it out" as you so quaintly put it, whatever the "it" might be?'

'Don't patronise me. We're not at work now. I've watched you in the class and at the pub –'

In the rear-view mirror, Carpenter could see Ned's Morgan – it was only three cars behind them. He accelerated. 'Have you really?'

'You despise everybody, yet you expect them to like you. You think you're superior. Look at your ridiculous pullover. Whatever made you wear it? Attempting to lower yourself for the evening to what you estimate our level to be?'

In his entire life he had never hated anyone as much as he hated Monica at that moment. He would have liked to lean across, open the passenger door and push her out into the oncoming traffic. Ned would run over her. Ned would then reverse back over her. Failing that, tomorrow he would sack Monica.

Up ahead of him he saw the Templar's Arms cow bell sign.

'I didn't realise you had such a poor opinion of me.' Now he hated himself even more than he hated her. What a pathetic, pusillanimous remark to come out with when he'd intended to verbally eliminate the ground beneath her metaphorical feet and send her plummeting down into the flames of hell! Definitely tomorrow he would find an excuse to get rid of her. But tomorrow was Saturday. By Monday, he knew his anger would have mellowed to embarrassment.

He braked in front of the pub.

As if she had all the time in the world, Monica took out a cigarette.

Of course she does have all the time in the world, Carpenter thought furiously. *She is looking forward to the rest of her evening, whereas I'd rather be lying unconscious in a flooded ditch.*

'Only the pathetically pretentious or the lowest of the low, smoke those nasty, evil smelling foreign cigarettes.' He knew he sounded exactly like his mother at her most nasty and snobbish.

Monica roared with laughter. 'Honestly Carpenter, you're such an idiot.'

The Morgan drew up beside them. Ned leapt from the car, tossed his Homburg onto the seat and began to sprint towards the pub door. 'Last man in gets the first round, Sir Fred,' he shouted.

Reluctantly, Carpenter pushed open the door of the pub and stepped into the saloon bar.

Ahead of him, Monica had already taken off her cloak but still wore the beret. She was seated at a table between Ned and Sandra, a middle-aged woman from their French class who Carpenter also detested.

‘Come on, Carpenter. You can squeeze in here.’ Sandra patted six inches of space remaining at the end of the horse-shoe shaped banquette.

‘No, no. This will do nicely.’ Carpenter picked up one of Laverne’s three-legged Swiss milking stools and carried it across to the opposite side of the table. He took his time placing it carefully and then searching his trouser pockets for his wallet.

Sitting down seemed an impossibility. How to lower his tall frame in a casual and unconcerned manner onto a circle of wood that was no larger than a dinner plate?

To cover his embarrassment he remained standing, looking down at them with a self-mocking smile. He concentrated his gaze on Sandra’s second chin. ‘So what’s it to be, lads?’

What had possessed him to call two women and an aging hippy, lads? He despised himself anew for not even having control over his mouth.

Ned banged on the table with his fist. ‘Pints, pints and more pints!’

‘And what will the ladies have?’ Carpenter bared his teeth.

‘Same for us please.’ Monica didn’t smile.

Standing at the bar with a ten pound note held out enticingly to catch the eye of the barmaid, Carpenter found himself thinking about his father. Physically he’d looked a lot like Junior, but he’d never seemed boyish, always very much a man. Carpenter couldn’t imagine Junior, at any age, actually becoming an adult.

His gaze focused on the back of Junior’s head in the lounge side of the bar. He would have recognised his brother’s greenish-brown hair and small ears anywhere.

A tall middle-aged man wearing a well cut tweed jacket lightly touched Junior’s shoulder as if steering him forwards. Carpenter recognised Martin Renshawe. They moved out of sight. What were the two of them doing out together? Yes, they could have bumped into each other by accident but Junior went to clubs not pubs. And the way Martin had touched his shoulder – almost paternally.

‘Wilful incontinence. What else can I call it?’ Sandra looked up at Carpenter. ‘I’ve just been telling Ned and Monica about mother refusing to use the toilet when she wants to go wee-wee.’

‘So, where does she go?’ Carpenter placed the glasses on the table – three beers and a double gin and tonic for himself. Carefully lowering himself onto the milking stool, he found his knees were almost on a level with his shoulders.

'Where doesn't she go?' Sandra took a tissue from her sleeve and violently blew her nose.

'Aren't you being a little hard on the old dear?' Ned picked up his glass of beer. 'When my gran began to lose control of her waterworks, she was mortified.'

Sandra's jaw jutted forward, the overhead light glinting on the thick glass of her lenses. 'My mother is not an old dear. Surely by now, you've gathered that?'

'Ned has a soft heart,' Monica said.

'He doesn't have to share a sofa with her. She's ruining the velour. If she starts doing "you know what" as well, she's going in a Home.'

For a second, Carpenter allowed his eyes to close. When he opened them again, Ned was wiping beer froth from his upper lip with the cuff of his jacket.

'No offence, Sandra,' Ned said, 'but can we talk about art, beauty, a new-born lamb, a field of ripe corn, the next round of drinks.'

Sandra drained her glass, her good humour returning. 'Ned, my love, you are a gentleman and a scholar.'

Ned bowed. 'I'm the first with my hands in my trouser pockets, whatever the reason.' He brayed out a laugh.

Sandra likes him as well, Carpenter thought. *How can that be possible?*

Aloud he said, 'Ned, I'll have another double gin and tonic if you're in the chair. Afraid I'm not much of a beer drinker. Never a cheap round where I'm concerned.' Under the table someone trod firmly on his toe. It had to be Monica, although she was rummaging for her cigarettes in the folds of her cloak.

'I'd rather you didn't smoke at the table. It's stuffy enough in here.'

Monica still didn't look at him. 'Actually, I was going outside for a breath of fresh air. Coming Sandra?'

'Why not?'

He refused to watch them making their way across the pub. So what if he was left squatting in front of an empty table? Being left alone with Sandra would have been purgatory anyway.

'Don't get cold, girls,' Ned called after them.

'We won't.' They both laughed.

What was so funny?

Against his will, Carpenter found himself surreptitiously observing Ned as he approached the bar.

Ned eased his buttocks onto the bar stool, crooked his right ankle negligently onto his left thigh and began to stroke the hairy expanse of skin between the end of his trousers and sock. A smile played across his lips as if he were recalling some fond memory.

'Penny for them, Ned?' The barmaid leant her elbows on the bar.

Don't offer him anything, you stupid woman. Whatever they are they're not worth the scraping off my boot!

But after not more than three words had left Ned's mouth, the barmaid was in hysterics.

The door to the car park opened and Sandra came in with a blast of chilly air. 'You look exactly how I was feeling ten minutes ago.'

Carpenter recoiled as Sandra gently touched his arm. 'And how would that be?'

'Angry.' She slid back into her seat. 'I was annoyed. It's all very well for Ned to play devil's advocate but he knows nothing of the real situation. I don't tell anyone the half of it.'

Thank God for that.

'Men don't understand these things anyway.'

'Your husband, John, seems an understanding sort.'

'He's marvellous. Solid as a rock. But incontinence can really take the shine off any relationship.'

Carpenter was dismayed to recognise real tears in Sandra's eyes and felt his own smarting in response.

She looked wistfully across to the bar, 'My John used to be just like that when he was Ned's age – the life and soul of every party.'

At a stroke, Carpenter's sympathy and tears disappeared.

'Of course John never had the knack with women that our Ned has.' Sandra smiled as Monica sat down. 'I was just telling Carpenter, I expect Ned has admirers queuing round the block.'

Carpenter decided that continuous immersion of Sandra's head in her mother's urine was almost too good a punishment.

'Honestly Sandra, I fail to see how you reach such conclusions about *our* Ned.' Carpenter attempted to cross his legs but failed. 'Is it his ruggedly ugly face, a certain down-at-heel charm or just the charisma of a dodgy jack-the-lad antiques dealer that has bamboozled you into taking him for some Byronesque figure? Anyway I thought all antique dealers were homosexual, so maybe you're way off beam.'

Impatiently, Monica pushed a strand of hair under her beret and leant forward. 'Sandra doesn't deserve this tirade. You've got some ridiculous bee in your bonnet about Ned, but I can tell you this –'

'Please don't.'

Sandra also leant towards him. 'Ned is as honest as the day is long. One of god's own.'

Beneath Carpenter's cricket pullover, shirt and vest he felt rage building up like – an engorged, reddened fist. He roared, 'One of god's own what? God's own antique dealers? Call me intellectually subnormal but that enlightens me not the tiniest jot.'

'Order, order, no bickering folks.' Ned put a tray of glasses onto the table. 'There's nearly a treble of gin in there for you, Carpenter. The barmaid's hands went all of a tremble just looking over at your masculine profile. She says you're a dead ringer for Lawrence Olivier in *That Hamilton Woman*.'

'Most amusing, Ned, but well before my time.' Carpenter poured a couple of inches of tonic water over the gin before saying, in what he imagined to be a dangerous tone, 'You think you're very witty, don't you, Ned?'

'Possibly. The same certainly couldn't be said about you.'

Sandra patted Carpenter's arm. 'Take no notice. It's just a bit of fun.'

How he hated anyone even touching him.

'Budge up, Monica, you gorgeous bint.' Ned eased onto the banquette seat and draped his arm around Monica's neck. 'Now tell me, what's misery guts like to work with?'

Monica removed Ned's arm. 'That's enough, Ned.'

'She doesn't work "with" me.' Carpenter stabbed a finger in Monica's direction. 'She works *for* me. I'm her boss; she's just one of my employees.'

Ned sat back. 'You ooze charm.'

Carpenter felt quite sick. Abruptly he stood up, sending their glasses sliding across the table and knocking over the three-legged stool. 'May you all rot in hell!'

He stumbled out into the dusk. Next to the car, he stood with the palms of his hands flat on the bonnet, a mild breeze ruffling his hair. That was the end of Adult Ed. On Monday he wouldn't have to sack Monica, she'd never want to work for him again anyway.

'Carpenter, I'm tired and I'd like to go home. If you'd just drop me off at the usual place.'

He didn't turn round. 'Monica? Aren't you staying with your friends?'

'I wouldn't be out here if I was.'

They both got in the car but he didn't switch on the engine. Instead he pressed his forehead against the steering wheel. 'I'm so sorry.'

'I do work for you, not with. You're quite right.'

'But the way I said it was horrible. What sort of monster am I?'

'You have an unfortunate manner but there's no real harm in you. Except to yourself.'

'I don't hate you, Monica, but I hate them.'

'How can you hate people you don't know?' Monica turned to look at him.

'Haven't you ever hated anyone?'

Monica slumped back in her seat. 'Yes, once. But that was a special case.'

'Nasty boyfriend?'

'No, not really.'

Intrigued, Carpenter found himself forced to break the silence that had fallen between them. 'So what happened then?'

'I had a breakdown, Carpenter. All I can say is that I was made very unhappy, put on a lot of weight and then got better.'

'I thought you'd always been a bit on the large side.'

'Well you thought wrong, and even if I had been, so what?'

'Point taken Monica – so what indeed.'

Carpenter was distracted. Illuminated in the doorway of the lounge bar stood his brother and Martin Renshawe. It was too dark for Carpenter to make out the expressions on their faces, but suddenly Martin's head jerked upwards as if something had startled him and he stepped quickly back inside the pub.

'But you've recovered from your… breakdown?'

'Yes,' Monica pulled the cloak around her shoulders. 'I'm fully recovered. Can we just drive?'

Chapter 15

1975

I've been at Mildmay's for several weeks. It is the first of August and the weather has changed with the month from wind and rain to blue skies and seventy degrees Fahrenheit. I've decided that if possible I shall spend the rest of the summer in Yorkshire. Common sense tells me that continuing this fictional romance with Doreen is foolhardy, but somehow I can't seem to call a halt to any of it.

I'm aware of a creeping intimacy – all creeping coming from Doreen's side. Arm-in-arm has graduated to hand-holding and there is now a slippage of Doreen's head to my shoulder when we are sitting on the sofa watching television together. There are two armchairs. I could have chosen either one but they are some distance from the television – the sofa seemed the sensible option.

The first time this slippage occurred, I allowed Doreen's head to remain on my shoulder for my silent count of twenty and then I muttered something about a ham sandwich being a nice idea, gently easing myself away from her.

'Venables won't like you interfering with the layout of her fridge,' Doreen said.

'I think I'm pretty good at returning items to their rightful place.' Actually meaning, returning *your* head back onto *your* own shoulders!

What the devil am I doing still sharing a bed with her? Each night I turn my back and then she cuddles up against me. 'Spooning' she calls it, which is a term I find offensive. Admittedly, I have grown accustomed to the sensation of her warm, rather comfortable body behind me. However, offered the choice, I would prefer a similar-sized and amiable dog to Doreen. A canine Doreen might just be acceptable.

I keep deluding myself that I can deal with her. Regain the upper hand. Bottom line – I can't. Nobody can. By hook or by crook, she invariably gets her own way.

There have been no further major outbursts apart from a small skirmish when Carpenter suggested inviting someone called

Monica to Doreen's ludicrous 'engagement' party.

'She's my PA and we get along pretty well,' he announced one dinner time. 'I think you'd both like her.'

The man has no understanding of his mother at all. Lesson one: telling Doreen that she's going to like someone, particularly another woman, guarantees that she'll dislike her intensely.

Doreen laid down her knife and fork, narrowed her eyes and said, 'She's an employee and we're not required to like her. She would be inappropriate as a party guest.'

'But you've invited Venables and her tribe.'

Lesson two: do not argue with the woman who pays your wages and whose roof you live under, particularly if her name is Doreen and she is also your mother.

'I can't imagine that Venables or any member of "her tribe" would want to marry my eldest son.'

'Monica doesn't want to marry me.'

'But do you want to marry her? It's Monica this and Monica that.'

'She's a good friend.'

Lesson three: never admit that another woman is your good friend.

'Which is what concerns me.'

'Actually, Ma, I can ask who I like.'

'Then I'll sack her.'

'Doreen!' I remonstrated.

Doreen enacted her impression of an angry bull, which is truly intimidating. Even Junior, her favourite son, looked anxious.

'Keep your nose out of this Oliver!' she snapped.

I've given up arguing with her. It's a fool's game. Instead I beat a retreat to the study across the hall, leaving the study door open. I could still hear Doreen's hectoring voice, 'Thank you so much, Carpenter – you've now chased Oliver out of the room and ruined our meal.'

A few minutes later he emerged looking hunted about the eyes and shoulders and still holding his napkin. I beckoned him in and closed the door.

'Have some sense, man.' I spoke quickly and quietly. 'Live your own life. Do not try to share it with your mother. By the time I reached my thirties I'd been independent for over fifteen years. If you like this young woman, then ask her out.'

At that moment Doreen had barrelled into the room, drink in one hand, expression mean. 'I will not have people ganging up on me behind closed doors. This is my house, and if the two of you don't like it, then get out.'

'Calm down, Ma, Oliver was just talking to me about buying your engagement ring.'

Her mood swing was immediate. 'Pet, you don't need to buy me a ring. I can dig out the one Peter bought me.'

'Doreen, I insist on buying you a ring. It's the least I can do.' In my head I was asking, *Have you taken leave of your senses, Oliver?*

But her outburst had been averted. Carpenter was off the hook for the time being and Doreen's good nature restored. I had taken one more step along a road I wasn't keen to travel.

I now know the layout of the house and garden pretty well. Mrs Venables' niece of the unlikely name Pandora comes in five days a week to clean, do the washing and ironing, and there is Dobbs, a silent elderly man in charge of general maintenance. Neither of these people impinges on me at all.

The kitchen is considered 'Venables Territory'. Since my fruitless search for the components of a ham sandwich weeks ago, when I'd found the fridge and larder padlocked, I have never re-entered it. However 'Venables Territory' isn't only about square footage. It covers many aspects of the daily life in the house.

'Oliver, if you want a snack – ask Venables. If you want a cup of tea – ask Venables. No point keeping a dog and barking yourself.' (That is a phrase I've frequently used in the past but until recently I'd never realised how unpleasant it sounded.)

First, it is a case of 'Find Venables'. There are no bells to ring, not that I would have liked ringing bells. To locate Venables means going into the kitchen, which means entering 'Venables Territory'. Enemy territory. Mrs Venables is never rude to me, but she treats me as if I am temporary – as I am. Her loyalty lies with Doreen.

They appear to communicate by some form of telepathy. If Doreen hankers after a pot of tea and a slice of Madeira cake, within moments there is Mrs Venables filling a doorway, enquiring,

'Would Mrs Mildmay like a pot of tea and maybe a slice of Madeira cake?'

I've even wondered if Doreen might be Mrs Venables' love child. Improbable but not impossible. I know so little of Doreen's background. Had she ever cooked a meal, ridden a bike, joined a library, or even read a book? At school she'd been unpopular. That much I knew.

'I was overweight but what could you expect on bread and dripping for lunch and suet pudding every bloody tea-time?' she'd told me.

'Surely your mother rang the changes?'

I'd thought my glib response had annoyed her, but her expression softened. 'Let's live in the present, Oliver. Dwelling on a miserable childhood doesn't change a thing.'

Today I try again. We share a pleasant lunch at the Templar's Arms. I am growing to like chicken and chips in a basket. It has come to represent Yorkshire's national dish. Returning home, we park the car in the drive and take the path next to the garage which meanders through the gardens at the back of the house.

I've never been interested in horticulture. From my time running the Bridal Salon, I've acquired some knowledge of the different varieties of wedding flowers: orchids, syringa, lily of the valley, rosebuds, gardenias, baby's breath and violets but real flowers I associated with muddy shoes, being cold and insect life. Now in the summer sunshine, the rain of the previous evening still clinging like jewels to the grass and leaves, I find myself moved by nature. Birds are singing. Many birds. A cacophony of rather pleasant notes.

I stand approximately six feet away from Doreen on a gravel path. She is talking authoritatively about dahlias, her face pleasantly animated – how they are prone to black fly and earwigs but I would see that they are well worth the effort in a couple of months.

'They'll have great big flashy flowers, purple petals edged with white.'

I stare at the insignificant green plants. 'Will they, Doreen? It's hard to believe. They don't look capable of supporting anything really big.'

'Wait and see.'

I am charmed by that instruction: 'wait and see'. I envisage the summer stretching out in front of me as I look forward to the day when the dahlias will begin to bloom.

Doreen takes my arm and we set off back towards the house. Suddenly I see a movement to my left. A flash of orange leaps off the kitchen windowsill and disappears amongst the bushes.

'I didn't know you had a cat.'

Doreen's rapt expression alters. 'Was it ginger? If Venables has adopted one of Laverne's litter of kittens, there's going to be trouble. I told her "no" and I meant "no".'

I pat her hand. 'This garden's enormous. Wouldn't it be a good idea to have an animal or two? My mother always had a cat. She said a cat on the hearth mat made a home.'

'Well I don't intend to have cat, dog or a hearth mat.'

'So did you have pets as a child? A rabbit or a guinea pig? I had a rabbit for a year but a fox ran off with it. I recall I was quite upset.'

I wait for Doreen's answer, follow her into the house and then into the lounge. She remains silent.

'Does that mean you didn't have any small animals as a child, Doreen?' I persist.

She shrugs. 'I've never been interested in small animals or any animals for that matter. I didn't much like my boys when they were babies. The best present I ever had was a five pound note. And that was when a five pound note was worth five pounds and more.'

'I don't believe you.'

'It's true.'

Doreen switches on the Berryflame electric fire, turning the dial to 'smouldering'.

'Surely we don't need a fire today.'

'But I think we do.' From behind the glass cabinet clock she takes a small lilac envelope and hands it to me. 'You've had a letter. It's been re-directed from London. Obviously from a woman. From the colour and quality of the envelope, I'd imagine quite a common person.'

I recognise Della's handwriting from the many sales dockets she made out during the twenty years she worked at The Store.

'Would you mind if I take my letter into the garden?'

'It wouldn't matter if I did mind.' Doreen laughs bitterly.

'Doreen, I am entitled to some privacy.'

'Do what you want. I couldn't care less.'

I step outside. I hope to read something life-changing in the letter, while having no real hope at all. There are just a few stilted lines.

'I'm thinking of a move to Swan & Edgar. It's not the same here anymore. Miss Frances has been made General Manager but remains Head Buyer. She's okay but will never replace you. Rumour has it that the Daker girl is lying low in Miss Frances's holiday cottage. Good riddance to bad rubbish. Best wishes, Della.'

Crumpling the sheet of paper, I stuff it deep in my jacket pocket.

As I thought: game, set and match to Miss Frances. The woman has not only taken my job but also swanned off with the prize. But my foolish heart beats faster. I'd played a hunch coming to Yorkshire and that hunch appeared to be the correct one. Suddenly I believe in fate taking a hand – I would see Claire Daker again. Somehow our paths would cross. But realistically, what could I hope for?

Behind me I hear the click of Doreen's heels on the York stone slabs.

She touches my elbow. 'Good news? Bad news?'

'I don't want to talk about it.' I shrug her hand away. For a moment I sense a spark of the old bullish Mr Oliver. 'You tell me nothing about yourself. I tell you nothing about myself. Agreed?'

Doreen stands quite still. She appears sad and unusually thoughtful. 'I think we'll have trays on our laps this evening.'

I follow her back inside.

*

Carpenter stood at his office window looking down into the street. There was no sign of Monica returning from Take-A-Break. Since the unpleasantness in the pub with her and Ned, he'd felt himself brought as near to suicide as a man who has absolutely no intention of ever committing suicide can get.

By Sunday night he'd decided to definitely sack her the following day. It was impossible to continue working with someone who had seen him make such a fool of himself. Right up till the moment when he'd arrived at the office that morning he'd held firm, and then he'd seen Monica's coat hanging on the back of the door. Somehow, the sight of that brown tweed coat with the rather worn velvet collar had flipped his anger into a feeling of great fondness. *What had she said about a breakdown?* He wished he'd paid more attention.

She had certainly crossed the line that existed between employer and employee. He could justly pick her up on tone of voice used, sullen behaviour and, added to that, misuse of office time and stationery – what had she been typing for the entire spring and early summer and then hiding away in the bottom drawer of her desk?

Quickly he stepped into the outer office. Her desk drawer was half-open. He eased out a sheet of copy paper and read the line: *I refuse to step into a dead woman's shoes.*

Outside in the corridor Carpenter heard the steady whine of the lift travelling upwards. Swiftly he replaced the sheet and began to study Monica's wall calendar – Goddesses of the Eastern Hemisphere. The lift stopped at the floor below and then began to move downwards again.

Carpenter studied the calendar, searching for clues regarding Monica's personal life. What had those words meant? He imagined a handsome widower, only recently bereaved, trying to persuade her to marry him and become a mother to his two grieving children.

June was empty apart from a brightly-coloured illustration of Kali, goddess of power and destruction. He checked the previous month: Lakshmi – fortune, prosperity and beauty; nothing happening there either. Where was the point of a calendar if nothing apart from 'must buy first class stamps' was written on it?

At the beginning of the year, when she'd first hung the calendar up, he'd been surprised. 'Monica, I don't see you as a "goddess" type of woman,' he'd said.

She'd adopted her particular aloof expression. 'It was a Christmas present,' she said.

'What, some dear but dotty aunt?'

'No, Carpenter. A friend.'

He'd waited for her to say something more but she hadn't.

Behind him the door swung open. He stepped away from her desk. 'I didn't hear the lift come up.'

'That's because I used the stairs.' She threw a greasy paper bag on the desk. 'Was there something you wanted?'

'I was distracted by the goddesses while searching for the office stapler.' He waved a hand towards the calendar. 'I wonder why these Eastern goddesses need so many limbs. Any thoughts?'

'The stapler is mine. You asked me to take money out of petty cash to buy a stapler but there wasn't any money in the petty cash tin.' From behind her typewriter she produced a stylish chrome stapler. 'I brought this from home.'

'Might I borrow it?'

'On this occasion but I'd rather you bought your own.' From the paper bag she took a pasty.

As the smell of cheese and onion filled the room Carpenter's stomach rumbled. Enviously mesmerised by the pasty, he watched her bite into it. 'I wish you'd mentioned that you were buying pasties.'

Monica licked grease from her fingers.

'I'd have asked you to buy me a couple.'

'You *are* capable of using the lift and walking a further twenty yards.'

'I'm not comfortable in queues.'

She ignored him, crumpling the bag and tossing it into the waste paper bin. Pulling out her chair Monica sat down and took the plastic cover off her typewriter.

'Monica, before you start typing… whatever it is you're typing.' He couldn't resist saying that. 'I wanted to apologise for last Friday. I behaved despicably.'

'Apology accepted.'

'Does that mean we're letting bygones be bygones?'

'I suppose so. Now is there anything else you want and why aren't we speaking in French?'

Carpenter eased his right buttock up onto the corner of her desk and looked smilingly down at her. 'I shall return to speaking French just as soon as I've got a couple of sentences out that I don't have enough French for.'

'Proceed,' Monica said, her fingers poised above the typewriter keys.

'My mother and her fiancé are throwing an engagement party at the Côte d'Or Hotel.'

Monica's expression was completely blank.

'That huge place just outside Harrogate. Next weekend. Would you like to come as my guest?'

'I don't think so.'

Carpenter smoothed the trouser material over his knees. 'Don't worry. You won't feel out of place. I'll personally guarantee my mother's civility – she can be a bit of an ogress.'

'Sorry, but not my sort of thing.'

'I appreciate that the hotel is rather high-toned. I'd be happy to advance next month's salary if you want to buy something appropriate in the cocktail frock line.'

'Carpenter, I don't want to go. I'm saying "no".'

'I thought you'd jump at the chance to get dressed up and have a sophisticated evening out. Most young women would.'

'How would you know? Will you please get off my desk?'

He stood up. He felt he should be annoyed but he actually felt relieved. 'You're bloody rude you know,' came out as a pleasant observation. Carpenter returned to his own office, closing the door gently behind him. His mood was quite agreeable. It had been a foolish idea to ask Monica; Doreen would have hit the roof. He could hear his mother's voice: 'First rule of business, Carpenter; you don't date the office staff.'

Ten minutes later Monica laid a greasy paper bag on his blotter.

'What's that?' he asked, although knowing exactly what it was.

'I should at least have given you an opportunity to order a pasty.'

'Actually, I wanted two.' He looked into the bag. Two pasties. 'That's very kind of you, Monica. Let me reimburse you.'

'No. Under normal circumstances I expect to be reimbursed, but not in this instance.'

He smiled up at her. 'There, you see – we couldn't have managed a conversation like that in French.'

She smiled back. 'But the intention is that eventually we will.'

Chapter 16

The Party
3pm – 4pm

'Martin, I'd like you to meet my fiancé.' Doreen lays her hand on my jacket sleeve. 'Oliver darling, this is Martin Renshawe – we've known each other since our school-days.'

It is a Saturday, mid-afternoon and we are standing with one hundred and fifty of Doreen's close friends in the Grand Ballroom of the Côte D'Or Hotel which, according to Doreen's guide book, 'Harrogate Revealed', is 'set within ten acres of woodland and countryside of unparalleled beauty'. Through tall Georgian windows, the sun pours across the highly polished parquet floor. Double doors, made up of squares of coloured glass, have been opened to allow guests to spill out onto the terrace.

'Congratulations.' Martin grips my hand. 'You're a lucky man.'

'I am indeed,' I reply, surprising myself with how convincing I sound. In no way do I feel 'a lucky man'. I am hurting in my head, heart and, above all, my feet. What had possessed me to wear new shoes? Hadn't I been long enough in the clothing trade to know better?

'And I'm a very lucky woman.' Doreen flashes her engagement ring at Martin. 'Platinum, with a single brilliant-cut diamond and diamond set shoulders, or that's what the bloke said in the shop. Not another one like it in Yorkshire.'

The ring has cost me nearly two thousand pounds.

Doreen takes firmer possession of my arm. 'I said to Oliver at the time, "Darling, are you absolutely sure you want to spend so much on your Doreen? I'm a simple country girl at heart – I'd be just as happy with nine carat gold." But he insisted, bless him.'

Martin Renshawe beats a hearty tattoo on my shoulders. 'We're all very pleased about this engagement. You better take damn good care of our precious Doreen or you'll have me to answer to.'

This is said with a boisterous masculine cheerfulness that requires me to respond in similar vein. But I am all out of boisterous masculine cheer. Fortunately Martin's attention swiftly returns to Doreen. He places a rough but tender kiss on her fuchsia lips. 'Love suits you. I can't believe you're the mother of two hulking great brutes.' As he spots Junior pushing his way through the crowd towards us, his handsome face splits into a smile. 'Junior, doesn't your mother look fan-bloody-tastic?'

Martin releases Doreen. He ignores Junior's outstretched hand, instead encircling the young man's neck in a playful arm lock. 'How are you doing, son?'

I would not consider myself an overly sensitive person, but I recognise a flash of distress in Junior's eyes.

Martin lets him go, fondly rumpling his hair.

'I'm pretty good.' Junior slips his rejected hand into his trouser pocket. He swallows. 'Martin, I wonder if I could have a word with you about our sessions –'

'Oh, darling.' Doreen is pouting. 'Not now.'

'What your youngest son needs is the love of a good woman,' Martin says.

There it is again. Hurt. There is some tension between the two men.

'That is not what I need,' Junior says quietly, before turning and walking away from us.

'Give him time,' Doreen says. 'It's taken me all these years to find the love of my life.' She looks up at me adoringly. 'I'm only sorry I can't give my Oliver a child.'

Diabolical thought!

'He'll just have to make do with my two boys.'

Diplomatically, I shift the conversation away from Doreen. 'So Martin, do you have children?'

Martin's face clouds. Doreen's adoring expression changes to one of womanly concern. 'He doesn't know, Martin. Forgive him.'

Martin squares his shoulders, tenses his admirable jaw and narrows his eyes.

Having hired and fired for decades I consider myself a good judge of men and I'm aware of not being satisfied with what I've now seen and heard of Martin Renshawe. He is good looking, has a certain charm, but there is something innately fake about him, which is a disappointment as I'd had hopes that I might have found a friend.

'Oliver.' I know that he is going to try to impress me with his sincerity. 'My wife Madge and I have tried for children. God knows, we tried! Alas the fates didn't decree. It broke our hearts.'

'I'm sorry to hear that.' *I couldn't care less!*

'No need. It's in the past and yet… ' He looks at Doreen with a reflective shake of his head. 'When I see your sons, Doreen, my heart is broken all over again. The tragedy is that I'm "born father material".'

Absolute tosh! I mull over just what sort of cloth 'born father material' might be? Dismiss corduroy and tweed (the latter might be 'born grandfather material') and settle, in Martin Renshawe's case, on a woven cotton polyester mix.

'How about you, Oliver? Are you "born father material"?'

'I've never given the subject much consideration.'

'Ah well, then you're not. Kids or lack of 'em has never left my head, even for a day, over the past three decades. One of each would have been perfect. Not to be. Not to be.'

I can't remember ever having felt so bored. Over a hundred people and I have nothing in common with any of them. In my head I keep repeating a line from an old school hymn, 'Lord, dismiss us with thy blessing', and I pray deeply and sincerely that the Lord, just this once, would prove a help rather than a hindrance.

A small miracle occurs. On the far side of the ballroom, his chestnut thatch warmed by a ray of sunshine, I see Steve Chambers. Two months ago I'd have been ready to tear a strip off Steve, call him a bloody interfering fool and to keep his advice to himself in future. Now I have to fight the desire to rush across the dancefloor, lay my head on Steve's newly acquired muscular chest and sob.

'Excuse me. I spy an old friend. I must have a word.'

I cross the ballroom, trying not to limp. The pain across my toes hasn't diminished an iota standing still for fifteen minutes.

'Steve.' I only just manage to keep a note of tearful gratitude from my voice.

'How you doing, old buddy?'

'Coping.'

'I'm thrilled for you.' Steve clasps my shoulder. 'You didn't let the grass grow under your feet, did you? That's the old Oliver we all know and love.'

'Steve, it's not as it seems.'

'Mind if I break in?' Carpenter eases his body between the two of us.

Steve gives him an easy grin. 'And you are?'

Carpenter returns his own easy grin. 'Carpenter. I'm going to be this guy's stepson. Can you credit it? Oliver, sorry to break in but your bride-to-be needs you.'

'For god's sake, Carpenter, Steve is the only friend I have at this party, do you mind if I enjoy five minutes' conversation with him?'

Carpenter grips my elbow so firmly that I find it impossible to wrench free. 'Carpenter, I'll come when I'm good and ready.' My voice lacks any real force.

'Best not to keep your lady waiting,' Steve says. 'We'll have plenty of time to catch up later.'

'But Steve.'

But Steve is already moving away.

Regarding Carpenter and Junior, one fact is now clear. However Doreen's sons felt about me initially, they are now united in actively wanting me to marry their mother. For some days I've felt like a valued and valuable business asset rather than a person. I have hardly been left on my own for a moment, as if they were expecting me to make a dash for freedom, which isn't far from the truth. At least half-a-dozen times I've come close to bundling a few necessities into my overnight bag and just leaving. But there never seems a moment in the day to make my escape. Even if Doreen is out of the house I still appear to be under surveillance.

This morning, emerging from the bathroom, I'd found Carpenter polishing the leaves of a giant cheese plant I would swear hadn't been in the corridor when I'd gone into the bathroom.

'Ma's up at the hotel checking for last minute hitches. She's over the moon.' Carpenter had said, waving a duster at me.

Would that she was!

'Not long now. Get the engagement party out of the way and on to the wedding. Clear that last hurdle and bingo!'

I'd wanted to roughly grasp Carpenter by his shirt collar and shout, 'Bingo? What is that supposed to imply? I've hit the jackpot? Is that what you think?'

With this Carpenter encounter still on my mind, I reluctantly accompany him back across the dance floor. 'I will not be bullied,' I remonstrate. Again, I sound ineffectual.

'I had no intention of bullying you but nor do I want my mother causing a scene.'

'Just because I don't jump to her bidding? I am still a free man.' I attempt to proudly toss back my widow's peak.

'Well, lucky you.' Carpenter nods in the direction of my shoes. 'You're limping. I noticed earlier.'

'My feet are lodged in the fires of hell and I blame your bloody mother.'

In the shop the shoes had fitted perfectly and I'd been overcome by the very real pleasure of finding a pair in patent leather. It isn't often a lifelong yearning is satisfied and I'd had the thought that perhaps that small triumph signalled an upward swing to my fortunes.

'Walk about, Oliver,' Doreen had said. Doreen is at her best in shops. She has patience.

I'd walked about, but space to walk about in had been limited. I've always been rather vain regarding my feet in spite of my fallen arches. They are neat – narrow and well formed. Admiring them in the mirror set at the end of each faux suede cube seat, the shiny black shoes had seemed a natural showcase: the perfect finish to a finely creased trouser leg and black or charcoal coloured silk socks. The shoes themselves had felt soft and giving.

'Oliver, with your background I'd have thought you'd know not to wear new shoes without breaking them in first,' Carpenter says.

I snap back, 'I don't need you to tell me about new shoes, smartarse.'

He drops my arm. 'Job done. Prisoner delivered. Keep going till you reach my mother.'

Watching his tall frame disappear into the crowd, I feel almost sorry for him. He appears completely friendless. In the weeks I've been staying at Mildmay's, he has hardly had a phone call and only ever goes out during the evening on Fridays, to his French class.

Even this appears to have been suspended over the last two weeks. He is a surly so-and-so but then I can't imagine what it must be like having Doreen for a mother.

The pain across my feet is now intense. Even the thought of soaking my toes at some distant time today offers me no comfort. Internally I am whimpering at the hellish discomfort.

The band begins to play. Many of the guests have formed a circle around the dance floor and are clapping in time to the music. For some reason everyone's attention is focused on me.

Five yards away, Doreen extricates herself from Martin Renshawe's embrace and moves skittishly into the centre of the empty dance floor. Now all eyes are on her. She turns to face me, her peach satin skirts swirling around her plump but shapely legs. Slowly she caresses her hips before raising her arms above her head. She clicks her fingers without actually producing any audible clicking sound, lowers her head and looks at me in what I take to be a seductive manner.

'Oliver,' she calls out. 'Come to me.' Rhythmically she stamps her feet on the ground.

I am incapable of movement.

In a piercing soprano, Doreen starts to sing along with the music, 'Love is lovelier the second time around.'

Encouraging hands are on my shoulder blades pushing me forward.

Another smouldering look from Doreen. She stamps louder and faster, which draws a roar from the guests who are now all lining the perimeter of the dance floor.

I remain rooted to the spot, welded as much by the pain in my feet as acute embarrassment. Appalled, I watch as her confidence falters. I see the girl she must once have been: plain and hefty and always too forceful to ever be liked. She repeats the same line of the song. If I don't act immediately, Doreen will be humiliated in front of all her friends. Damn and blast the woman but I can't let her down.

Without bothering to untie the laces I kick off my shoes. The relief is instantaneous. With a couple of debonair dance steps I hadn't realised I knew, I sashay across the floor to join her.

She curtseys.

I bow.

'Those shoes have been murder all afternoon,' I tell her as I take her in my arms.

'Why didn't you say? I'd have sent Carpenter home for your Hush Puppies.'

'Never mind.'

The music changes to The Blue Danube Waltz. We sail across the floor. Doreen's face returns to an expression of rapture. My own agony alleviated, I allow myself a diversion. In my head I return to a scene from the previous year that even at the time had seemed significant.

From my favoured standpoint at the top of the Bridal Salon staircase, I gazed down at the stark white carbuncle that marred the colour and order of my precious shop floor.

'Big day tomorrow,' Della murmured as she passed behind me, a shade closer than was strictly necessary.

I'd ignored her. I was determined to appear as if nothing about the boutique opening interested me. I would play my required part, meet and greet the Beverley Sisters, smooth out any inefficiencies and I had no doubt that there would be some, but that would be the extent of my duties.

Outside, on Oxford Street, the window-cleaner moved steadily from right to left with his bucket and sponge. There was Rosa bustling through the swing doors on her way to her domain at the cash desk. She exchanged nods with Mavis as she emerged from the boutique, a pair of cream and tan check trousers over her arm.

'I'll try a dab of carbon tetrachloride, but I can't guarantee it will get the stain out,' Mavis called over her shoulder to someone unseen.

A shadow hesitated in the white doorway. My heart beat so fast I felt it might choke me.

Claire Daker stepped out of the boutique and stood next to Mavis.

'Just do your best, Mavis. I shouldn't have left my Coke bottle there.'

Greedily I watched her. The expression on her face was mischievous. Never had she looked at me like that. She grinned. I couldn't call it a smile. It was too young and careless to be anything as adult as a smile.

Mavis was unimpressed. 'Strictly speaking, sales staff aren't allowed to bring drinks onto the shop floor.'

'Miss Frances said I could.'

'Well, what a surprise!' Mavis seemed to sense that I was watching; she'd looked up at me, an unpleasant smile on her face.

I ignored her. It was Claire Daker's voice carrying across the shop floor that interested me; the voice of the girl on the stairs during the power cuts in March, frightened of the dark yet demanding so much information before she would allow herself to trust me. Claire Daker and I had already met.

4pm – 5pm

Slowly, Madge Renshaw sipped her warm gin and tonic. She'd been hanging onto this one drink for over half-an-hour. At the table, her remaining companion was Laverne's mother, Paddy, who looked at least ninety, although Laverne insisted that she was in fact a 'glorious seventy-three'. Madge watched as Laverne, partnered by her husband, jived enthusiastically to the five-piece band's rendition of the Supremes' 1960s hit, 'Stop! In the Name of Love'.

Here I am at the premiere engagement in Harrogate's social calendar, yet I might just as well be sitting alone at my own kitchen table.

She searched the crowd for just one friendly face and saw Carpenter breaking cover only yards away.

He fell into the chair next to her. 'Ah Madge. I feel as if I've been circulating for days rather than hours. I've used up every platitude in the book.'

Madge smiled. 'What book would that be?'

'The elder son's book of benign platitudes. They are inculcated into us at birth. Sorry, Madge. I should have said, mind if I join you and what are you drinking?'

'Another gin and tonic, please. I shouldn't, but make it a double.'

From the other side of the table, Paddy thumped her empty glass.

'And anything with a kick in it for you, eh Paddy?' Carpenter pushed back his chair. 'No peace for the wicked. Save that seat,

Madge.'

She watched Carpenter broad-shoulder his way through the crowd at the bar. Now if her husband had shown a partiality towards him instead of his whey-faced brother she could have better understood it. For a moment she considered going in search of Martin, but what would she say if she found the two of them together? *The game's up. Martin, how could you? He's young enough to be your son!*

No, she couldn't say that. Could she?

'Gangway everybody.' Carpenter put the tray on the table. 'Sorry Madge, no ice. One bottle of gin, two bottles of tonic, slices of lemon and lime, a pint of Guinness for Paddy and three fresh glasses. That should keep us going.'

He began to pour the drinks, winking at Paddy. Paddy winked back at him.

'Thank you, Carpenter.' Madge put her hand over the top of her glass. 'I'll skip the tonic water.'

Raising her glass to her lips, she savoured the clean taste of Bombay Sapphire gin, the sharpness of the lemon and lime, and the tonic water bubbles making her ears pop pleasurably. Her shoulders relaxed.

'Cheers.' She clinked her glass against his.

'Cheers! So Madge, where did you buy that nifty little outfit? It's got the stamp of London rather than frumpy old Harrogate.'

'More platitudes?'

'No. I mean it. The colour suits you. Hasn't my mother's fiancé commented yet? He appears to know everything there is to know about women's clothes.'

Flattered, Madge touched the beaded embroidery on her jacket. 'Believe it or not, I found this in Eileen's Costumes in Burnside.'

Several hours had been spent rejecting the style of suits and dresses that Eileen (previously plain Joan Hardwick of Woolworth's greetings card counter) had been fobbing her off with for years.

'But Madame has always had the dove or lilac with Peter Pan collar – so flattering for the older neck,' Eileen had cajoled, aware that for the first time ever mousy but wealthy Madge Renshawe was in danger of taking her custom elsewhere.

'This is a very important occasion. I'm looking for something rather special,' Madge had said firmly. 'Perhaps in burgundy or forget-me-not blue. A more dressy fabric than wool. Satin perhaps?'

'Surely not satin? It wouldn't do for madam to overshadow Mrs Mildmay.'

Madge had reached for her fawn kid gloves and matching handbag.

'Of course there is the Charlotte Rose model.' Eileen had looked doubtful. 'Although Madame isn't really a Charlotte Rose person.'

This had annoyed Madge and piqued her curiosity. She couldn't bear to leave the shop without at least knowing the type she so definitely wasn't.

'Could I see this Charlotte Rose model in a size ten?'

Eileen disappeared into the stockroom at the back of the shop. There was a rustle of polythene and then a flimsy object of great beauty floated towards Madge. The colour was deep vibrant burgundy, the material shot-silk. A fitted jacket, single breasted with an edging of tiny black beads, the skirt bias cut so that under the right conditions, if she could master a swing of her hips, it would flare out – insouciantly!

Madge had swallowed, her eyes prickling horribly. In her chest she recognised the ache of unrequited love. Eileen was right. She was not a Charlotte Rose woman. A Charlotte Rose would be young with perfect skin, soft wavy hair and a clear yet confident gaze. Such a woman would be a little like the Margaret who had fallen in love with Martin Renshawe twenty-two years earlier.

Out of the corner of her eye she caught the twitch of Eileen's mouth. A tiny movement but definitely the quickly suppressed beginning of a smirk.

'I'll take it.'

'Don't you want to try it on first? Burgundy isn't an easy shade to carry off.'

'Pack it and wrap it.' Madge was proud of her emphasis on each consonant.

Carpenter had now returned to the bar twice. He didn't think he could make the journey again unless he crawled on all fours.

On the other side of the table, Paddy was fast asleep, one side of her face pressed against the linen cloth. From her open mouth trickled just enough liquid to form a small damp circle. She might have been dead except for her loud snoring.

He idly wondered if her nasal passages might be blocked. Still it was none of his business. Laverne could sort her own mother out at the end of the evening. But where was Madge? Ah, there she was, sitting next to him but with her chair turned towards the open French windows. He'd never taken much notice of Madge before, but several drinks earlier he had decided that he liked her. He suspected she had hidden depths, although it had been a mistake to provide a second bottle of gin. Madge didn't look well. Her naturally pale complexion had become a mottled red, with a band of colour that was almost purple across the bridge of her nose.

Realising that Carpenter was watching her, she scraped her chair back to face him. ' …of course, then I might have felt differently,' she muttered. 'Cut me and I bleed. I'm a woman – if you cut me I bleed. That's true isn't it?'

'What was the question again, Madge?'

'I said, do I bleed, or don't I?'

'I don't think I know the answer to that one. Actually Madge, I don't much like the look of your eyes. Are you on drugs?'

'Damn you, I wish I was.'

He patted her hand, 'There there, Madge.'

'There where, Madge, more like!' She snatched her hand away.

'There where, Madge?' Carpenter repeated. 'Do you mean, there but for the grace of god, go I?'

'Something like that.' She held the empty gin bottle up to the light before upending it over her glass. A few drops fell out. She reached across the table and drew Paddy's glass towards her.

'It doesn't look like Guinness any more. It's cloudy.' Her voice was friendly. 'There's something floating in it.'

They both lurched forward. Madge poked the liquid with a cocktail stick. A bruised pink hump rose to the surface.

'It's a denture,' Madge said.

'Top or bottom?'

Madge prodded around a bit more and suddenly the hump keeled over onto its side and another hump appeared next to it.

'Both.' Madge reached for a second cocktail stick, then pressed both humps down into the liquid. They disappeared from sight and then bobbed up again, two tiny coral islands floating in a dark brown sea.

Paddy's eyes opened.

Carpenter thought he'd never seen a human being before who had bright yellow eyes. He eased the glass gently across the table towards her.

'Paddy, you ought to look after those.'

'Mind your own bloody business,' she lisped. Her eyes closed again.

Abruptly, Madge staggered to her feet. 'I've had enough of this. I'm going to find Martin.'

'Is that wise?'

'I have been left on my own all afternoon. He hasn't even had the grace to check up on me. Not once.'

'By "is that wise", I meant that sometimes discretion is the better part of valour.'

Madge hammered on her bosom: 'For your information I trust my husband. The love between us is sacred. Do you know the meaning of the word "sacred"?'

He nodded, hoping she wouldn't require a definition.

Madge rested the palms of her hands on the table and leant towards him. 'It's that pasty, creepy brother of yours I have the problem with. He wouldn't recognise the words "sacred trust" if he was slapped in the face with them. Ringing our home at all hours, thinking that I don't recognise his silly nervous voice. I recognise it all right. I recognise him holding his breath when it's me who answers, waiting paralysed on the other end of the phone before putting the receiver down. Sidling, simpering and sliming around my husband. He's the one I don't trust.'

Carpenter was filled with admiration for her – to be so articulate after so much alcohol. 'You're magnificent, Madge. Martin is a fool if he can't see it.'

'Go to hell.'

She grabbed her handbag and set off, steady as a rock for four paces, then veering acutely to right or left for the next two. Carpenter watched as the waves of his mother's guests parted and then closed behind her.

6pm – 7pm

'You want to have your cake and eat it.' Junior slumped sulkily in the passenger seat of Martin's Land Rover.

'Don't we all?' Carefully, Martin eased the car out of its parking space. 'Give me a break. At least I'm dropping you home. If I don't get back to the revelries before Madge realises I've gone AWOL, I'll be in serious trouble.'

The car slid smoothly between the iron gates that led out onto the main road. Junior reclined his seat and relaxed, admiring Martin's profile as they joined a slow moving line of traffic.

'Sorry.' Junior squeezed Martin's thigh.

'Not while I'm driving.' Martin frowned, his attention diverted from the road ahead.

'Darling, we're almost at a standstill. Couldn't we pull in at Haresbridge Copse? Just for an hour. We haven't been alone together in days. Please Martin, don't say no.' He kissed Martin's tanned cheek.

There was a furious pounding on the back window. Martin and Junior broke apart.

'Open this door, you little bastard!'

As Madge's angry face pressed against the glass, Junior quickly locked his door.

'Martin, what shall I do? Can't you drive on?'

'We're stuck. Nothing's moving. Just open your window. Don't worry about Madge. She wouldn't hurt a fly.'

Junior wound the window down six inches.

Madge's hand shot through the gap and grabbed his ear. 'I saw you. All over my husband. Martin, stop this bloody car.'

'The car is stopped,' Martin said, reasonably putting on the hand brake. 'Let go of Junior.' He looked sternly at her. 'Now, Madge!'

'So he can close the window again? That's my seat he's sitting in. I'm the passenger. I won't be displaced by some snivelling public school boy. I want him out of our car.' She began to twist Junior's ear.

'Martin, help me.' Junior clawed ineffectually at Madge's hand, tears of pain pumping from his eyes.

Martin leant across him and grasped her wrist. 'Stop it! This is most unbecoming behaviour.'

'He kissed you. I saw it!' said Madge.

'Ow!' cried Junior.

Martin let go of her wrist. He took a deep breath. 'Very well. I will pull over onto the grass verge. Junior will leave and you will get in. Then together, we will go home.'

Martin looked at her steadily. He had always been rather proud of his wife. Her delicate features and ladylike way of dressing he'd considered to be an excellent foil for his own suave good looks. The woman at the window was a stranger and he didn't like her one bit.

Madge's lower lip trembled. 'I'll have my seat back?'

'Yes, you will.'

She released Junior's ear.

The car mounted the verge and stopped. 'Junior, open the door.' Martin paused. 'Please.'

Wordlessly, Junior did as he was told.

Madge stepped aside to let him get out of the car, then, with her face averted, she took his place. Before the car door had properly closed, the car had re-joined the stream of traffic.

7pm – 8pm

On arriving home, Madge spent an hour prostrate on her divan bed (one of a matching pair with olive green velour headboards, olive green being Martin's favourite colour). Her Charlotte Rose jacket lay crumpled on the floor. She still wore the skirt but with the zip undone to relieve the pressure on her stomach, which churned, rose or fell depending on whether she lay on her sides, back or front.

Still furious with Martin, Madge was becoming less sure of her ground. By the time he'd parked the car in their driveway Madge was aware that an aggrieved tone was replacing his earlier conciliatory one.

I know what I saw, she told herself, pressing an eau-de-cologne soaked handkerchief against her forehead.

She couldn't quite bring herself to accuse Martin outright. *Look here, that boy's hand was on your thigh. He did kiss your cheek.* Or: *Do you realise that Carpenter Mildmay and god knows who else, is aware of your dubious relationship?*

But was Martin allowing another man's hand on his thigh and being kissed on the cheek absolute proof of a dubious relationship?

Her head ached so much she could hardly bear to open her eyes but eventually she swung her legs off the bed, picked up her jacket and hung it back on its padded hanger.

She'd say nothing but tonight and every night for the foreseeable future, till Martin realised just how much he was harming their marriage, he would have to sleep in the spare room. That would teach him a lesson. There was nothing Martin liked better before switching out the light than sharing titillating scraps from his patients' case-notes with her. Of course he never named names. He was too honourable for that. A fond smile surprised Madge and she shut the cupboard door sharply.

As she stepped out of her skirt, Martin came into the bedroom carrying a mug of coffee. She ignored him. It was going to take more than coffee to smooth things out between them. She took her dressing gown from the hook on the back of the door and slipped it on, yanking the belt tight around her waist. Madge hoped Martin noticed the way she'd tied the belt: with anger.

'Glad to see you're on your feet,' he said, putting the mug down on the glass-topped dressing table. 'I'll be sleeping in the spare room for the time being. Here, you'd better drink this.'

'Thank you,' Madge said, her voice catching. 'Actually I was going to tell *you* it might be better if you slept in the spare room.'

'Fine by me.' Martin shrugged. 'While I'm in here, I'll get my pyjamas.'

'You don't have to do that immediately.'

'You're surely not suggesting I sleep in the nude? Another penance?' He rummaged under his pillow for his pyjamas. 'I'll take some of my clothes as well.'

'Don't be silly, Martin. There's no need.'

'I'm afraid I think there is.' He sounded almost sorrowful. 'You see, Madge,' Martin crossed to the chest of drawers, 'as long as you're harbouring these nasty, derogatory delusions about your own husband and one of his patients, I believe it would be unwise, yes even psychologically damaging, to continue sharing a room with you.'

He added several shirts, pairs of socks and boxer shorts in maroon, olive and navy candy stripe to his pile of clothes.

'I'm not harbouring –'

'But of course you are. We need space. No, correction, I need space! My reputation, my personal integrity, is being questioned by my own wife. I can't deny it's been a crushing blow.'

Madge tried to take his arm but he batted her hand away. 'Don't come near me. I feel peculiarly alienated towards you this evening.'

'I've never questioned your personal integrity. If anything you have too much personal integrity for your own good.'

Again she reached for his arm.

Martin side-stepped over the corner of his divan leaving Madge sprawling across the candlewick bedspread, one hand clasping a handful of flock bird of paradise, the other raised imploringly.

'Martin, please listen to me. Junior Mildmay is evil but you're too kind and decent to see him as he really is.'

'You know nothing about him.' Martin paused dramatically in the bedroom doorway. 'He is an innocent young man. The son of a woman with a spotless reputation in this county. Spotless! A woman who would never disgrace her husband as you did today. Look at yourself – eaten up with jealousy.'

Obediently, Madge turned to look at herself in the dressing table mirror.

'I feel deeply sorry for you, Madge. In my innermost heart,' over the pile of clothes Madge saw Martin's reflection indicate his left breast with his chin, 'I fear for our future. As for the boy, let me ask you this, Madge; if he does care for me, what's so wrong in one human being's love for another?'

'Do you love him?' she whispered.

There was silence in the room. Madge spoke first, her voice trembling. 'I won't condone a relationship between the two of you.'

'Condone, Madge? Nobody's asking you to condone anything. I don't need your permission to come and go as I please. I never have. It has merely been a courteous formality. One that I will have to reconsider allowing you in the future.' Martin stepped out into the hall, pulling the bedroom door shut with the heel of his shoe.

Chapter 17

1974

On the morning of the boutique opening, Miss Frances arrived at The Store by eight-thirty. Under normal circumstances she rarely came in before ten, which she considered to be the prerogative of a head fashion buyer. She acknowledged her reflection in one of the many mirrors as she made her way via Day Wear towards the white wooden cube that was the boutique, or THE SUGAR CUBE! as she referred to it in all the press releases.

She wore more make-up than usual, had added a slash of eyeliner and a new fibrous mascara from Miss Selfridge's cosmetic counter. A fine lurex thread ran through the weave of her linen jacket. This would have been unacceptably frivolous for work under normal circumstances, but Dusty Springfield arriving by limousine direct from Heathrow Airport at ten forty-five required that special extra glitz.

Miss Frances felt inclined to clap her hands at her own cleverness. *Everything was going to plan. What a coup! What a smack in the eye for Mr Oliver!*

Gus would have loved a day like this: Dusty, a limo, a red carpet and an attractive young woman called Claire Daker to flirt with. Miss Frances knew that *she* personally would not have been part of the equation but, right now, Gus laughingly embracing every female she could lay her hands on would have been so right.Sensing someone watching her, she looked up.

Mr Oliver stood at the top of the Bridal Salon staircase – one hand in his jacket pocket, the other gripping the gilt balustrade.

Their eyes locked.

'Good morning, Miss Frances.' His tone was chilly.

'Good morning, Mr Oliver.' She glanced again at the mirror before adjusting the reveres of her jacket, raising them slightly so that they framed her neck and face.

'What time are the Beverley Sisters expected?'

Still studying her reflection, she answered, 'Let me check that everything is in order and then I'll pop up and discuss the arrangements.' She fluttered her hand at him before striding briskly towards the boutique.

'You'll find me in my office,' he called after her.

Claire had obviously been in the boutique for some time, she noted with approval. A half-full bottle of Coke rested on the glass display cabinet and the boxes of accessories that had arrived the previous afternoon were now empty, the cardboard stacked neatly to be collected by Jim Patterson once he'd finished sweeping the forecourt. From her shoulder bag, Miss Frances took out two packets of balloons, pink and black. Another job for Jim: blowing them up and tying welcoming bunches each side of the glass double doors.

'Am I invisible?'

The voice startled Miss Frances.

Mavis, tape measure draped around her shoulders, pin cushion tied to her plump wrist with a length of bias binding, stepped out from behind the Twiggy mannequin.

'Well, yes, you were for a moment. Good morning, Mavis.'

Had anyone asked her for a light-hearted reference for Mavis, she would have said: Excellent seamstress and garment passer, admirable taste in wrap-around cardigans, possesses some knowledge of basic medicine due to looking after a perpetually sick mother. Negative qualities: bad tempered, unhelpful and a gossip.

'I don't get paid extra for coming in this early,' Mavis responded.

'I am very grateful. Management is very grateful.' Miss Frances patted Mavis's pin cushion. 'I'm sure Claire is very grateful.'

'Gratitude doesn't pay the bills.'

From the store side of the boutique wall a voice called out, 'Oh stow it, Mavis. You only arrived ten minutes ago.' Claire Daker appeared carrying a cup and saucer.

Miss Frances's eyes widened. Surely that cup and saucer was for the sole use of Mr Oliver?

'There you are, Mavis – milky tea with two sugars. Don't say I don't spoil you.'

Miss Frances's eyes widened even more. Did she detect a softening in Mavis's expression as she took the cup and saucer from Claire?

Mavis made an unattractive gobbling movement with her jaw.

'What about biscuits, or do you just save them for your favourites?'

No, Mavis was as hostile as ever; her eyes as she glared at them both, resembled two shiny pieces of coal!

*

On several occasions during the final weeks before I was sacked from The Store I thought that I might be losing my mind, but after a lifetime of self-control my iron will still functioned and it would not allow me to exhibit the smallest public display of rage, jealousy or awareness that I was being undermined by a chit of a girl.

The morning of the boutique opening arrived. It was ten-thirty and where was my coffee? Where was Miss Frances? Had my status over two decades just been dependent on a profitable balance sheet? Finally I'd erupted out of my office, crossing the salon at speed and snatching up the receiver of the internal phone. Impatiently I dialled the number of the cash desk.

Rosa answered immediately. 'Mr Oliver,' her tone was apprehensive.

'Rosa, I fully realise that The Store has been reduced to pandemonium this morning, but if I could draw your attention to the time. I still haven't had my coffee.'

'Give me two minutes.'

'That's all I will give you.' I replaced the receiver and wasted a few seconds thinking how I would make good my veiled threat. *That's all I will give you. After that, you're out of a job and don't look to me for a reference.*

Behind me, I was aware of Della rustling something in a solicitous manner. The last thing I wanted was for her to see that I was rattled. Calming myself, I'd returned to the head of the staircase and surveyed the shop floor. It had never been so crowded, even on the first day of a Summer Sale. The level of noise was incredible. Only the Bridal Salon was empty.

'Will you be going down for the boutique opening?' Della's voice oozed sympathy at its most repellent.

I shot my cuffs, admiring the solid gold cufflinks as I played for time before answering. 'Most certainly. I may not approve of this mayhem, but the Beverley Sisters would naturally expect me to be there to greet them. We've known each other for many years.' I'd given Della my thinnest smile. 'And just what time does your colleague Gwen intend to honour us with her presence?'

'She was in early, Mr Oliver. Her daughter's coming up from Croydon especially to see Dusty. Gwen was thrilled when Miss Frances asked her to help out in the Sugar Cube.'

Silkily, I'd continued. 'But I spoke to Miss Frances only two hours ago and she said nothing about this.'

'You were in your office and she didn't want to disturb you.'

'Why didn't *you* tell me?'

'Miss Frances said you wouldn't mind. She said that we're all in this boutique venture together.'

I was literally rocked back on my heels as if I'd received a physical blow. I touched my jaw half expecting it to feel tender.

'How dare she!' My outburst prompted Della to begin her glide towards me, a look of concern struggling through her vibrant make-up. 'Stay where you are!' I ordered.

Della stopped, took a step backwards.

I concentrated my gaze on the shop floor again. In the past, just meditating on the busy, colourful movement of store life has soothed me. It is like watching the ebb and flow of the sea. Customers wash in. An hour later, burdened with carrier bags bearing our logo – a black and white image of a woman holding a single rose – they wash out again onto Oxford Street. I looked across to the boutique. No sign of movement, although I could imagine the excitement building up inside the small square room, Miss Frances, Gwen and Claire chattering and laughing.

From the Fire Exit, Stanhope emerged, a smile of surprise and delight dawning on his face as he saw how busy it was.

My gaze shifted to where Jim Patterson was setting up chrome bollards each side of a red carpet. Two lengths of thick silver rope lay coiled on the floor, waiting to become a barrier between the Beverley Sisters and their public. I began to feel better. My anger drained away. I was in control again. After all, nothing lasted forever. Let Miss Frances have her day. The higher she flew, the more painful her descent would be.

On the point of turning back towards Della to ask, 'And who is Dusty?' I spotted Rosa bearing a mug and a saucer of digestive biscuits, making slow and erratic progress towards the staircase as she tried to push through a noisy group of young women.

One of them, holding up a Chanel-style, boucle wool suit with faux oyster pearl detail, cackled derisively, 'Even my old gran wouldn't be seen dead in this. If the boutique's rubbish, we'll go over the road to Top Shop.'

Clumsily, the girl knocked against Rosa's arm. Coffee splashed over the suit. 'Soreee!'

With a vengeance, my anger rolled back. How I hated these young women: hated their brash confidence, their spending power and shining enthusiasm to be their horrible, loud, tasteless, common-as-muck selves. I slapped the palm of my hand against the balustrade. 'It's a madhouse. A glorified rugby scrum down there.' Two at a time, I descended the stairs, my fury filling me with energy.

'Mr Oliver, I tried,' Rosa appealed.

'Indeed you did. Sterling stuff.' I whisked the mug from her raised hand. 'And where is my special cup and saucer?'

'Miss Daker commandeered it. I said it was your property. She said "property is theft". I've no idea what she meant but she seemed so sure of herself.'

Holding the mug above me, I executed a pirouette which seemed exactly in keeping with my strange, mad mood. I was now facing away from Rosa and staring at a horde of at least fifty women, running and jostling each other towards the front of the store. The tide had turned. Rosa and I stood alone. There was no one left to abrade.

Over the sound system a song began to play.

I checked my watch. Ten-forty. The Beverley Sisters would never arrive early. They knew how to make an entrance, keep an audience waiting till they were just the heightened side of anticipation. I raised the mug to my lips, not caring that the coffee was cold. Head to one side, I concentrated on the music. Over the noise in the store all I could catch were a few words: *crazy, true – want to be with you*. The words were unfamiliar; their introductory song was always the same, 'Sisters'.

'That isn't the Beverley Sisters.'

Rosa held out the saucer of biscuits. 'It's Dusty Springfield. She had a big hit with this one in the –'

From the Bridal Salon I heard Della's laughter. She tripped lightly down the staircase, her fan-pleated skirt billowing out, gaze fixed on the boutique.

'Just where the hell do you think you're going?'

'Oh, Mr Oliver. You won't mind if I just sneak a peek at Dusty. My Stan wanted me to get her autograph. She's one of his favourites.'

'Then let him get his own autograph. On a day when the world seems to have taken leave of its senses I'd like you to remain on duty, on the outside chance that there may be a customer amongst this rabid mob!'

Della faltered. 'But Mr Oliver, Dusty Springfield is a huge star.'

'What has Dusty Springfield got to do with anything?'

'She's opening the boutique.'

My head, chest and limbs began to fill with a hot, sulphurous and highly inflammable liquid, while above the hum of voices I heard Jim Patterson's raised voice, 'I can see the limo! Stand by your beds!'

'How can this be?' I looked from Della to Rosa, knowing as I posed the question, how foolish it sounded. It was too late for pretence. *Oh, so they opted for the second stringer, this Springfield woman after all!* Whoever was arriving to open the boutique, it was imperative that the store manager was at the front of The Store to greet them. Fighting a desire to break into a run, I walked briskly away. Ahead of me, the crowd surged forward.

Stay calm, man.

'Oliver.' Stanhope was cutting across my path, a detestable beaming smile on his sweating face.

'This is not a good time.'

'A favour?'

'Good god, I have guests arriving at any moment.'

'Leave them to it.'

I feigned bewilderment. 'What do you mean? Why should I leave *them* to it'?'

'Those young women don't want a couple of old fogies like us in the mix. The boutique is about youth and nothing at all to do with chaps in their fifties.' He gripped my arm.

Without descending into a physical tussle with my Sales Director, I would have to comply. I was left with no plan of action except to appear normal.

At the front of the store, someone screamed.

My body tensed, but then the scream was taken up: screams, yelps, cheers and shouts of 'Dusty'. I swear I heard women sobbing.

Side by side, Stanhope and I began to walk towards the mirrored wall at the rear of the store. Oxford Street, the crowd, the boutique, were all mirrored in the glass and then, as if my eyes were a camera lens focusing on its subject – enlarging, making every detail sharp and clear – Claire Daker filled my vision. Not the Claire Daker of the quirky cheap fashion items, motley ragbag of clothes gleaned from jumble sales and charity shops.

An unbidden sound emerged from my throat: a gasp, gargle, groan of frustration.

'Bloody hell,' Stanhope said, adding a low, admiring whistle.

The dress she wore was superb. It had a green satin ruffled bodice, tied on one shoulder only with spaghetti straps. From a distance the skirt appeared to be made of a leaf-patterned silk chiffon arranged in panels so that the material moved yet wrapped around her body, making me think of the slender stem of a flower.

'Zandra Rhodes if I'm not mistaken,' Stanhope said. 'One of the bright new kids on the block.'

Inside I felt chilled. How could any woman design such a beautiful piece? Women were made to wear clothes created for them by men. Claire Daker, the dress, a female designer with an outlandish bloody name – I was being well and truly left behind.

'Too extrovert for our customers of course but there's no denying she's a brilliant designer – don't you think?'

I didn't answer. Mesmerised, I watched as Miss Frances stepped out of the boutique and joined Claire Daker on the red carpet. They were almost the same height – Miss Frances perhaps only an inch or two taller. I studied their profiles as they turned to exchange a few words with each other. Miss Frances tucked Claire Daker's hand under her arm and together they began to walk towards the open doors.

The music from the sound system built up.

I broke free of Stanhope's restraining hand. 'I'm quite capable of returning to my office unaided.'

Apparently unaware of any animosity, he followed, chatting amiably. 'Just store gossip of course. A little bird by the name of Mavis whispered that Miss Frances got that dress at a discount from a friend of hers in Selfridges.'

Brusquely I replied. 'Who or what are we talking about?'

'The Daker girl's dress. And her shoes. Probably her underwear as well. You do know that our Miss Frances is a les-bi-an?'

I hadn't known. My brain absorbed the word and then the phrase 'probably her underwear'. I saw two white, lacy articles soaring up into a blue sky like a couple of liberated doves. The image was unbearable.

'I always had my suspicions of course. An unmarried woman of a certain age wearing flat shoes.' Stanhope took out his handkerchief and wiped sweat from his forehead. 'But she's brilliant at her job and frankly I'd hire a donkey if it could keep The Store in the black.'

I was no longer listening.

Could Claire Daker be bought? Was that how to do it?

I turned on my heel to look back at her. The yearning must have shown clearly on my face.

'Easy tiger!' Stanhope said.

I could see the crowd, a dozen deep around the open doorway; only Claire Daker and Miss Frances stood on the red carpet. I was a king again. An emperor. If spending money was what it would take, I had more money put by than that dried-out dyke could ever dream of.

A roar went up. Half-obscured, a woman was entering the store – her hair a brittle blonde bee-hive style.

Almost playfully I clapped my hand on Stanhope's shoulder. 'I had no idea about Miss Frances. Fascinating.'

While Dusty Springfield had come and gone, taking at least half of the crowd with her, I'd bided my time watching Miss Frances return my cup and saucer to Rosa; waiting for Claire Daker to emerge from that tawdry white box as eventually she must.

She was on her own, returned to normality in a short white

dress, cheap tapestry bag over her shoulder. She'd crossed the store, passing only feet away from the salon staircase. 'Miss Daker, a word.'

She'd looked up at me with such dislike. 'I'm going home. I'm late.'

'Only a word.'

She'd stopped.

'Come on up.'

'I shall miss my train.'

'You'll certainly miss your train if you keep prevaricating.' As she ran up the stairs, I noticed that she wore grey loafers with creamy lacy tights – no knee socks today.

'Yes, Mr Oliver.' Unsmilingly, she stood in front of me, staring over my shoulder.

'I wanted to congratulate you. You did very well this morning.' How I'd enjoyed saying that. The warm note in my voice had been as far away from genuine as night from day.

From the back of the salon I heard the approaching click-clack of Della's ill-fitting sling-back shoes.

'I'm off now, Mr Oliver,' Della called out. 'I've locked up the stockroom.'

I didn't take my eyes from Claire Daker's face. 'Good night, Della.'

Carrying her raincoat over her arm, Della headed for the staircase. 'Good night, Mr Oliver. Good night, Miss Daker.'

'Hang on. I'll come with you.' Claire Daker moved quickly, joining Della on the stairs. 'I managed to get Dusty's autograph for your Stan.'

The following day, on my bus ride from Earls Court to Oxford Street, there were plenty of seats available, which was rare, but I couldn't sit. I wouldn't sit.

Having to keep quiet was one of my chief agonies. I despised every single person on the bus. What a relief it would have been to bawl into the face of the woman wearing a headscarf, an anorak, and minding her own paltry business: *I'm not like you – you poor, colourless, tepid-blooded cretin.*

I felt like a crazed yet potent Old Testament prophet, filling the aisle with MY body, head raised, vigorous beard sprouting along my jaw line. I longed to bellow at the bus driver and passengers: *I pulsate with heat. My blood – head, lower regions – are on fire!*

My inner vocabulary had never been so colourful. Words overflowed – some of them ludicrous. They gushed, spouted and spewed, even as I maintained my normal rigid reserve. At least I hoped it was maintained. There were moments when I feared my heightened state was visible to the outside world. BUT SO WHAT? I internalised in capitals, bold type, italics, exclamation marks and asterisks, looking no further into the future than that unfolding day.

A few months earlier I'd known nothing of Claire Daker. I had added precisely nil to my knowledge and had no desire to find out more. It didn't occur to me to wonder where she lived, what her interests were, her favourite colours. Did she like animals, chocolate, town or country? I didn't care.

In one sane moment, as the bus stopped at Marble Arch, I asked myself, *Should I pluck out the eye that is Claire Daker?*

The woman in the headscarf stood up. 'I'm getting off here if you want my seat.'

I studied her face. It was pale, lined, haggard, hollow-eyed. She would be in her forties. The last woman I'd taken to Cyprus for a week had been in her forties. Not a success, although at the time I'd imagined it had been a success of sorts. We hadn't argued. Our views had coincided. However, when we were ready to go our separate ways at the airport, I'd noticed she'd seemed eager to leave me. But I had been keen to leave her.

'I prefer to stand,' I said.

'Suit yourself.'

I did not want what was allocated to me. I did not want what was appropriate to my time of life. I had never experienced emotions like this before. Inadvertently I had overlooked something important or counted it as an irrelevance, as in the reality of me touching another's warm and desired skin. Having her touch me.

That final thought, which extended no further than to Claire Daker laying her cool fingers against my cheek, made me groan inside. Not just from desire but at the expectation of a tenderness received. The word ‘tenderness’ brought tears to my eyes. Was it madness to continue with this… madness? Or lunacy to stop, cauterise, turn away?

Fact: she disliked me. Even detested me. But wasn’t that the stuff of romance? When the reluctant heroine is finally brought low and only then able to acknowledge her true feelings?

Chapter 18

1975

For some time, while Doreen monopolises the bathroom, I have been musing on what I'd really like to be doing at eight o'clock on a summer's evening. Playing cards with Steve Chambers comes back as the reply. Although I've never in my life played cards, it seems a companionable, manly occupation for the evening ahead.

I hate the hotel room. What fool decided love seats were a good idea?

'Enhance your Côte d'Or experience by partaking of our Food of Love Buffet' the hotel brochure had boasted. On a hostess trolley is a stainless steel platter of fruit, bowls of pick-n-mix and cashew nuts, some wafer-thin mints and a raffia basket with sachets of cheese and biscuits. A tray of rapidly cooling coffees, brandy decanter and glasses waits on a low coffee table supported by four gasping, gilt dolphins. Should I pour myself a drink? No, Doreen will be annoyed or hurt, or annoyed and hurt if I start doing almost anything without her.

Gathering up a handful of pick-n-mix, I limp over to the window. Outside, it's not properly dark yet. Doreen's friends are probably still carousing in the bar downstairs. I watch the lines of slow moving traffic on the road below; hundreds of cheerful people starting out on their evening or going home for their dinners. If only I could be a passenger in one of those cars. With a sigh, I let the heavy brocade curtain drop back into place.

I sit on the edge of the bed and ease off my Hush Puppies and socks. Across my toes a weal of reddened skin marks where the patent leather of the shoes has contracted. Puzzled, I stare at my feet framed by cream shag pile rug. Surely they don't belong to me? I remember them being tanned and smooth, pressed into the sand of a Mediterranean beach. While I hadn't been paying attention, those youthful, healthy feet have been replaced. How could I imagine that Claire Daker would be attracted to a man with old feet?

Doreen's presence, an area of green chiffon, impinges on my daydream. I don't look up immediately. The only response Doreen wants is one that I am incapable of giving. None of this is her fault – but it is mine. I've gone along with the charade when any sane man would have walked away the moment he'd left the cruise ship and stepped back on *terra firma.*

The area of green chiffon approaches me at speed. I move quickly away from the bed and go on the attack. 'What the devil have you been getting up to in there? I've been hanging around for the best part of an hour.'

She alters her trajectory to pour herself a brandy. 'You could have started your new Hammond Innes novel, pet.'

'I can't begin a book when I'm not relaxed and nothing in this room is relaxing. Have you seen these sheets and pillowcases?'

'Satin bed linen is romantic, my darling.'

I ignore the implication of her voice having dropped by at least two octaves. 'I won't get a wink of sleep.'

'Then we must find something else to keep us occupied through the wee small hours.' Holding a brimming brandy glass in one hand, she peels back the counterpane. 'Why don't you just have a quick shower and then hop in *au naturel.*'

Diabolical idea! I am a man who looks best wearing at the very least a pair of sturdy underpants and short-sleeved vest. With dignity, I gather up my tartan toilet bag, pyjamas and dressing gown.

'Oliver, you could undress out here.' Doreen moves towards the coffee table, blocking my route to the bathroom.

'I wouldn't dream of it.'

'Well don't be long in the bathroom,'

'You've not exactly been Speedy Gonzales.'

She smooth's chiffon over her hips. 'Rome wasn't built in a day.'

'Gangway please, Doreen.'

I dodge around her, into the bathroom, close the door and turn the key.

Nearly an hour later I emerge. With eyes lowered so I can't actually see Doreen, I head for the wardrobe and slowly and methodically begin to hang up my clothes.

Please make her be asleep.

She isn't. Doreen is in bed, framed by cerise satin pillows, her brandy glass balanced on her chiffon breasts.

I close the wardrobe door. 'Coffee no good?'

'It's stewed,' she replies icily.

'Shall I ring down for a fresh cafetiere? Yes? No? Well perhaps not.' I pick up the decanter and pour myself a measure of brandy. I wave the decanter at her. 'Refill?'

'I've had four bloody refills waiting for you. If I have any more brandy I'll pass out, which would suit you very well, wouldn't it?'

Without replying, I carry my drink over to the love seat. In retrospect the 'S' shaped design is really quite clever; accommodating two people yet ensuring neither can get too close to the other.

'Are you going to sit there in a trance all night?'

Thoughtfully I sip brandy. 'You're probably wishing I could be exchanged for someone of the calibre of Martin Renshawe.'

'Get into bed.'

'I don't like taking orders. It doesn't improve the situation.'

'*Please* will you get into bed?'

I approach the bed carrying my brandy glass. Doreen has left my spectacles, my Hammond Innes novel, a clean folded handkerchief, indigestion pills and a glass of water on my side table. There is no space left. Reluctantly, I put the glass down on her side table. I remove my dressing gown, draping it neatly over the arm of the love seat before easing under the covers.

'You see, Oliver,' Doreen says as if continuing an earlier thread of conversation, 'while you've been doing whatever you needed to do in the bathroom that has consumed more than an hour, I've been taking stock.'

'You took forty minutes yourself.' I draw the counterpane up to my chin.

'During my forty minutes I removed my make-up, bathed, moisturised and talcum powdered my whole body. I then combed and lacquered my hair, re-applied makeup and I hope successfully transformed myself into a desirable woman.'

'I did at least three of those things.'

'It's not a competition.'

'It sounded like one.'

She gulps brandy. 'I have respected your wishes about physically holding back, although I'm amazed that any red-blooded man could lie next to a woman night after night without becoming aroused.'

My toes clench.

'I've held any passionate feelings in check but, as far as I can see, you have no passionate feelings to hold in check. Have I got that right?' Doreen turns to look at me.

'This sort of dressing down isn't exactly endearing you know, Doreen.'

She drains her glass.

'Could you pass my drink?' I ask.

'Get it your bloody self.'

I consider my options. I don't much like brandy but that is all there is on offer and I sense that I'm going to need Dutch courage to get me through the next hour. I can't actually see my glass as it is obscured by the swell of Doreen's breasts. I could get out of bed and walk round but that might trigger a full-scale row.

'If you'll excuse me,' I say in my politest, least likely to arouse, voice. Sitting forward, I lean across her.

'Got you.' Doreen's arm snakes around my shoulders, pinning me against her.

With difficulty I lift my head, shaking my mouth free of chiffon ruffles. 'This isn't the way to achieve anything. You know how fond I am of you –'

'Fond? All my life I've had fond. I thought you'd have hidden fires – fires we could ignite together. The first time I saw you – so vulnerable, but oozing sexual charisma – I imagined how it would be between us.'

'But you imagined wrongly, Doreen.'

'Why did you kiss me, say you loved me?'

'I didn't do all that. It was you that did the kissing and when you said you loved me, I merely concurred.'

'You merely concurred?' She shoves me away from her and throws back the covers. 'You have cheated your way into my affections. Do you think I wanted yet another man who was just looking for a mother figure? Did you think I was that desperate?'

Doreen picks up her glass and rushes towards the brandy decanter.

Yes, no, possibly, not at all – all these options present themselves to me but I'm saved from making a choice by loud knocking on the door. We look at each other, both of us appalled at the thought that maybe this could be the hotel management team come to see what all the noise is about.

'Better answer it, Doreen. Put my dressing gown on.'

She slips it on.

My feelings of mild fondness for Doreen, resurface. If only she would wear a metaphorical dressing gown at all times.

'Ask who it is, before you open the door.'

'In case it's an axe murderer?' Doreen says dryly.

'You never know.'

'As the man shouldn't you answer the door?'

'You're wearing my dressing gown.'

The knocking comes again, louder and more forceful.

'Who's there?' Doreen asks.

*

'She pulled my ear, Mummy.' Junior slumped onto a plastic chair next to a fire extinguisher in the corridor. 'She almost tore it off.'

Just for once, Doreen felt irritated – almost annoyed – with her favourite son. She tightened the sash of Oliver's dressing gown and glanced along the hotel corridor towards the lift. It was stationary on the third floor but at any moment could begin the journey upwards to spill guests out onto this landing. She should have insisted that Oliver book the Bridal Suite occupying the entire top floor. There, they would have enjoyed total privacy, even from Junior.

'Darling,' Doreen said distractedly. 'She doesn't sound like the right type of girl for you. In a few days' time you'll realise you've had a very lucky escape. Ask Reception to get you a cab home. They can put it on Oliver's bill. Get Venables to make you a creamy hot chocolate, then go to bed.'

'But you don't understand. Look at my ear.' He flapped his scarlet earlobe at her. 'It's bleeding.'

What bitches young women were these days, Doreen thought. She slipped her hand into the dressing gown pocket and felt inexplicably pleased to find one of Oliver's pristine Irish linen handkerchiefs.

'Just a tiny scratch.' She held the folded handkerchief against Junior's ear. 'The little minx certainly likes to play rough.'

He pushed her hand away. 'Mummy, I'm talking about Madge Renshawe.'

The number above the lift doors changed. The lift was moving upwards. It stopped at the floor below.

Doreen heard voices and laughter. 'You'd better come inside.'

'Won't Oliver mind?'

It was on the tip of her tongue to say, *He'll be relieved.* 'Of course not.'

Junior followed her into the hotel bedroom, which smelt slightly of brandy. On one of the bedside tables he noticed a glass lying on its side. Dark liquid had dripped onto the carpet. The bed was empty, the sheets rumpled. A satin counterpane lay on the floor. He had a momentary image of Oliver, naked and aroused, rushing to hide in the bathroom. A more physically attractive Oliver – tanned and at least ten years younger. Junior glanced quickly at his mother. There had been a time when she had been able to read his thoughts.

'Sit down, darling.'

He chose the love seat. The other chairs looked too comfortable. He didn't want to sink into upholstery. Not now. His head was full of images: Martin going home with Madge, sharing a bed with Madge. A woman his mother's age. It was disgusting!

Doreen crossed the room to the bathroom door. She stood listening for a moment before tapping lightly. 'Oliver, are you in there?'

'Where else would I be?'

She ignored his sarcastic tone. 'Junior's here.'

There was a silence.

Doreen imagined their ears on each side of the door pressing against the wood. 'I said, Junior's here.'

'I heard you the first time. Do you want me to stay in the bathroom or come out?'

'Could you give us ten minutes to talk? Is that okay?'

'I shall be fine sitting on the lavatory. You and Junior go ahead.

Don't mind me.'

'Are you annoyed?'

'No, I'm not annoyed.'

'Would you like your book?'

'That's not a bad idea.' His tone softened. 'Thank you.'

She picked up the note of relief in his voice. Oliver preferred to be shut in the bathroom with his book than with her. She felt too disheartened to be angry.

Junior handed her the book from the bedside table.

'Oliver, I have your book.'

He opened the door just enough for her to pass it through.

She willed his warm fingers to brush hers, but that didn't happen. 'You're sure you don't mind?'

'Not in the slightest.' The door was shut firmly in her face.

Before turning around to deal with Junior, Doreen closed her eyes. They felt sore and tired. At that moment, she wished it could be Carpenter, her least favourite son, waiting for her on the love seat. Carpenter would have understood completely had she announced, 'Carpenter, I am at my lowest ebb, ever.'

Come on Doreen. Get it over with. She sighed and opened her eyes again.

Ignoring the temptation of the half-full brandy decanter, she pulled up an armchair opposite Junior and prepared to listen. 'So, darling?'

Junior put his head in his hands. 'I don't know where to begin, Mummy.'

Doreen opened her mouth to say, 'Begin at the beginning.' But the thought of Junior telling her a story that might last hours was unbearable. Gently, she drew his hands away from his face. 'How long have you been in love with Madge Renshawe?'

'You don't understand.'

'Oh, but I do. You and I have always had such a close bond. It's only natural that you would be attracted to an older woman.'

'Men, Mummy. Older men.'

Doreen tilted her head. *Was Oliver running a tap? Was he dehydrated? Was he ill? Did he need her but was too proud to call out?*

'You're not listening.' Junior pulled his hands from hers and began to tug at his hair.

'I have listened to every word.' *Was that a groan coming from the bathroom?*

'Then what am I saying?'

She was relieved to hear the rush of water followed by the sound of the toilet cistern filling up. 'You're telling me that you feel attracted to older men. I've got that right, haven't I?'

He nodded.

She patted Junior's knee. 'That is perfectly natural. In the past I've found my friend Laverne attractive. I wouldn't want to…' Doreen searched for the right words, 'have anything to do with her in that way. However, when she makes an effort with her clothes and make-up, I tend to think she's rather pleasing to look at.'

'Finding Laverne attractive but not wanting to "have anything to do with her in that way" isn't what I mean at all.'

'And of course, you're young and inexperienced.'

'I've done something "that way" with a man, dozens of times already.'

She removed her hand from his knee. 'I'd rather you didn't make up mucky stories at this time of night.'

'I'm not making anything up. I am in love with Martin Renshawe!'

Doreen almost laughed with relief. 'But of course you are. Who isn't a little bit in love with Martin? He's a marvellous role model for any young man. I promise you these feelings will pass. Perhaps cancel your sessions with him for a few weeks. You wouldn't want to upset the Renshawe marriage applecart?'

Junior left the love seat and began to pace the carpet, picking up a handful of cashew nuts and throwing them one by one into his mouth. Finally, fists clenched at his sides, a euphoric expression on his face, he threw back his head. 'Martin is in love with me.'

Daylight still filtered through a gap in the brocade curtains but Doreen felt exhausted. She leant her head against the cushioned back of the chair and forced herself to consider the possibility of her oldest friend being in love with her son. She had never truly found Martin sexually attractive, but had always assumed that he found her irresistible. Surely a man couldn't be attentive, tactile, complimentary and flirtatious for so many years and not be genuine?

'You're talking nonsense,' she said wearily. 'On countless occasions, Martin Renshawe has assured me that I am his first and only love, including on the day he married Madge!'

They both heard the key turn in the lock of the bathroom door and Oliver emerged clutching his Hammond Innes novel.

'Doreen, will you shut up and listen to what your son is trying to tell you?'

'Don't you dare tell me to shut up.' Energised by his entrance, she slid her shoulders out of the dressing gown and got to her feet. She imagined her upward movement was a graceful one. 'Brandy, anyone?'

'No!' Oliver felt ready to wrestle Doreen to the ground if she offered him one more drink. 'I'm sick of brandy. In fact I've just been very sick on brandy.'

'My poor lamb. Are you feverish?'

'Don't come near me.' He held up his hand. 'My name is Oliver and I'd thank you to use it. I'm not some cuddly animal.'

'Oh, but you are.' Doreen lowered the decanter.

'Mummy, please? I need to get this off my chest.'

'Can't it wait till the morning?' She forced herself to look at her son when all she wanted to do was look at Oliver. He was so forceful, so dynamic, reclaiming his dressing gown from the armchair and shrugging his broad shoulders into it. As much as she loved Junior, she would have been quite happy to see him spirited away to the other side of the world. Given an option she would have chosen Australia as a land where her son would thrive.

'Junior, it's been a very long day.' Taking Junior gently by the arm, Oliver began to guide him towards the door. 'Earlier I heard your mother advising you to jump in a cab and go home. Why don't you do that? You've said what you needed to say. Give her time to think about it.'

Doreen, watching them both, was visited by the strange notion that she might be somehow akin to the goddess Venus. Many years ago, during her honeymoon in Florence with Peter, she'd seen a painting of Venus, completely nude, standing on an open oyster shell with a backdrop of calm green sea. Doreen felt completely nude. Her green chiffon nightdress was nothing more than the sea lapping against her aging, yet surely still desirable body?

There is my man. She smiled inside at her own foolishness. *And my son.* Both insubstantial, yet how she loved them.

'Wait!'

In the open doorway, they turned to look at her.

'Junior, I suggest that you ask someone at the reception desk to make up our bill. I think we should all go home. We could be dressed and packed in ten minutes. Agreed, Oliver?'

He looked surprised. 'Whatever you say.'

'But would you like that?'

Their eyes met.

'Yes, I would.'

When Mr Oliver, immaculately dressed, once again emerged from the bathroom he found Doreen still wearing her chiffon nightdress and gold high-heeled sandals.

Junior sat on the end of the unmade bed, already some way into Mr Oliver's temporarily discarded novel. He looked up. 'Was Hammond Innes a homosexual?'

Doreen's smile was efficient rather than warm. 'I've no idea.' She slipped on her full length fur coat on and fastened it low enough to reveal the green ruffle that framed her breasts.

'I believe he was happily married,' Mr Oliver said. 'Doreen, you're surely not driving home dressed like that?'

'I surely am.'

'You'll be hot and uncomfortable.'

'Which is my choice.'

'Where is my suitcase?'

'The cases have been taken to the car.'

'But what should I do with my pyjamas?'

Doreen shrugged. 'That is your choice.'

Shoulders back, head held high, the silver mink pelts that made up the coat fanning out behind her, Doreen sailed from the room, Junior in her wake. Mr Oliver hesitated, not knowing quite what to do with his pyjamas. Outside in the corridor he heard the lift arrive, he dropped the pyjamas on the bed and hurried after them.

There remained some light in the sky. On the horizon were streaks of red and the same pale green as Doreen's nightdress.

'They're bringing the car round,' she said.

'When did you arrange that?'

'While you were getting dressed.'

The Jaguar saloon pulled up in front of the steps. Doreen tipped the hotel driver. In silence they climbed into the car, Junior stretching out on the back seat.

Before switching on the ignition, Doreen rolled the window down – the cool night air would sober her up. 'Oliver, go to sleep if you like. In this traffic, the drive will take at least half an hour.'

Doreen liked to drive, particularly at night. She liked the quiet, the isolation. She liked the idea of Oliver and Junior asleep in the car, completely reliant on her. Patiently she waited for a break in the traffic before turning the car towards Burnside, then gathering speed and settling to a comfortable fifty miles an hour.

Reaching the town, all the shops were closed; only a string of multi-coloured fairy lights still glowed outside the Milvern Tea Rooms.

At a zebra crossing Doreen slowed down as a young woman stepped off the kerb. Doreen sighed. All she now wanted was to be at Mildmay's, in her bedroom with a comforting drink in her hand. She revved the engine impatiently.

The woman stepped back onto the pavement.

Doreen leant out of her window and shouted, 'Make your bloody mind up!'

Hesitantly, the girl began to cross the road again.

'I've had enough of this.' Doreen pressed her foot down on the accelerator and the Jaguar shot forward.

'Doreen, be careful.' Mr Oliver's hand gripped her wrist.

She shook him off. The car swerved around the woman and sped away. In her driving mirror Doreen saw a white frightened face.

'We need to go back,' Mr Oliver insisted.

She drove faster.

'I believe I knew that woman on the crossing. Would you mind either turning the car round or letting me out here?'

She ignored him, sensing how much he wanted to go back. Something told her – a woman's sixth sense – that girl on the crossing was the one. Or very like the one. She knew the type: tall, slim, pale and pretty. And young of course. No way was she turning the car round.

'Doreen, I repeat, I want you to go back.'

'We are going home.'

From the back of the car, Junior chimed in. 'Come on, Oliver. I don't know about you, but I'm starving.'

'Please Doreen?'

'No.'

Chapter 19

1974

Over one weekend, I planned out my strategy in much the same way I planned out the sales strategy for The Store each season: by dividing an A3 piece of graph paper into individual months, then weeks and days.

It was now the end of August. I set myself a time frame running from the first week of September to Friday the fifth of December, the date of The Store Christmas party. Space was limited but my handwriting is small and neat from years writing out price tickets and filling in sales dockets. Neatly, I marked in every Thursday late night shopping, the autumn fashion shows and my own absences. From the Head Office's executive diary, I discovered Miss Frances's in and out-of-store work commitments.

Knowledge is power, I thought, as I added Claire Daker's and Miss Frances's birthdays – these taken from my own staff files. As an afterthought I added home addresses, noting that Claire Daker lived in Tottenham, while unsurprisingly Miss Frances resided in an increasingly salubrious part of Islington. To my delight (being thorough has been very much a contributor to my business success) I also found Miss Frances's holiday home address, Foulkes Cottage in the village of Hampsthwaite in north Yorkshire. There was no telephone number.

In the Bridal Salon, making my rounds from department to department, I watched and listened, surprised by the revelation that in the past I hadn't watched or listened at all on any personal level. Yes, from a distance of ten yards I could recognise a customer who intended to buy rather than one who had only come in to browse or get out of the rain. I could spot a best-selling style and a quality cut. I knew when I was being lied to, manipulated, who was extending their tea or lunch breaks and which member of my staff throughout the store, wasn't pulling their weight. So much knowledge at my fingertips yet I knew very little and cared less about anyone's private life. Gwen had two children – boys or girls – no idea. Someone had a demanding mother; a woman from coats liked anything in trousers. Jim Patterson had body odour. This was the level of my information, most of it gleaned from my head saleswoman, Della.

What did I know about Della? Well, actually quite a bit. She was married to Stan, who I imagined to be a thin weasel-like type of husband. Even after nearly thirty years of marriage, according to Della, Stan was still mad about her. And so he should be!

There had been a time in the past when I'd found Della sexually attractive. I'd always known she cared for me. I imagine most of the long-time staff were aware of it as well. Probably a standing joke. I'd never taken advantage of this knowledge – to me, Della was worth far more as a saleswoman than a passing dalliance.

She would have been in her thirties when she first joined the Bridal Salon, before the effects of extreme sun-tanning and cigarettes took their toll on her skin and she'd begun to dye her hair that unnatural shade of bronze. I still admired her. From a distance she remained a fine looking woman. She'd kept her figure and dressed well, apart from an over-fondness for plunge necklines that revealed too much. Anyone could see that Della had once been stunning.

But next to Claire Daker, there was no contest. Claire Daker was perfection.

It was a sunny Sunday but inside my lounge the temperature was chilly. I decided to set aside my chart, my coloured felt-tip pens (Magenta to indicate Claire Daker's information, Burnt Sienna for Miss Frances, black for myself) to make a cup of Nescafé. Adding two plain digestive biscuits to the saucer I carried my coffee out onto the balcony.

Steve Chambers, on his one and only visit to the flat, had observed that my balcony was cramped but I considered it a perfect size – just room for a table and a couple of chairs, with a bit of space in front so that I could lean on the wrought ironwork and watch the world hurrying by down below on the Earls Court Road.

I dipped a biscuit into my coffee. As I bit into its sweet softness I recalled a quiet morning during the previous week when Della and I had watched Miss Frances enter the store. I'd spent much time considering what, if any, my reaction was to be after the boutique opening dishonesty and had finally, reluctantly, decided to say nothing. Apart from relieving my own angry feelings, little would be achieved. Stanhope's information had given me power. I would bide my time.

Miss Frances isn't a woman who strolls, ambles or saunters. She moves at a fast pace, head and shoulders back, emanating complete confidence. Over her trouser suit (she always wears perfectly cut trousers of the finest cloth) she'd thrown an off-white trench coat, the belt and buckle flying behind her as she'd burst through the swing doors. I'd thought that she looked pre-occupied but quite cheerfully so.

When she reached the foot of the staircase she'd glanced up.

'Good morning,' I called out, receiving a cool nod of acknowledgement. 'How fares the boutique?'

'Out-pacing every other department, I believe.' Her expression smug, she moved on towards the lift but then hesitated and turned back. 'That mix-up with Dusty Springfield – at the last moment The Beverley Sisters cancelled…'

'Not a problem, Miss Frances. I'd assumed as much. Dusty Springfield proved an excellent alternative.'

Miss Frances had looked delighted, although I've no doubt she was as little taken in by me as I was by her. '*Au revoir*,' she called out.

I didn't bother with a reply. As the lift doors closed on her, Della glided to my side. 'That trench-coat must cost a fortune in dry-cleaning bills,' she observed.

'Without doubt.' I'd studied my watch before saying carelessly, 'Is it true that our Miss Frances is a lesbian?'

Della had tittered. Not a sound, nor a word I liked, but that was exactly it.

'She certainly used to be.' Her tone became more serious and confidential. 'Apparently, she was with the same woman for years and then, over a matter of months, the woman fell ill and died. Her name was Gus. A tragedy.'

I'd waited as Della plucked a tiny scrap of lace handkerchief from her bodice and dabbed away moisture threatening to ruin her eyeliner.

'That is very sad,' I said solemnly.

'She was devastated. I've seen a photograph in her office. She says it's of her sister but it's Gus. She brought her to the Store Christmas party once. Such an attractive woman. Got on with everybody.'

'I expect Miss Frances found a replacement eventually?'

'I don't think she has.' Della shot me a quick anxious glance.

I'd known exactly what she was thinking: that Miss Frances liked Claire Daker and that I more than liked Claire Daker. My ever faithful Della had seen through my subterfuge.

'Funny old world,' I said. 'I never for one moment suspected that Miss Frances liked women. I thought she was totally committed to her career.'

'It's easy to be committed to a career when you've got nothing else in your life.'

Had there been a note of criticism in Della's voice? Of bitterness? Fighting my need to ask about Claire Daker, I brought our conversation to an abrupt end. 'Della, how many times do I have to tell you, the display cabinet isn't the place for your make-up bag? Please remove it – now.'

I believe we were both relieved to return to our manager–saleswoman roles. However, Della remained quiet and a little reserved with me during the rest of the day. I sensed that I'd hurt her feelings.

Finishing my coffee I returned to my task. Already, my chart indicated that certain days or parts of days were showing up as intervals of opportunity, when The Store would be relatively quiet and Miss Frances elsewhere. I considered whether I should also squeeze Mavis in somewhere. For a young woman who was supposed to be managing a boutique, Claire Daker spent an incredible amount of time in her company, up on the Mezzanine floor. I decided that any Mavis information would be signified by a small grey asterisk.

Using a ruler and yellow felt tip pen I began to draw lines across the 'clear' sections. Early October was a particularly yellow month, representing what I referred to as a 'pause' period, before The Store began to accelerate towards Christmas. I felt a tremor of excitement. I imagined myself arriving at the Christmas party with

Claire Daker. It could happen. There were many instances of spring to autumn romances, most of them featuring an older, sophisticated man. People would sneer. People would talk behind my back. I didn't give a damn about people!

From my briefcase I took out the thick file that contained the holiday rota for the entire store. I'd almost not bothered to retrieve it from my filing cabinet. The peak holiday time was during July and August, when the hiatus in Oxford Street following the summer sales and staff holidays caused the least disruption.

I opened the file at September and my heart lifted. Miss Frances was away during the first week of the month! It didn't give me much time but I would strike when the iron was hot. A whole Miss Frances-less week.

My index finger ran over the list of names. Miss Frances was the only member of store staff taking a holiday in September. But where was Claire Daker's name? Did she still come under Head Office staff?

The light in the room grew darker. I felt chilled. I looked down at my forearms (the morning had been sunny and I'd worn a sports shirt) and seen that the hairs had lifted in quite an extraordinary manner.

Grimly, I turned to the required page. There was no need to search for her name. Claire Daker was the only member of Head Office staff going on holiday in September. The first week was scored out in scarlet. Were they holidaying together? I needed to move quickly, but what move should I make?

Chapter 20

1975

I arrive at The Templar's Arms just after eleven the following morning. The lounge bar is empty apart from Steve Chambers.

'Got you one in, old buddy. A pint of Thwaite's Best Bitter, okay?' Steve holds up his glass. 'Laverne's looking for some salt and vinegar crisps out back.'

For just a moment, my old rivalry surfaces as I absorb Steve's powder blue pullover. Cashmere. Expensive. The colour – not one I would have chosen – only enhances Steve's healthy tan and the gleaming whiteness of his teeth as he smiles a welcome.

But in that same moment, I notice another man reflected in the mirrored glass behind the optics. His hair is attractively tussled as if from a brisk walk. During my time spent at Mildmay's I've let my hair, moustache and eyebrows revert to their natural iron grey. *My* face is tanned from sunny afternoons spent in Doreen's garden. I approve of my clothes – a complete departure from dark business suits. Thank god I had the sense to take a pair of slacks, fawn pullover in virgin wool, and tan velvet-cord sports jacket from my wardrobe in Doreen's bedroom the night before. My shoulders visibly relax. I like that man in the mirror.

'Bitter's fine by me. Do you mind if we take our drinks outside?' I gesture towards the open door leading to the beer garden. 'The sun's attempting to break through.'

'Good idea. You carry the drinks; I'll hang on for the crisps.'

I reach inside my jacket for my wallet. 'Let me…'

'Get out of here. I downed at least a bottle and a half of your good wine at the shindig last night.'

In a sunny spot against the pub wall I find a bench and table. With a slight tremor in my hands, I put the glasses down and lower myself gingerly onto the bench. I am still shaky from all the alcohol last night, and of course from the certainty that I had seen Claire Daker. She was nearby.

Imagine the addict less than a year in from abstaining. The drug, if not in their blood, remains in their senses. The temptation is once again within reach. I forced myself for the moment to think of other things: the blessed relief of waking up earlier in the guest bedroom, turning my head and seeing no sign of Doreen. Not her head on the pillow, not an item of chiffon, no black satin mules with marabou pom-poms – there had been absolutely nothing personal of Doreen anywhere in the room. Beneath the covers, I'd stretched my legs, flexed my toes, thrown an arm out each side, then just lain back against the pillows, luxuriating in my freedom,

'You look a happy man this morning.' Steve drops two packets of crisps onto the table.

'I am.'

Quietly I wait for Steve to drag a chair across from the lawn and fall into it.

He immediately reaches for a bag of crisps. 'Mind if I open these? I had breakfast at the hotel but you know how it is with alcohol.'

My stomach rumbles. I nod. I've eaten nothing since the cashews and pick-n-mix in the hotel room last night. My hoped-for sandwich when we arrived back hadn't materialised. There was no sign of Mrs Venables and Doreen had been in no mood to cosset me or Junior. She'd thrown her car keys on the hall table before heading into the lounge. Seconds later, she reappeared carrying the brandy decanter and one glass.

'Junior, go to bed.'

'Goodnight, Mummy.'

'Goodnight, darling.'

I'd wondered if I could get away with also saying, 'Goodnight, darling,' and following Junior up the stairs. Emphatically not, I decided.

The eyes Doreen turned on me were mean; Doreen at her nastiest. As she advanced, I'd edged backwards till my spine pressed against the hall table.

'You've got two minutes to get your night stuff out of my bedroom. The guest room's all yours.' She tapped my chest with the rim of her glass. 'That's what you've wanted all along, isn't it?'

'Now Doreen –'

'Fuck off and get moving!'

I lean forward. 'Steve, might I have a few of your crisps? The house was like the Marie Celeste this morning – not a sign of anyone and a locked kitchen.'

'Help yourself. If we're still here at twelve-thirty, Laverne will rustle us up something up...' He grins. 'Hey, I'd have thought you guys would have breakfasted *a deux* in your suite.'

I open the remaining packet and rummage inside for the largest crisp I can find. 'We didn't stay at the hotel last night. To be honest, Doreen and I weren't getting on very well and then her son turned up. It seemed easier to come home.'

Steve rocks back in his chair. 'You rowed? What happened? The two of you seem like a perfect match. The woman is obviously mad about you.'

I glance nervously back over my shoulder towards the open pub door. 'But I'm not mad about her. I'm not even sure I like her.'

'Then why get engaged? Why the party?'

'I seem to be on an unstoppable trajectory into chaos.'

Steve rubs his chin with a tanned hand.

My eyes widen, distracted for a moment. On Steve's wrist is a Rolex Oyster which must have cost several hundred pounds. I adjust my jacket sleeve over my own modest Seiko.

'Nothing's unstoppable.' Steve's mouth forms a lopsided grin. 'Except maybe a runaway steer.'

Irritably I wonder why Steve, when I most need him to be supportive and sensible, chooses to adopt the persona of a cod cowboy. But then again, Steve is the one who is as free as air. Whoever he chooses to be, it appears to be working for him.

'It seems that I'm going to be forced to ride the steer till it throws me off and probably tramples me underfoot,' I say ruefully. 'There's something else I need to talk about, if you care to listen.'

'Go right ahead.'

I have his full attention. Why have I never noticed before that behind Steve's bantering, there is real kindness? And patience. An ability to stop the clock and concentrate on someone else's problems. What had I ever done for Steve to warrant such decency? Bought him a few dinners, but only to make me feel magnanimous.

I help myself to more crisps before blurting out, 'As we were driving back last night, I saw Claire Daker.'

'Phew!' Steve raises his glass to his lips. 'Are you sure it was her? She'd be a long way from home.'

'I'm a long way from home. It was her.'

'Did she see you?'

'I don't know. She looked startled but it was dark and the way Doreen was revving the engine would have startled anybody.'

'You recognised her in the dark?'

'There was the light from the headlights and a tea-shop. It was Claire Daker all right.' My hand is shaking again as I reach for my glass.

Steve gets up. 'Another one?'

'Why not?'

I lean back in my chair, trying to enjoy the warmth of the sun on my face. From feeling almost euphorically happy twenty minutes earlier, my mood is now dipping. Behind me in the bar I can hear both Steve's and Laverne's voices but not what they are saying. Laverne laughs, then he laughs. Are they laughing at me? No, he would never do that.

Steve steps back out into the sunlight. 'There you go. More crisps as well.' This time Steve straddles his seat. Carefully he says, 'She seems like a very nice woman – your Doreen.'

My shoulders tense. 'Steve, whether she's nice or not, I don't have any inclination to sleep with her, which is what she wants me to do.'

'Personal question, old buddy, but are you usually okay in that department?'

'I imagine I'm a normal man with normal instincts.'

'Is that a yes?'

'It most definitely is a yes. I wish I could find Doreen attractive, but I don't.'

'But you find Claire Daker attractive?'

'Yes.'

'Even though she's almost young enough to be your granddaughter?'

'Go easy!'

'Just answer the question.'

From his jacket pocket Steve takes out a cigarette case. He flips it open and offers it to me. 'I shouldn't smoke, but old habits...'

I shake my head. 'I simply…want her.'

Steve blows smoke thoughtfully into the still air. 'That doesn't sound like love.'

What can I say? *What do I know of romantic love? I love cloth and good design. I can appreciate a spectacular view. I might become fond of a small friendly animal. None of these apply to how I feel about Claire Daker.*

Somewhere out on the road that runs past the front of the pub I hear a car approaching at speed. I stiffen.

Steve's eyes are questioning.

I wait for the car to pass the pub and drive on towards Burnside. With a squeal of tyres it turns into the car park. 'Doreen. Damn it! I don't want to see her now.'

Steve picks up the crisps. 'Grab the drinks and follow me.'

He makes straight for the dense six-foot-high beech hedge at the end of the beer garden.

Out in the pub car park a door slams.

I grab our glasses and chase after him, feeling like Alice in pursuit of the White Rabbit.

Steve pushes aside the beech branches and steps through. The branches spring back.

Clutching the glasses against my chest I turn around and press back into the hedge. For a moment the branches resist me and then they give way. I push through. There is Steve, already in his Ford Capri, throwing open the passenger door, and in I get.

Steve leans across me to shut the door. 'Hang onto those drinks, old buddy,' he shouts, gunning the engine. The car accelerates out onto the road, the speedometer racing upwards: seventy, eighty, ninety.

Just as I'm beginning to think that I'd rather face the wrath of Doreen than end up dying in a car accident, the car slows and Steve turns into a country lane. A hundred yards further he swerves onto a leafy cattle track and brakes.

I balance the glasses on the dashboard and wind the window down. Immediately I am assailed by bird song.

'Just breathe in that air.' Steve opens the car door, twisting in his seat so that his long legs stretch out across the grass. 'You know, there isn't a future with that girl. There never was, and whether you saw her last night or not and imagine that this is fate taking a hand on your behalf – she's past history.'

I reach for my beer but suddenly I have no real appetite for it.

'You don't have to stay with Doreen if you hate the idea. But you've made the break from London and your old life and something, god, the universe is offering you a chance. Take it!' Steve tosses his cigarette butt into the bushes. 'Shall I tell you about my Damascus moment?'

'I didn't realise you'd had one.'

'We all have them. It's recognising the moment in the first place. About three years ago. I was as near rock bottom as I've ever been. A five-day bender but I just couldn't get drunk enough. Finally the bartender refused to serve me. He said, "You know, Steve, even when you're out of your head, you're still likeable." I said, "What? Are you a pansy?" He said, "I said you're likeable. I didn't say I liked you. You have a way with people, which is why you're never short of someone to buy you drinks. It's a talent. You should use it."'

I couldn't help but think of all the times I'd lent Steve money.

Reading my thoughts, Steve grins at me. 'Yes, you've bought me enough dinners. Maybe out of pity, or perhaps it gave you a kick to feel superior, but you wouldn't have wasted your money on someone you disliked.'

'True,' I said. 'But what talent do I have?'

'You know just about everything there is to know about women's' clothing. That's a weird talent but you've made it work for you. Why turn your back on it now?'

'I want more than that. I want …' What did I want?

As if by mutual agreement we both get out of the car and walk a little way down the track. It is muddy but the mud has dried. We come to a gate and a fence and a view of fields and distant hills and pale blue sky. We stand and contemplate. I think about the excitement I've felt in my gut from the moment of seeing Claire Daker again. I recognise that feeling as a false friend but still cannot quite bring myself to… annihilate it.

Steve looks at his watch. 'I'll need to make tracks soon. Can I drop you anywhere?'

'No. I'll be fine. A walk will clear my head.'

Having waved Steve and his glossy Ford Capri goodbye, I set off on foot I know not where. The randomness of my action pleases me. I peer over fences and hedges, admire sheep, wonder at the provenance of 'virgin wool', enjoy the sun on the back of my head and shoulders and feel inclined to sing. I pass country cottages and decide that although they are picturesque, given a choice I prefer the ugly newness of Mildmay's, with all its modern conveniences, to the dark small rooms I imagine behind the dark small windows.

Initially I stroll carelessly along, but as twenty minutes becomes an hour and I haven't spotted a single road sign or seen a vehicle, I'm aware of a niggling anxiety. Where the devil am I? I've worn my comfortable Hush Puppies but they are beginning to rub against the weals caused by yesterday's tight shoes. Even though it is only just after one o'clock in the afternoon, I imagine night falling and being forced to search for shelter.

And then behind me on the road I hear a familiar car engine and I know there will be no need for that. The vehicle slows and stops.

Through the open window Doreen looks at me. She's wearing sunglasses so I have no idea what is going on in her head. There is a stillness about her that I instantly find reassuring. Doreen isn't angry any more.

'Get in.'

We drive back in silence. As the car turns into the drive, Doreen says, 'I must have covered more than sixty miles trying to find you.'

'I'm glad you did. I was well and truly lost.'

She takes the key out of the ignition and drops it into her handbag. 'I thought maybe at some point, you might give me some advice on the Martin and Junior situation. Something must be done but I'm not sure quite what.'

'Certainly, Doreen.'

We get out of the car. From the boot she lifts several bags of shopping.

'Let me.' I take the bags from her and together we walk towards the house.

By tacit agreement, while Doreen drives out again to visit her hairdresser in Burnside, I enjoy a pleasant few hours removing all my clothes and any luggage from Doreen's bedroom and arranging everything in my new room. I unpack a box of books and put them in alphabetical order on the window sill.

Not much but my own, I say to myself, and then vow never to use that phrase again. It reminds me of the pokiness of my Earls Court flat and the browbeaten, defeated man I'd become. But not anymore.

I am on holiday. A strange sort of holiday but a change is as good as a rest. I will jettison that phrase as well. Steve's words of wisdom have lifted my spirits. If Steve could climb back up from being an alcoholic and general loser, surely I can become my own man again.

Chapter 21

1974

From the moment I saw Miss Frances's and Claire Daker's coinciding holiday dates, any remaining sane judgement I possessed flew out of the window. I turned my back on methodical planning, keeping a cool head, making no rash decisions, in fact every lesson of self-promotion, people handling, when to bully and when to roll over and pretend to be a good and friendly dog, I wilfully set aside.

By the close of summer all the ranges for the following season are already arriving in the store and the new spring styles are on order. The period from late August to the end of September represents a hiatus in the fashion world, filled with summer sales and the frantic build-up towards Christmas. Suppliers have all been visited, orders placed, stipulations and alterations put in writing; from then on the only correspondence between us is via brief telephone calls. I needed an excuse for a buying trip at a time of the retail year when buying trips were no longer needed. One requiring an overnight stay.

Every week I am inundated with brochures and mail-shots, fashion companies trying to attract my attention in the hope of becoming a stockist to the prestigious brand name that is The Store. Ninety-nine percent of these communications are unsuccessful and end up in the waste-paper basket. The few that make it through are those that keep on trying – but politely and with respect.

A few days earlier I'd received an amateurish little brochure, the pages cut and bound together by hand, a ribbon instead of staples or a proper binding. On the sepia tinted pages, small designs had been painted in watercolour – bride and bridesmaid hats and head-dresses. As an object of artistic merit, the brochure was a pretty enough concoction. While not wishing to go within a mile range of the supplier, I could appreciate that the illustrations and designs they represented possessed some flair. If the final product looked as picturesque as its painted equivalent, each hat, flower garland, headband would be perfect for some free-spirited bohemian wedding.

However, I'd been impressed before and then disappointed. Experience told me that anything I ordered from them would turn out to be a tawdry version of the painting; the materials used would be cheap, garish and insubstantial. Promised delivery dates would be missed, artificial flowers would come adrift, the supplier would bleat endlessly about needing to be paid well before The Store's policy of twenty-eight day minimum. The little brochure had all the hallmarks of a disastrous short-lived business relationship but I'd held onto it. There was a charm and an innocence which for some reason made me think of Claire Daker.

I took the brochure from my pending file and studied it again. The firm was based in St Ives down in Cornwall – much too far to come and go in a day – good. All I needed now was a solid excuse for asking the boutique manageress to visit a bridal wear supplier.

Luck was with me! Previously overlooked, the final page was devoted to illustrations of hand-painted scarves with an art-deco theme. Even with my limited knowledge of the 'youth market' I knew these to be very similar to a line being stocked at the new Biba flagship store in Kensington High Street (the old Derry and Toms).

I rang the supplier and was put straight through to a female managing director who sounded young, breathless and overwhelmed to be speaking to the general manager of a West End store. I set up an appointment, for me and my assistant. We would be staying overnight. The woman immediately suggested that she would make the hotel bookings on my behalf.

'Adjoining rooms,' I told her. I couldn't help myself. I made those two words heavy with intimacy, so she knew or at least surmised that the assistant and I were lovers.

From that day on I was particularly pleasant to Claire Daker. The date was set and rail tickets bought, it was imperative that I win her trust. Our meeting with the supplier was arranged for Friday morning of the following week but I was in no immediate hurry to let the cat out of the bag. Yes, Claire needed sufficient notice, but should she take fright, not enough to invent her own escape strategy. So I was… gracious. While on the shop floor I allowed her more bodily space, although for weeks I'd been intentionally crowding her.

When in my company, Claire Daker was generally monosyllabic. I now let these silences continue between us and sometimes – because she was young and certainly had no experience dealing with older men – she found herself obliged to fill an awkward pause. In return, I treated any opinion she might have with serious consideration, whereas again in the past I'd taken pleasure in heaping sarcasm on the young woman. Added to this ploy I adopted an air of absorption, as if more pressing problems than baiting Claire Daker assailed me.

Only once did I overstep the mark, but it was irresistible. She was invariably immaculately dressed even when her clothes were obviously cheap and poorly made. One morning I noticed a label sticking up above the collar of her blouse. Rather a large flashy Top Shop label. I said in a deferential tone, 'Claire, do excuse me, but….' I lifted up her pony tail (it felt like a skein of silk) and with my free hand tucked in the offending label.

Startled, she shied away from me.

I let her hair run through my fingers before smiling apologetically. 'I can't bear visible labels,' I said.

She'd touched the back of her neck as if to check I hadn't left some viscous deposit on her skin.

'I'm sorry, Claire. I didn't mean to offend you. Better get off to the boutique now, there seems to be quite a crowd of young women milling around downstairs.'

For the rest of that day I avoided her. Just before five-thirty I noticed her waiting for Della at the foot of the Bridal Salon staircase – they now walked to Oxford Circus tube station together.

'Della's on her way,' I called out.

She nodded but said nothing.

'Well, good night.' I turned back into the salon and began my evening ritual of switching off the many spot-lights.

The following morning I asked Rosa to send Claire to my office. I left the door open and didn't look up when she walked in.

'Sit down,' I said, my head bent over The Store diary. 'I think it's high time you began visiting suppliers, don't you?' *Then* I looked at her, my expression entirely business-like.

'Yes, I would find that experience useful.' Her voice was low and she wouldn't meet my gaze.

I allowed my expression to soften fractionally: the good-natured uncle treating his favourite niece. 'Well, I'm sending you off to St Ives. Ever been there before?'

She shook her head.

I pushed the brochure across the desk. 'A small company. I thought you might be interested in their scarves for your boutique. While you're there, you might check out the millinery for me? Would that be acceptable?'

'Of course, Mr Oliver.'

Still no enthusiasm in her voice, but no hostility either.

'You'll set off next Thursday afternoon. No need to come into work first.' I placed a folder in front of her. 'Here are your travel tickets and hotel reservation. Take a cab to the hotel. I'll get Rosa to give you some petty cash to cover evening meal and breakfast. I've made the appointment with a Mrs Abrahams at 11am on the Friday. Watch and learn. Don't commit to an order no matter how impressed you may be.'

'But who will look after the boutique?'

'Oh, I'm sure Miss Frances will sort something out – she's a big fan of yours. So would you like to go?'

She didn't answer immediately.

I thought she was going to turn the offer down but then suddenly Claire Daker smiled at me. 'Yes, I would,' she said.

It was a quiet week. I kept my distance from both of them. I spoke to Miss Frances just once, when she approached me in the staff canteen to thank me for arranging the trip.

'It's exactly what Claire needs,' she said. 'The boutique is fine for her now but really it only represents a starting point.'

'Very true,' I answered gravely, as if she wasn't just stating the obvious.

On that Thursday afternoon, using the pretext of visiting a sick elderly aunt in Bishops Stortford, I left The Store with my overnight bag containing pyjamas, a change of underwear and socks, a shirt, and my capacious toiletry bag. In the interior zippered pocket was a newly purchased packet of condoms.

What an idiot I was! I remember actually mulling over whether to take just one condom and then, in my mad optimism, thought 'just supposing an evening of passion runs into a morning of more passion'? The word I'd used in my head had been 'coupling' – a sexual linking together.

At Paddington I lay low in the station bar, a place I knew she'd never enter. I sipped a bitter coffee then cleansed my palate with a shot of whisky. With only minutes to spare, I boarded the train at the door nearest to the ticket barrier. Although the train was crowded I managed to find an empty seat next to a window. I took out my Telegraph and attempted to read it, but knowing Claire Daker was only a couple of carriages away made this impossible. Several hours passed, the next stop was Plymouth. By now she would be relaxed. Surely I could get away with my excuse of at the very last minute realising I had been unfair to expect her to make the journey and appointment on her own. I would stress that I wasn't here to interfere, just to offer any support if needed. In a crowded train what could she do about it?

I stood up and stretched my cramped legs. I felt hungry – a little snack from the buffet car perhaps, but first I'd claim my reservation. As I pulled my case from the overhead rack I was smiling. Claire Daker would be startled then no doubt furious but I felt I'd put in some excellent work over the intervening days. Even Della had been fooled. She and I had returned to our old camaraderie that in the past sometimes surfaced: me teasing her, Della responding with just the tiniest hint of cheek. Several times I'd been aware that the Daker girl was watching us curiously, seeing a different, more relaxed side to her arch enemy.

Folding my newspaper, I slid it into the side pocket of my case and began to make my way along the aisle, heading for Coach D. I was forced to step over bags, around bicycles and baby buggies, but with good humour I excused and apologised my way through the train. There were hours of journey-time left to us so I didn't try to hurry. 'Savour these moments, Oliver,' I told myself and I did. The train rocked gently. I looked down with affection on family groups, children – their heads bent over comics, some teenagers playing cards, and an elderly couple holding hands – what was their story?

Before pushing open the door to Coach D I took a deep breath. This was it, whatever the outcome.

Claire Daker wore a pale grey silky blouse, a skirt of an identical shade, dainty black ankle boots; one leg was crossed over the other rather elegantly. I had never seen her with her hair loose about her shoulders before. It was like the moment when I saw her wearing the Zandra Rhodes dress on the day of the boutique opening – I realised again just how beautiful, how perfect she was.

Her eyes were closed and her head rested on the shoulder of the person who had claimed my seat. That person was gazing out of the window, hands folded in her lap. That person of course was Miss Frances.

Without hesitating I passed smoothly on through the carriage and into the next carriage where I sat down.

Imagine this: a man like myself, who had always been in control of himself and others, with no idea what to do. Should I make a scene, demand Miss Frances vacate the seat immediately, treat the situation and them as if they were all part of my own private joke? I had built my hopes so high that their descent was catastrophic. My courage completely failed me. I might be able to fool Claire Daker, but never Miss Frances – she'd see straight through my artifice. The thought of them spotting me was unbearable. I left the seat, trailed onwards till finally I found a place with my back to anyone coming from the direction of their coach and huddled down. At Plymouth I joined the hubbub of passengers getting off the train and hid in the waiting room till the train pulled out, then I crossed over the footbridge and after half-an-hour caught the connection back to London.

On Monday morning a sparkling, enthusiastic Claire Daker gave me a full report: the supplier had been most helpful, the quality of the products first class, although the scarves were too expensive for her boutique customers.

'Really?' I said. 'Would they be suitable for The Store?'

'Definitely.' She awarded me with her second smile ever. 'I've passed on the details to Miss Frances. She's placing a trial order.'

'I'm surprised Miss Frances would even consider buying a product she hasn't personally checked out first.'

Another smile from Claire Daker, but inward looking, smug. 'She trusts my judgement.'

'I don't doubt it. And did *you* enjoy your trip?'

'Very much.'

'Not lonely at all?'

'Mrs Abrahams took us – me – out to dinner.' She didn't even have the grace to look embarrassed at her obvious slip-up.

'How kind. I must admit I almost changed my mind and joined you.'

A cloud crossed her face but she said nothing.

'Well thank you, Claire. And the bridal millinery? Did you find time to look at that?'

The expression on her face told me that my bridal millinery hadn't once entered her head. 'The meeting was so rushed, Mr Oliver. Mrs Abrahams had another appointment to go to and I didn't want to hold her up.'

'Of course not. I quite understand. Well, that's about it.' I smiled a dismissal. What a little liar she was!

Needless to say, I dropped all the information in the bin. When the company began pestering me on the telephone for feedback I instructed the switchboard to tell them I wasn't available.

Chapter 22

1975

Arriving back in a taxi from a congenial lunch at Harry Ramsden's with an old colleague from my Marshall & Snelgrove days, I join Doreen in the lounge. She is curled up on the sofa reading the newspaper. She wears a pair of horn-rimmed spectacles which I find almost endearing.

I say, 'Doreen, I've decided to put my Cruikshank prints into auction. You're right, they are depressing. However, the Lowrys will return home with me.'

Doreen's head is bent over an article I read earlier, about the new concept of timesharing apartments recently launched in America.

'Unless you'd like them.' I suppress a smirk. 'Although they might spoil the effectiveness of your *Toile de Jouy* wallpaper.'

'Definitely "no" to any of your pictures, Oliver. You know I do believe I introduced *Toile de Jouy* wallpaper to the north of England. I may do the same for this timeshare idea.' Doreen sighs and takes off her spectacles. 'Would this be a good time to discuss the Junior and Martin Renshawe problem?'

'I don't see why not. I was only thinking this morning that I do have some experience of this sort of malarkey.'

Doreen's small eyes sparkle.

'In my twenties I went for a meal with the buyer at Stella Stephano's Bridal Accessories. His name was Edward Flynn. I found him very elegant. In those days I was quite naïve. He treated me to an excellent dinner at Sheekey's fish restaurant. Afterwards, he invited me back to his flat behind Marble Arch for coffee. Anyway, he went into another room to dig out his collection of antique guipure lace scraps and came back wearing a bath towel.'

'What happened after that?'

'Nothing really. He sat on the arm of my chair and re-arranged the quiff I had at that time. I scalded my tongue on piping hot coffee, then made my excuses and left.'

We both laugh.

'Oliver, could you get me a brandy?'

'Of course.'

'Are you going to have one?'

'Not at the moment.'

As I head for Doreen's drinks cabinet, I'm aware that my pleasant lunch combined with Doreen's un-confrontational mood has put me in excellent spirits.

When I first arrived at Mildmay's I took an instant dislike to the drinks cabinet: a reproduction of a medieval Venetian book – about the size of a large child – with a blue vellum cover embellished with semi-precious stones. I compared it to my coffee table at home in Earls Court, fashioned to resemble a stack of antique books, and found it inferior and garish. However, as I've come to admire Doreen in many respects, so over the weeks I've found myself admiring the workmanship, the semi-precious stones, the bald fact that the cabinet alone shouts, 'My owner is loaded!'

I'm smiling as I twist the key in the gilt padlock and step back as the book's front cover swings open. The interior lights come on, shining down onto shelves of bottles and glasses. I pour Doreen a modest brandy, placing the glass in front of her on the coffee table.

Before I leave in a few weeks' time, I am determined to speak to her about the amount of alcohol she gets through each day, but not now when we seem to be rubbing along so well. There is so much that is good and admirable about her and I'm only just beginning to appreciate this now the pressure of sharing a bed has been removed.

'Shall we have some music?' Earlier today I found a box of her late husband's LPs in the garage. As I remove a Barbra Streisand record from its sleeve, Doreen is monitoring my every action.

'I can't stand that woman,' she says irritably.

'Barbra Streisand has one of the greatest voices of the twentieth century.' With my handkerchief I polish the disc.

'I thought we were going to discuss my son.'

'There's no rush, is there?'

'Well, if you insist on playing records, I'd prefer some Herb Alpert.'

'Let's listen to Barbra first, shall we?'

'She's got a voice that would puncture eardrums.'

'An incredible voice.'

'That's what I said – a voice that would puncture eardrums.' She puts her spectacles on again and turns to an inner page of her newspaper before saying loudly, 'My Rio Tinto shares aren't doing too well. Do you think I should sell them?'

'I have no idea. My money's in government bonds. Do you mind if I concentrate on Miss Streisand?'

Doreen tries a change of tactics and pats the sofa cushions. 'Why not come and sit next to me? Then I can concentrate on Miss Streisand as well.'

'You can just as easily concentrate on the music with me standing over here, Doreen. Do give her a chance.'

I take the armchair, link my hands across my chest and prepare to give myself up to the music. Halfway into the song I tell her, 'You're humming "Big Spender".'

'Isn't that what she's singing?'

'No, she's singing "People". You may be unmoved, but I find these lyrics extremely poignant.'

Doreen kicks off her shoes and tucks her stockinged feet under her. 'I'm well aware that you find these lyrics poignant, which is why I'd rather you played something else.'

'Meaning?' As soon as the query is out of my mouth I regret it. By now I should know, never ask Doreen a question that I might not like the answer to.

She doesn't respond immediately, leans her head to one side and listens carefully before exclaiming, 'There you are! That bit about people who need people being the luckiest people in the world. That's why we're so bloody miserable. Because I do need someone and that someone certainly doesn't need me.' She upends the brandy glass, drinking every last drop.

'Doreen, go easy. You'll make yourself ill. It's only mid-afternoon.'

Slumping back against the sofa cushions, she stares resentfully at me. 'I know what's brought on all this sentimentality – it's that young woman you imagined you recognised the other night, isn't it?'

'It was probably a trick of the light.'

'You don't really think that.'

'Leave it, Doreen.'

The song finishes.

'Now can we have some Herb Alpert?'

'I thought we were going to talk about Junior.'

'If Barbra Streisand means something to you, Herb Alpert means something to me.'

'What exactly?'

Her voice softens. 'On the Artemis. The first time we danced together. We danced to Herb Alpert's "This Guy's In Love With You". It's hard to find a man who dances well, I was delighted.' She smiles at me. 'Let's not spoil my one and only good memory of us together – by this becoming the record I played to cancel out your record, on the afternoon we had the flaming row over just who it was you were pining for.'

She refills her glass. Her expression is serious and sad. Any make-up she wore earlier seems to have leached away.

I find Herb Alpert's *Music To Watch Girls Go By* LP and search for the track she wants.

She says, 'I do remember how unhappy you were when I met you. I'm not a fool. I am able to understand that if you love someone and then lose them, it's not that easy or even possible to just cheer up and get on with your life.' Holding her glass up to her face, Doreen inhales the smell of brandy. 'Are you sure you won't have one?'

'I was always a beer man, Doreen. And then only at weekends. A good red wine for special occasions.'

We both fall quiet and consider this.

I'm bewildered by the way I'd gone along drinking spirits for so many weeks. What had happened to that fist of iron in the velvet glove that I'd been renowned for for over twenty five-years?

'I'm sorry. I should have made sure there was always beer for you.' She balances the glass in her lap. 'Before I drink this and the ones that will come after, I'd like you to tell me why you looked so lost and vulnerable that first evening in the bar.'

I put down the record and return to the armchair, arrange the creases of my trousers and loosen my shirt collar.

'Tell me the truth for once, Oliver.'

'I'll do my best.'

*

Leaving Oliver in the study musing over his lost love, Doreen made her way tiredly upstairs, shadowed at a discreet distance by Mrs Venables. At her bedroom door she turned abruptly. 'I'll have a pot of tea at six. Till then I don't want to be disturbed.'

'Will you require biscuits?'

'I have no idea whether or not I shall require biscuits. I'll let you know when you bring up the pot.' Even to Doreen's ears her tone sounded unpleasant. 'That will be all.'

Mrs Venables inclined her head, took three paces backwards before turning to walk away.

Entering the bedroom, Doreen remembered her husband's gentle reproof. 'That's no way to talk to another human being.' He'd said that to her, the very first time she'd been rude to Mrs Venables. Laverne and Michael had come over for dinner and Doreen had hated him telling her off in front of them.

The room was immaculate, all clothes put away or taken to be laundered or dry-cleaned. Her dressing table, which she left in chaos each morning, was tidy and dusted. No powder, no blobs of nail varnish, no make-up tissues. The bed cover was turned down the way Doreen required it to be: a triangle of satin counterpane revealing toning bed linen. Not one single sign left of Oliver. Not even Ollie and Dorie bear.

A slight breeze moved the net curtains where Mrs Venables had opened one of the sash windows. *I am horrible*; she told just one of the reflections in her three-way mirror. Taking her time, she unbuttoned her jacket and draped it on a padded coat-hanger before placing it in the wardrobe. She stepped out of her shoes and arranged them side-by-side in the rosewood shoe-rack. She crossed the room to the other wardrobe, the one she'd designated for Oliver. It was empty. He'd even taken the coat hangers with him to the guest bedroom. If she'd just kept her mouth shut he'd still be sharing her bed, however sterile their relationship was.

Once again her anger had taken her off at a ridiculous tangent.

It was only mid-afternoon. Quietly and reasonably she could have suggested they walked across the fields to the Templar's

Arms, to clear the air. They could have driven into Burnside for a cream tea. She could have suggested any number of options rather than feeling constrained to remain in her bedroom till a pot of tea arrived at six. Was it too late to get dressed again and go back downstairs? She thought of Oliver's face as he'd reached the end of his story. He'd looked old and pathetic. She despised him.

She sat down at the dressing table.

Doreen, the last thing you need is another drink, she told her reflection. She drew open the shallow middle drawer and peeled back a layer of silk underwear. A small crystal tumbler glinted next to three vodka miniatures. Her mouth felt dry. Just imagining the sensation of the alcohol on her tongue made her feel happier about herself. Three tiny bottles. Not a drink problem. They would do no more than help her sleep. Sleep was what she needed.

Ignoring the tumbler she opened the first miniature. She'd sip it. Make it last. Oh, it tasted wonderful. Felt wonderful. If she had to die, let Doreen be drowned in a vat of vodka. All gone. She'd definitely sip the next one. She didn't. Had her tongue been slender enough, she'd have snaked it inside the bottles and licked out every last remaining drop. The last one she'd savour. She didn't. Carefully, as ever, she placed the bottles in the wastepaper basket and hid them beneath a handful of paper tissues.

She felt better. Almost cheerful. The miserable feeling between her breasts had dulled. She padded across to the side window and lifted the net curtain just as Oliver entered the summer house at the lower end of the garden. She knew he wouldn't choose one of the comfortable rattan loungers. No, he'd rather settle himself stiffly in the wicker Peacock chair. Countless times she'd told him, 'Kick off your shoes. Make yourself at home here.'

He'd taken no notice. But then he'd probably been equally uptight in his miserable Earl's Court flat. She couldn't imagine him putting his feet up on his leather sofa with a couple of cushions behind his head. She could no longer even imagine him in a prone position, awake or asleep.

She watched as he pulled the Peacock chair forward, positioning it in a band of sunlight in the open doorway. He disappeared inside again. She waited. A minute passed before he reappeared carrying the paperback he'd been reading earlier, Nevil Shute's *A Town like*

Alice. From that distance, she couldn't make out the expression on his face, but somehow just from the way he settled himself in the chair, she knew he was looking forward to an hour or two of peace and quiet with his novel.

As if aware of being watched Oliver looked up at the house. Doreen let the net drop. He might see its movement but she didn't care.

Lying on the bed, she tried to summon up the vivid daydream she'd had on The Artemis, the first evening they met. Closing her eyes she tried to summon Oliver of the wolf hands, lounging Oliver, brutal yet tender Oliver. It was impossible. She knew too much about him now. He was like a child, wanting everything: new clothes, outings, a summer house to read in, her husband's novels and records, a comfortable double bed in his own room to retire to every night after an excellent dinner.

He's as happy as a pig in shit, she thought. *He's even growing fond of my boys – but me, he can do without, apart from my value as a sympathetic ear when he needs to pour out his unhappiness over a girl less than half his age.*

Doreen woke into darkness. While she'd slept, Mrs Venables had crept in and drawn the heavy curtains.

She switched on one of the bedside lamps. It was nearly six o'clock. With a groan she got to her feet and went to the window. The garden was still filled with bright sunlight but the summer house doors were shut. Turning away she saw that her waste paper basket had been emptied. She opened the middle drawer of the dressing table. Three fresh miniatures lay next to the crystal tumbler. Where would she be without Venables? She pushed the drawer closed. The very thought of vodka now made her feel nauseous. Heavily, she sat down on the stool and began to comb her hair.

When Carpenter and Junior had been young, right up till their md-teens, they'd eaten their tea in the kitchen. Another house of course. Much smaller and semi-detached, near the centre of Burnside. She could only afford to have Venables three afternoons a week to clean, iron and cook for them.

In her head she had a clear image of a smiling Venables standing at the stove frying bacon, eggs and chips for them; Peter bounding in full of energy in those early days. 'Something smells good. Mrs Venables, you're a treasure.'

Venables cheerfully retorting, 'And you're a flatterer, Mr Mildmay. One egg or two?'

Doreen couldn't bear the smell of fried food any more. It represented poverty, a Doreen linked to a working-class background she'd rather forget.

Now Oliver always smelt terrific. She loved that mix of Brylcreem, Old Spice and male sweat. Sometimes it was all she could do not to press her nostrils against his neck, the palm of his hand, the inside of his wrist – against all visible areas of skin. Would she ever see him naked? More to the point, would he ever see her naked and not want to run a mile? She gave her reflection a rueful smile.

Behind her she heard a tap at the bedroom door.

'Come in Mrs Venables. There's never been a need for you to knock.'

The door opened.

'I thought I'd bring up the tray,' Mr Oliver said. 'I've added a couple of your favourite custard creams.'

Quickly, Doreen pushed the drawer shut and got to her feet, suddenly aware that her skirt and blouse were creased. She felt flustered and near to tears, disproportionately overwhelmed by his thoughtfulness.

He'd changed into a dark suit and wore a tie with a fine silver-and-cream thread he'd bought a few days earlier.

'There was no need to put on a suit, Oliver. I could have asked Venables to knock us up a scratch meal.'

'Old habits die hard.' He set the tray down on the bed. 'Anyway, I believe roast chicken is on the menu.'

'But you've eaten an enormous lunch.'

'A few slices of chicken, er, breast can't hurt.'

They smiled at each other, both acknowledging his embarrassment.

'You could have said: a few slices of the white flesh.'

'That sounds rather cannibalistic.' His eyes twinkled. 'Shall I see you downstairs in a bit?'

'Give me fifteen minutes.'

Mr Oliver withdrew, almost in the manner of Mrs Venables' withdrawals: a lowering of the head combined with small backward steps. Doreen leant against the closed door. Was there anyone she didn't intimidate?

Chapter 23

1975

I don't consider Carpenter to be an ally. He's far too in thrall to his mother to ever risk overtly taking my side; however, I'd say that he's found much to respect in me. I like him. He is certainly easier to get on with than Junior, who I fear will never become an adult.

Doreen's sons have suffered not only from their father's death but because of the poor opinion Doreen had of him. The man is rarely mentioned but I see real pain in their eyes when she starts one of her bitter diatribes (usually fuelled by alcohol), blaming her late husband for everything that has gone wrong in her life.

But it is Carpenter I turn to when finally I succumb to – you might call it weakness, although the word doesn't come close to describing the emotional turmoil I've endured since Doreen almost ran over Claire Daker on the crossing.

Carpenter already knows something of my past history, or at least my sanitised version of it. I've told him that the female buyer and I locked horns and, through no fault of my own, I'd been the loser.

We have taken two deckchairs onto the lawn. In companionable silence we read our books for almost half an hour. Fearing that at any moment Doreen will return from her hair appointment in Skipton, I lay aside my novel and say, as if I've been mulling the subject over for some moments, 'Extraordinary, but I believe the woman who plotted and succeeded in getting me fired last year has a cottage near Hampsthwaite. That's only a few miles from here, isn't it?'

I know full well that we are just over a mile away, having looked it up in Doreen's road atlas.

'No more than five minutes in the car,' Carpenter says.

'I don't know if I've mentioned that she was a rampant lesbian.' This secures Carpenter's full attention. 'A most unpleasant character.'

'Good grief.' Carpenter drops his book. From the expression on his face, I don't believe anyone has used the word 'lesbian' in front of him before.

I almost expect a cloud to blot out the sun. *Leave it alone, Oliver.* But I can't, even though I have come to accept that Miss Frances had as much right to love Claire Daker as I did. More so. My emotions were never healthy, never sprang from loving intentions and, god help me, still don't.

'I wouldn't mind taking a look at her house.' I laugh pleasantly. 'Morbid interest on my part, I suppose.'

Carpenter looks pleased at my confidences. 'I'd be happy to drive you over if you fancy a snoop.' Then he remembers his mother. 'I presume you don't want Doreen to know?'

'There is no reason why she should. My dealings with this person originate from a part of my life that has nothing to do with your mother.'

We agree to go immediately. It is a Wednesday and I reason that if Miss Frances is using this cottage she will most likely be there at a weekend, and if Claire Daker is installed *she* will probably have some sort of job to go to during the day.

It takes us a full fifteen minutes to find Foulkes Cottage. It is on the outskirts of Hampsthwaite and we drive past it twice before realising that there is a building tucked behind a high hedge of rose bushes.

Carpenter parks the car in a layby. 'Want company?' he asks.

'No, I won't be long. A quick decko should satisfy my curiosity.'

I stroll back the twenty-odd yards. The garden seems to be all at the front but a footpath leads to a side gate and continues on behind the house. Bramble suckers criss-cross the narrow path, pulling at my trouser cuffs. I am able to approach quietly, unseen from the downstairs windows which all face the road.

Everything about the cottage is still and empty: late afternoon shadows fall at odd angles on the grey brickwork. My hand resting on the gate I stand and just look. It is a lovely cottage – nothing like the gloomy, small-windowed, mean-looking houses I'd passed on my walk. I can see money has been spent on it. The paintwork is fresh, the windows clean; the wooden table on the terrace looks expensive.

In the centre of the table stands a jug of dried hydrangea blossoms. I can so easily imagine Miss Frances and Claire Daker seated together at that table, the sun warming their heads as they talk quietly, sipping coffees, wine, even a simple, perfect glass of water.

I consider myself a strong unsentimental man and yet I am experiencing a devastating pain in my heart and head. Never before have I seen with such clarity that I don't fit in. I can't fit in. My presence at that table, in the cottage kitchen, in one of those bedrooms would be… inappropriate, ugly. It would erase all the light and happiness.

Still I push the gate open and step into the garden, saunter across to the terrace as if I lived there. I surprise a magpie loitering on a stone bird bath. It flashes past me in flight. *Is it bad luck to see one magpie?* On the table is a postcard with a view of Hampsthwaite church, a book of stamps and some magazines: Honey and Marie Claire. A young woman's choice and nothing to do with Miss Frances, Claire Daker *is* living here.

'Oliver, what the devil are you doing?' Carpenter hisses from over by the gate. 'This is trespassing.'

I ignore him and turn over the postcard. It is addressed to Miss Frances.

Frances, I tried to telephone you from work but you were in a meeting. Guess what, I saw someone who looked just like Mr Oliver – how horrible is that? Two Mr Olivers! This one had grey hair though, but being reminded of him has made me anxious again. Hurry up. Come soon. Come now! X

There is already a stamp on the card. I am tempted to post it for her. Instead, I place the card under the jug of flowers so that it doesn't blow away. I'd give anything to be able to stay for a few more minutes.

'For god's sake Oliver, someone is coming. We have to leave now.'

In silence we hurry back to the car.

'Would you drive slowly past the front of the cottage, please?'

'Is that wise?'

'Please.'

Reluctantly he does as I ask. Too late to see her, but I glimpse a flash of tartan as the front door closes. I check my watch. Five-forty-five. She'd be coming home from work.

Carpenter is frowning. 'So do you think that was the rampant lesbian?'

'No. It may have been her niece. Do you mind if we don't talk?'

That is surely it. No more stupid hope to cling to there. That postcard is so typical of Claire Daker – her mix of cheek, bravado and vulnerability. I can take the jibes but I cannot bear the thought of making her feel anxious. Perhaps it is only now that I begin to understand the true meaning of selfless love. Or am I still bamboozling myself?

Chapter 24

1975

We are in the conservatory. Doreen is standing in a patch of what is left of the afternoon sun and is studying her face in a gilt hand-mirror, while I am settled in a comfortably cushioned corner of one of a pair of cane sofas. I keep an eye on my Telegraph cryptic crossword, the other on Doreen. Had I a third eye, it would be trained on Mrs Venables waiting in the open doorway.

'More lipstick, Oliver?' Doreen asks.

'Definitely not.'

'Too much perhaps?'

'Doreen, Mrs Venables is waiting for instructions regarding where to put Martin Renshawe when he arrives.'

'I am well aware of that. I asked whether I am wearing too much lipstick.'

'Your lipstick is perfect.'

'Thank you.' Satisfied, Doreen gives her attention to Mrs Venables. 'You can show Doctor Renshawe into the study.'

Mrs Venables nods. 'Will you want tea immediately?'

'Possibly. Wait within earshot. That will be all.'

Silently, Mrs Venables backs out of the conservatory, closing the glass door in front of her.

'So, Oliver?'

'Yes, Doreen?'

Reluctantly, I lay the newspaper next to me on the cushions. Something more is required but definitely not *Doreen, what do you make of 'overcome on dangerous ground', five letters, second letter 'w'*?

Playing for time I unbutton then re-button the cunning small-change pocket in my recently purchased khaki slacks, as if the properties of buttons and button-holes are a novel concept.

Under Doreen's guidance, I have expanded my wardrobe to include both outdoor and indoor leisure-wear. Initially I'd been anxious about relinquishing my uniform of formal suit, shirt, tie and pocket handkerchief, but discovered that buying quality ensures no loss of status. Watching Doreen flick through a rail of expensive summer shirts in Dunn & Co., I had felt the stirrings of respect.

'Oliver, you could carry off a zigzag print. Even a floral, provided we keep to a russet palette.'

'Could I, Doreen?'

'Oh yes. I think I know what's acceptable in the north of England.'

Doreen has even introduced me to Yves Saint Laurent, although at first I had been dubious. Wasn't the man a homosexual? How could a fellow in his twenties know anything about design?

For an engagement present, Doreen bought me a perfectly cut YSL double-breasted blazer in grey wool and I'd been forced to acknowledge that my own two existing blazers looked shabby and badly tailored by comparison.

I imagined how it might have been had Doreen teamed up with my ever-faithful Della in the Bridal Salon. The two of them would surely have sent Miss Frances and her head office cronies packing.

Restlessly, Doreen moves to the open sliding doors that lead out into the garden. From there she has an oblique view of the dual carriageway, just visible on the far side of the tall hedge.

I reach forward to retrieve my Parker pen from the coffee table.

'Aren't you even the slightest bit concerned about this afternoon?' There is an edge to her voice.

I withdraw my hand. 'Of course I'm concerned. What time is the bloody man due?'

'He is not a "bloody man". He is a well-loved family friend.'

'Rather a too well-loved family friend.' I smile inwardly. *Bravo, Oliver!* My mood feels surprisingly buoyant.

'I don't intend to rise to your bait.' Doreen clicks her nails impatiently on the door frame. 'Martin will be here shortly and I have no idea how we are going to broach this subject.'

'Must we broach it?' I sigh quietly. 'Couldn't we just send him some kind of warning shot across the bows?'

'What exactly would you suggest?'

'Obviously adopting a serious tone, how about: "You do realise Martin that it takes two to tango?"'

With an exasperated shrug, Doreen turns her back on the view of the garden and approaches the sofa. 'Now you're being silly.'

Straight away I sense the alteration in her voice, the change from business-like to affectionate. Her fingers rest on my shoulder. Although these instances are becoming less frequent, there are still moments in every day when Doreen feels she must tweak, stroke or adjust something about me so that we have a physical connection.

To distract her, I pick up the newspaper and flick through in search of the financial pages – the only section that Doreen ever reads.

A headline catches my eye, a blurred photograph. The London Hilton in Park Lane has been bombed, two people killed, sixty-three injured. I feel sick.

'Of course I trust Martin to do the right thing,' Doreen says.

Two people have been killed with a further sixty-three injured.

'Doreen, did you see this?'

'I read it earlier. I didn't tell you in case you got upset. I know that's your old stamping ground. Thank god we're well out of it up here.'

She leans forward so that her hair is almost brushing my cheek as her hand slips into the breast pocket of my shirt. 'Oliver, I wonder if you realise how unhappy I am.'

'Unhappy?' I shake the newspaper at her. 'The families of these people are unhappy. You're just dissatisfied.'

'And since when did you start worrying about other people?'

'Doreen, as Martin is such a close friend, perhaps you should see him on your own,' I say stiffly. 'I'd like to watch the six o'clock news if you don't mind.'

'But I do mind.'

'Look, as far as I can see, you and Renshawe have had a special relationship for years. Nothing I can say could make you see the man as he really is.'

'I believe you're jealous.' Her lacquered hair crackles against my ear.

I almost choke. The idea is ludicrous. Were I not so upset I would find this laughable. That for one moment, Doreen could imagine that I am in any way bothered by the two of them! I remove Doreen's hand from my breast pocket then find I cannot disentangle my hand from hers.

Passionately she insists, 'Martin and I are two friends of long standing, nothing more. You must believe me, Oliver.'

'I couldn't care less.' Just to annoy her I say, 'I have a similar set-up with my good buddy, Steve.'

Which does the trick. Doreen drops my hand. 'Hardly the same. Steve Chambers is a man.'

'He is indeed.'

'So possibly not quite the same depth of feeling.'

'Deeper. Through thick and thin. We're almost blood brothers.'

Behind my words, I am aware of some further subtle change – as if I am breaking free. There is no time to analyse this sensation because Mrs Venables is back, tapping on the glass.

'Come,' Doreen calls out.

The door swings open while Mrs Venables remains in the hall. 'I've installed Doctor Renshawe in the study as per instructions.'

Doreen frowns. 'I didn't hear his car arrive.'

'He said he walked across the fields.'

'I wonder which fields they would be, Doreen?' I raise a querying eyebrow. 'Surely Mildmay's is pretty much surrounded by motorway.'

'Don't be cynical, Oliver.' The foolish woman is smiling fondly at the image of Martin Renshawe walking – no striding –across fields. 'Tell the good doctor we'll be with him in a moment.'

Reluctantly I put on my jacket. Returning to the mirror, Doreen applies yet another coat of lipstick. Her eyes sparkle as she blots her lips on a tissue. 'Ready, Oliver?'

'Yes.'

Following her out, I concentrate all thought on Martin Renshawe and how he intends to play the next scene. Perhaps crouched in a chair, face in hands before raising his leonine head of annoyingly tawny curls – a broken man? Or will he be ready for battle, hands clenched into fists as he rises up onto the balls of his feet like a prize fighter?

Doreen pauses to smooth her skirt over her hips before opening the study. She advances into the room, her hand held out in welcome.

'Martin, I'm so glad you came.'

Martin Renshawe appears to leap from a standing position by the window to land directly in front of her. He clasps her elbows, looks deep into her eyes, 'Doreen.' A quick glance in my direction. 'Oliver. You both look glowing.'

Like a flower bud sensing the warmth of the sun, Doreen's face opens.

Martin releases Doreen and grabs my hand. He attempts to crush my fingers.

'Oliver. Ollie.' He thumps me between my shoulders.

'Easy tiger.' The extraordinary two words that Stanhope had used on me after the Boutique opening debacle now flow easily out of my mouth. I catch a flicker of anxiety in Martin's grey eyes. Smoothly, I reclaim my hand and turn to Doreen. 'Perhaps Venables could bring in some tea now? I expect Doctor Renshawe will be parched after his cross-country slog. And a plate of cakes? You do indulge, don't you, doctor?'

'Please, call me Martin.'

'Oh, I rather like the "doctor" sobriquet. Doreen?'

'Aye aye, sir,' Doreen answers with a snappy salute before marching out into the corridor.

'Shall we sit down?' I lay a light hand on Martin's arm and steer him towards the window. 'Just park your butt on that window seat. It might be better if I take the chair behind the desk.'

Awkwardly Martin perches on the narrow sill.

From the desk drawer, I take out a note-pad and write the date then underline it. I position a silver paper knife at an exact parallel to the top of the leather blotter. I give Martin a brief smile.

He doesn't smile back. The expression in his eyes is hostile but warms as Doreen comes back into the room.

'Tea and a selection of cakes are on their way,' she sings out. 'Martin, are you comfortable over there?'

'Leave the man alone, Doreen.'

For once she doesn't argue as she sinks into the only armchair. We two men wait in silence while she arranges her skirt, jacket; her rather fine legs encased in grey fishnet stockings.

Finally, Doreen relaxes. She beams at us both, enjoying the drama. Her response as Mrs Venables staggers into the study with a laden tray is almost girlish. 'Mrs Venables, you are a treasure. Just leave the tea things on the desk.'

Again we wait till Mrs Venables departs.

'Shall I be mother?' I don't wait for a reply. I hand Martin a plate and a linen napkin. 'Doreen, will you have cake?'

'I will indeed.' She throws Martin a dazzling smile. 'I'm rather partial to a finger of Battenberg.'

'If you could take round the cake-stand, Doreen, I'll give the teapot a stir. Martin. You're frowning. Is there a problem?'

Martin runs a finger between his neck and shirt collar. 'As a rule I steer clear of cake.'

Doreen swings the three tiers of cake temptingly in front of him. 'Do make an exception. Venables does make an excellent Victoria sponge.'

Martin makes a strange sound, half sigh, half snort. It is as if Doreen is offering him poison.

'Oh go on, man. A piece of cake that size won't hurt you,' I tell him.

Desperately, Martin looks at Doreen before grabbing a thin sponge wedge. He tosses it into his mouth and swallows. 'Satisfied?'

I begin to pour the tea, aware of Martin's total discomfort.

'As I recall it's only a drop of milk and no sugar for Martin,' Doreen says brightly. 'Am I right?'

Martin nods.

'Darling.' She leans forward and pats his knee. 'We shouldn't have insisted on you trying the cake, only Venables would have been so disappointed. She made it especially.'

I wipe my hands on a napkin. 'Never mind cake – I think we should get to the point.'

'Gently, Oliver.' Her eyes are pleading.

'Doreen, if you find this too painful, perhaps you'd better wait in the lounge?'

'Can I just say?' Martin waves his teacup at us.

'No, you can't. Not yet. Staying or going, Doreen?'

'Of course I'm staying. Martin, I'm so sorry – this is very embarrassing.'

I pick up the paper knife and rap twice on the desk. 'To cut to the chase, Doctor Renshawe, are you having an affair with Doreen's son?'

'I'd just like to put this into context –'

'Well, I'd rather you didn't. Personally, I couldn't care less who you carry on with. But in this instance, a relationship with Junior – who I believe is a patient of yours – strikes me as unprofessional conduct.'

Doreen half rises out of her chair. 'That's very harsh, Ollie.'

'My name is Oliver. Please sit down. Over to you, Doctor.'

Martin leans back against the window and makes a steeple of his fingers. He takes a moment to organise his thoughts before turning to face Doreen.

'My dear, it is a well-known fact that patients frequently develop crushes on their doctors.' Voice like warm treacle, Martin allows himself a self-deprecating smile. 'Or even mentors. This can lead to further fixations, mistaking warm concern for a reciprocation of feelings, even to imagining that certain situations have occurred. Which I assure you, haven't.'

With relief, Doreen looks at me. 'There you are. I knew there was nothing in it. What a storm in a teacup.' She reaches for a second finger of Battenberg. 'My son's a sensitive, impressionable young man, who unfortunately lost his father at a time when he was most needed. Martin, I didn't for one minute think –'

'Subject closed.' Martin pulls a packet of cigarettes from the pocket of his sports jacket. 'Nobody minds if I smoke, do they?'

'Go ahead.' Doreen jumps to her feet and hurries towards the desk. 'There's an ashtray in here somewhere.'

As she pulls open a drawer, I take hold of her wrist and pull her hand away. I pass Martin the ashtray and slam the drawer shut. 'We haven't finished yet.'

'Surely we have? Let's leave the mucky subject. I don't want to put Martin through any more of an ordeal.'

Martin lights his cigarette and exhales a perfect circle of smoke. 'I might remind you, Oliver, that I've known this family for years. Since Junior was a babe in arms. Obviously I'm extraordinarily hurt that he should concoct such a farrago of lies about me, although as I've explained, this type of behaviour is well-documented. What has been most heart-breaking,' he inhales deeply, 'was that my dearest woman friend should believe his lies.'

Doreen is devastated. 'Martin, I never believed it, but Junior is my son. If you'd seen him the other evening. He was distraught. I couldn't just sweep his insinuations under the carpet. You must understand that.' She holds out her hands in supplication.

Again, I rap sharply on the desk with the blade of the knife. 'Doreen, will you please sit down?'

'I'm having palpitations.'

'Then have them in the comfort of that armchair.'

Martin stubs the cigarette out in the ashtray. 'I'm amazed that you let Oliver talk to you like that. He's nothing but a glorified bully.'

I smile thinly. 'May I remind you, Doctor Renshawe, that your wife also asserts that you are having an affair with Junior?'

Martin is on his feet. 'My wife is none of your damn business.'

'It is my business when she tries to twist Junior's ear off in broad daylight. It is my business if she tells all and sundry at a party to celebrate mine and Doreen's engagement. Surely you didn't expect to have your cake and eat it?'

'As I said earlier, I steer clear of cake.' His face is contorted into an expression of dislike.

'Madge never told all and sundry, did she?' Doreen looks horrified.

It is my turn now to get to my feet. 'I heard it from at least three different sources, including Carpenter.'

Now Doreen is standing.

The study seems suddenly very crowded.

She takes a hesitant step towards Martin. The top of her head is level with his impressive biceps. Enviously, I note that they are bulgingly visible even through the sleeves of a shirt and corduroy jacket.

Martin looks tenderly into Doreen's upturned face. 'Doreen, dearest Doreen, you must know who holds the Number One spot in my heart?'

Her eyes fill with tears. Her lips tremble.

Martin throws his arms wide for her to enter his embrace.

She takes a second step towards him. The large diamond of her engagement ring seems to throw out a shower of sparks as her hand shoots up and slaps Martin's left cheek.

'Don't you dare "dearest Doreen" me! You're a bloody philanderer and I'm the fool to have paid you thirty quid a week to help my poor innocent lad for the last two years. All you've managed to do is turn him into a homo-sexual.' Her chin juts forward aggressively.

In the past I've found Doreen's jutting chin unappealing but on this occasion I am inclined to applaud.

Martin's eyes have narrowed to unpleasant slits. 'Your son *is* a homosexual.'

'And what does that make you?' I ask quietly.

It is Martin who finally breaks the silence.

In a completely altered voice he says, 'I really don't know.' The anger has left his face, all energy drained from his frame; even his broad shoulders sag.

He looks his age. Rather than triumphant, I suddenly feel sorry for the man.

Head lowered, Martin buttons his jacket with meticulous care. 'I apologise to both of you. My position at the moment is untenable. My own fault. A weakness of character. Call it what you will. I take complete responsibility for whatever occurred between Junior and myself. Believe me, it was foolish but it wasn't a foolish whim. I do – did care for him. Now if you'll both excuse me.' He thrusts past Doreen, opens the study door and strides out into the corridor.

'Oliver, stop him.'

'Let him go.'

I step out from behind the desk, take her gently by the shoulders and draw her towards me. 'The facts remain. He has made your son and his own wife very unhappy.'

'He's always behaved like such a gentleman towards me,' Doreen whimpers into my jacket lapel.

We hear the front door slam and the crunch of hurrying footsteps on the gravel path outside. Over Doreen's bent head I survey the room; the debris from the afternoon tea, crumpled cushions on the window seat, the discarded napkins, the half-smoked cigarette in Martin's saucer and the crumbs on the Persian rug.

'Let's get out of here. Leave it for Mrs Venables to clear up. What say you, Doreen?'

'I'll just pop upstairs and get my car coat.'

Doreen will be some time. No doubt she'll re-apply powder and lipstick or help herself to a vodka miniature. She may even change into something different. I return to the lounge and slowly read the newspaper article. This entire summer I've spent sheltering within a protective and pleasant bubble. I've rarely watched the news on television or bothered with anything in the newspaper that seemed serious.

I feel sick with a sense of loss and disloyalty. I want to be back in London, sharing as I'd always shared – the celebrations and tragedies of my city. At a stroke, I've had enough of lunches, afternoon teas, being chauffeured around Yorkshire, seeing all that was agreeable and nothing that truly matters.

'Ready?' Doreen calls from the hall.

My holiday is over.

Chapter 25

1975

'I love Yorkshire,' Martin said with apparent relish.

Junior desperately wanted to reply, 'I love you,' but didn't. It was clear that the space he had occupied in his beloved's heart was now given over only to a fondness for the county and memories of a long-haired dachshund called Jed, pet friend of Martin's youth. Martin had brought down a barrier between them. For self-preservation – Junior understood that.

'Coffee, Martin?' Junior took a flask from his rucksack. He had spread his tartan travel blanket on a patch of dry grass on the flat outcrop halfway up Burnglas Point. The winding hill path, popular with walkers was merely twenty yards away but the two men were shielded from sight by a hedge of straggling juniper bushes.

Martin shook his head. Before making the trek up the hill an hour earlier he'd come to a decision: he would avoid looking directly at Junior. A start must be made on erasing Junior from his life.

That morning he had concentrated his thoughts on dressing as the type of man he most wanted to be – a man of incredible inner strength who savoured a solitary hike. He'd chosen a brushed cotton shirt, thorn-proof trousers and dusty leather walking boots. The boots had only ever been worn on one godforsaken holiday with Madge. It had been during the early days of their marriage when she'd expressed a yearning to spend a fortnight in Berwick-on-Tweed. After four days of torrential rain, spending interminable hours with Madge visiting antique and tea shops, he'd bought a map of the local area and strode out alone each day after breakfast.

'I'm an outdoors man,' he'd told her. 'I need to commune with the elements. I can't be caged.'

Wistfully, he recalled finding a sheltered spot on the beach about two miles outside Madge's possible jurisdiction, where he'd sat for hours demanding of the grey sea and matching sky whether this was all he could expect from his life?

He'd never cleaned the boots and now he was glad that he hadn't. Any mud had dried and fallen away years ago, but the boots still looked scuffed and well used – the footwear of a man who had possibly earned his walking stripes in the Andes. Martin made a mental note to check on 'walking in the Andes' before he used that line in public. He realised that he was smiling at the perceived complexity of his own character. *This won't do, Martin.*

He allowed himself the smallest peek at Junior. Dressed in white trousers, an embroidered collarless shirt and royal-blue espadrilles, he looked ready for some light clothes shopping in Chelsea.

Martin thrust his hand through his thick brown hair, for once not congratulating himself on how thick his hair remained. How he would miss the boy. He returned to his study of the horizon. Burnside shimmered in the heat on the far side of the neat fields of green and gold. He could even make out his own house. Had he brought binoculars, it might have been possible to spot Madge working in their front garden.

Over breakfast she'd threatened to clear away his petunias, which she knew *he* liked to do in the second week of September. Martin had kept his head bent over the newspaper aware that she was willing him to look up and say something. Keeping silent had taken all his willpower.

He liked and respected Madge. Madge was reliable and a good sport. She was an excellent listener, which, for a man like himself who loved to talk, he acknowledged as of priceless worth. But married life with a loving Madge stretching on till death, the lack of excitement for ever and ever – how would he bear it?

'Martin?' Junior laid a hand on his knee.

'Please don't touch me.' Martin brushed Junior's hand away. He closed his eyes, blotting out Yorkshire and tried to imagine himself somewhere else with Junior Mildmay. It wouldn't work. Wherever they went, Junior would be mistaken for his son. Or a client. There would be no settling down to an accepted Madge equivalent. Through gritted teeth he said, 'Junior, we cannot see each other anymore. We cannot pretend to be client and counsellor. I'm telling you this as a friend.' Martin gulped, his eyes filling, 'Someone who deeply cares about your welfare.'

'What about *my* happiness?'

Junior surprised him by not sounding sulky, hurt or even annoyed.

'There is no promise of happiness for any of us, damn it. I am not going to be happy. Madge is not going to be happy. There may be a chance that, at some point in the future, you will find happiness.' Awkwardly, Martin clambered to his feet, brushing non-existent grass from his trouser legs. He pulled a clean white handkerchief from his pocket and waved it at Junior. 'Ironed and washed by my wife,' he shouted before blowing his nose loudly with it.

'I can wash and iron handkerchiefs,' Junior said.

'You can do a damn sight better than that with your life. Bottom line, leave. Get out. Do me that one favour.'

'You'll miss me.'

'I'll get over it. I have to. I'm going now. If I meet you in the street I won't acknowledge you. As far as I'm concerned, you're dead to me. Sorry, but it has to be that way.'

Martin parted the bushes and pushed through. He almost ran back to the path, barged between a group of walkers and their dogs, went slithering down the hill, his boots sending up plumes of dust. Finally he paused for breath. He couldn't help it, he had to look back, just the once, before he reached the bend in the path. Junior remained as he'd left him, sitting cross-legged on the blanket, his head bent in concentration as he poured himself a coffee from the flask. Martin would have preferred to make his way homewards with the image of Junior's pale, stricken face staring after him, lodged forever in his memory. Not even that wish would be granted. He wondered how his own face looked and feared it must be drawn and old.

One hand on the gate, Martin paused to survey his front garden. The tubs were empty. His petunias were gone.

The front door opened and there stood Madge wearing one of her many aprons, a trowel in her hand.

'Are you coming out to do more damage?' he snarled, pushing the gate open.

Her gaze travelled upwards, stopping at his hot, sweating face.

Defensively, he said, 'I've been for a walk. Presumably, I am allowed time outside my home or the practice rooms?'

'Martin. Please don't use that tone of voice with me.'

'God, Madge, you're laughable. I see you've even bought yourself a cheap trowel. What are you trying to prove?'

She ignored him and began to turn over the soil in the nearest tub.

'Leave that alone,' he barked.

The only sign that she'd heard him was the pink colour creeping up from the neck of her blouse. In two strides Martin reached her and grabbed the trowel.

'You do realise those petunias had at least another two weeks of life left? It is still summer. You've managed to transform this garden into a bloody desert.'

Madge stood her ground on the gravel path. 'I'm putting in winter pansies and spring bulbs.'

'The soil is contaminated.' He waved her trowel to take in all eight of the wooden tubs. 'Probably rotten with disease and hibernating aphids.' He would have liked to have made this a metaphor for their marriage but felt he needed some time alone in his study to construct it effectively.

'Give me back my trowel.'

'No. I'm confiscating it. A cheap trowel like this won't last a season anyway.' His voice softened, became almost affectionate: 'I suggest you go indoors and attend to the duties you so excel at.'

'Don't you dare patronise me.'

Taking a deep breath, Martin said, 'I was attempting – unsuccessfully – to diffuse a difficult situation. What I'm trying to say is that normal service is now resumed. The affair with Junior Mildmay is over. Finished. I've ended it.'

Madge's eyes filled with tears. He couldn't help feeling just a little irritated. *What more did the woman want? Blood?*

'I expect he's heartbroken.' Madge wiped her eyes with a corner of her apron.

'He's young. He'll get over it. Can we go inside now?'

He felt horribly tired. The anger expended over the petunias had exhausted him. He wondered if Madge would mind if he went to lie down in the cool and comfort of the spare room. With the curtains closed, and a pillow under his head he could try and make some sense of a future for himself. Tentatively, he put an arm around her shoulders and they walked into the house.

'I'll make tea. We could sit in the sun lounge.' Madge smiled up at him. 'I know you don't eat very much cake, but I've made a Victoria sponge. It's very light.'

Only an effort of supreme will kept Martin's arm about her shoulders. He thought of the cake he'd been forced to eat the previous afternoon at Mildmay's. He could have laughed wildly, he could have had a mid-life crisis – he certainly felt that he deserved to indulge in one. That was how women destroyed you – with cake and kindness.

At that moment he hated Madge. She made him think of a drab, yet plucky little sparrow. Had he owned a gun he would have shot her dead and felt not a twinge of remorse. Didn't she appreciate the sacrifice he was making?

They reached the kitchen and he was able to remove his arm and slump into a chair, letting Madge's trowel drop to the floor.

'Madge, you'll have to make some allowances for me over the next few weeks. Junior is out of my life, but obviously our relationship did not just represent a passing whim. It meant something to me.'

Cradling the kettle against her pinafored breast, Madge said, 'Do you mind if we don't talk about this anymore? I'd rather not think of you and him together. Ideally I'd like this to become a misunderstanding. Nothing more than a dalliance – someone long ago who had a crush on my good-looking husband. An affair that never went further than 'what if?'.'

'That's all very well, Madge –'

She held up the kettle to silence him. 'Otherwise my life will be unbearable. Surely you understand how I feel? As a counsellor as well as my husband?'

His shoulders drooped. He was well and truly beaten. Nothing was a game anymore. More than ever he needed that darkened, silent room.

'Of course I understand.' He tried to smile but his mouth refused to follow instructions.

'You go out into the sun lounge. I'll bring in the tray, darling,' Madge said softly.

Martin winced.

'You'll find the new Unwins flower catalogue on your chair,' she continued. 'I've earmarked some plants you might like to order for the front borders and the tubs. I didn't realise *astroemaria* came in such gorgeous blues. In clumps they could look quite extraordinary.'

Chapter 26

1975

As the train pulls into Brockstead Station, I am jolted awake by a neighbouring passenger manhandling her shopping bags from the rack above my head. For a few seconds I have no idea where I am or why I'm on a train. In my dream I was very definitely still in my Earls Court flat having a row with Doreen. Her 'I've had just about as much as I can take' rings in my ears.

There is something about this train journey from Liverpool Street out into Hertfordshire that has a soporific effect on me. Perhaps after living in the Yorkshire Dales for several weeks I find the scenery of small houses, small back gardens, small parks and even small trees unimpressive. There hasn't been much sky either. I've grown fond of the Yorkshire sky. Having rarely taken an interest in anything that didn't concern London, the northern sky has come as a fresh wonder. So much of it and forever changing.

Although it's only early September, I'm glad that I've brought my alpaca overcoat. I slip it on then wait patiently behind a group of cyclists and cycles jostling each other good naturedly to be first off the train.

I judge them all to be in their late twenties, early thirties, but they seem incredibly young and fresh faced. Their voices are full of laughter and affection for each other, although this may be sentimentality on my part as I am in a strange sad mood. They spill out onto the platform and I follow along slowly, letting a distance develop between us.

Today, there is a porter at the barrier. 'If you need a taxi, you can get one at the pub,' he says, punching my ticket.

'It's no distance. I shall walk.'

Something in my voice, or perhaps the sombre clothes, prompts the porter to look more keenly at me. 'Are you here for the funeral?'

My eyes prickle. 'No, just the – whatever comes afterwards – wake, reception.' I fight a desire to mention Steve by name.

'Mr Chambers will be missed,' the porter says.

'He will indeed.'

Outside the station, I pause. The cyclists are now a fading spot of colour in the distance. There is the telephone box I'd used to ring The Club on my first visit. How hot that day had been. I look at my watch. As always I am far too early. Many of the mourners won't be back from the funeral for at least three-quarters of an hour.

I'd made a conscious decision not to go to Steve's funeral. The idea of Steve being dead, when one of my most recent memories is of him vigorously pushing his way through a beech hedge at the Templar's Arms and in a way saving *my* life, was too vivid and... magical. I wanted it to always stay fresh for me, as if he hadn't died – just gone to live abroad.

I take a few steps in the opposite direction and open the wooden gate leading to the muddy towpath. It has rained for several days but a weak sun is struggling through the clouds. The temperature seems to have dropped into the low fifties.

I seem to feel the cold more. I blame Doreen's central heating. The house has been like a furnace all summer. But I don't want to think about Doreen; this is Steve's day. I find the bench facing the canal that Steve and I sat on only a few weeks ago. It is almost dry.

Hot and cold. Dry and wet. Then and now – how fortune can turn on a sixpence. All the years I've spent patronising the man, but by god, he lived his life to the full.

My newly discovered sense of humour raises its head as I acknowledge that I am not so distraught as to demand of any hovering deity, 'Lord, take me. My friend, Steve, is by far the better human being.' Although, hand on heart, there is no doubt in my mind that Steve *was* by far the better human being.

It is painful to remember him as he was that very last time I was down here. He'd been too thin and the skin around his eyes seemed stretched unnaturally, but with his tan and thick mop of brown hair, the impression at a glance was of a man still in perfect health. But only at a glance. Anyone who'd known Steve well could see how ill he was.

Steve had surprised me; he'd never met me off the train before. 'Hello, old buddy,' he'd drawled. 'You travel mighty light!'

We'd both laughed as Steve took over the handle of my heavy black Samsonite suitcase. Stepping out into the sunlight, he'd stowed the case on the back seat of a vintage Armstrong Siddeley Sapphire saloon.

Once I'd have been jealous of Steve owning such a car, but not anymore. 'You must be making money hand over fist,' I'd said admiringly.

'An old aunt died and left me a pile of the filthy stuff.' He'd grinned.

I still don't know if the 'old aunt' dying was true or not.

'That's my life.' Steve started the car. 'Feast or famine! How's the world treating you?'

'Blood is trickling back into my veins,' I'd replied. For some reason that had amused us both.

I watch a figure step onto the path about twenty yards away. It could easily be Steve, except he'd never walk along a muddy towpath. Or perhaps he would, but not with me. Steve rightly assumed that I wasn't a man who liked getting his shoes dirty!

The man on the towpath is almost level with the bench. He also wears a dark suit, the trousers tucked into Wellington boots. On his back is a smart canvas rucksack.

'Not a bad morning is it?' the man says, without slowing his brisk pace.

I pull off one of my leather gloves, clench my fingers and raise my thumb as Steve would have done. The man passes me by.

I consider our exchange. Is this grey dampness really considered 'not a bad morning' by the people of Brockstead?

The man is moving away at quite a pace. In the summer, down by the canal, it is a scenic route but not today. Today it is miserable. The couple of houseboats moored along the bank look uninhabited or as if any occupant has chosen to hibernate and won't crawl out till warmer weather arrives. I shiver. The cold is getting inside my coat. Doreen told me to wear a scarf. Foolishly, I'd refused on principal.

'Don't fuss,' I'd said.

'I like to make a fuss of you, my pet,' she'd answered.

At the moment, she and I are allowing ourselves to drift. She wears her engagement ring and I haven't the heart to suggest she takes it off. She knows I'm going but refuses to acknowledge it.

Once I leave, she'll no doubt concoct a story. Knowing Doreen, she won't make herself the victim. She'll tell everyone that I'm useless in bed and she's been forced to send me packing. I won't blame her. She deserves more from life than being stuck with a permanent house guest.

I put my leather glove back on and stand up. For a moment I consider following the man in the Wellington boots to arrive at The Club looking like a chap who enjoys brisk walks beside deserted canals. I decide against it. I would rather arrive looking fresh, immaculate, well-heeled. Steve would approve.

'Oh fuck,' I say aloud, just to relieve the intensity of the sadness washing over me. I thrust my hands deep into my coat pockets: my eyes full, throat swallowing. I set off for The Club.

I'm surprised to find the car park already crowded. People stand by their cars in couples and noisy groups, chatting and laughing as if they've known each other for years. Some of the men wear suits but many more are dressed quite casually. Even if I had my life to live again, I would never turn up on the day of a friend's funeral wearing slacks, open-necked shirt and a linen jacket with the sleeves rolled up almost to the elbows. But then, I remind myself, Steve had adopted this very same style of rolled-up jacket sleeves.

'Miami Vice,' I recall him telling me the last time we met. 'Don Johnson. He's a cool dude.'

I had replied with a hint of amusement, 'He may well be a "cool dude" but he'll have the devil of a job getting the creases out of those sleeves.'

I'd been gratified when Steve roared with laughter. That had been part of our newly-arrived-at-friendship – me. Finally discovering irony. Each time I'd seen Steve or spoken to him on the phone recently, I'd tried my damnedest to be amusing. By then I knew he was dying.

'I'm handing in my chips, old buddy. Joining the invisible choir up-top.' Steve had any number of phrases to make light of his advanced prostate cancer.

I've tried to imagine myself in the same predicament. What would I say? Very little, probably. 'Doreen, I have a rather unpleasant illness. I don't wish to talk about it but I think I need to get my financial affairs in good order within the next six weeks. After that I'll book into a private hospital and not see or speak to anyone till my death is a *fait accompli*.'

In the men's cloakroom I hang up my coat and scarf and smooth my hair in the mirror. It is incredibly vain of me to be even having such thoughts at a time like this, but I look better than I can remember looking in my entire life. I no longer feel as if a puny body is hiding inside my clothes. I've filled out. Not fat – muscle. I wash my hands. Behind me, someone else comes into the cloakroom. It is the man from the towpath. In the mirror, we nod at each other.

He sits on the one chair and takes a pair of black leather shoes from his rucksack.

I leave him pulling off his Wellington boots. I'm suddenly embarrassed witnessing the vulnerability of another man's socked feet. I follow the sound of conversation and glasses being clinked, out onto the deck. As I step through the open French windows again I feel an emotional tug: I would never again come to this deck, to this club, to this 'benighted hole of Brockstead', never see Steve striding towards me waving an overlarge Whisky Sour and hailing his 'old buddy'.

Someone lightly touches my elbow. 'Mr Oliver.'

Irritably I turn round. 'Yes?'

The woman is almost as tall as I am. At least the same age, I hazard. Her hair is a strange metallic orange but not unattractive. From force of habit I assess her navy skirt and matching bolero jacket. Stylish and a good cut but not top quality. Probably from a mid-price chain store. I approve of the discreet glimpse of lace at her neckline and wonder, not for the first time, why Doreen is so incapable of managing, or even understanding, 'discreet'.

'Don't you recognise me?'

I concentrate on her face. Of course! I know that smile. It had welcomed me morning after morning every working day for the best part of twenty years.

'Della!' I feel inordinately pleased to see her.

She appears to be inordinately pleased to see me.

I pat her upper arm.

She looks delighted.

I feel that kissing her on the cheek would be the right and gallant thing to do. Again, she looks delighted.

'Let me get you a drink,' Della says.

'No, let me get you a drink.'

'Gin and tonic, then. Ice and a slice.'

'*Mais naturellement*.'

As I push through the crowd – they are all too cheerful and noisy to be described as mourners – to the outside bar area, I wonder where that had come from. Possibly Carpenter's influence. Although he's given up his French evening class, he still comes out with the odd phrase. I believe the silly devil thinks it makes him seem sophisticated.

Making my slow return across the crowded deck, our drinks held aloft, I am able to better appraise Della. She has found an isolated table overlooking the canal; her chin rests on one hand as she watches a barge moving upstream. I am struck by her rather fine profile. The word 'heroic' comes into my head, followed by the question, 'But what is she doing here?'

As I move closer, I realise why I hadn't immediately recognised her: apart from the signature dyed hair, Della isn't wearing make-up. No black eyeliner, no thick mascara, no orange tan. As I approach the table, she looks up at me and I cannot read the expression in her eyes. Assessing? Critical?

There is a moment's awkward silence as I sit down. I have the oddest feeling that our drinks call out for a maraschino cherry each.

Della reaches for her glass. 'If you don't mind my saying, Mr Oliver, you look terrific. Leaving The Store seems to have done you the world of good.'

I feel as if the sun has broken through the cloud. 'Why, thank you Della.'

Should I return the compliment or would that deplete Della's compliment?

'How has it been in London?' I ask instead. 'I can't believe that I wasn't even aware of the Oxford Street bombing. My city, my part of London.' Just saying these few sentences to Della upsets me. They bring back memories of the IRA bombings the year before, how I'd made light of them. What the devil had changed?

Lightly Della touches my hand. 'We live with it. You know we do. Worse this summer, so many false alarms as well.'

'But nobody from The Store was hurt?'

The woman read my mind. I swear she almost smiled. 'They're all still alive and kicking, including Miss Frances.'

We sip our drinks companionably, and slowly I recall why I'm here and begin to wonder why Della is also here

'Had you known Steve long?' I ask.

'Steve?'

'Steve Chambers. The man whose wake this is.'

'I didn't know him at all.' Della reaches for her handbag.

Soft-grained navy leather. A Chanel copy, I decide.

'Chanel.' Della catches my glance. 'Cost a fortune. A present from my late husband, Stan, on our thirtieth wedding anniversary.' She takes out a sheet of Club notepaper and hands it to me. 'I received this about ten days ago. It was posted to The Store. For Della c/o Bridalwear.'

I recognise Steve's scrawl, only even more untidy than usual. He must have written the letter only a day or so before he died.

'Dear Della, you don't know me, but I've heard a bit about you over the last few months. I've rather taken on the role of guardian angel looking out for my good buddy, Sydney Oliver. But life being the wayward bitch it can be, I'm on the point of hanging up my spurs any day now. I've arranged a post-funeral shindig, high noon on the twelfth of September. I know he will be there and I'd appreciate it if you could have a few words, remind him of the old days before The Fall from Grace. If you can't make it or feel it's that hoary old chestnut of being 'not appropriate', nil problemo. All best, Steve Chambers.'

The letter flutters to the table. I turn my chair to face the canal. Della takes a paper tissue from her handbag and presses it into my hand.

'Thank you,' I say.

A few minutes later I put the tissue into my pocket and begin to sip my drink. As if I'd known Della, really known Della for most of my life, I begin to talk.

*

So this is what I'm reduced to – hanging about in the kitchen with Venables. Carpenter's at work, god alone knows where Junior is and Oliver's gone off gallivanting to a funeral.

Doreen sank onto a chair at the scrubbed pine table.

'I heard it from the postmistress.' Venables spooned plain flour into a sieve over a mixing bowl. 'If she wants to deny it, let her come and deny it to my face. As you know, ma'am, I am not a carrier of gossip, but I felt you should be aware of what is going on behind your back.'

Why wasn't I invited? The man had been a guest at my party. How typical of Oliver to keep this death a secret, right up until the very last moment.

'All I need to do is change into a darker outfit.' I'd cornered him at the front door. 'I won't take more than five minutes.'

'No Doreen.'

'But why not?'

'Because I want to go on my own. I have a taxi waiting.'

'But I want to go with you.'

'It's a funeral, not chicken and chips in the pub.'

'We could go for chicken and chips afterwards. They never provide much food at funerals.'

He'd shaken his head. 'I'll be back in the evening. There might be time to pop down to the Templar's Arms for a late supper.'

'Don't do me any favours,' I'd shouted.

'I should think half Burnside must be talking about it by now.' Venables began to weigh out margarine.

'Talking about what? Personally I'm not fond of tittle-tattle.'

'Not tittle-tattle at all. I don't take kindly to being branded a liar by a woman who doesn't know her seven times table and can't find a husband for love nor money.'

Doreen felt the novel urge to reach across and soothingly pat Venables' hand, but the difference between her own smooth manicured hand and Venables' rough blunt-fingered one, made her feel very slightly uncomfortable. 'If you like, I can ask my solicitor to write to the postmistress demanding a retraction.'

'That won't be necessary. I'm more than capable of dealing with Lizzie Baxter.'

Doreen tried to look animated. 'And who is Lizzie Baxter?'

'The postmistress, of course.' There was a note of unfamiliar irritation in Venables' voice. 'You went to school with her.'

'Did I? I don't remember.'

'That's because in those days, you only had eyes for Martin Renshawe.'

'Martin and I were certainly school friends, which isn't quite the same thing. Can we leave the pastry till later? I have a terrible headache. If you could just sit down for a moment.'

Venables wiped her hands on her overall. 'I'm making a pot of tea. Do you want a cup?'

'Yes please.' What she badly needed was a drink but she couldn't bring herself to just ask for one. Or get it herself.

Doreen waited, her hands folded in her lap, while Venables boiled the kettle and laid out cups and saucers. With an interest she rarely felt, she looked round the kitchen. Every item, every utensil, tiles, cooker, hob, furniture, she'd personally chosen at least five years earlier. Yet they were all unfamiliar, as if they'd belonged to somebody else's life. Extraordinary to think there had been a time when she'd possessed a stock of crisp patterned aprons. She recalled matching oven gloves. With a pang, she remembered that the brand new family kitchen had been one of the house's main attractions

'He indulged me,' she said.

'Pardon?'

'Peter.' She almost smiled. 'My husband. He indulged me and I got lazy.'

Venables put the teapot in front of her. 'Why don't you pour our teas?'

'Do you think I got lazy?'

'Not for me to say.' She pulled out a chair on the other side of the table and sat down.

'But you must have an opinion?' Picking up the teapot, Doreen began to fill her own cup. She hesitated before reaching across for Venables' cup and saucer, filling that instead.

'Well, do you want to know what's happened or don't you?' Venables folded her arms.

Doreen didn't want to know what had happened, nor did she like Venables' rather aggressive tone of voice. But somehow

Venables, for the moment at least, represented the responsible adult, and she, Doreen, was turned into the fourteen-year-old schoolgirl sitting in a small kitchen with her mother and her mother's friend. Audrey. That had been Venables' name.

'Please go on.'

Venables raised her cup to her lips, sipped, then grimaced. 'You should have let the pot stand for a few minutes.' She lowered the cup back onto the saucer. 'On Wednesday, just as Lizzie – the postmistress – was drawing down the shutters for half-day closing, Martin Renshawe came in. He handed her a form to re-direct his mail to an address in London. "Off on holiday?" Lizzie asked. "Family business," he said. "Will Mrs Renshawe be travelling with you? You've only made the re-direction form out in your name." Lizzie said. "I'm speaking at several conferences discussing the male menopause and its effect on the economy. Not a subject for my wife."'

Venables scraped back her chair. She picked up her cup and Doreen's cup, carried them across to the sink and threw away the tea. 'Let's begin again. I like a strong cup and this is more like gnat's piss.'

I must be in a bad state, Doreen thought. *Under normal circumstances, Venables wouldn't dream of using a phrase like 'gnat's piss' in front of me and I wouldn't dream of letting her.*

Instead, Doreen waited patiently while Venables made a fresh pot and left it to stand – produced clean cups and saucers, dropped in two sugar cubes for herself and sweeteners for Doreen. After exactly three minutes Venables stirred the tea and poured it, then added milk.

'You'll feel better if you drink it while it's hot.'

Doreen did as she was told. Again she felt like a child.

'As you know, I'm generally in the kitchen by seven every morning.'

Doreen nodded. *To get here by seven must mean getting up at six. How horrible!*

'This morning, just after seven, I heard a car turning into the drive. I went to the kitchen window. The front door opened and Junior came down the steps with his overnight bag. He was followed by your Mr Oliver – who was carrying a suitcase.'

'But Oliver has gone to a funeral. He certainly didn't take a suitcase with him.'

Venables blew on her tea. 'Only Junior got into the taxi. The driver stowed the suitcase in the boot and then Mr Oliver handed him two ten pound notes.'

'I don't understand.'

'Martin Renshawe was in the back of the cab.'

Doreen pushed her cup and saucer away. It was two o'clock. She now desperately needed a drink, followed by Venables slowly and concisely repeating the bit about Martin in the post office.

Venables sighed deeply. 'Your son and Martin Renshawe have gone away together.'

'Surely not? Junior wouldn't leave without saying goodbye.'

'But he has left. He's taken most of the clothes from his wardrobe and some from the laundry room.'

Doreen sat very still. Her head ached, her eyes were sore and her mouth felt completely dry. Was she coming down with flu?

'Might I trouble you for a drink, Mrs Venables?'

'More tea?'

'I was thinking of something with a kick in it.' Doreen knew her smile was ingratiating but she felt quite desperate.

Venables didn't immediately answer. She appeared to be considering and then she said, in a firm yet gentle voice that Doreen couldn't remember having heard before, 'I'm going to say "no".'

Chapter 27

1975

Martin stood in the bedroom doorway, a towel knotted at his waist. He watched Junior – asleep, lying on his stomach, one bare arm hanging from the bed, his pale hand almost touching the carpet.

Have I ever slept like that? So completely? Martin asked himself. *I don't think so.*

They'd been at Mr Oliver's flat for three days. It seemed almost laughable to Martin now that he'd packed a pair of pyjamas. They were still at the bottom of his suitcase. A pyjama-less life beckoned. He imagined himself in some idyllic future, padding barefoot around an airy, stylish apartment – Madge either conveniently dead or happily married to a sheep farmer in South Wales. He saw glass double-doors thrown open onto a minimalist garden, the starkness relieved by topiarised box hedges rearing out of brutalist stone cubes.

Martin shook the images from his head. He had rarely allowed himself to daydream. Artistic people, literary types, creative thinkers, had always seemed contemptible to him. There was no room for daydreaming or 'what-ifs' in psychology. 'Search and ye shall find' had been the mantra of one of his university professors. That phrase offered a certainty that had satisfied him – until now.

Pleasurably he unknotted the towel around his waist and let it drop to the floor. A slight breeze filtered in through the open window and played on his bare skin. The sensation was – sheer bliss! Another first. No furtive feelings, no underlying sense of guilt, he could actually stand stark naked in a bedroom and feel this was the natural way for a man to be. Of course, deep down he had always known it, but marrying Madge, flirting with Doreen, all the ploys he'd developed to create the illusion that he was a man who adored women, had inevitably resulted in a barrier between what was real and what was his carefully created fiction.

Martin, you are becoming over-fond of analysing yourself! But am I?

Since creeping out of his house just after dawn three days earlier, Martin had found himself with time to just think. He had been amazed and relieved to find that Junior didn't expect to be amused every moment of the day. Junior was able to sit quietly and read a book, could be trusted to go down onto the Earls Court Road and return an hour later with ingredients for a meal and a good bottle of wine. Martin had experienced the novelty of genuine laughter. He had never realised how insincere his own laughter had been till the real stuff had spilled out of him. He was unnerved. Was this all too good to be true, or too damn good to ever again turn his back on?

Pulling on his clothes, Martin padded into the dark galley kitchen. The flat told him a lot about Oliver. He could have prepared a thorough case history just by spending five minutes contemplating each room. Here lived a man who had chosen to spend his time in a series of small, gloomy boxes that little natural light ever reached. Within the few kitchen cupboards, Martin had discovered everything a man might need but nothing he would have greatly desired. In the unlikely event of Oliver ever popping in for a drink he would be greatly surprised by the additions to the cupboard shelves: bags of pasta, jars of olives and pimentos, packets of herbs, and a bottle of virgin olive oil. New pans and kitchen knives had been purchased from Habitat. In the even more unlikely event of Madge popping in for a drink, she would be equally surprised.

'But Martin, you've always loved your roast beef and Yorkshire pudding. You said I made the best gravy in the county.'

As Martin waited for the filter coffee to drip into the cup, he realised that he was humming. The melody was familiar but he couldn't immediately place it.

Madge had frequently accused him of being tone deaf. That had been one of the clichés of their marriage – one partner laying claim to music, books, hobbies that automatically cancelled out any claim the other might have had on them. Madge loved 'serious music'. She went to concerts, tuned in to the Proms concerts, and was up to 'S' for Sibelius in her LP collection of 'An A to Z of Classical Music'.

After an interminable evening listening to Brahms, Martin had once stated, 'Of course, I'm more of a Mahler man, myself.' She'd given him a look which had clearly said, *Don't try your phoney tricks on me, Martin Renshawe. I see right through them.*

In the nineteen-fifties, early sixties, he had genuinely liked the Everly Brothers; not Elvis who he'd found too overtly sexual. Then suddenly The Beatles were everywhere and he hadn't liked them at all. They'd seemed like callow boys, not men. He remembered being furious when Madge had owned up to having a favourite Beatle – Paul McCartney.

'And exactly what is his appeal?'

'I'd have liked my son to be like Paul McCartney.'

'Then thank god we never had a son.' Martin walked out of the room but all his anger had gone. At the time he remembered being quite upset because Madge had still been young enough to have a child, and there she was, already assuming that she never would.

Martin took a small carton of cream from the fridge and added a dash to his coffee. He'd have to be careful or the pounds would begin to pile on. He thought of Oliver – dapper rather than physically masculine. Something of an enigma. He could imagine a certain type of woman being attracted to him. Doreen, for one.

He snapped his fingers. He was humming a Strauss waltz, The Blue Danube. Doreen and Oliver had danced to it at their engagement party.

'Da-da-dadada,' he sang out as he reached for an enamel tin marked 'Biscuits'. Inside was an unopened fresh packet of chocolate biscuits. He would allow himself just one. He took his coffee and the packet out onto the balcony and placed them on the wrought iron table, then went back inside and returned with a cushion for the cold iron chair. He sat down. Another first. He had never sat on a balcony before.

Across the road, a mere twenty yards away, there were other balconies, some of them occupied. A woman was watering several pots of petunias. *Of course it's warmer in London*, he thought. Directly opposite, two men about the same age as Martin sat each side of a very similar table, their faces almost touching. As Martin assessed them, one of the men turned his head so that he was looking directly across the road at him. Quickly Martin averted his gaze, moving his chair slightly.

He raised his coffee cup to his lips. There was no reason for the coffee to taste like the finest in the world, but still it did.

Martin reminded himself sternly that all these few days

represented was a sublime holiday. Madge, divorce, definite shame and a ruined professional career would have to be faced. Martin closed his eyes and savoured the warmth of the afternoon sun. For now, at least, he'd bask in the glow of having taken a risk, stepped out of line, off the beaten track, attempted to be true to himself.

Thank you, Oliver. You old bastard.

And Carpenter as well, standing with them on the platform at Harrogate Station, looking awkward and embarrassed but also concerned.

'Are you okay for money, Martin?'

Martin had patted the breast pocket of his corduroy jacket and produced his most genial smile. 'Plenty of cash, but thanks for asking.'

'Madge can't close your bank account or anything like that, can she?'

Martin hadn't been able to keep the genial smile in place. Actually Madge could easily close their joint bank account. In fact he expected her to do so within a very few hours of realising that he'd left her. 'Oh, don't worry about me. I shall be fine.'

'It's my brother I'm worrying about.'

They'd both turned to look at Junior hurrying towards them with what looked like a paper bag full of sweets.

'For the journey,' Junior said, rustling the bag at them.

Carpenter had taken out his wallet and peeled off a fifty pound note and five tens. He'd handed them to Junior. 'Let me know if you run short.'

Junior stared delightedly at the money as if he'd suddenly become a millionaire. 'Carpenter, thank you. I've never had so much.' He glanced at Martin as he slid the notes into the back pocket of his jeans. 'I'll buy our lunch on the train.'

Carpenter looked alarmed. 'Haven't you got a wallet?'

'I've never needed one.' Junior jingled a pocketful of change.

'No problem,' Martin had said. 'I'll buy him one when we reach London.'

He couldn't remember ever having seen Carpenter look distraught before.

'Junior should have his own wallet. He's got to start being a man. Right now. Junior, are you listening to me? What you are doing isn't a joke. There will be repercussions.' As Carpenter emptied out the contents of his own wallet, the London-bound train came in. 'Put the money in there.'

'I'll pay you back,' Junior said cheerfully.

'I'll hold you to it. Oliver's arranging an interview for you with someone called Edward Flynn, a job in bridal accessories.'

'But I want to be a male model.' Junior struck a pose, head back, one hand on hip.

They'd ignored him.

The kindness of men, Martin thought, as he finished his coffee. Yet all his life he'd avoided close male friendships. He'd nipped any attraction in the bud, choosing to alienate rather than get involved. Apart from Peter Mildmay. But that had been an accident neither had been able to avoid.

'Martin!' Junior called from the bedroom.

Martin got to his feet. 'Do you want a coffee?'

There was a pause as Junior considered his options. 'Eventually.'

*

Carpenter had now missed two evening classes and was surprised to discover that he *did* miss them. While driving home one evening, listening to a radio programme on 'dealing with elderly parents', he'd actually found himself wondering how Sandra's mother was faring and if Sandra knew not to allow her any liquids after five o'clock in the evening? Even Ned now seemed more to be chuckled over than vilified.

In theory he was back on his old footing with Monica but they'd stopped conversing in French, nor did they mention the evening class. Each Friday he drove back to Mildmay's, while she set off on foot towards Burnside College. It felt awkward. The rest of the week he'd grown used to passing her in his car, hooting the horn as she turned into a narrow lane heading for wherever it was she lived; now he began to wonder where she did live. There was nothing in her personnel file. In fact there really wasn't anything in her personnel file. Doreen would have a fit if she found out that he'd employed someone he'd known nothing about.

Brandishing his rock bun he stood in the doorway of his office.

'Monica, do you have far to walk to get here?'

She didn't stop typing. 'It's do-able.'

How her constant typing irked him. 'I could always collect you and drop you to your door.'

'Not necessary.'

'I realise it isn't necessary but I don't like to think of you having to walk miles in the dark now that we're getting into winter.'

'It's only September and really, Carpenter, I like walking.'

He took a bite of bun; talking and chewing at the same time, he continued, 'So where exactly do you live?'

'I'm staying with a friend at the moment.' A burst of staccato typing. 'No fixed abode you could say.'

'Is that a worry?'

'Nope.' Monica paused to Tippex over several words and then blew on the paper.

'Actually Monica, I am just trying to open up a line of conversation. Things between us appear to have been strained recently. My fault I'm sure.'

She didn't reply.

'Would you object if I drank my coffee out here in the general office?'

'You're the boss.'

By the time he'd retrieved his coffee from his own desk, Monica had cleared away all signs of typing and was bent over the open drawer of the filing cabinet. He was staring at the back of her legs, including at least four inches of tanned and perfect thigh.

During winter and spring he'd approved of her berets and cloaks, maxi-skirts and laced boots phases. Presented with his own mother's powdered cleavage every morning at breakfast, he'd felt at ease with a woman wearing more clothes rather than less.

He carried his drink over to the window. It was a hot day. The north of England was enjoying an Indian summer. Three storeys below, the pavement heaved with people wearing skimpy summer clothes. Obviously he couldn't expect Monica to continue wearing woollen maxi-skirts with temperatures reaching eighty, but did she have to wear such a short skirt?

She straightened up, placed one hand in the small of her back, tensed then relaxed her shoulders. She made him think of a pure bred horse, although he knew nothing about horses of any kind.

'Isn't your skirt a tad on the short side?' He poured the dregs of his coffee into the office umbrella plant.

'It's a kilt.' From the cabinet she took out a bulky sales ledger. 'Can you not do that Carpenter? She doesn't like caffeine.'

'Since when?'

'Since her leaves started to wither and turn yellow.' Approaching her desk, the pleats of Monica's kilt swung as if in a brisk breeze before settling several inches above her knees.

'I've not noticed any other young people wearing skirts that short in Burnside.' He pulled out her chair and sat down.

'That's because Burnside is at least twenty years behind the times.'

'Or Harrogate.'

'Thirty years behind the times. Sorry Carpenter, I'd like my chair back now. I've got work to do.' Her voice was unfriendly.

Reluctantly, he got to his feet. In her open bottom drawer he could see the clear plastic file full of typewritten pages. Carpenter put his head on one side and tried to read the top sheet.

Monica nudged the drawer shut with her tanned knee.

His irritation surged back. Monica was no longer a pure bred horse – she worked in a subordinate role for his family firm. 'My mother and her friends buy all their clothes in Harrogate.'

'Exactly.' Unfazed, Monica sat down. 'You're crowding me. Could you stand in front of my desk rather than behind it?'

'I am the boss and you the employee.'

She linked her hands on the typewriter carriage. 'Here we go again.'

'Don't be so damn cheeky.'

Monica fed a fresh sheet of paper, a carbon and a sheet of copy paper into her typewriter and began to type very fast.

'What the devil are you typing now? I wasn't aware that I'd given you any letters.'

'I'm typing "the quick brown fox jumps over the lazy dog".'

'Well stop typing and listen to me.'

Their eyes met. Hers were clear blue, not angry – but challenging.

Any affection he'd ever had for her was gone. It would return, but in its absence he would strike while the iron was hot, take the bull by the horns and leave building bridges for another occasion. He thrust his hands into his trouser pockets in an attempt to look forceful. 'My mother – Doreen – Mrs Mildmay – will be making a visit to this office on Friday.' He removed his hands from his pockets. Monica might think he was playing trouser billiards.

'Your point being?'

'I'm not bothered what length of skirt you wear but, at the end of the day, she is the managing director. She may be bringing her fiancé with her and I'd like us to make a good impression.' He tried to laugh carelessly but instead it came out as a bitter snigger. 'After all, this is an office, not a fashion boutique.'

Monica lowered her head, sat back, her fingers linked together. 'Would she object to trousers?'

'She certainly would. What sort of signals do trousers give out?'

'You wear trousers.'

'Now you're being silly. I'm a man. Women in trousers…'

'Yes?'

'I don't intend to argue with you on this – but please do not wear trousers.'

'In that case I'm sorry, but I will continue to wear a skirt and fashion dictates shorter.' She resumed typing, but slowly with one hand, picking out each letter with her index finger.

Focusing his gaze on Monica's Goddesses of the Eastern Hemisphere calendar, Carpenter considered whether he could get away with saying something along the lines of 'How dare you, you little guttersnipe,' but knew he couldn't. To control his temper, he concentrated on September's Ishtar, goddess of love. He read the caption: Mother of the fruitful breast.

'And that calendar will have to come down. My mother won't find "fruitful breasts" particularly edifying.'

He strode past her and into his office, slamming the connecting door. A few seconds later he came out again. 'I am in charge here and I dictate a longer skirt for my mother's visit. And while I'm in the mood to dictate I'd like to dictate some letters. A good time would be right now!'

From the shoulder bag under her desk, Monica took out her dictation pad and a biro. 'What happened to us both speaking in

French?'

Carpenter hesitated. 'I thought we'd given up on all that.'

She swivelled around in her chair to face him.

For the first time he realised how remarkably pretty she was. He felt uneasy. The last thing he wanted was to start finding Monica physically attractive rather than a comrade to squabble with. And yet, he must have found her attractive, otherwise why had he been so jealous of Ned?

'Why don't you come back to the class?' Her voice was gentle.

'I'd be miles behind.'

'You've always been miles behind. Come on Carpenter. We miss you.'

Carpenter felt as if he'd been landed a blow to the chest. Automatically his shoulders buckled protectively forward. 'I can't imagine your pal Ned missing me in the slightest.' He hated his voice sounding so needy.

Gathering up her notebook and pen, Monica got to her feet. She avoided looking at him. 'Think about it, Carpenter. You could have a life outside. Anyway it's none of my business.'

As he followed her into his office he wanted to ask, 'Outside of what? Let's skip dictation and talk about me for an hour or so.'

Instead he opened a random file, took his time to read the top page and then dictated a letter to the director of a mythical firm at a mythical address about a mythical delivery of faux Victorian skirting boards.

Chapter 28

1974

It had been a ferociously hot summer and now, only late September, the foliage on the trees along Oxford Street was already turning an unhealthy yellow.

The Store was unpleasantly humid, as young boutique customers jostled with more sedate (and well-heeled) regulars. 'Youth merchandise' as Miss Frances chose to call it, had spread its cheap and nasty tentacles into the ladies fashion and cocktail-wear departments. The boutique, celebrating six weeks of stupendous trading, was officially a success. Champagne had been drunk in the boardroom that lunchtime and Miss Frances's promotion to marketing manager while retaining her position as chief buyer, no doubt duly toasted. Claire Daker was tantamount to being the Boutique Manageress, although this didn't officially come into effect till her return from holiday in ten days' time, when she would no longer be obliged to help out in the Bridal Salon or anywhere else in The Store.

I shared none of the celebrations. Yes, I was invited and under normal circumstances would have gone, if only to feed my resentment. But I was not experiencing 'normal circumstances'.

Standing next to the bank of cash registers, I watched each succeeding sale, nearly all of them (in my opinion) cheap and tawdry garments. It would have been satisfying to say as much to the fresh-faced customers but I remained silent.

What had happened to my strategies, my graph paper covered with yellow, grey, every bloody colour of the rainbow ink? What had happened to my mad idea to heap fine clothes, jewellery, anything a young woman could desire, at Claire Daker's feet? Had I fallen at the very first hurdle? Well, yes I had. That image of the two of them together on the train and the implications were burnt into my imagination.

Those of you – and I know that means most of you – who have had some success with relationships, may think me weak. I've laid out my desires, my resolutions and hopes for a sort of future – these remain in my heart but not splendidly so any more. They are like a love-letter penned at the height of an affair – every word is still true yet this letter-writer feels bitterly embarrassed and ashamed. Nothing in my life over the previous twenty years had prepared me for serious failure.

Clear-eyed I saw that Claire Daker couldn't be bought. Lined up on her side were youth and beauty and the careless confidence that these attributes bring. She had no need of anyone she hadn't chosen and thus Miss Frances, a mere twelve years my junior, had stepped in to claim her. I was left with no plan of action but the reckless determination that, to save myself, I must act. In some sane corner of my mind, I knew this to be not just foolish, but dangerous. I smote that small sane corner with a metaphorical sword, annihilated it. I had been sane all my life and where had that got me?

I felt a light touch on my shoulder and swung round.

'Are you all right, Mr Oliver?' The expression in Della's eyes was one of concern.

'Never better. Has Miss Daker come down from the boardroom yet?'

She looked uncomfortable. 'I believe she is back.'

With an exaggerated spreading of my hands I asked, 'Then where is she?'

'She's only a youngster.'

'Am I missing something here?'

'I don't want to get anyone into trouble, Mr Oliver.'

'I'm not asking you to reveal state secrets. I would just like to know what has happened to Miss Daker?'

Della glanced furtively over her shoulder as if she really was about to reveal a state secret. 'According to Mavis, Claire had a bit too much champagne earlier. She's taking a ten minute break in Hanover Square to clear her head.'

'Must I remind you, yet again, that her name is Miss Daker and at three o'clock in the afternoon, boutique manageress or not, she has no right to be taking a ten minute break anywhere?'

Della lowered her head, giving me a bird's eye view of her carefully arranged bronze curls. At the roots her hair was grey. My gaze travelled further to rake across her face. Cruelly, as if examining her under a microscope I drank in every age line, every clogged pore.

She looked up. Our eyes met. Confused, she took a step away from me.

I relented. 'Did I frighten you with my brusqueness?'

'I'm concerned about you, Mr Oliver. You don't look well. Can I get you anything?'

'I've never felt better.'

'You've gone very pallid,' Della said. 'It's the heat.'

'It is not the heat.' Awkwardly, I turned away from her and barged into a woman holding one of the boutique's angora cardigans.

'Look where you're going, mate,' the woman said.

'I wouldn't mate with you if you were the last woman left on the planet; now get out of my way.' With the heel of my hand I pushed her aside.

She looked startled. 'Who are you pushing?'

'You, my dear. And as for that cardigan, it's rubbish. Not real angora. It will shrink, mat and turn yellow under your armpits the first time you wear it.'

'Fuck off!'

'No, you fuck off. You dirty little...'

Della stepped between us. 'Madam, this is the Bridal Salon. If I could take you down to the cash desk.' Gently, she steered the woman away. 'The gentleman is not well. Heat stroke.'

I pulled my handkerchief from the breast pocket of my jacket and mopped my forehead. 'I have not got bloody heat stroke,' I muttered. 'Bitch. Cow.' At that moment I didn't know whether I referred to the customer or Della. Black shapes flickered across my vision. I took two steps towards a chair but could go no further. The floor seemed to be shifting.

'Come on, Mr Oliver, take my arm.' Della had suddenly re-materialised at my elbow.

I despised her red talonned hand as she tried to link my arm through hers. Angrily, I shook her off. 'I'd rather take poison.'

'Gwen, get a chair and a glass of water. Mr Oliver's dehydrated.' Della's voice came from a great distance.

Through clenched teeth I said, 'I will dash any glass of water out of your hand. Do you understand? Can you understand?'

The ground steadied. I felt powerful again. Omnipotent, while everything around me, from Della and Gwen to the actual furniture, dwindled in size. I grasped Della's wrist.

'Mr Oliver, you're hurting me.'

Who cared about hurting Della? Certainly not me. I drew her towards me. 'Della,' my voice was gentle. 'Do you know how it feels to love someone so much that you would risk everything to have them?'

Our mouths were almost touching. I did not want to kiss her, but I wanted her to want me to kiss her.

'I do know.' Her breathing was ragged; her lower lip trembled.

'How would you know?' I could have bitten into her lip. Drawn blood.

'If my Stan was dying in the road, I would step over him – just to get to you.'

That took a second or two to sink in and then I roared with laughter. 'You foolish, foolish woman. I'm talking about Claire Daker. Surely you didn't think I was in love with you?'

She wouldn't look at me. 'I was joking.'

'Are you sure about that, sweetheart?' I was at my nastiest best.

'That's enough, Mr Oliver.' She glanced at her watch. 'If you want to see Miss Daker, I expect she'll be upstairs by now.'

'Thank you.' This time I touched her arm gratefully before striding away towards the lift.

*

Pulling on calfskin gloves – unnecessary in the heat but the perfect complement to her mustard-coloured suede jacket – Miss Frances observed herself in the mirror above the filing cabinet in her office. Remembering that moment in the boardroom earlier, when Claire Daker had turned and hugged her, she should have felt triumphant; instead she was thoroughly miserable.

'Well done us,' Claire had murmured against her ear.

Once again, Miss Frances berated herself; she had taken a phrase out of context and begun to build a foolish castle in the air. What exactly did those three words mean other than 'congratulations'?

'So Claire, where are you off to for your holiday?' Miss Frances had kept her tone light.

'Nowhere special. See friends, start looking for a flat. Time to leave home.'

'I know so little about you.'

'On the train back from St Ives we hardly stopped talking except when I fell asleep.'

Miss Frances immediately felt better. 'True.'

Their eyes met and then they both looked away.

'You're off to your cottage?' Claire asked.

'Yes. I'm thinking of selling it. It's rather remote.'

'I think I would like "remote".'

Again, her heart had lifted. *Frances, you're such a fool.*

That was the point when she'd stepped back from the brink of asking Claire Daker to join her for the week. 'It wouldn't suit everyone.'

Conveniently, a waiter arrived with a tray of fresh drinks.

'No thank you,' she said, as Claire helped herself to another. Miss Frances put her empty glass on the tray. The alcohol was making her talkative. For once she'd felt relieved when Mr Stanhope positioned himself in front of them.

'Well, dear ladies?'

She was tired – of the daily cut and thrust with Mr Oliver, the diplomacy needed to keep men like Mr Stanhope sweet – most of all she was tired of her own pathetic indecisive behaviour with a woman almost young enough to be her daughter.

Setting off alone seemed just too challenging a task. Should she spend her week's holiday at home, phone switched off, sleeping till further sleep became an impossibility?

'Miss Frances, I noticed your door was open.' Mr Stanhope's smooth pink face loomed behind her in the mirror. 'I would have imagined you halfway to Polperro by now.'

'My cottage is in Yorkshire, Mr Stanhope. I'm sure I've told you that before.'

'You may have done, but when I think of cottages I always think of seaside. I don't know why that is.'

'I must run – I only came back for my gloves.' She stepped away from the mirror. Invariably Mr Stanhope stood too close. Miss

Frances didn't ascribe this to any sexual attraction towards her on his part, more that he found the body warmth of women a comfort. She wondered if he was married.

'Miss Frances, are you wool gathering?'

'Yes, I was.'

'If you could restrain yourself for half-an-hour, I'd like your help with a small crisis around vermin on mezzanine.'

'Would that not be a job for Jim Patterson?'

'Vermin do come under Jim's jurisdiction, but the man has a tendency to gossip. The next thing I know, the entire company will be on red alert, imagining every grain of dust to be mouse droppings. If the female staff in particular get wind of this, there will be mass hysteria.'

'I am a member of the female staff.'

'No, Miss Frances. You are a member of the management team.'

But I am still a woman! What was the use? She began to peel off her gloves and then changed her mind. Her suitcase was waiting for her at the commissionaire's desk. She could go straight from Mr Stanhope's small crises to where her car was parked behind John Lewis.

'Are we ready?'

'Not quite.'

Mr Stanhope had supplanted her in front of the mirror. His head was tilted back and he appeared to be checking his nostrils for hair. 'We'll pick up torches and a plastic bag on our way down. To be honest, I also need your support on this mission, dealing with a dragon of a woman who works there. Our paths rarely cross but when they do, it often results in unpleasantness.'

'That would be Mavis.'

'Mavis?' Satisfied with his nostrils, Mr Stanhope stepped away from the filing cabinet. 'Not a fashionable name. Nothing "swinging" about it. Do people still use that term?'

'I have no idea.'

Stepping out of the lift, she tried to quell a thrill of euphoria. From personal experience she knew that thrills of euphoria generally led to disappointment. It refused to be quelled. Would she see Claire Daker once more before she left? More importantly, would Claire

Daker look up from whatever she was doing, allowing Miss Frances to catch an unguarded expression on her face? A pleased smile would reinstate her *joie de vivre*; a frown could send her off on holiday feeling unbearably depressed.

'After you, dear lady.' Mr Stanhope held open one of the swing doors for her.

As Miss Frances entered the stockroom, she had a fleeting image of Gus's face, just a few days before they'd realised that she was seriously ill.

Intending to surprise Gus, she'd come home early from a buying trip. She hadn't used her front door key, just rung the bell and waited. She remembered her smile of anticipation, how she'd swung her carrier bag containing pizza, champagne and a bunch of yellow tulips. She'd heard Gus's feet on the stairs, had wished that their door panels were made of glass so she could see Gus rushing towards her. The door flew open.

'Ta-dah!' Miss Frances had posed on the front step, the hand holding the shopping bag resting on her jutting hip, the champagne bottle held triumphantly above her head.

Gus's expression had been all she could have hoped for – a smiling mouth ready to exclaim, 'Hello you! What a surprise! I'm so pleased you got back early.' But the animation had drained from Gus's face. 'Could you lower that bottle? You look quite threatening.'

Like the puppy-dog Miss Frances knew herself to invariably become in the face of Gus's disinterest, she'd pressed on. 'Pizza delivery! Pleased to see me?'

'You're early.' Gus turning and walking away from her into the gloom at the back of the house. 'Actually I was expecting someone else. I need to make a phone call.'

'Miss Frances.' Mr Stanhope's tone was irritable.

Before he could again accuse her of 'wool-gathering' she marched firmly into the stockroom. 'Claire? Mavis? Anyone at home?'

*

Mavis sat at her desk eating chocolate bourbon biscuits and

thinking enjoyably unpleasant thoughts about Claire Daker. Whatever Mavis's faults, she had an eye for beauty. She liked deep red tea roses, mature oak trees, tiger and leopard cubs but not lion cubs – she accepted that Claire Daker, caught at a certain angle, under a certain light, with a certain expression on her face, was beautiful. In an objective discussion of the physical merits of Claire Daker, Mavis would have asserted that in a few years' time, with maturity, Claire Daker would become a stunning young woman. However, she would have felt forced to add the rider that the Daker girl's personality was at odds with her looks. As far as Mavis was concerned, there was no charm, no true womanly depth. Mavis prided herself on possessing true womanly depth.

With her index finger, she dabbed around her mouth for crumbs and moved her thoughts on to a reverie on whether or not and under what circumstances she would have had an affair with Mr Oliver.

Her mother's approval would be of paramount importance. That went without saying, although Mavis always felt the need to say it in her head – as if she believed her mother could tune in to her thoughts and might be devastated by her middle-aged daughter's disloyalty.

Mavis guessed that she and Mr Oliver must be about the same age. Time had perhaps been kinder to her, which was gratifying. Of course, a man could get away with wrinkles and a general exhaustion of the features. Mavis patted her second chin lovingly. The little extra weight she carried had ensured her skin stayed smooth with a youthful plumpness. Mavis swore by Camay soap. She had the television presenter Katie Boyle to thank for that. *Camay – the only soap with moisturising cream – it's the secret of soft skin.* Although even Katie's neck was on the slide. When presenters started wearing knotted silk scarves they had to be hiding something.

Helping herself to another biscuit, Mavis warned herself that this must be the last one if the packet was going to last till Tuesday.

The physical side of their relationship might have proved problematic. There was no denying Mr Oliver's virility. Della had vouched for that and if she wasn't a woman of the world, who was?

Mavis didn't feel she'd been born with the energy to be one of those. She was too fond of settling into her dressing gown, slippers and an armchair, while her mother cooked the dinner and looked after her needs: house cleaning, laundry, dry-cleaning.

Yes, the dry-cleaners have provided an excellent re-texturizing service for my winter coat and very reasonably priced, she mused.

Mavis realised she'd drifted from the physical side of her and Mr Oliver. She attempted to haul herself back by conjuring up Mr Oliver naked. Not possible. The picture in her head was of Mr Oliver, but he wore his shirt, tie, underpants and socks.

Men's naked body flesh – what exactly did it look like?

'Claire? Mavis? Anyone at home?'

Guiltily, Mavis dropped her half-eaten biscuit into the desk drawer and brushed the remaining crumbs in the direction of the waste-paper basket. 'Why Miss Frances!' She pushed back her chair. 'And Mr Stanhope. To what do I owe such a privilege?'

'Just continue with whatever you're doing, Mavis.' Miss Frances began to push aside one of the dress rails. 'We're on something of a mission.'

Staring curiously at Mr Stanhope's black bin bag, Mavis then noticed his pink rubber gloves. 'But surely I can be of help? After all, this is my domain. I'm *au fait* with every inch of mezzanine.'

Miss Frances looked at Mr Stanhope.

He shrugged. 'The cleaner has reported finding mouse droppings on this floor.'

Mavis tugged hard on one of the two tape measures strung around her neck. 'I assure you there are no mice here. I keep an immaculate ship.'

'Nevertheless, mouse droppings equal mice. We will just give your nooks and crannies a once over. Could you open a window? It's stifling in here.'

Mavis crossed her hands defensively on her stomach. 'I don't want traffic noise.'

'Perhaps an exception could be made for a brief few minutes.' He reached forward to pat Mavis's shoulder. She recoiled so sharply that his rubber-gloved hand appeared to trail lingeringly over her breast. Horrified, Mr Stanhope snatched his hand away.

Mavis clutched the front of her cardigan and glared at him. She stormed towards the nearest window and pushed it open to a gap of three inches.

'I think I can do better than that.' Miss Frances heaved up the sash, letting in a rush of air.

Papers from Mavis's desk fluttered to the floor.

Miss Frances looked only slightly apologetic. 'So sorry, Mavis. Perhaps it would be better if I left you to deal with the mayhem. By rights, I'm on holiday.' She smiled at Mavis, who didn't smile back. 'Mr Stanhope, shall we begin in the left-hand corner?'

'You won't find mice in the left or the right-hand corner!' Mavis folded her arms.

'I'm sure you're right, dear lady,' Mr Stanhope soothed. 'Miss Frances, perhaps you and I could make a start in the ladies' lavatory and work our way forward.'

'You certainly won't find mice in there!' Tight lipped, Mavis watched them disappear between the dress rails. Awkwardly, she squatted on the dusty parquet flooring to gather up her scattered invoices. Had Mr Stanhope's brush with her breast been intentional? Her breast still tingled pleasantly.

From behind her, she heard a 'crash' as the double doors were simultaneously flung open, and an avalanche of dresses, swinging on the tall chrome rails like the advancing ranks of headless brides, swept into the room. The new season's bridal wear stock had arrived.

'Hold everything right there,' Mavis bawled. Scrambling to her feet, she ran at the incoming tide. 'I've had no notification. They'll have to go back down to dispatch.'

'I spoke to Miss Daker yesterday afternoon. She said to send them straight up.' Jim Patterson emerged from behind the rail. He wore a khaki boiler suit and a wide grin on his face.

There was something about a man in a boiler suit. Thirty years ago, Mavis could remember Jim telling her she was a pretty little thing - which had made her feel light-hearted and a little in love, until she'd heard him say the same thing to Beryl from the coat department. Beryl was long gone but Mavis still retained feelings for Jim – fondness, disappointment and resentment in equal portions.

'Jim,' her voice was almost gentle, 'I don't care if the Pope himself told you to bring these dresses up. Nothing comes onto the mezzanine floor without notification.'

His grin broadened. 'Miss Daker says she's left the documentation on her table.'

'I can't imagine Miss Daker has spent enough time in mezzanine these last few days to have organised the correct notification.'

Claire's table was scrupulously tidy. In the middle of the blotter, under a heavy chrome stapler, was the documentation in triplicate as required and duly signed, *Claire Daker, boutique manageress.* Mavis stared at it for a minute and then looked up at Jim. He was trying not to laugh.

'I fail to see the joke. Is this the lot or are there more?'

'Hundreds more.'

'Then you'd better get on with your work.'

She looked around for Miss Frances and Mr Stanhope. There was no sign of them. The telephone rang. As she lifted the receiver she checked her watch against the mezzanine clock – exactly three-thirty.

'Hello Mother. Anything in the post? Oh, Mr Oliver, it's you again. No, she isn't here. Yes I will tell her.'

*

Most tragedies – serious illness aside – emerge out of farcical situations. As I step from the lift on mezzanine, I see Miss Frances and Stanhope entering the women's toilet; incomprehensibly he carries a torch and a dustbin bag. I pause, waiting for the toilet door to swing shut behind them.

Despite my desire to confront Claire Daker, I know myself to be – and I'm smiling ruefully as I recall it – in a sorry state. The disparity between us has never been more marked: young, fresh and beautiful compared to middle-aged, jaded and sweaty! I sweep back a strand of hair that has fallen forward and take several deep calming breaths before entering the stockroom.

It is crammed to the hilt with the new season's bridal dresses; it won't be easy to push my way through without them hearing me. From the far side of the room, muffled slightly by the density of polythene, I recognise Claire Daker's voice. 'Mavis, I feel nauseous.'

'Hah! *I* should have the luxury of feeling nauseous.'

'I'm suffocating in this heat.'

'Nothing to do with heat – you've been drinking. I can smell alcohol on you.'

I hear Mavis's self-important footsteps, and possibly the sound of a kettle being switched on.

'I'll have a cup, Mavis. No sugar.'

'You can make your own tea. I've had to check in four-hundred-and-seventy units and write out twenty-two delivery dockets. It's not work I'm paid to do.'

'Then you shouldn't have done it.'

I can't help smiling inside. Daker never fails to hold her corner. Stealthily, I ease two rails apart and slip between.

'There was no rush. I had all that earmarked for when I got back from holiday. Could I get to my desk? I must sit down for a few minutes.'

'Don't get comfortable. Mr Oliver's looking for you.'

'Did you hear what I just said? I don't feel well.'

'And did you hear what *I* just said? Your boyfriend's been ringing on and off for the past half-hour.'

I stand stock-still. My heart beats at a painful rate – to be described as Claire Daker's 'boyfriend' – ludicrous, untrue, but I feel as happy as if it *is* true.

Back comes Daker, her voice deadly. 'I don't have a boyfriend.'

'Agreed! He's certainly no "boy".' Mavis sniggering.

'I advise you not to go around repeating stupid gossip.'

The scraping of a chair.

'So you know there's gossip? No smoke without fire.'

Light footsteps – Claire's? – moving away towards the window.

'Cat got your tongue?' Mavis opening her desk drawer, the rustle of a packet.

'Please don't eat those biscuits. Just the thought of food in someone's mouth makes me feel sick.'

'Then don't think about it.'

'Why are you being so spiteful?'

The click-click of dinky heels, a kettle boiling – water poured into a cup? 'You, madam, think you're the bee's bloody knees. You may have fooled everyone else with your pretty vacuous face but you've not fooled me.'

Galvanised by the malice in Mavis's voice, I dispense with stealth and shoulder my way roughly through the rails. On purpose, I make the white shrouds dance and the metal hangers clatter. My introduction. Will they even notice?

'I think you've got a visitor,' Mavis says.

As if parting the curtains of a stage, I draw back the dresses and step out into sun-filled light. By the window, Claire Daker stands, her face deathly pale. Mavis is sidling out from behind her desk, a chocolate bourbon biscuit in one hand.

'Mr Oliver.' She makes a ridiculous half-curtsey.

'Mavis.' I take the hand not holding the biscuit, look deep into her eyes as I kiss it. 'I see the new bridal range has arrived.' My voice is just above a whisper.

'I really should have had notification,' she says, but with no real conviction. I know the women in The Store who have a soft spot for me and Mavis has always been one of them.

'My deepest apologies. Could you, would you, do me one final favour?'

Mavis looks cautious. *Bravo*! The woman may have had a crush on me for years but that doesn't mean she's a pushover.

'Might I trouble you for a cup of coffee?' I relinquish her hand and take out my wallet. 'From the Copper Kettle. Also a tuna and cucumber sandwich.'

'I shouldn't really leave the stockroom unattended.' Reluctantly, Mavis takes my crisp pound note.

'Let me go,' Claire Daker says, which galvanises Mavis.

'I thought you were feeling nauseous.' She gives me a horrible, knowing look. 'Shall I take the circuitous route?'

'Perfect.'

She drapes her cardigan around her shoulders and leaves the two of us alone. I remain unmoving, staring at the floor, until out in the corridor I hear the lift arrive, open and depart.

Then I turn my attention to Claire Daker. 'You're not well?'

She nods.

'I'm so sorry, and after all the excitement of the day.'

'I think it's best if I go home.'

'And get started on your holiday?'

Another nod, with a relieved expression. The foolish girl actually believes I'm going to let her off the hook.

'But first we should at least make a start on checking these dresses.'

'I can't. I feel too ill.'

My voice is gentle. 'A member of the management team is required to do their job even when feeling worse for wear. So, shall we not waste any more time? Miss Daker –' I hold out my hand.

She ignores it and tries again. 'But I'm not well.'

'While you're on holiday you can recuperate. Going away with friends or is it just one special friend?'

She doesn't answer.

'Of course. None of my business. But don't worry. I'm here to catch you if you feel faint.' I smile, knowing that any smile of mine repels her.

She shudders and looks towards the window.

No escape, Claire. Not this time.

Reluctantly, she picks up her notebook and pen from her desk, then suddenly, hoping to leave me behind, she sets off at a healthy dash towards a distant rail of dresses.

It takes me three strides to catch up with her. 'Not so fast – I'm not as young as you are, my dear.'

Her mouth pulls wide in a grimace as she reacts to that 'my dear'.

I feel a powerful desire to chuckle at my own cleverness as now, together, we make our slow progress between the packed rails. They provide the perfect excuse to let my hand, elbow, shoulder constantly graze against some part of her body. I can see that she is disgusted by my proximity but I don't care. I wind my tongue around words like *guipure, skirt, bodice, ruching, bust dart, collar bone* – using the words as if they are a secret sensual language between the two of us as I observe her increasing distress.

'I need air,' she says. There is perspiration on her upper lip.

'But you've already spent part of the afternoon sitting in Hanover Square.' I split the polythene cover of one of the gowns from neck to hem. The bodice is made of lace scattered with tiny crystal beads. 'Beautiful workmanship.'

Slowly, suggestively, I raise the chiffon skirt to reveal the thin, slippery satin petticoat underneath. I bend my head to inhale the scent of fresh, sensuous fabric. A tiny spot the colour of dried blood stains the satin, then another, then a shower of drops. Questioningly, I turn to look at Claire Daker.

'It's coming out of your hair. I'm going to be sick.' She twists violently away.

'Don't go –' I reach for her.

She slaps my hand and begins to push back through the dresses.

With my handkerchief I wipe away the blend of Grecian 2000 and sweat on my forehead; then calmly, at a measured pace, I follow.

She has reached Mavis's desk. She picks up the metal wastepaper basket – shoulders heaving, she bends her head over it. Then she screams and the bin crashes to the floor, scattering crumbs, biscuit and sweet wrappers, and finally a tiny grey mouse. Bewildered, it sits on its hind legs as if assessing the situation, then dashes towards the sanctuary beneath the packed rails.

Claire Daker heads for the open window. She leans out. I hear her groan as a stream of vomit rains down onto Hanover Square. The shower seems to last for several minutes and then finally, wiping her mouth with the back of her hand, she turns around.

I step forward and offer her my stained handkerchief.

'Get away from me.'

I will not get away from her. She is shivering, her hair is lank and her skin has turned a greenish shade and yet I desire this depleted young woman even more. I take hold of her arms. She doesn't resist me.

'No,' she pleads.

I am lost. There is no point in subterfuge and nothing to be gained through best intentions. 'Claire, you must know how I feel about you.'

I draw her closer. It doesn't bother me that she's just been sick. I like the smell, the intimacy of it. I let my tongue flick across her chin.

The ice maiden wakes, twisting her head away, her hands pushing hard against my chest.

'Steady,' I croon. 'Nothing to fear.' And then, god help me, I kiss her soft warm lips. I am drowning. I am dying. I press my body into hers. As my tongue forces a way into her mouth, I feel as if I am entering her. I press against her. She knows exactly what is in my mind.

'You filthy bastard, let me go.'

And I do let her go. My knees buckle and I sink to the floor, hands clutching the front of my trousers. 'Aah,' I moan. Such pain is unbearable but, even so, a saner Oliver is observing somewhere in the back of my head, *A first Oliver. You've never been kneed in the balls before!*

Claire Daker stands over me. 'Now will you leave me alone?' Her face is a mask of hatred; no fear or vulnerability – she is ready for battle.

My hand shoots out to grab her ankle.

She kicks me, a hard blow to my shoulder.

Impervious, I try again but only succeed in removing her shoe. She rains blows down on me, weak ineffectual female blows. I welcome the physical contact after so long with none. With all my strength I scramble to my knees and throw my arms around her waist. I press my face against her skirt and breathe Claire Daker in.

'Oliver, have you gone mad?'

I recognise Stanhope's voice. I shut my eyes, blot him out.

'Let her go, you bastard.' A woman's voice – this time Miss Frances.

Within my grasp, Claire Daker writhes.

'I told you to let her go,' Miss Frances says.

Something hard cracks against my skull.

Still I hold on.

Miss Frances hits me again, harder this time, and Claire Daker steps free. I begin to topple sideways. I hear Mavis's voice singing out 'We have coffee' and then, as they say in old novels, everything went dark.

Chapter 29

1975

Winding a fresh sheet of notepaper into the Remington typewriter, Miss Frances paused and glanced down at her five-year desk diary: on this very day a year ago her life had truly begun.

Just about now she would have been standing next to a sobbing Della. They and the rest of the Store staff had assembled to watch Jim Patterson escort Mr Oliver from the building.

'He's holding up his head like a bloody guardsman,' Della had sobbed through her tears.

Miss Frances had seen that he was doing just that. She even conceded that he looked almost heroic, a large sticking plaster adhering to his left temple. Wearing his double-breasted raincoat and carrying a briefcase and a Store carrier bag, to a cacophony of voices, he'd walked – straight backed and unsmiling – down the bridal staircase. Someone had called out 'Shame!' and this cry had been taken up by several others. Possibly during his entire career Mr Oliver had never been so well liked.

There would be no farewell ceremony. No celebrating his two decades as the successful manager of a top London store. No padded card crowded with well wishes (sincere and otherwise) and no promises of postcards sent from his favourite holiday resorts.

'I can't bear it.' Della stepped forward, her hand outstretched.

He'd ignored her. Looking neither to left nor right, he made his dignified progress through coats, daywear, accessories, and finally past the Sugar Cube Boutique. The Store's newly electrified double doors swung open and he stepped out onto Oxford Street. As if a starting pistol had been fired, Mr Oliver broke into a run, plunging into the rush-hour traffic.

'Stop him somebody,' Della shouted. 'He's going to throw himself in front of –'

But no, Mr Oliver hadn't intended to throw himself in front of anything. Nimbly he'd jumped onto a bus travelling in the direction of Earls Court.

Della had turned towards Miss Frances. 'And for what?'

'Della, he behaved disgracefully.'

'Your pal, Claire Daker, has ruined the reputation and career of a wonderful man. From the very beginning she led him on.'

'That just isn't true.' Miss Frances checked her watch. 'I must go.'

'Holiday?' Della's voice had been bitter.

'Eventually.'

Of course, the police should have been called and Mr Oliver at least charged with assault. But Claire hadn't wanted that, a relief to Mr Stanhope who had immediately begun burbling about bad publicity.

'You must sack him,' Miss Frances said firmly. 'Have Mr Oliver removed from the premises right now.'

'Should we not give him a month's notice? Allow The Store a chance to find a half decent replacement?'

Miss Frances had steered Claire into the corridor and left her by the lift before hurrying back to him. 'He could and should go to prison. No months' notice. The man leaves today or I phone the newspapers.'

'Miss Frances!'

'I mean it.'

'I for one shall be sorry to see him go,' Mavis interjected. 'Out of the two of them I know which one I'd prefer.'

They'd both ignored Mavis.

She'd taken Claire up to her office. 'Nobody will disturb you. Sit here and calm down. Would you like tea, coffee, something stronger?'

Claire shook her head. She was shivering.

Miss Frances took off her own jacket and wrapped it around Claire's shoulders.

'Thank you.' Her voice was small, not a Claire Daker voice at all.

'I'm sorry we didn't get to you earlier. I was on a fool's errand in search of mice. Mr Stanhope suggested that we check out the ladies' toilets first. I think he just wanted to be in a lavatory with a woman. Any woman.' She stopped herself. 'Claire, forgive me, that was a stupid remark to make. Are you sure you're warm enough?'

'Please, I'm fine now.' Claire picked up the photo of Gus and studied it. 'Who's this?'

'Gus.'

'And she is?'

Years later, Miss Frances remembered her reply as marking a defining moment in her life. She said, 'She was my girlfriend. She died. I loved her very much.' Miss Frances swallowed. 'Probably far more than she loved me.'

Claire put the photo back on the desk. 'Like Mr Oliver and me? That's how everyone will see it.'

'Of course they won't. '

'But everyone believes I encouraged him.'

'Claire, that is just not true.'

'For months the shop staff have been gossiping about me.'

Which hit home. Of course she'd known there was gossip but perhaps she'd chosen not to take it seriously. While the staff were discussing Mr Oliver and Claire they wouldn't be discussing her. Fine for an older man to be infatuated by a younger woman – Stanhope and the board would understand and even envy him – but linking Claire with her could jeopardise her whole career. Was that the reason she'd ignored how serious the situation was becoming?

'I should have stepped in weeks ago.'

'Mavis spread the rumour all over the store.'

'Nobody takes any notice of Mavis.'

'But they did. Even Della.'

'Claire, you've done nothing wrong.'

'I might just as well have. You told me once that the women on the shop floor loved him and I didn't believe you, but they do. They won't ever forgive me.'

At that moment, when Miss Frances thought herself to be the most selfish, cowardly woman in the world, Claire Daker touched her hand. 'Frances, could I come with you to your cottage?'

And there was hope again. She felt some affection for this hope of hers – sturdy child with grazed knees and rosy cheeks, searching a room or a crowd for that one special person. Hope had been disappointed in love so many times.

'You are going to be all right. I will make it up to you, Claire. I promise.'

That evening in 1974, Miss Frances hadn't set off alone to her cottage; she took Claire Daker with her.

Lowering her hands into her lap, Miss Frances turned slightly to face the window. Autumn was on its way. She imagined herself walking with Claire as they had the previous autumn, in the woods behind the cottage, kicking their way through the fallen leaves, picking blackberries, swinging their arms, holding hands, looking forward, looking backwards, laughter, sadness shared. It had been a special week, the best week ever until the last day.

'Gus is still part of your life,' Claire had said.

'Not really. I'm ready to move on.'

Claire hadn't believed her then.

Miss Frances reached for Claire's postcard. The postman had handed it to her as she'd left the house. Would Mr Oliver have followed Claire? Well yes, it was possible.

She studied the photo of Gus. She couldn't just throw Gus away. It seemed unbearable even to consign Gus to a drawer or an album as if she'd merely been one of many friends who come and go within a lifetime. She removed the photograph from the frame and slipped it into her pocket. Then, a creature of habit, she got to her feet, carried her cup and saucer into the executive toilet, and washed and dried them. Back in her office she tidied magazines and files and left her desk absolutely clear.

From behind the door she took down her jacket – she hadn't deserted Jaeger. The jacket was cashmere and wool mix in a deep rose colour. The door pressed against her and Mr Stanhope peered in. 'Can you spare a moment, Miss Frances – something of a crisis down on the shop floor?'

'Afraid not. I have to leave immediately.'

'But it's only mid-morning.'

'Some distance to travel,' she murmured and picked up her car keys.

It was chilly in Hanover Square. The brisk breeze made Miss Frances tighten the belt of her coat as she made for their bench – Frances and Gus's bench. It was busy in the square but the bench was empty. Miss Frances sat down and waited for the memories to come: watching Gus walk towards her, sometimes pleased, at others as if the two of them meeting was such a trial. But when they sat together on the bench, their shoulders touching, eventually they'd talk, communicate, be the deep and dear friends Miss Frances wanted to believe they were. The bench and Hanover Square had never let her down. She tilted her head back to look up into the trees. Leaves in citric green, orange, burnt ochre and golden brown were spiralling onto the grass.

From her pocket Miss Frances took the photo. She couldn't bear to look at it again.

Goodbye Gus. I'm letting you go.

When Miss Frances left the bench, she left Gus behind. The wind gathered up the photo and it was lost amongst the leaves.

The sky was grey and there was rain in the air by the time she reached her car.

From the dashboard her plastic sunflower encouraged her. 'Come on Fran. Keep me company. No fun sitting in a car and going nowhere.'

Miss Frances got in the car, put the key in the ignition and started the engine. In the rear-view mirror she caught her gaze – brown eyes shining.

Chapter 30

1975

I'm hungry. I wish I'd asked for two buttered scones. I also wish I'd said, before Doreen had disappeared down that alley leading to the front entrance of Mildmay Executive Properties, 'Can you arrange for my refreshments to be delivered to your car before you start demanding facts, figures and criticising Carpenter's female staff?'

However, I settle myself more comfortably in the passenger seat and inhale. Doreen's brand new Austin Princess 1300 Vanden Plas smells strongly of leather and money. I reach forward and stroke the mahogany veneer of the dashboard. The sedate style suits my temperament far better than Doreen's unwieldy Jaguar – late of her late husband. When I get back to London I may take driving lessons. Over the summer I've been a passenger in so many luxurious cars that I find myself wanting one for myself. The world would then be my oyster.

The car park to the rear of the office block is half empty. Doreen is making a 'flying visit' to Mildmay Executive Properties on the third floor and has already been away over half-an-hour. Which is okay as, desire for sustenance aside, I need time to think.

I haven't mentioned anything to Doreen, but on this very day, September of last year, I was dismissed from my managerial position at The Store. At the time I believed that my life was ruined forever. This has not been the case.

Whatever I feel for Doreen – and it is not love – she deserves my gratitude. In a different, yet no less beneficial way than Steve, she has presented me with options. Even her affection, which so frequently I've declared an anathema, has encouraged me to contemplate rebuilding my life.

The proverb 'you can't teach an old dog new tricks' may well be true, but this 'old dog' can still entertain the genuine desire to make changes. When I remember what I put Claire Daker through with my boorish, bullying, sexual behaviour, I could howl. I revelled in damaging a vulnerable young woman while calling my behaviour 'love'. There will never be any making matters right. An apology from me would no doubt open up painful wounds for her. But that is the better side of my character talking; despite any regrets I still visited the cottage. And perhaps if I stay on at Mildmay's, I'd visit the cottage again. The temptation is too great and I don't trust myself. Not yet anyway.

It is now imperative that I return to London. Take myself out of temptation's way. I'm ready to leave Doreen in the least upsetting manner possible but I won't go back to the Earls Court flat. Martin Renshawe has offered to buy it and I've decided to accept his offer.

Today, I am reasonably cheerful. We've spent the day in York and I enjoyed walking around the city walls with Doreen on my arm. She knows a surprising amount of history, whereas I know absolutely nothing.

'These walls are medieval. Ninth century. The Romans were bloody marvellous at getting things built. I expect they used slaves for the heavy work. I could do with a slave or two myself,' she'd said, which had made me laugh.

I like York. I like Harrogate. In fact I like every single town and village Doreen has introduced me to: the shops are interesting, the cafes and restaurants genuinely welcoming.

I don't want to delude myself that everything is hunky-dory but even Doreen's mood swings have lessened. She seems to have stopped drinking. In fact we have all stopped drinking. Mrs Venables is in charge of the alcohol at Mildmay's and at mealtimes she no longer provides any. Carpenter appears to accept this change, or perhaps he knows something about the situation that I don't.

A bright red Volkswagen Beetle has pulled in a couple of cars away. The driver hasn't got out. I might like a Volkswagen but not in red. Grey or black would suit me. I attempt to peer across to see what sort of person is driving such a car but the driver is obscured by a plastic sunflower hanging from the mirror. A yellow flower in a red car – what an awful colour combination.

I wonder if I should I go in search of Doreen. I don't much like the look of the alley. It is dark and dingy and possibly an excellent spot in which to be hit over the head with a brick and have my wallet snatched. Perhaps, even now, Doreen is lying in the shadows, her life-blood trickling out of her. A place like that should have lighting even during the day. I lean forward. Initially, I'd thought the alley empty but there seems to be a slight re-arrangement of the shadows. My spirits lift; perhaps it is Carpenter's secretary bringing my tea and scone.

Not wishing to appear the type of man dependent on afternoon tea and scone, I study my newspaper. Has Doreen realised that measures to deal with the drought have been introduced in Yorkshire? If she does know, she's made no attempt to rein in Mrs Venables, who is busy with the hose-pipe and lawn sprinkler every single evening. But that is Doreen and Mrs Venables – they are a law unto themselves.

Someone has emerged from the alley. I hear light footsteps approaching the car.

'No doubt my son's typist will be some little tart with a skirt up to her waist,' Doreen has predicted. I'm predicting a woman in tweed and a twin-set.

Will getting out of the car appear presumptuous? Even threatening? But what if Carpenter's typist doesn't know about Doreen's new purchase and delivers my tea and scone to the red Volkswagen by mistake?

Sunshine glances across the front window and I'm momentarily dazzled. There is a woman walking towards me holding a cup and a paper bag. About time too!

I open the door and get out, brushing the creases from my jacket. 'I'm Oliver. Over here,' I call out and wave cheerfully.

I'm startled by a cry.

A long drawn out, 'O-o-oh.'

Five yards away, the woman stumbles and starts to fall. In slow motion, bag and cup begin to spill, the cup lid flies forward.

By the time I reach her, she is lying on the ground, completely still. Coffee stains her skirt and cream cotton blouse. I hunker down next to her. Her face is turned away from me. Blood oozes from a cut at her hairline. Tentatively, I feel for a pulse at the side of her neck.

'Claire,' I whisper. The skin beneath my fingers feels like satin.

She doesn't answer.

Someone has got out of the red Volkswagen and is running

across to us.

Without looking up I shout, 'Can you telephone for an ambulance? She's unconscious.'

'No, Mr Oliver, *I'll* stay with her. You get the ambulance.'

Who else would it be but Miss Frances? I could almost laugh.

*

The outer office seemed unnaturally silent once Doreen and Mr Oliver had finally left to drive back to Mildmay's.

Something of a cataclysmic afternoon was Carpenter's verdict, as he pulled out the chair from behind Monica's desk and sat down. Immediately he felt cramped. Her desk was only a third of the size of his own. Crossing one leg over the other knee – his favourite sitting position – was an impossibility. He made no effort to move. It wouldn't hurt him to be uncomfortable for a while.

Would he ever see her again? Of course, he could just drive over to Burnside Hospital, ask what ward she was in – but he knew he wouldn't. Oliver's 'rampant lesbian' might be with her.

Looking around the room, he experienced a strange sense of loss, almost as if Monica was dead. Her office had never seemed so empty. She was always there, or coming in and going out again. Monica had made this part of his life real.

He was glad she hadn't taken down her Goddesses of the Eastern Hemisphere calendar for his mother's visit.

'You'll have to get rid of her,' his mother had said once the ambulance had driven away and they'd returned to the office. 'She's too young. Far too sure of herself. I didn't like her at all. I thought you said she was inordinately fat.'

He hated it when his mother spoke to him like that: hard-nosed and bullying. 'Show a little charity, Ma. The poor girl's on her way to hospital with a possible fractured skull. She's my friend as well as an employee.'

'She can't be both.' Her laugh wasn't pleasant. 'You don't mix friendship and work. You'll back me up there, won't you, Oliver?'

'Yes, Doreen's right. Up to a point.' Mr Oliver pushed back a strand of greying hair.

Carpenter noticed a smear of dried blood on his shirt cuff.

'I almost ran over that young woman the other day,' Doreen announced.

Which was when Carpenter picked up the tension in the room.

'Didn't I, Oliver? What a coincidence or did *Claire* follow you up from London and that story you told me was just a pack of lies?'

'Her name is Monica. She's been working here for at least six months,' Carpenter corrected her. 'Well before you met Oliver.'

'Claire Monica Daker,' Mr Oliver said. 'Doreen, you saw Miss Frances. I didn't make *her* up.'

'I saw a concerned friend and nothing else. Carpenter, your typist and Oliver have history.' With her head on one side, she looked at Mr Oliver. 'I'm disappointed, pet. The way you raved on about her. I'd expected someone pretty spectacular. She wasn't much at all.'

Mr Oliver ignored her. He walked across the room and stared at the calendar. 'You can take that down right now,' Doreen said. 'It's disgusting. Heathen.'

He read out: 'Buy milk and brown envelopes. Evening class.'

Carpenter had felt despairing. Here he was, a grown man in his early thirties, yet he couldn't even manage to clear the two of them out of the office to carry on their squabble elsewhere. All he wanted was to sit quietly and think about losing a friend, perhaps someone he might have been able to love had he not been so emotionally stunted.

His mother was unrelenting. She'd positioned herself between Oliver and the wall. Even wearing high heels she only reached his shoulder.

'You're in your fifties. She's a kid. Not a proper woman. What did you see in her? What did you think she'd ever see in you?'

Mr Oliver remained silent.

'Cat got your tongue? I'm worth a dozen Claire Dakers, you blind bastard.'

Taking a step away from her, Mr Oliver held out his hand to Carpenter. 'Will we see you back at the house later?'

'I'm not sure. I may go to my French class.'

'On your own?' This was his mother at her worst, lashing out, if not with her fists, with her tongue. 'Without your little girlfriend? What is it with men these days? Are they all frightened of real, warm blooded women?'

Mr Oliver clasped her shoulder. 'Home now, I think.' He propelled her through the door and out into the corridor.

Carpenter slid open Monica's top desk drawer. She'd liked her biros: red, green, blue, black. That had been one of her contradictions; a woman meticulous to the point of fussy about keeping up the full complement of colours; her HB pencils sharpened and paper clips divided into colour, then sub-divided into large, medium and small. Monica had been efficient in the extreme. A reliable timekeeper, a boon to any office; in fact she'd excelled at any criteria that Doreen could stipulate. A young woman like that, on paper or described by an employer – Carpenter would have expected her to be dull, drab and wearing sensible cardigans and shoes. Monica couldn't have been more different.

He was already thinking about her in the past tense. Months ago Monica *had* been dull, drab and worn sensible cardigans and shoes. But even then he'd known on some level that her turning up in his back-of-beyond office in back-of-beyond Burnside was too good to be true. As she'd altered, he'd thought that maybe some time in the future she'd head for London. But no, she'd come from London. That must have been where Oliver had met her. Carpenter considered Miss Frances. An attractive woman. Very well dressed. Whatever his mother said, there had definitely been more than just friendship between the two of them. He shied away from using the word 'tenderness'.

He felt sad and rather lonely, which he was sure wasn't anywhere near as rewarding as feeling solitary.

The telephone next to his elbow rang. He picked up the receiver and listened.

'Carpenter?'

'Ned?'

'How are you?'

'I'm okay. I'm afraid Monica's not here.' *Now sod off and leave me alone!*

'I know. I've just seen her at Burnside hospital. She asked me to ring you.'

'For why?' He slapped his forehead in frustration. Where did these awkward phrases spring from?

Ned sounded amused. 'To remind you of the class tonight.'

Carpenter packed his response with fake heartiness. 'I believe I'm double-booked his evening. A pal down from my Uni days.'

'Monica said, if necessary, I'm to drag you to college by the scruff of your neck.'

Carpenter swivelled the chair round so he faced his own office. Suddenly he couldn't bear to look at Monica's umbrella plant for a moment longer. 'I don't think she's coming back,' burst out of him.

Ned didn't miss a beat. 'All the more reason for you to come to class. I'll collect you.'

'Thanks, but I have my own car.'

'Loosen up, you stupid sod.' Ned's tone was not unpleasant.

'I'm not good with people, as you well know. Probably it would be best if I call the class a day.'

'*Un jour* or *une jour*?'

'Most amusing, Ned. Now really.' He despaired of himself. This must be how it felt to endure a nervous breakdown, although common sense told him that he wasn't enduring anything half as serious, but how sick he was of himself – so incapable of bloody loosening up. When had he ever been given the opportunity?

'See you at six-thirty,' Ned said amiably.

'But Monica – how is she?'

No Ned on the line.

Carpenter unwound himself from the chair and telephone cord. His head was still full of words and theories: that whatever affected his ability to connect with others – which, if questioned by a psychiatrist, but definitely not Martin Renshawe – as to what that looked like, he'd have said a large chocolate Easter egg that was cracking and melting. Which made no sense but didn't stop the sensation being painful, even frightening.

He did what he felt he shouldn't do but which was something he'd wanted to do for weeks – opened Monica's deep, lower desk drawer and lifted out the bulky plastic file he knew to be in there. He carried it back into his own office and made himself comfortable, legs stretched out, feet on his executive desk. The file contained at least a hundred typed carbon copies of letters Monica had written to Frances or Fran. He began to read. Once, forgetting, he looked up to ask Monica to get him tea and a rock bun. Quickly he went back to the letters. When he read 'Carpenter's not bad, just his own worst enemy', his throat constricted. But that was the only time Monica mentioned him.

Outside in the corridor he heard the lift approaching. His desk-clock said six-thirty. He returned the letters to the file, slipped the file into a large envelope, and wrote CM Daker on the outside. Grabbing his jacket and brief case, he met Ned in the doorway. That was difficult. Always hard to keep emotion in check in the presence of someone who recognises just how hard you're trying. Carpenter found himself incapable of speech.

Ned grinned. He was dressed in overly tight denim jeans and a leather biker jacket. 'Message from Monica. Leave home. Don't slouch. *Profiter du présent*!'

'What the devil does that mean?'

'Seize the day, man!'

*

'I thought perhaps a softer hairstyle, a warmer colour?' Doreen flipped through a copy of Woman's Own. 'A little more modern than Margaret Thatcher's.' She was relaxing (never easy for her) on a cushioned wrought iron bench in the garden. Some distance away, Venables was tending a bonfire.

'What about Jane Fonda? She has lovely hair.'

Doreen frowned, but with good humour. 'Venables, I'm hoping to become a local councillor; I don't think transforming myself into Jane Fonda would be a good idea. Also, there is a small age difference. In a quiet way I want to emulate some of the coming women politicians. Barbara Castle is very attractive. I'm not so keen on Shirley Williams. On occasion she can resemble an unmade bed.'

Venables stopped poking the fire with a walking stick and turned her attention to a pile of cardboard boxes. One by one she tore them open then tipped their contents on the ground. All the late Peter Mildmay's Nevil Shute and Dennis Wheatley paperbacks, and the more recently acquired works of Hammond Innes tumbled out. She paused at the last box – Mr Oliver's favourite books, brought with him from London.

'Should we?' Venables raised an enquiring eyebrow.

'He didn't take them with him and I'm certainly not paying postage and packing to send them on. Anything he's left behind goes on the bonfire.'

'Would it be symbolic if you tossed the first few?'

Doreen put down her magazine. 'No, you do it. I've thought of something much more symbolic in the conservatory.'

Determinedly, she walked back across the lawn to the house. She wore brogues, rather similar in style to the brogues Venables favoured, although much more expensive and of real leather. The wearing of these was just one of the differences Venables was encouraging her to make in her life. Her initial complaint had been on finding herself three inches shorter, but after a few days wearing them around the house, in the garden and for any brief car journeys, she began to enjoy not just the comfort, but that they made her feel more energised – zippy. Like a bullet from a gun, she saw herself entering the Post Office at speed; arrive at the counter – no pleasantries – then out, back into the car and up to the garden centre. A concise few words with the manager, an exchange of money, sacks of compost loaded in the boot, home in under thirty minutes.

Of course she would never give up heeled shoes. Wearing heels, she became a sharp, sexy, feminine, womanly little titch, whereas wearing flats she was just titchy. Flats or heels, they both gave her a different but equally enjoyable sense of power.

Since Oliver's departure, Doreen had spent rather a lot of money. With Madge Renshawe for company she'd booked a suite at The Savoy in London for a week. They'd bought clothes, lunched, dined, seen A Little Night Music at the Adelphi Theatre and got on rather well. Madge had turned out to be anything but a timid mouse. She had spirit, a sense of humour, ideas for Doreen's future. Plans for her own. There could easily have been awkwardness between them, Junior as good as eloping with Madge's husband. But after some initial stilted conversation they'd found the topic endlessly fascinating. In retrospect, Madge discovered numerous signs of Martin's homosexuality, while Doreen acknowledged that Junior had never shown the slightest interest in the opposite sex and perhaps she should have wondered why.

There had been other reasons to choose Madge as a companion. For years Laverne had been her closest friend but Doreen was no longer drinking and, until her resolve to remain sober became more established, she'd decided to avoid both Laverne and The Templar's Arms.

The image that Doreen could not shift out of her head when she thought about Laverne was of her bouncing on Oliver's lap on the day he'd got drunk – the two of them enjoying themselves in an easy relaxed fashion that she and Oliver had never achieved. She'd known – as only a mature woman can know – that he found Laverne attractive. Had *they* shared the same bed for the best part of a month something would have happened between them. Neither would have settled for a peck on the cheek and cuddling up platonically. As far as Doreen was concerned, that memory had spoilt their friendship forever.

She opened the door to the conservatory. Venables had already started packing – the move to the new house only weeks away. The cane furniture was stacked against one side of the room, the cushions wrapped in polythene. In a corner she'd left the plants in pots: the fig, bougainvillaea, fuchsia and lemon geranium that had been with the family for years. Overseeing these stood the two wicker donkeys, Napoleon and Josephine.

Hopes and dreams, Doreen thought. Aloud she said, 'The two of you have got to go.'

But still she didn't attempt to pick them up. She realised immediately that she should have asked Venables to deal with them. Or Carpenter on one of his flying visits, becoming rarer since he'd moved to Harrogate. They could have gone to a jumble sale or a charity shop.

Looking at the donkeys, trying to block out memories, what she desperately needed was a drink. For days she'd kept the pain in her heart under control. With the help of sleeping tablets, she'd managed the nights. She looked round for something to sit on. Unless she was prepared to dismantle the stack of chairs there was nothing.

'It's all right, Mrs Mildmay.' Venables gently eased her aside.

'You want to get rid of these donkeys, don't you?'

Doreen nodded. 'I was going to put them on the bonfire.' Her voice was shaky.

'Good idea.'

'But am I burning something that has an importance?' She didn't know exactly what she meant, but implicitly trusted Venables to understand.

'What if instead, I take them away? Out of your life?'

'But they're me and Oliver.'

'Well no, they're not.'

'To me they are. Were. Please, can I just have one drink? Just a brandy. I won't ask for another. Just the one.'

'There is no alcohol in this house, Mrs Mildmay. You are a strong woman, but if you keep drinking your strength will be lost and you're not young enough anymore to get it back.'

Carrying a donkey under each arm, Venables walked out into the garden. The bonfire had died down, the flames struggling with the thickness of the books.

Doreen stood in the conservatory doorway watching her. Getting rid of the donkeys seemed momentous. An end. No space left for hope or dreams.

'Please don't burn them.'

At the edge of the fire Venables hesitated. 'Then what shall we do with them, because they can't stay here?'

Doreen Mildmay had no intention of crying. She never had cried, she never would. It was a surprise when she understood that genuine tears had crept up on her. They streamed down her cheeks. 'I really loved him.'

'I know you did.'

Doreen sank onto the grass. She hugged her knees, pressed her face against the sleeve of her jacket; her shoulders shook. For ages she sobbed as the sun moved behind the house and she sat, huddled in shadow.

Venables looked up from feeding cardboard into the flames. 'Do you know Doreen, you look about fourteen years old.'

With the heel of her hand, Doreen wiped the tears from her face. 'It's still Mrs Mildmay, if you don't mind.'

They both laughed.

'Whatever suits you.'

Doreen joined her at the bonfire. 'What happened to the donkeys?'

'They're gone.'

'Thank you.'

'Here's an idea. Why don't you tidy yourself up? I'll sort out some cake and sandwiches. Perhaps ring Mrs Renshawe to see if she wants to come over for tea?'

'But you've been here since six this morning, aren't you very tired?'

Venables shook her head. 'I enjoy a good bonfire and we haven't had one in years.'

*

Miss Frances sat on a hard plastic chair at Claire's bedside, waiting. Thin gingham curtains moved slightly at the open window; there was the rattle of a tea trolley entering the ward. It was nothing like her previous experience with Gus; no monitoring machines, no desire to feed Claire spoonfuls of yoghurt.

'Frances?'

'Oh, you're awake.'

'Will he ever leave me alone?'

'If he doesn't we'll just have to plan a nasty accident for him. However, your friend Carpenter tells me that the vile Mr Oliver has returned to London and won't be coming back.'

They both smiled.

'Can I stay at your cottage for a little while longer?'

'Of course. Would you mind if I stayed there with you?'

'What about The Store?'

'That part of my life is over.' For a moment Frances was amazed, but it was true. She was ready for a change.

Claire looked neither surprised nor curious – but why should she be? Unacknowledged between them, but still there, was affection. Miss Frances almost laughed aloud at that ludicrous tepid word. She took Claire's hand. Could she risk it?

Such a painful memory intruded. 'I love you, Gus,' she'd said, only once, by accident because she'd always known the phrase would be unwelcome. There was Gus's face: her mouth tightening and the expression in her eyes changing from warm to hostile in a second. 'Not reciprocated,' she'd said and walked out of the room.

'What are you thinking about? You look so sad.'

'No, in many ways I'm feeling positive. Ah, the trolley has arrived. Tea or coffee?'

'Hot chocolate if they've got it. And biscuits.'

Miss Frances took her time, thinking carefully as she queued with other hospital visitors and patients, for their chocolate. Ten minutes later, she placed the tray on Claire's bedside cabinet and sat down again.

'It's too hot to drink yet.'

Claire offered Miss Frances her upturned hand. 'Carry on,' she said.

'Carry on with what?' Miss Frances took Claire's hand in hers.

'Carry on with whatever it was you wanted to say.'

'This may not be an appropriate moment.'

'Just say it.'

'Supposing you don't like –'

'Frances!'

Miss Frances leant forward and said quietly, 'I love you.'

'I'm glad.'

Of course, there was part of Miss Frances that would have welcomed an 'I love you too', but surely for Claire to be glad she was loved was an excellent beginning?

Claire said, 'Do you remember that day when you were reading the canteen menu and I came and stood beside you?'

'Of course I remember. You were wearing bright yellow socks.'

'I'd had a crush on you for months.'

'That is very good news, Claire.'

And then they both started to laugh, although Miss Frances could just as easily have cried. With happiness.

Chapter 31

1976

Imagine this if you will: an immaculately dressed middle-aged man wearing a bespoke suit by Hardy Amies, pale blue shirt and navy-and-silver jacquard tie. He – I have dispensed with the matching breast pocket handkerchief. Carrying a black leather briefcase, I emerge from Marble Arch tube station into sunlight. My iron grey hair is fractionally longer than I've worn it in the past and I've grown sideburns. Nothing flamboyant – two neat, stylish wedges that lend my face a piratical air.

As I stride along past Marks & Spencer's flagship store, I'm aware that my body feels comfortable within its carapace of clothing. I no longer have a problem with perspiration. Flesh no longer adheres to cloth. I'm not flabby any more. Extraordinary to now appreciate that I had been flabby before. I never noticed. Claire Daker had become all-important, the state of my body secondary.

I slow my pace. As always I'm early. There is no reason to rush. *Learn to saunter, Oliver.* The idea amuses me. I catch sight of my reflection in a shop window. Amongst the tourists and shoppers in their brightly-coloured summer foliage, I look incongruous, but correctly so. I'm neither shopper nor tourist – I am a Londoner, born, bred and returned to the fold.

Daydreaming, I almost miss St Christopher's Place. This isn't a street I would ever have visited while managing The Store. The small shops are expensive and stylish, as are its restaurants and wine bars. In the past I would have sneered, but inside felt intimidated. The people are better dressed than on Oxford Street. Here *are* saunterers, leisurely browsers, all looking forward to a chilled glass of wine, lunch, conversation. I doubt that any of them have ever looked forward to 'chicken in a basket'.

My shoulders twitch and I shrug the thought away. Foolish to feel nostalgic, yet suddenly I see Doreen's face as she stood on the platform at Harrogate station. We'd both exhausted ourselves. Surprisingly, I would have liked to remain friends with her, but that wasn't possible or fair.

'Don't worry about me,' she'd said. 'I don't intend to spend the rest of my life alone.'

'Nor should you.' I'd summoned up genuine enthusiasm.

'And don't patronise me either.'

'Doreen, I wasn't. You deserve –'

'Oh stow it.'

Although tempted to, I didn't apologise for letting her down. I'd been through hundreds of apologies already. This is something I've learnt: if one apology isn't enough, there aren't sufficient apologies in a lifetime to make amends.

Charmed by a display of women's jewel-coloured silk shoes and matching woven handbags, I stop in front of a boutique window – Jane & Dada. I can imagine a young woman like Claire Daker wearing such shoes, carelessly swinging the dainty bag as she dances her way through life – at least for a few years. I am tempted to enter the shop. Through the open doorway the clothing beckons, brilliant colours, fragile silks, taffeta and chiffon. Not styles I'd ever consider stocking. They are meant for the young and lovely, but I completely understand their appeal.

With the exception of bridal wear, the youth market has never attracted me. My ambition has always been to take an older woman – complete with the flaws that time has added – and make her look stunning. Incredibly, up until the last few months, I'd never fully worked this out. Time spent in or outside Doreen's summer house, only half-reading the novels of Neville Shute, clarified what really mattered to me. My *raison d'être.*

I spot Della before she sees me. Or maybe she's been watching my slow progress for some time but is pretending otherwise.

She sits at a table in front of a wine bar, her head bent over the menu. Already, she's ordered a carafe of water and two glasses.

As I walk towards her, she raises a glass to her lips. Our eyes meet. Yes, she'd known I was there. Standing in front of her, the idea that I should kiss her seems, for a moment, an impossibility.

'Greetings, Della.'

She looks surprised, then a little amused. 'Greetings, Mr Oliver.'

'You'll have to call me Sydney, now.' I make rather a production of sitting down – arranging my briefcase between chair and table leg, undoing my jacket, pretending to loosen my tie. I am assailed by thoughts and emotions, about life, letting in life and how could I have spent nearly two decades working shoulder to shoulder with this woman without realising how wonderful she was.

Della *does* look wonderful. Adjusting my cuffs, I take several quick glances at her. She's retained her light summer tan, which I thoroughly approve of. Also her fine head of faux-bronze curls. Other than a dash of eye-shadow, she wears little make up. Why have I never noticed her cheekbones, her elegant nose, her sensitive top lip, her full, sensuous bottom lip? I think that the film star, Sophia Loren, would look very like Della when she reaches her mid-fifties.

We order a salad and new potatoes and talk desultorily about my rented flat in Acton.

'You never thought of going back to Earls Court?' Della asks.

'No. I sold that flat to the tenants – Doreen's son and one of her family friends.'

The waiter clears away our plates.

For the first time in my life, I wish I smoked. A cigarette would be perfect to smooth the transition from generalities to more personal matters.

Folding my arms, I lean them on the table. 'So Della, is it to be champagne or do we go our separate ways?'

She sits back in her chair.

I watch her mouth.

'I think we can make a go of it,' she says.

'Is that the best we can do?'

Before Della can answer, the waiter returns with a dessert menu. He places it in front of her.

She looks at me. 'We don't want a dessert, do we?'

'No.'

She hands the menu back to the waiter. 'I think we'll have the champagne now, please.'

I pick up my briefcase and open it, draw out several documents and put them on the table. 'The shop lease is for one year, with an option to increase it to ten if we're happy. We can negotiate a price for the shop fittings and existing stock.'

'We don't want to do that, do we? I don't think I could sell a garment made from bonded jersey or polyester.' Della smiles at me and then we both laugh.

Ignoring the waiter solemnly filling the champagne flutes, I begin. 'Della.'

'Sydney.'

'I'm not quite the man I was when I managed The Store.'

'There would be no point my being here if you were. I don't believe I'm quite the same woman.'

I twirl my champagne flute. 'The Daker girl –'

'Yes?'

With my free hand, I lightly touch my breast pocket. I experience no pain, no sadness or regret. 'Any feelings I may have had are gone. A few months of insanity. I am my own man again.'

'Good.' Della slips the papers into her slim leather handbag. 'I'll have everything signed, witnessed and back to you by the weekend.'

'*Salud.*' Our glasses touch.

'To our new venture.'

'Adventure.' I lean across the table and kiss Della lightly on the lips.

'To us?' she says.

'Of course."

Anxiously, the waiter watches us. I'm sure he is used to observing his customers, picking up on highly charged situations. Here he senses some strong emotion, some tension. Are we old friends, business colleagues or middle-aged lovers? We both seem serious. Surely there is a connection going back many years? Whatever we two are planning together, he can tell that there is nothing light-hearted about it. He drops the champagne bottle back into the ice bucket and withdraws.

Acknowledgements

Mr Oliver's Object of Desire has been a long time in the writing and many people have supported me along the way. In particular, I'd like to thank Robyn Vinten – her enthusiasm encouraged me to turn the original story into a novel over twenty years ago; D.J. Connell and Paul Burston, whose constructive criticism and support inspired me to turn this novel on its head and edit out at least a hundred extraneous pages; and my dear friend Mary Vassallo, who has listened to me droning on about plot and character for decades!

Thanks so much to Ward Wood Publishing for believing in this book and for yet another lovely cover.

Mr Oliver, after twenty-three years I'm setting you free!